"Suspenseful, powerful, thought provoking—straight from today's headlines. *The Dolphin* reads like a movie with no waiting to cut to the chase."

Dean Rowe, *Producer/Director Member, Director's Guild of America*

"Hallenstein demonstrates a remarkable gift for creating rich, engaging, and wholly human characters. In the sexually frank and terrifying world he creates, important social questions beg to be addressed."

Rebecca Pastor, *Writer/Educator/Editor*

"Amidst the twists and turns of a first-rate thriller, a revelation occurs about the way we raise kids. Bold storytelling. Greater than the sum of its parts."

Ellyn Wrzeski, *Award-Winning School Superintendent*

"Enlightening in its depiction of lives torn apart by over-reaching laws. From start to finish, *The Dolphin's* one wild ride."

Carol Fetzner, *Psychologist*

"*The Dolphin's* going to make a terrific movie!"

Michael Denneny, *International Award-Winning Editor*

To Dr. Jean Kennedy
Best Wishes,
Craig

THE
DOLPHIN

CRAIG BENNETT HALLENSTEIN

Storyville Press * New Orleans

Cover Design by Derek Murphy
Interior Design by Jake Muelle

Library of Congress Control Number: 2015917916

ISBN-13: 978-0-692-57883-4

Storyville Press
P.O. Box 3876
New Orleans, Louisiana 70117

Printed in the United States of America

Dedicated to…

Ruth and Ralph Hallenstein

loving parents who had the wisdom to know
when to step in and when to step aside

Chapter 1

GUILT

THE instant the explosion shattered the heavens, sending his bicycle reeling, newspapers tossed to the wind, the eleven-year-old knew: His grandfather had something to say.

Sean Andrew Jordan had grown accustomed to his grandfather's messages since the patriarch died the previous spring. They contained useful problem-solving advice that furthered his education and made him feel not so alone. But this morning he hadn't asked any questions, posed any problems, or sought any advice. Still, his grandfather had spoken and in a most dramatic way.

Sean lay sprawled on the sidewalk, wrists skinned, blood oozing from both knees. He heard a siren and saw a fire engine race by with the words "Chicago Fire Department" emblazoned on its side. As quickly as the wailing began, the siren stopped, replaced by others howling in the distance. Minutes later, a squad car flew past—then another—then a third. Sean righted his bike and retrieved the papers, knowing he had to hurry with school about to begin.

"Mr. Compassion!" Miles Abbito called, brakes squealing to miss the curb. "You hear it? Bet it's the Citco on Grand. *C'mon!*" Sean angled in Abbito's direction, but Miles rode on, shouting, "Your house tonight. The big psychology meeting!"

Sean was glad Miles hadn't waited. He had papers to deliver and a message to decode. *If you're trying to tell me Wit Creed's being abused or that Blain Milner's still thinking about killing himself, I handled those. Is there something else you want me to know?*

Sean turned and pedaled up Ms. Fincher's walk, positioning her paper squarely on her porch. He was used to putting papers wherever his customers wanted instead of flinging them haphazardly from the middle of the street. But today he placed them with even greater care, pausing after each to inspect the results. *She'll appreciate that*, he decided, satisfied with the spacing on all four sides. *What's a few extra seconds to make a customer happy?* Slackening further on his way to the Turbachevs, it dawned on him: He was looking for reasons to slow down.

Why?

A strange foreboding made him want to avoid the question, but his knowledge of psychology—"Extraordinary for someone so young," his grandfather often boasted—wouldn't allow it. Some truth lay beneath his desire to slow down. And truths needed to be faced sooner rather than later.

Sean's Grandfather Vincien—"Vince," Sean called him—was a nationally known psychologist respected by his peers. He was the first to call attention to Sean's intellect and curiosity—"'Remarkable' in a word"—anointing himself Sean's mentor as soon as the boy turned eight. "Take charge and live large," he'd say. "And be honest with yourself. Honesty is the cornerstone of integrity, and integrity is the cornerstone of life."

In response to Sean's asking why people did the things they did, Vince gave the eight-year-old elaborate explanations, drawing examples from his clients without divulging their names, recounting their complaints and the advice he provided. He'd then quiz Sean about the source of each problem and shake with glee when the boy got it right.

Every day after school, Sean raced to meet Vince, who opened a portal to adulthood, revealing its secrets and joys. Many things Sean didn't understand, but he asked the right questions, for which he was rewarded with full and honest answers. When talk turned to sex, he felt uneasy at first, but was quickly drawn in by Vince's unabashed enthusiasm. If there was anything Vince was better at than being a psychologist, it was being a teacher and an explainer of things.

"Are you sure he isn't too young to be given so much information?" Sean's father asked *his* father on a number of occasions.

"The truth never hurt anyone," Vince replied, "especially when one asks and comprehends so well. That boy'll be quite a psychologist someday. Hell, he's already better than a lot of my colleagues."

Parental apprehension gave way to pride as Sean's knowledge and skills became increasingly apparent. At eight, he was settling disputes between neighbors. By nine, he was counseling the parents of friends. Vince died in May of the following year, leaving a grief-stricken Sean his collection of books—Shakespeare, Dickens, Hemingway, and Twain, along with Freud, Jung, Ellis, and Perls. Nearly every page was dotted with tears as Sean poured over each, learning all he could.

I didn't want *to follow Miles,* Sean admitted to himself. *Whatever it is, I don't want to know.* He felt strangely anxious and didn't know why. Maybe he was wrong; maybe there *was* no message. Maybe whatever had happened had nothing to do with Vince.

"Hi, Sean," Wendy Glidden called, riding up the sidewalk on her pink and white Schwinn, fiddling with a Walkman clipped to her jeans. "I'm bringing Jamie to the meeting tonight. What do you call them again?"

"Psychology salons." Sean stared past her, lost in thought.

"Yeah, *that's* it. I told her about the stuff we talk about. She wants to come along. There's this boy, Clayton Rice . . ." Wendy rode next to Sean, lowering her voice to keep the world from hearing. "She's starting to like him—"

". . . And wants him to know. But she's sure she'll die if he actually finds out."

"Wow!" Wendy gushed.

"She needs to just *tell* him."

A prodigy in psychology, Sean sought to empower friends, helping liars get real, wallflowers take action, gossips drop drama, and freaks fit in. "Stop caring that you're a freak and you don't fit in. *Everyone's a freak*," he'd say. "*No* one fits in," To that, he'd add: "Being different, in fact, is a really good thing. If you love yourself and value your uniqueness, others will want to fit in with *you*." Vince had said so hundreds of times.

Sean was the go-to kid at school from fourth grade on whenever threats were made or fights broke out. Others stopped fights by charging between parties. Sean succeeded by talking parties down, guiding them to realize the pettiness of their disputes while helping them appreciate the things they had in common. Then he'd prevail upon them to give each other hugs, taking in the support of a cheering crowd. Fights, he determined *without* Vince's advice, nearly always arose because a kid needed a hug. That's why he launched the salons in the first place—to provide occasions when everyone could get hugs.

Wendy smiled. "I told her you'd know just what to do."

Sean always knew exactly what to do—except, of course, when the problems were his.

"It's easier to help others than it is to help ourselves," Vince said. "In fact, helping ourselves isn't always wise. According to Sir William Osler, the Father of Modern Medicine, 'A physician who treats himself has a fool for a patient.'"

Sean's biggest problem was Wendy Glidden. He liked her in the way boys like girls while transitioning from hating them to thinking about them incessantly. But her crush on him, laden with rising expectations—walking to and from school, sitting next to her at lunch—was an annoyance on its way to becoming a full-blown irritation.

"Did you feel it?" she asked. "My whole *house* shook."

"Yeah, I felt it," he replied.

"Let's go see."

"Naw, you go ahead."

"I'll wait 'til you finish."

"*Wendy.*" Sean heard the impatience in his voice and felt a tinge of shame. "Maybe tonight we can sit together at the meeting."

"*Deal.*" Wendy beamed, turned, and peddled down Pleasant Street.

Sean grimaced, Vince's words echoing: "Skirting issues is how problems hang on."

Sean's anxiety increased as the remaining papers dwindled, each delivery nudging him closer to knowing. Classmates raced by, heading toward Grand, with its auto repair shops, pinball parlors, currency exchanges, and comic book stores.

Sean reached the corner and turned onto Pleasant as a second fire truck screamed past, followed by an ambulance. He heard a bicycle sprocket, clattering behind him, and turned to see Wendy who'd circled back, her presence ghost-like, her demeanor vapid. She was cutting figure eights at the end of the drive, leaning on the handlebars, eyes to the ground. "Wendy?" he said, expecting her to look up, but she kept on pedaling without raising her head.

Sean's fingers trembled. His heart began to race. He knew he had to ask, despite not wanting to know: "What's wrong?"

Wendy sped off without saying a word, away from Grand and away from school.

Dread descended.

Sean approached Fred Hunter's house, the last paper of the day tucked under his arm. He positioned it on the step, nudging it this way and that, until the door flew open and Ms. Hunter shooed him on his way. He returned to his bike and looked in his baskets, hoping in vain that another paper remained.

Dizziness set in. Time had run out. Regardless of his wishes, there were no more delays.

Sean mounted his bike, rode down Pleasant, turned right onto Jennings, and squealed to a halt. Emergency vehicles cluttered the block with dense, black smoke choking the air. He dropped his bike and walked ahead, haltingly, as if mired in quicksand. He passed the Bryants' house, anchoring the corner, and started toward the Litchfields', the house before his.

"You can't go any further," a police officer commanded, pivoting quickly to block Sean's path.

Peering up the block and across the street, he spotted classmates and parents, gawking and pointing at what he couldn't see. Several glanced toward him and diverted their eyes. No one moved. No one came near. They were the friends he'd known his entire life, the friends he'd helped whenever they asked, the friends who'd poured out their secrets in his living room, gathering hugs along with advice.

Sean found comfort in the policeman's arms. As long as they remained, holding him at bay, he'd continue to be spared whatever awaited him. *Maybe the policeman will stand guard forever, people'll keep staring, and time'll stand still.* The thought felt more like a plea than a pondering. He wanted to believe that such things were possible, but knew deep down life wasn't that way. Smashed cars got towed. Flooded basements got drained. Messes didn't linger. Time moved on. Sooner or later he'd be forced to know.

Face your fears promptly, he heard Vince say. *Delaying does nothing but fuel your suffering.*

Sean tried to dodge, but the officer moved swiftly, grabbing his jacket, holding on tight. When the policeman took a second to glance over his shoulder, Sean seized the chance and wriggled free.

The sight. The smell.

Sean's lower lip quivered. His knees began to quake. Smoldering before him where he'd laughed and learned, thought big thoughts, and dreamed big dreams, was a thirty-foot crater filled with burning debris.

The street fell dark. Time did stand still. Sean stood, dazed, uncomprehending, struggling to resolve where tonight's meeting would be held. Thoughts turned to his parents. He wondered where they were. He'd left while they slept an hour before.

The unworldly sight began to sink in, Sean acknowledging the garage and the charred brick chimney. He noticed something and stooped to retrieve a small china plate with a butterfly border, belonging to his mother and her mother before her. Tracing his finger around the edge, he found it warm and smooth like his mother's kind hands.

If your message was to warn me, you were a little too late.

Sean's slight frame trembled. His eyes blurred with tears. He knew in his innermost place of knowing that his parents were dead, the life he loved was gone, and that nothing again would ever be the same.

He knew as well . . . it was all his fault.

Chapter 2

THE CELEBRATION

HENRY Toussaint downed the last swig of beer before tossing the bottle into the Mississippi. He reached for another and laughed out loud. *Who else'd steal a ship to impress a broad?* He pictured her waiting on the other side. *Steal? HELL!* The thousand tons of iron were practically his, having shuttled them for years between Algiers and Canal Street. And even if they weren't, Henry thought, *So what! We in New Awlins love breaking the rules almost as much as bending the truth. When we get caught . . .* His lips broke wide. *Lies pour forth like improvised jazz.*

Henry peered skyward through eyes crowded by crow's feet, steadying himself while the ship pitched below. He studied his reflection in the pilothouse window—*Not too bad for a guy turned sixty*—and glimpsed the tattoo of a dove atop an anchor, peeking from beneath his rolled-up sleeve. He recalled his twelfth birthday, a sweltering Fourth of July, when he met a young sailor, strolling along the riverfront. Henry followed the man like a pesky gnat, quizzing him about sailing, life at sea, and what it was like to get a tattoo, having spotted one on the sailor's neck. Claiming to provide tattoos himself, the sailor agreed, in exchange for a favor, to initiate Henry with one of his own.

In a vacant building, just off Decatur, with fireworks painting the evening sky, Henry winced first at the taste of semen, then at the pain of needles, piercing raw nerves. While he never tasted semen again, he went on to accumulate enough tattoos that little of his body remained untouched. His favorite was one of Jesus, hanging on the cross, centered precisely above his heart. Henry's greater triumph came the following day when dozens gathered in disbelief, having heard a *kid* had scored a real tattoo. Standing on a milk crate behind St. Louis Cathedral, Henry exposed his tortured flesh, turning skepticism and ridicule into credence and admiration.

"Molly. That's your name—right? Molly?" Sean Jordan called, waving a finger insistently in the air, alerting the goth-inspired bartender he was ready for the check. Her clothes ranged in color from charcoal to black, her cheeks lined with metal forming hearts intertwined. Upside down crosses hung from both ears and a voodoo doll medallion dangled about her neck. Sean admired her style and personal expression, laughing with-her rather than at-her in a respectful sort of way.

He'd heard locals sing the praises of Shannon 'N Molly's since arriving in New Orleans two years before. They were the same people who taught him to properly pronounce the names of the streets that anchored the pub: Conti with a long *i*, and Burgundy with the accent on *gun*. He hadn't spent a minute in the bric-a-brac littered establishment before spotting an Illinois license plate hanging on the wall beneath a photo of Elwood Blues and Joliet Jake.

Ignoring his gesture, Molly refilled his drink, breasts straining to break free from her sheer lacy bodice.

Sean thought about his wife, Laurie, and four-year-old daughter, Ren, and the classes he had to be prepared for in the morning. Still, he decided to linger a bit longer.

"You always wear black hats with long green feathers?"

"Always," Molly answered, licking her lips sensuously. "S'pose *next* you're gonna ask if I'm *the* Molly."

"I just assumed—"

"Well, you assumed wrong." She cocked her head, feather bolting upright. "I'm merely the latest in a long line of Mollys. And no, there's no Shannon—never was." She reached across the bar and tousled his thick brown hair, cascading in curls toward long silky lashes. "Gorgeous," she proclaimed, as if wishing he were hers, "though I'd lose the vest with Santa's eight reindeer." Sliding the drink in the twenty-eight-year-old's direction, she studied his face. "I think it's your eyes."

"They're cobalt blue," the man next to Sean said. "Take a good look. You'll never find another pair like them."

"How do you know?" Molly purred . . . "I see a lot of eyes."

"For years I sought a woman with eyes the color of his. Since she doesn't exist, I settle for him." He extended his hand. "I'm Doug—*his* best friend."

"But I *like* reindeer," Sean said, playing along.

"For his birthday, I got him a subscription to *GQ*."

"It came free when he re-upped with *Tiger Beat*."

Molly laughed and shook Doug's hand. "You have nice eyes, too."

"Too late," Doug said, head snapping back. "It's clear how you feel. You made your choice."

Sean rolled his eyes at the mock play for sympathy, knowing very few people were as well grounded as Doug. At six foot one, he beat Sean by two inches, possessing a hearty face, square jaw, and eyes that opened with invitation. The tattoo of a parrot on his sinewy left shoulder appeared to move its beak whenever he flexed his muscle.

"Everyone chooses him over me," Doug went on. "I thought about therapy, but he's my therapist."

"No, I'm not. We're friends."

"You're looking at the once-youngest psychologist in the entire world. On one single day in seventh grade, he led a seminar on bullying, saved the principal's marriage, and talked the janitor down off the roof."

Molly reached forward, sweeping a curl from Sean's eye. "I'm a psychologist, too, you know. All the crazies come in here—the wife

| 9

beaters, the beaten wives, the derelicts, and the desperados. Had a guy threaten suicide the other day. Whined on and on about it. I finally told him to go fuck himself. How would you have handled it?"

Though not a psychologist, Sean hastened to reply. "I suppose I might have asked him if he had a method in mind."

"I didn't care!" Molly exclaimed.

Glancing at each other, Sean and Doug shrugged, repeating in unison: "She didn't care."

Doug's grin segued to a serious expression—the one Sean remembered from years before when Doug broke from the crowd on Jennings Street to comfort a boy he'd never met. From that day forward, the two were inseparable, joining forces to discover the ways of the world. To their myriad of discoveries, they could now add Molly.

Molly opened a storeroom at the end of the bar, inadvertently freeing a Jack Russell terrier. The dog raced to the bar and bounded into Sean's lap, licking lavishly every inch of his face.

"Who are *you*?" Sean asked, nuzzling the dog's face.

"Satan! Get down from there!" Molly growled.

The terrier barked once as if to say *no* before coating Sean's face with a second round.

"Strange, he never goes near customers," Molly noted.

"Actually," Doug said, "he's an *animal* psychologist. Great with pets. It's people who confound him."

Molly scooped Satan into her arms, cooing and rubbing noses on their way back to the storeroom. "If it's meant to be, you'll find each other again someday."

"I'll send you a text," Sean called to Satan.

"The ones he likes best contain naked pictures."

Sean turned to Doug. "Listen, I have to go."

"But we just got here. Relax."

Guilt stalked Sean like a road rage warrior, charging from the rear, braking in front, circling in an effort to fill him with dread. "Laurie's waiting. Lately, things have been rocky." Leave or stay, he'd disappoint someone.

Molly returned with a frozen Irish Coffee, swirling coffee beans on top with the tip of her tongue. "So whatcha celebratin'?"

The image of a tarot card reader popped in Sean's head, like those dressed as gypsies in front of the Cabildo. "What makes you think we're celebrating?"

Molly tipped back her hat. "Like I said, I see a lot of eyes. Yours were troubled when you first walked in—blue slits with dark bags underneath. Soon as I saw them I knew it was a celebration."

"Because I looked troubled, you knew it was a celebration . . ."

Molly leaned forward, bringing her lips to Sean's ear. "In New Awlins . . . the two go hand in hand."

Henry's gut churned with serious misgivings as wispy white ghosts gathered all around. Their numbers swelled, and in no time at all, an ominous fog settled over the river. He gripped the wheel firmly with weather-worn hands, looked to the heavens, and prayed for a clearing. As if God were listening, moonlight pierced the haze followed by thousands of accent lights up and down the Riverwalk. The brightest among them were three giant beams, spotlighting the centerpiece: the Aquarium of the Americas. Air spilled profusely from Henry's lungs.

He spotted a rowboat bobbing on his right. *What's something that small doing in a place like this?* It was the kind of boat he'd used as a kid to explore the river near Baton Rouge. The kind he'd slept in alone and with friends on the nights his father was too drunk to find him. The kind he'd lost his virginity in time and time again to the girls who believed when he swore they were his first. What it wasn't was a boat for the river's busiest channel, bent in the shape of a crescent moon, giving rise to the nickname *Crescent City*.

Henry donned his glasses and let loose with a howl, sounding more like a pirate than a ferryboat captain. Wriggling about in the boat below were a pair of lovers—*Who else'd risk their lives?* They were going about their business, blissfully engaged, like the ones he paid to see over on Iberville. Henry strained to maintain his view, the fickle mist wafting between him and them.

White again surrounded him. Fearing for the couple, Henry tightened his grip and tugged on the wheel to ensure a safe margin.

But when visibility returned, he realized: despite his efforts, the boat had nearly capsized. He yanked the wheel feverishly and checked once more. He'd widened the gap but by just a few feet. He drew a quick breath and seized the wheel mightily. The ship screeched and yowled as if breaking in two. Henry held tight. The ship kept turning, clearing *finally* by less than a yard.

Hands shaking, Henry thought to turn back—blow off the woman and head back home. Then he considered the additional investment. *Not now. Not after that!* He reached down and raised the hem of his shirt, using it as a rag to mop sweat from his forehead.

"So, c'mon. Tell me. Whatcha celebratin'?" Molly cracked open a pack of cigarettes, offering to share before helping herself.

"Doug," Sean pressed, anxiety mounting.

"Hang on. The lady asked a question." Waving away the cigarettes, Doug coiled his legs around the old wooden bar stool. "Just got out of the slammer, Moll. If we're celebrating anything, I guess it's my freedom."

Molly pitched forward. "What'd you do? Somethin' *terrible*, I hope." She took a drag, smoke rising toward the ceiling.

"I dropped trou in the middle of the French Quarter. Treated my cock and balls to a moment of fresh air."

Molly's mouth fell open in a disbelieving grin. "No you didn't. I mean of course you *did*, but nobody goes to jail for that. This is New Awlins, for Christ's sake."

"So I've been told. You just happen to be looking at the exception to the rule."

"But *how*?" Molly asked, anchoring her elbows on the bar.

"Go ahead," Doug said, waving Sean to center stage. "I like how you tell it."

Sean clinked Doug's glass. "When I first moved to town, I asked my best friend to visit. He waited until Mardi Gras because he'd heard all about it."

"*And . . .*" Molly waited.

"Blew his mind the minute he got here. Girls were standing on every corner—their shirts pulled up, their pants pulled down. It was better than anything he could have imagined."

"Rather limited imagination," Molly huffed, smoke billowing from the corners of her lips.

"Half a billion dollars," Doug said, throwing back his drink. "That's what this town makes in a single week. People don't come from all over the world for Bible lessons and religious retreats. They come for music, food, booze, sex."

Sean hoisted his glass. "To being free again to enjoy all four."

Doug lifted his. "How about: To the millions of sex offenders from 1700 forward who made this town what it is today?"

Molly cheered. *"It's in our DNA!"*

Sean continued. "Doug had been watching people up and down Bourbon Street, exposing themselves in exchange for beads. He was considering doing the same when a well-built brunette leaned over a balcony and pointed straight at him. 'Show me!' she hollered."

Doug shrugged. "Who could refuse a lady?"

"He had an idea what an indecent exposure rap might have brought him back in Chicago, but he thought, fuck it! This is New Orleans. It's a tradition. He'd have felt like an asshole if he *hadn't* partaken. So he unzipped. Flashed his junk for all of two seconds."

"Encore!" Molly applauded, eyes a shower of sparks.

Sean placed his hands over his heart. "In a dazzling moment of deep connected love, the brunette waved, blew Doug a kiss, and sent beads tumbling toward his outstretched hand. Unfortunately, with his eyes glued to hers, Doug failed to notice the cop who'd strolled up beside him. Next thing he knew . . . handcuffs clamped down around the wrist that held the beads, while his free hand scrambled to pull up his pants."

"Shit," Molly said. "Cops handcuff guys once in a while as examples to others, but they always let 'em go. It's called a Signal 21—'less than criminal activity.'" She winked at Sean. "We get a lot of cops in here."

"Right. *Minor*," Doug jumped in. "I kept looking around when they booked me at the station, hauled me into court, and locked me in my cell. Not once did I see any of those girls or the guys who'd stood around flashing their dicks. What I saw instead were gangbangers and pimps."

"That's fucking bizarre," Molly said.

"According to Doug's attorney," Sean went on, "he pulled the harshest judge in Orleans Parish. On top of that, a couple appeared, testifying they were there with their seven-year-old twins at the precise moment Doug unzipped, damaging the kids so severely that they'd since suffered acute post-traumatic stress. Based on the judge's temperament, the parents' testimony, the mood of the country, and the alignment of the stars, my best friend spent a year in OPP."

"Fuck!" Molly said.

"He did his time and walked out four days ago." Sean checked Doug lightly on the arm. "As much as I like you, try not to stay a whole year next time you visit."

Molly snatched Sean's glass and filled it again. He thought to stop her but held his tongue. What was the point at this late hour? Besides, he was enjoying himself. It was the first time in a long time.

On her return, Molly stopped along the bar, lighting fresh candles in carbon-charred holders.

"Wouldn't you think I'd given enough—" Doug commented to Sean as he stared at his drink. "My attendance at their annual world-renowned party, my enthusiastic participation in their tribal rituals, and my pound of flesh as an example to others? But no. They want my *life*. They've given me ten days to register as a sex offender. Not 'sex offender: Mardi Gras partier' to distinguish me from 'sex offender: child molester.' Just 'sex offender.'"

Sean wanted to protect Doug, but knew from experience Doug would do exactly as he pleased.

Henry turned his attention again to the couple, his heart racing, his penis growing heavy. The man on top was clearly visible, but it was the woman beneath him he really wanted to see. *Must be tiny as a bird.* He craned his neck but couldn't see a thing.

A cry rang out—reed thin, high-pitched. The bone-chilling plea sobered Henry in an instant. He looked again and saw there was no woman. The man was forcing his way with a *child!*

Henry sounded his horn—a violation after midnight—and activated the fire bell, rivaling the horn in decibels. He switched on the radio, turned off to avoid detection, grabbed the mic and called for help, praying the harbor patrol would arrive in time.

"Doug, this is important," Sean said.

Doug glanced down the bar, as if to make sure Molly couldn't hear. "I'm not gonna register and let some unwarranted label dictate where I can live, who I can hang out with, and when and where I can take a leak. Fuck all that. I've rented a place under an assumed name. If I get caught, they'll send me back for another year."

"If you get caught in *New Orleans*, it's a thousand-dollar fine and two years hard labor."

"Then I'll have to make sure they never find me. Make sure I stay lucky." Doug's eyes held Sean's. "Luckier than you."

There was a brilliant flash of light—then a second and an explosion. The concussive force obliterated the pilothouse windows, slamming Henry against the glass-splattered floor. With considerable effort he pulled himself up, balancing precariously on watery legs. He blinked repeatedly to bring into focus shimmering shapes dancing on the horizon. Eventually he realized the shapes were flames and understood at once: the Riverwalk was ablaze. Heat, singeing his hair and searing his cheeks, he pictured his face orange in the fire's glow. He remembered the rowboat and peered over the side. There was no boat in sight in the dark choppy water.

He spun the wheel frantically to return to Algiers to restore the world to the way it had been. He glanced over his shoulder at the fire in the distance, realizing something had changed. Something about the skyline . . . .

Shockwaves careened through Shannon 'N Molly's, throwing Sean, Doug, and Molly against the ballast-tile floor. "What the fuck was *that*?" she exclaimed, clinging to a keg as she struggled to stand.

"Hell if I know," Doug shouted. He scrambled to his feet and rushed for the door. "We'll circle back and let you know."

Sean rose from the floor, righted his stool, sat back down, and stared at the bar.

"What the hell are you doing?" Doug yelled, one foot in Molly's, the other in the street.

Sean sat motionless, cobalt blues vacant.

Henry's knees buckled. He slumped to the floor, blood darkening his chest in a rapidly expanding circle. He ripped open his shirt and looked down in horror at the dagger-shaped glass imbedded in Christ's side.

Irrevocable darkness descending, he reflected on his life, but the change in the skyline interrupted his thoughts.

HAH! It came to him, affording eternal peace.

The Aquarium of the Americas had been blown to bits.

"You've been pushing to leave for the past couple of hours." Doug called to his friend from across the room. "Now you want to *stay*?"

Sean remained still. He was aware only of the candles extinguished by the blast, smoke mocking him in its spiraling ascent.

"Aren't you the least bit curious?" Doug sniped.

Curious? The word seeped slowly into Sean's brain. *Sure . . . I guess . . . Curious how boys with such promising futures could have their dreams dashed and end up like this.*

Escaping from the storeroom, Satan settled in Sean's lap, and barked as if he, too, were trying to get his attention.

Doug's look of impatience yielded to concern. He glanced at Molly and Molly glanced back. He drew a deep breath and returned to the bar, placing his hands on Sean's shoulders, gazing into his eyes.

"It's a different explosion," he said, in a reassuring manner. "It's not the one that killed your parents."

Chapter 3

EYES IN THE NIGHT

DETECTIVE Lieutenant Owen Dupree knelt over the naked body and began to weep. He recognized the seven-year-old's petite oval face, long pointed chin, and tortoiseshell eyes, one with missing pigment in the shape of a horse, rearing gallantly on its hind legs. He'd seen those eyes hundreds of times and knew them as well as his daughter Jenna's. "Mattie, I'm sorry," the detective said. He reached to close them, disbelieving what he was doing, imagining a hysterical Jenna begging him not to. Completing the act, his big hands shook. His body convulsed. His eyes filled with tears. He pictured, too, Mattie's parents' eyes, anguished, terrified, and void of hope. He was no stranger to the task, terrible as it was, of informing parents of the death of a child. But this was different. They were his friends. He wondered where on earth he'd find the strength.

Dupree recalled the first time he saw Mattie, cavorting with Jenna in the middle of the living room. "Who's the tow-head?" he asked his wife, Sandy, disappointed that the girl's presence would defer lovemaking again.

"Mattie Daniels," Sandy answered. "She's spending the night. Seems nice."

Dupree pictured the girls sitting on his lap, Mattie asking to see his badge amid endless interrogation: Why didn't Jenna have brothers and sisters? Why was Mrs. Dupree so much younger than him? Why was his hair so short, his ears so big, his nose so long, and his stomach so fat? *Fat?* That was the one that got him. At six feet even and 195 pounds, he considered himself trim, perhaps even good-looking in spite of his wife's waning interest. Sure, he'd added a few pounds over the years. Who hadn't at the age of forty-eight, especially in New Orleans where people actually eat? But *fat?* When he realized he was defending himself to a kid barely six, he smiled, informing her that she was on her way to becoming a first-rate detective. Mattie could be a handful twenty-four hours a day, which was why he found her so endearing.

Dupree swept a hand down the back of his head and retrieved a notepad from his left coat pocket. "Suffoca—" he scribbled. More tears flowed, blurring his vision.

"Lieutenant?"

Dupree recognized the voice of Trevor Jas, his junior partner for the past two years. Most days he'd fuck with the twenty-six-year-old's head about his towering height, pencil-thin waist, long choppy hair, and rookie enthusiasm. Not today. "I can't do this," he said without looking up, adding snot mixed with tears to the sleeve of his jacket. "Her name's Mattie Daniels. My kid's best friend. Played at the house before the divorce. S'pose she still does. She and Jenna . . ."

"Jesus." Jas stooped, taking in the scene.

"I gotta get outta here. Get over to their house." Dupree thrust a finger in Jas's face. "Don't miss a thing, you hear me?"

"But the aquarium . . ."

Dupree looked up from the rocky shore at the catastrophe lying yards in front of him. Hundreds of cops swarmed the area, along with firemen, politicians, and maritime officials, grappling with the enormity of the catastrophic explosion and still-smoldering fire stretching on for a mile. Adding to the scene was a twelve-story cruise ship with a New Orleans ferryboat embedded in its hull. Dupree had taken a wider swing. Doing so, he'd stumbled across the young girl's body.

"I don't give a *fuck* about the aquarium. There'll be time enough in the morning to consider all of that. I've got other things to do."

"Yes, sir. Sorry, sir."

Dupree peered across the river at a brightly lit Algiers. Any other night he'd be staring into darkness. But tonight both shores teemed with activity, everyone trying to make sense of what happened. Everyone, that is, except the third-shift revelers still cruising Bourbon Street, too drunk to know that anything had occurred; the monster who'd stolen the life of a young girl; and the Daniels. Dupree pictured them in their family room, sitting on the gold plaid couch he'd always hated, holding each other while awaiting word and a tidal wave of relief that would never come.

Dupree spun at the sound of commotion behind him. A cameraman and a reporter had topped the levee and were sprinting rapidly in his direction. *"Christ, Jas! Where's the tape?"*

Jas shouted at officers who'd begun cordoning off the scene. They dropped what they were doing and dashed toward the intruders. They were able to block the reporter but the cameraman slipped past, making his way to within yards of the girl. Dupree lunged. The cameraman flew in one direction, his camera in another.

"What the hell are you doing? That's an $18,000 camera!" the man shouted, lying prone on the rocks.

"I'm protecting my crime scene," Dupree fired back. "Now get the hell outta here." It was his friends, Hal and Lynette Daniels, he really wanted to protect but knew that was impossible. What the press was about to do to them sickened him further.

Crouching beside Mattie one last time, Dupree recalled the tortured look of a mask he'd once seen and judged his own expression a near perfect copy. He wanted to scream but laughed instead, a little at first followed by a deluge. He'd watched others laugh uncontrollably in the face of tragedy and never understood why. Maybe the pain center of the brain spilled over to the laugh center when the volume of pain could no longer be contained. Or perhaps the world had grown so insane that laughter was the only rational response. Regardless, he felt embarrassed, tried to stop but couldn't. Finally hysteria gave way to exhaustion.

"You're gonna pay!" the cameraman shouted from outside the perimeter.

Dupree closed his eyes. "I already have."

Chapter 4

KNOWING TOO MUCH

A different explosion . . .

Sean considered Doug's words while heading home, dazed from consuming too much booze, wrestling over loyalties between a wife and a friend, and suffering the evening's brutal finale.

No, it wasn't. All explosions are the same, erupting without warning, tearing through the ether, and punishing innocent people with merciless fury. No one understood. Not even Doug.

"I'll take a look around," Doug said outside the bar. "I'll let you know what happened soon as I find out."

But Sean didn't want to know. He knew too much already.

He knew what it was like to lose one's parents without having a chance to say goodbye. He knew what it was like to stand in a street, waiting endlessly to be told what to do. He knew what it was like to be locked in a squad car with a cop turning and saying, "Tough break, kid. *You* didn't have anything to do with this, did you?" . . . knowing full well that he did.

Knowledge informed every cell in Sean's body—useful knowledge to possess as a psychologist—still knowledge he wished he didn't have.

He knew what it was like to be taken to a police station and left in a room for more than an hour, picturing cops figuring out what he'd done before bursting through the door, guns blazing.

A lone officer finally entered the room and appeared startled by Sean, sitting in a corner. "Who are you?"

"I'm the kid whose parents died."

"Oh," he said, with the emotion of a paperweight. "Can I get you something to drink?"

"Coffee. Black." The words surprised Sean as soon as he said them. He'd never tasted coffee and didn't want to. But coffee was the drink his parents liked. Black was the way they drank it.

He knew what it was like to lie to the police—despite Vince pressing him to be honest at all times—landing him in a shelter for runaway kids.

He swore to authorities that he had no relatives when the truth was he had—*blood* relatives—the kind who ventured out at night to feast on others' blood. Sean's parents detested the Hardys, his mother's sister, Arabeth, and her arrogant husband, William, every bit as much as Sean did. Four days after he was sent to the shelter, the Hardys, with sons Russell and Trent in tow, showed up to claim him, informing everyone within earshot that it was their Christian duty to give him a proper home. Sean had come from a proper home. He couldn't imagine William Hardy providing anything close.

Sean returned home at a quarter past two. He was glad he decided to spend time with Doug. How glad Laurie would be remained to be seen.

"'Laurie.' I *like* the name Laurie." It was the first thing he said to her after they met. How lucky he was, he later decided, to have kicked things off with words fondly remembered. He just as easily might have said something stupid, leading to years of regret and endless embarrassment. He filed away his first words to Laurie with several other firsts that occurred that year—graduating first in his class from Darnell College and being the first to graduate in two and a half years.

He'd gone on to enroll in the Midwest School of Psychology and met Laurie in the hallway after attending the first class.

The class, Therapeutic Strategies, was taught by Jesus Rivera, Dean of Clinical Studies, a man so stout, his girth rivaled his height. Dr. Rivera entered the auditorium, marching brusquely to center stage.

"A man and a woman get married," he began. "She for safety, security, and a good father for her children. He for love and sex." Students chuckled. "Both get what they bargained for and live happily for years. Before they get married and for years after, the woman tells the story of her abusive father—how he routinely terrified her and her siblings, who'd hide in the attic when his car approached. After fourteen years, the woman tells her husband she can no longer have sex with him because he reminds her of her father. Soon after, she leaves. The husband's devastated and not a little perplexed because he's anything but abusive and nothing like her father. In fact, he's given her everything she wanted." Rivera scanned the room. "What's going on?"

"They got married for different reasons. She didn't want sex with him right from the start," a young man called out from the second row.

"Repressed memories are finally coming to the surface, and anything having to do with sex reminds her of her father," a redheaded woman ventured from the back.

Sean raised his hand and was acknowledged by the teacher. "She misses the excitement."

The doctor crossed the stage to Sean's side of the room. "What's your name?"

"Sean Jordan."

"Tell us more, Mr. Jordan."

"There's a razor-thin line between terror and excitement. Because of the abuse inflicted by her father, she can't access excitement without the presence of fear. Her frequent retellings of the story of his abuse aren't to purge her soul but to relive the thrill. She chooses to marry a nice guy—the good father she never had—who keeps her safe, provides a good life, and never frightens her in any way. But her craving for excitement laced with fear goes unfulfilled. Eventually, while making love to her husband, she thinks of her father—not because her husband is like him, but because he isn't like him enough.

| 25

She yearns to make love to someone who can scare her. She leaves her husband in search of a bad boy."

Rivera cleared his throat. "Which, Mr. Jordan, is exactly what she found."

"I like what you said in there," a voice rang out after class. Sean turned and saw a stunning young blond, her smile so dazzling it could turn cocoa beans into chocolate. "I'm a nursing student across the street. Thought I'd take an hour to see how the other half lived."

Sean nodded, taking stock. *Independent . . . a rule breaker . . . wearing not two, but a single pierced earring."*

"Oh, the earring." She gave it a tug. "My tomboyish identification with pirates and thieves, dating to a rebellious phase between fifth and sixth grade. Hi, I'm Laurie."

"'Laurie.' I *like* the name Laurie."

Sean checked on Ren and found her asleep with her green-and-gold alligator clasped in both hands. He curled a blanket under her chin and kissed her forehead half a dozen times.

Creeping toward his bedroom, he hoped Laurie was asleep—that his late-night return would pass unnoticed. But as soon as he walked into the room, she spoke, facing away. "It's late," she said, her voice wide awake.

"Doug wanted to stay."

Laurie didn't answer.

Sean's words lingered, adding to his pain. Despite their problems having nothing to do with Doug, he knew the words were badly chosen.

Sean wanted desperately to cut to the core, Vince maintaining, *You have to go deep for a payoff to occur.* But he recalled Vince also saying: *We can't be psychologists to the people we love. For them, we need to be regular guys.*

I'm sorry, Sean rehearsed, in a regular guy sort of way. *You know I didn't mean for any of it to happen. I love you and want things to be like before.* But he refrained from saying so, fearing Laurie's response.

Sean thought again about the things he knew—the anguish of missing parents and the pain of missing his wife.

He climbed into bed with his back toward hers, choosing once more to suffer in silence.

Chapter 5

GOOD MO'NIN' N'AWLINS

"GOOD mo'nin' . . . *N'Awlins!"* Burn Breneaux crowed, like a rooster heralding a brand new day. He sat in his perch in a soundproofed studio in a relic of a building on North Peters Street, home to WFQT Radio—French Quarter Talk. He hit the defeat button and cleared his throat, priming his unmistakable baritone, richer than roux. "And good morning to the rest of you straight-thinking Americans from the Florida Keys all the way to Alaska. This is Burn Breneaux, voice of conservative talk radio, burnin' up the airwaves like nobody else can."

An intern displaying the eagerness of a puppy slid a water bottle to the center of his idol's desk as if dropping a newspaper at his master's feet. *Bet if he had one, he'd wag his tail,* Breneaux thought to himself as he shook his head. An editor followed with news clippings in hand, arranging them with great care next to the bottle.

Breneaux was used to being treated like a prince, adored by fans, and sucked up to by the press since his days as a quarterback for LSU. His once rugged face and toned six-foot-two body had begun giving way to the ravages of age and too much of everything wealth can provide. His pitch-black hair was now snow white, his thirty-two inch waist an augmented thirty-six. The transition had occurred so gradually, however, few seemed to notice and fewer seemed to care. But Breneaux knew and lamented the changes. To bolster his image and sense of himself, he shunned the clothes most radio jocks wore—boots, leather jackets, and raggedy pants—choosing instead the finest clothes money could buy: handcrafted suits, lizard-skin shoes, European-fit shirts, and luxurious silk ties. It pleased him to look like the über success he was—*How better to pique the conservative imagination?*—despite being a man often heard but rarely seen.

Breneaux's broadcasts originated from New Orleans, but millions tuned in daily in all fifty states.

He lowered his glasses to the bridge of his nose, scanning for updates on last night's events. "Of course, when I say 'Florida to Alaska,' I'm excluding the entire Pacific Northwest—*Sad* Francisco all the way to Canada. Not that I and our sponsors wouldn't like you to tune in, it's just that you won't 'cause you're busy with other things—un-American things—angling for gun control, advocating for illegals, killing babies for stem cells, and helping child molesters go free. Has anyone tested the water up there? Collective psychosis doesn't just happen."

Breneaux continued to improvise. "Most of you probably know we had a little excitement last night. There was an explosion of unknown origin at New Awlins's Aquarium of the Americas. If you've ever thought of heading our way for a visit, consider this the perfect time. We've got more fish on hand than you can possibly imagine!" He pressed a button, sounding a rim shot.

He spotted an item that filled him with glee, underscoring perfectly his sardonic persona. "You're gonna love this. Last week, the FBI busted a couple from West Texas for swapping sex with their six-year-old for free use of a *condo*." He peered through the glass from the studio to engineering, grinning at the handsome woman with headphones over her ears. "Marilyn, my engineer, is shaking her head disapprovingly. What's the matter, Ms. Mandolet? You've got a four-year-old. He's gotta be worth *something*." Breneaux snickered disdainfully. "Now she's really giving me a dirty look. Didn't we have another story like this a few years ago? Seem to recall a couple trading their kid for a car."

Marilyn, dressed in black leather slacks and a black silk blouse, with black lacquered glasses and iridescent turquoise sneakers, threw a switch and joined Breneaux on air. "I think it was a Corvette."

"That's right." Breneaux's face glowed. 'Gee, Jimmy Bob, I'd sure like to test drive that fine lookin' 327. How 'bout I leave ya my kid as collateral. While me and the ol' lady are out, kid's yours. Take 'im for a spin. Lemme know what he's worth.'"

Marilyn smiled, adding to his glee. "Says here, the plan was cooked up by the mom's boyfriend. Why is it always the boyfriend? Doesn't anyone have husbands anymore? She said she and her boyfriend thought cavorting with the 'landlord' would be something her daughter would really enjoy—that she'd have 'a positive experience.' Compared to what—being plunged into a volcano? Imagine the 'positive experience' awaiting *them* when they finally check into the Folsom Hotel.

"Okay, show of hands. This question goes out to all the unmarried women in our audience. That includes you, Marilyn." Breneaux looked up and saw that she'd left the room. "If you were dating a guy who suggested—for fun and a housing upgrade—that you hand your six-year-old to a stranger to do with as he pleased, and you were willing to go along because you thought she'd have a positive experience, raise your hand. With your other hand, call us to explain why. If instead, you'd say 'no,' believing your daughter would rather attend a boy band concert than hop into bed with Freddy Krueger, and that the guy you were dating deserved to have his head shot off, raise your hand and call. Lines are open." Music swelled. Marilyn cut to a commercial.

Breneaux loved setting the trap, leading to the final gotcha that was his every time. Reading a book about Abraham Lincoln, he learned his rhetorical skills were so great, his arguments rendered opponents speechless, driving at least one of the many to tears. Lincoln would take time to gloat over their defeat, then circle back and make his apologies. Apologizing, however, wasn't Breneaux's style. He felt it his duty to skewer half the country while rendering the other half helpless with laughter. How else could he "reset the national dialogue" and "reshape the American agenda" like his followers expected? *Reshape the American agenda—Ha!* He grinned at the thought of conservative legions looking to him to spearhead a movement, when the only movement he truly cared about was the movement of cash into his account.

Marilyn pointed at the newspaper lying on his desk and pressed a button, accessing his headset. "Page one."

Breneaux read the headline: "Whale of an Explosion." He was mildly taken aback by the lighthearted tone. *He* could make fun of chaos in his city, but winced when editors did the same. "Explosion of unknown origin," he read on. "Algiers Ferry rams Danish Star: 3,800 evacuated." "Ferry pilot investigated for terrorist links." He'd heard all that before. Marilyn continued to thrust her finger downward. He reached paragraph three and continued to read. His face fell. His energy plummeted. The body of a seven-year-old girl who'd been raped and strangled was found on the rocks near where the explosion occurred. He removed his glasses and leaned back in his chair.

Murder was commonplace in Breneaux's beloved city, particularly among gangbangers, drug dealers, and thieves. "Let 'em kill each other!" he often railed. "Who cares? Do the town a favor." But this was a child lost to a sexual predator. He couldn't remember the last time it happened. He thought about Charmaine, his thirteen-year-old daughter, and Maggie, his wife, whom he lost the previous June.

He repositioned his glasses on the tip of his nose and scanned the article a second time. This time he recognized, with guilty pleasure, commercial potential in the young girl's death.

"America is listening." Breneaux intoned.

"Burn, this is David from Seattle. I just wanted to take issue with what you were saying about the Northwest."

Jesus! Kids are being sold in West Texas and murdered in New Awlins and this guy wants to debate geography. "Let me guess. You're going to try to convince me that you're the exception."

"Me *and* my wife. We both own guns. So do most of our friends."

"Do you have kids?" Breneaux asked.

"A boy and a girl."

"Then let me ask this. If a guy wanted to exchange his Jeep for your kids, would you go home and *get* your guns, or direct him to seek therapy?"

"Well—"

"That's what I thought." Breneaux cued Marilyn, and Marilyn dropped the call. "America is listening."

"Burn. How's it goin'?"

"It's goin'." Breneaux bristled, as always, at the inane expression. "What's on your mind?"

"We laugh at crazy stuff like parents selling their kids, but I guess it really happens. Maybe someone ought to teach parents how to parent. You can't drive a car without a license. You can't teach kids without a teaching certificate. Seems like to do just about anything, you have to go to school. But to become a parent, all it takes is ten minutes in the back of a car."

"Let me guess: you live next to David in Seattle." Breneaux felt blood, rushing to his brain. "I'm a dad. Everyone knows that. What people don't know is I'm a really good dad. I know what the job entails and knew from the start without spending five seconds in some liberal's wet dream of a classroom. The *last* thing we need is a bunch of socialists lecturing us on how to raise our kids. If you think you need parent training, get some, but keep it to yourself. If you actually believe there's a parent class in the world that could influence a mom who'd swap her kid for a condo, forget parent training and consider a lobotomy. Sex offenders don't need training. They need clinics specializing in castration, employing a combination of razor blades and salt.

"Case in point. Last night a seven-year-old girl was found murdered in New Awlins, blocks from our studios. Wake up, America. It can happen in your neighborhood like it happened in mine. There are monsters everywhere attracted to children. They go to prison, make friends with other monsters, learn advanced techniques for abusing kids, and get set free." He signaled Marilyn to drop the call.

"Keep your eyes open, America. They live right next door. Call your congressmen. Call the cops. Call an exterminator . . . before it's too late. It's time to stoke the ovens. These guys deserve to burn."

Breneaux signaled Marilyn and music swelled. *'Call an exterminator.' That's pretty good.* He smiled and settled deeper into his chair. Few things he enjoyed more than rousing his minions, stirring their passions, and getting them to care, even though for the most part, he couldn't care less.

Chapter 6

AWARDS AND ACCUSATIONS

SEAN paced nervously in the office of the chancellor, wondering why he'd been summoned to the hastily arranged meeting. He'd met with Sloan Erikson on only one other occasion, when interviewing for a job at Barataria Bay College. Erikson hired him as an adjunct instructor— then seemed to disappear until today. Sean stood alone, gazing out the window, unable to see Lake Pontchartrain due to the insistence of the rain.

"A morning shower. Should blow over by noon," the weatherman reported earlier in the day. Sean hoped he was right, having promised Ren he'd take her to a park after school. If New Orleans had anything, it was plenty of parks: parks for people, parks for dogs, and parks you just looked at through black iron gates. It was one of the first things Laurie and he noticed after moving there, answering the city's call for professionals in the wake of Hurricane Katrina. They packed the car and headed south, hoping to help others while cleansing themselves of all that had gone wrong in their native Illinois.

The chancellor's office, trimmed in mahogany and rosewood, boasted gaudy gold carpets and red velvet drapes. French chandeliers, ripe with pear-shaped crystals, hung high overhead beneath floral medallions. The building had been hastily rebuilt after the storm to assure jittery parents of the school's viability. Even after four years, sawdust hung in the air, mixing noxiously with the scent of Old Spice, the aftershave used by William Hardy.

Sean ran a finger along the edge of the desk that dominated the space in the center of the room. An oversized chair stood behind the desk, towering over smaller ones on the opposite side. One needn't know psychology to grasp the *big* chair occupant's intent—to create the illusion of power over puny, insignificant guests. Sean had felt exactly that way, positioned to look up at the five-foot-four chancellor. He recalled the man reaching over the top of the desk, grasping his hand with a bone-shattering crunch, making up in grip what he lacked in stature. Landing the job required paying a price: spending time in a puny chair, bearing the intended humiliation.

Sean continued to pace, the hour drawing near. There was still a chance Erikson could arrive on time, unlike Hardy, who was perpetually late. Sean shuddered at the mere thought of his nefarious uncle, a small-time Chicago attorney, bully, and bigot—the most despicable person he'd ever known. Gray-haired and bespectacled with an overhanging gut, he projected the image of a hanging judge, absent the rope hidden inside a sleeve. In public, he acted the loyal servant. But behind clients' backs, he sabotaged their aims. Claiming, "Only the righteous deserve a competent defense," he relished bragging to the family about the maneuvers he employed to punish the sinners he swore solemnly to protect. Hardy's competence could generally be seen; it was his heart that was obscured, as it was never in the right place. From his uncle, Sean learned to avoid all vice. One thing was certain: William Hardy knew who the sinners were.

"*Sean!*" Erikson roared, powering into the room. "How long has it been? Almost two years?"

Accompanying the chancellor was a strawberry blond, a student Sean had taught the previous spring. Marci Evans, wearing a tank top and jeans, glanced in his direction, but only for an instant. Sean recognized the dodge and knew it meant trouble.

"I believe you know Ms. Evans. Have a seat." The chancellor powered toward his perch, relegating them to the puny chairs.

Sean's pulse quickened. Thoughts filled his head. *Marci Evans. Average student. Did well on tests but failed to turn in homework.* The one time she came in to confer during office hours, he told her she had the potential to do well in psychology but that there was no free pass for failing to turn in assignments. She shocked him by giggling and running her finger along his arm, pausing at the sweet spot opposite his elbow. He pulled away in a panic, feeling vulnerable and exposed, but the memory of her touch lingered, distracting him for months.

Following the incident, Sean avoided her outside class, but felt her finger on his skin whenever he lay in bed. He felt guilty not only for straying in his mind, but for lusting after a student, risking years spent overcoming his past.

As the semester progressed, Marci's behavior changed. She turned in assignments and kept her hands to herself, causing Sean to conclude his message had been heard. Due to her improvement, he'd given her a B.

That's it. She thinks she deserved an A. She's here to challenge her grade. Relief flowed from the logical explanation.

Marci gazed at the floor, hands at her sides, pushing up and down incessantly on the red leather seat. Each time she pushed down, she sank a little lower, adding to the puniness on their side of the desk. Snapping sounds revealed a mouth full of gum, no doubt accumulated since second semester began.

Despite her childish behavior, Sean continued to be charmed by her bright cheery face, long shapely legs, narrow curving hips, and firm young breasts. *How can I be turned on by someone so immature?* He waited, hoping Vince would explain.

Erikson sat with his hands on the desk, sighting Sean down his long Roman nose. His silence implied it was Sean's turn to talk. But Sean remained quiet since nothing had been asked.

"We've got a problem," Erikson said, breaking the silence.

Oh, God. Sean's chest seized, Marci's expression remaining vacant. He'd given her a disappointing grade *and* rejected her advance. To get even, she'd twisted things, made up stories, perhaps gone online and discovered his status.

"Ms. Evans says she came to you for help last semester." Erikson paused again, as if waiting for an answer to another question not asked.

"That's right." Sean's hands trembled.

"According to her . . ."

Sean braced for the worst, his life flashing before him—Vince, William Hardy, and the girl he abused.

"You helped her pass the class."

Sean failed to comprehend.

"Because of that . . . she's nominated you Teacher of the Year."

Sean's face blanched. His throat constricted.

"Ms. Evans spearheaded a drive and found a lot of other students who felt the way she did. Turns out, you won. Congratulations, Jordan."

Sean sat stunned, not knowing what to say.

"There's just one problem . . ."

Sean's gut clenched again, the roller coaster approaching its next descent.

"We don't know your middle name."

"Middle name?"

"For the plaque . . . in the hall."

Marci reached in her mouth and pulled out the gum, wrapping it foil, wiping her hands on her jeans. "You saved my butt, Mr. J. You were so nice and helpful. I wanted to do something nice in return."

"I . . . ah . . ." Sean stammered.

"You're to be recognized a week from today at the annual faculty luncheon. Well done." The chancellor stood and smiled, extending his hand.

Sean staggered to his feet. "Thank you," he said, hand seized by the chancellor's. Sean turned to the girl and tentatively offered his hand. Ignoring that, she hugged him soundly, pinning his arms tightly to his sides. After years of dodging children, Sean was horrified by the embrace of a young woman who *acted* like a child, especially in front of the chancellor. He broke free, thanked her, and started for the door.

"Hold on a minute," the chancellor called.

Sean stopped and turned. Erickson's smile vanished.

"Thank you, Ms. Evans. You're excused."

Heading for the door, she discarded the gum, throwing a last glance at Sean with the doe eyes of a seventh-grader.

The moment the door shut, Erikson's eyes narrowed. "What gives, Jordan? I thought we had an understanding."

Sean's knees weakened. "What do you mean?"

"You informed me of your status before you were hired. The faculty committee found that admirable and we gave you a chance. But *this*. The girl's clearly enamored of you. I assumed she nominated you for your teaching ability. But seeing the two of you together . . . I need to know if there's something going on."

Sean's mind reeled, anger and guilt vying for supremacy. "I barely know her. There's nothing going on. I didn't even know we had a Teacher of the Year award."

The chancellor shook his finger. "I have no choice but to look into this. If I find you've taken advantage of Marci Evans, or any other student, for that matter, I'll relieve you of your duties and see to it you never teach again."

Bile rose from Sean's depths. He pictured his uncle in Erikson's place, waving a Bible in place of a finger, recounting a litany of imaginary sins. The ceiling inched lower; the walls closed in. *What more do you want?* Sean wanted to scream. Hadn't he avoided children and complied with the rules? Hadn't he gone ten years without a complaint? Hadn't he contributed to the education of his students? He wanted to proclaim his innocence, defend his actions, and extol his virtue. But he said and did nothing as doubt intervened.

What if I am *attracted to young girls?* It was the question that wouldn't go away.

Sean knew who he was from the time he was eight—a good kid with a mission and a passion to help. But at eighteen, upon conviction as a sexual offender, the world handed him a different read. He believed in his heart that he hadn't hurt anyone, and if he had, he certainly hadn't meant to. But it all became a blur as the voices grew louder, negating his goodness, asserting the bad. "An animal," he'd hear whispered as he walked down the street. "Less than human." He began to doubt his innocence. He began to ask the question.

There was no denying his attraction to Marci Evans, in spite of, or perhaps because of, her youth and immaturity. "It's perfectly natural," Vince had professed, "for men to be attracted to girls of child-bearing age starting at twelve to thirteen when their bodies begin to change—the blueprint written in our genes eons ago." But Sean didn't care what was natural or not. The only thing that mattered was proving the voices wrong.

Yet in attempting to do so, the voices grew louder, the question arising ever more frequently. Sean found himself asking it when girls walked by, obsessing over them while trying to cull them from his mind. Pushing thoughts of them aside was like rolling boulders uphill, denying their existence—ignoring the elephant in the room. He'd pose thought experiments, asking if he was attracted to each. When he was, guilt surged. When he wasn't, doubt negated knowing. He'd find fault with the results and, like a moth drawn to fire, push the experiments further by imagining having sex with them. The fantasies sickened him on most occasions. But when they brought him pleasure, guilt turned to despair.

"Now, if you'll excuse me," Erikson said, showing Sean the door.

There were so many things Sean wanted to say, but didn't know how without exploding in anger. *The little boy would have handled him without spilling blood.* The little boy, however, was nowhere to be found.

Chapter 7

BUSINESS AS USUAL

OWEN Dupree squinted in the early morning sun, pissed for having wasted still more time. Twice in two days, he'd caved to post-Katrina protocol, attending press conferences to convince the world that the city was on top of things, this time around. Dupree tried to imagine something he hated more. He glanced at his boss, Clarence Dodd, the city's self-important Chief of Police. Dodd stood at a podium spitting platitude after platitude, attempting to reassure tourists that despite recent events, New Orleans was ready to get on with Mardi Gras. Four gold stars on each of his shoulders made clear his status: one heartbeat below Mayor Jason Vincennes. Each time Dodd moved, the stars captured the light, reflecting it in Dupree's eyes, blinding him in microbursts of white. *Fuck!* Again he veered to avoid the light. *As if I need another reason to loathe this guy.*

Dodd had been lured back recently from LA where he'd risen to deputy police superintendent when gang violence declined. Dupree knew, however, that during that time, gang violence decreased in nearly every American city. What Dodd actually was, was a really good talker, dispensing dirty jobs to others to keep his own hands clean. That attitude was underscored by his ever-present gloves—white, in contrast to his coal-black skin.

Dodd, together with Mayor Vincennes, presented the face of reassurance to the city's black community and the face of black achievement to the rest of the country. They'd been friends since childhood and lived on the same block, attending Francis Nicholls High School and the University of New Orleans. No one was surprised when Dodd got the job. In New Orleans, friends took care of friends, and the rich got richer. Tradition determined outcomes and nothing ever changed.

Take murder, for instance. Dupree rocked on his heels, preferring to talk to himself rather than listen to Dodd. *Murder never changed.* It was one of the ugliest truths of the city Dupree adored. Murder was ingrained in its very fabric, dating to the early 1700s, when pirates settled scores with pistols and daggers, and runaway slaves were beheaded or hung. Contemporary murder—mainly black and drug related—was viewed as akin to natural selection, ridding the gene pool of dangerous pathogens that could adversely affect future generations. It wasn't right, but it wasn't going to change. In New Orleans, nothing ever changed.

Same with the environment. Dupree kicked a rock from beneath his foot. Disregard for coastal habitats had put the city at risk, again and again over the past hundred years. But despite coastal scientists' efforts and environmentalists' pleas, no one seriously believed anything would change. Not with thousands of jobs tied to the petrochemical industry. Not with politicians' reelections funded by oil and gas. Not with the State of Louisiana counting on billions in revenues from dozens of refineries still to be built.

And of course, graft in the French Quarter. Dupree couldn't remember when calls *hadn't* gone out to whitewash the warts of the city's oldest enclave. "Sanitize it like Disneyland." "Plasticize it like Vegas." Yet no one really wanted anything to change. Not the corporations that owned the bars that generated the cash that flooded the Quarter. Not the mayor and other officials who, like the pirates before them, protected the status quo for their own handsome rewards.

Dupree glanced at Dodd, recalling the shenanigans he'd seen, which had steadily grown during his years on the force. He'd gone his own way and been threatened as a result for not caving in and playing the game. His paycheck was sufficient, he'd always told himself. But he couldn't shake the question: Would his choices have been as clean if he hadn't come from money?

Dupree had come from a lot of money, flowing from his great-great-grandfather's sugar empire that, in the early 1800s, spanned five Southern states. Yet despite his family's fortune, he'd chosen to distance himself from the elite in reaction to the snobbishness of the Gulliars, relatives on his mother's side, and the pretentiousness of the Duprees, permeating the entirety of his father's side. He'd never been to a ball in his life. A ballgame was more like it, followed by a couple of shots of rye at one bar or another. A detective was what Dupree had wanted to be. Surviving in the position without selling his soul was among his life's greatest achievements. It wasn't his soul, however, that kept him employed. Rather, it was the quality of his work and the results he attained. If there was anyone in the department who made his superiors look good, it was Detective Lieutenant Owen Dupree.

"Let me be clear," Dodd said, scanning the reporters standing all around, his mustache dripping sweat, his gloved hands gripping the podium. "We think the explosion was due to natural gas. According to our engineers, a gas line runs beneath the old CSX freight lines now being used by the Riverfront Trolley. That line lies beside the aquarium, the IMAX Theater, and all of the Riverwalk. Why *just* the aquarium and theater were affected, sparing the majority of the marketplace, is unknown. We'll keep you posted."

A young reporter waved her arm.

"This'll be the last question," Dodd said. "Go ahead."

"With the exact cause of the explosion still unknown, should out-of-towners planning on attending Mardi Gras have any reason to be concerned?"

Dupree knew Dodd well enough to know that the reporter's challenge, with its implied threat to Mardi Gras, had lit a fuse. The press conference had been calculated to draw attention *away* from people thinking there might be a terrorist running loose. It had been staged not in front of the aquarium's remains or the listing Danish Star, but midway between, along a portion of the marketplace that had largely been spared, its broken windows quickly repaired. Dupree wished he could walk over and shake the young woman's hand for providing the first bit of glee he'd felt in days.

"No reason whatsoever," Dodd answered, flashing a Louis Armstrong-wide smile of reassurance. "Families, couples, one and all—come join us this year for Mada Gras. We regret that two of our entertainment venues are temporarily closed, but there are hundreds more ready for your enjoyment."

As soon as the press conference drew to a close, Dodd darted for Dupree, took him by the arm, and led him downriver in the direction of the aquarium. "What the fuck was that? I'm bustin' my hump to keep everything under control and we got reporters takin' potshots at us during the biggest event of the year." They swung under the police tape, stepping over glass, twisted steel, and noxious debris. Dodd motioned toward the crater. "Gas. Not in a million years. It was some crazy son of a bitch. Couldn't wait 'til July or the beginning of November. Had to hit us now when it hurts us most." Stepping outside the yellow perimeter, Dodd stumbled on the uneven ground, breaking his fall with an outstretched arm, his hand grazing a rock covered with charred wood. "God *dammit!*" he yelled, removing both gloves, slapping one against the other to expunge the dirt. "So . . . where are you?"

Nowhere. Not yet. Not this early, Dupree wanted to say, but knew he had to keep the thought to himself. "Sheldon and Thames are working on the explosion. I've got Santos on the ferry. Brisbane's looking for witnesses. They're poring over evidence and calling me hourly."

"*And . . .*" Dodd's impatience was palpable.

"Jas and I are heading the Daniels murder. Weinstat provided a list of sex offenders, half of which I interviewed yesterday. The rest I'm seeing today." Dupree tracked the scowl broadening across Dodd's face. "One thing's been settled: Henry Toussaint was no terrorist— just a ferryboat captain run amuck. He stole the boat to impress a woman—wrong place, wrong time. Paid for it with his life." Dupree braced, feeling it coming.

"That's *it*? Christ, Dupree. So what if everyone's working. Think that's gonna impress the mayor? He wants this business settled *now*." Dodd lowered his voice. "Every day this case goes unsolved— particularly if the media starts hinting at terrorism—more tourists'll stay home. You know what that could cost us this year?"

"To within a five bucks," Dupree said, spitting with sarcasm.

"Just south of half a billion dollars. Gone. Nothing can replace that. Not Jazz and Heritage. Not Essence. Not even Decadence. Shit, it'd take five years of Southern queer Decadence to make up one fucking *Mada Gras!*"

Dupree had heard enough. He unzipped his jacket and slung it over a bench, loosened his tie, and brought his face to within an inch of Dodd's. "You think half a billion dollars is impossible to replace? Try replacing a seven-year-old. Let me make this simple. My job's yours any time you want it. I don't give a fuck about you or the mayor or your billion-dollar weekend. What I care about is the safety of this city's citizens and bringing a tiny measure of relief to the Daniels, knowing their daughter's murderer won't get a second chance. Any problem with that?"

Dodd bowed his head. "Yeah . . . the Daniels. Sorry. Heard they were friends. How did that go?"

"Fuck you, Dodd. How do you *think* it went?" Dupree draped his jacket over his arm. "Unless there's anything else we need to discuss, I've got work to do."

Chapter 8

A NEW GUN IN TOWN

"GOOD mo'nin' . . . *N'Awlins!* Weatherman's promised us a beautiful day. Unusually warm for this time of year. Should stay nice straight through to Mada Gras. Speaking of which . . . to those of you who've never been to New Awlins, pack your bags and head to the French Quarter. What's that? You can't afford to travel? Not since the Democrats raised your taxes so you could buy health insurance for the poor?" Breneaux and Marilyn exchanged smirks through the window. "What would *you* like to talk about? America is listening."

"Mr. Breneaux," a woman began, "I'm calling about my husband. He's twenty-four. He served time in jail for having sex with a sixteen-year-old. He was a senior in high school and eighteen. Now he can't get a job and we're having a hard time finding a place to live. We've been married two years and have a one-year-old son who the authorities are threatening to take away. My husband's a good man. That's what nobody understands. The girl said she was eighteen, but she lied."

She lied. Breneaux loved the excuse. "When 'the girl,' as you called her, claimed to be eighteen, did your husband ask for her ID before he had sex?"

"I don't know."

"Sounds like a question that ought to be asked." Breneaux said.

"But she lied."

"Listen, honey, if I got a nickel every time a caller told me someone lied about her age, I'd be a million dollars richer." He signaled Marilyn, who released the call. "America is listening."

"Burn, that last call you had, I believe her. The same thing happened to me," a male voice said.

"See what I mean? A million dollars and five cents. I'm listening."

"I met this girl in a bar."

"That was your first mistake."

"I figured, no way would a bar let an underage girl in. Right?"

"That was your second."

"They would have checked her ID at the door to make sure she was twenty-one like she said."

"And how old *was* she?"

"Fourteen, but believe me—"

"Oh, I believe you."

"—she totally looked twenty-one in makeup, high heels, and falsies."

"And you had sex with her?"

"Yeah . . . thinking she was twenty-one."

"When you had sex, was she still wearing makeup, heels, falsies?"

"Just makeup."

"So let me get this straight. You're staring at the naked body of a fourteen-year-old who's no longer padded, no longer decked out like a twenty-something hooker, and you can't tell she's not twenty-one? With all the kiddie porn you have lying around your house, surely you're an expert." Breneaux waited to see if he'd provoked a response. The absence of one meant he'd hit the nail on the head. "I can sort of understand if a girl's seventeen and says she's eighteen, and you're a confused kinda guy and too dumb to ask for proof. But expecting us to believe you were taken in by a fourteen-year-old is beyond belief. Did you talk?"

"What do you mean?"

"You know, words strung together: 'Hi, how are ya?' 'Wuz up?' 'How come your legs are so skinny?' Stuff like that."

"Sure."

"Well, did she sound like a college girl, spouting Chaucer, discussing Poli Sci, comparing and contrasting Christian and Buddhist traditions? Or did she like sound sorta, um, you know, well kinda like, dah . . . middle school?" The caller remained silent. "And would you know the difference?" More silence. "What did you talk about?"

"Her friends, mostly."

"Her *friends*. Did you have sex with any of them?" The phone went dead. "Whoops, there he goes. The caller who objected to being lied to apparently couldn't handle the truth."

Breneaux glimpsed Arthur Manning, general manager of WFQT, entering the engineering booth, followed by a young man wearing slacks and a blazer. The kid was good looking with wavy black hair and an air of confidence verging on conceit.

"You know what?" Breneaux said, suddenly animated. "If I woke one morning to discovered that scientists had found a way to tell which eggs and sperm would combine to become sex offenders, I'd consider changing my position on abortion. That's right. You heard it here: Burn Breneaux, pro choice."

Breneaux glanced up, just in time to see the kid give him two thumbs up. He resisted waving back with a different set of fingers.

Marilyn cut to a commercial. The imperious Arthur Manning, spitting image of Ichabod Crane, pressed a button on the engineer's console. "Burn, when you wrap, come to my office. There's someone I want you to meet."

Breneaux smiled, masking his contempt. He'd known a hundred Art Mannings—coaches, agents, managers, and execs, who earned a fraction of what he did yet tried to tell *him* what to do. Twenty-four months. That's how long each of them lasted, while he'd stayed put for twenty-one years. He remembered simpler times when *he* handled engineering, accompanied only by a secretary for coffee, phones, and mail. Then came a string of worthless general managers whose *raison d'être* he never fully grasped. None had ever posed a threat, but each had annoyed him immensely.

Originally, the station was privately owned—then later acquired by a regional chain. Eventually it was purchased by a network for millions to capture the revenue generated by Breneaux. The only thing that *hadn't* changed over the years was the shithole suite of offices in the dilapidated brick building, built by slaves before the Civil War. Breneaux knew in his heart he deserved much better. But if push came to shove over tuck-pointed brick, he'd choose cash over brick all day long.

Manning exited the booth with the young man in tow, the kid waving a salute in Breneaux's direction.

Breneaux hated punks like him. "America is listening."

The remainder of callers, rounding out the morning, was made up of sex-offender haters lobbying for torture. Breneaux felt increasingly disturbed by such calls, confusing fantasized violence with the real thing. He thought about Maggie, the love of his life, recalling her antipathy toward violence of any kind. He rubbed his eyes, staring at the ceiling. *Maybe it's me. Maybe I'm too old for all this.*

"Be alert, be prepared, be Americans. God Bless America. See you tomorrow." He sighed deeply, like a man heavily burdened, rather than one who'd just scored another twenty-two grand.

Breneaux noticed, upon entering Manning's lair, boxes of reel-to-reel tapes atop NAB carts that had lain in the same pile for thirty-some years. He'd forgotten that Manning's office was an even bigger pit than the others. The kid held up a cartridge with a quizzical expression.

"Don't ask!" Manning barked. "You hadn't been born." He turned to Breneaux. "Burn, I'd like you to meet Del LeGrande." The young man quickly extended his hand. Breneaux took stock of his stylishly trimmed hair, high cheeks, square jaw, and deep-brown complexion. He'd either spent months on a beach in Tahiti or weeks under lights at a tanning retreat. His black eyes gleamed, crackling with excitement, while at the same time appearing strangely vacant. "I've brought Del from our affiliate in Santa Monica to be our new ten-to-two man. He thinks like you do. You have a lot in common."

Breneaux grasped the kid's hand and stared into his eyes, trying to imagine what commonalities there could possibly be.

"This is an honor," LeGrande said, glancing at his hand still held by Breneaux. "I'm in radio because of you. Every night from the time I was twelve, I climbed into bed and listened to your show, trying to anticipate how you'd respond to each call."

"Did you wait until later, or jack off *while* you were listening?" Breneaux asked, belittlingly.

LeGrande seemed stunned but recovered quickly, laughing along good naturedly.

"'LeGrande'—French . . . They'll love you down here," Breneaux added, finally releasing his grip.

"Actually, Spanish and French, with a pinch of Italian added for flavor." LeGrande exercised his fingers, recirculating the blood. "Is it okay to call you Burn?"

"Well, seeing as how we'll be working together, I think you should feel free to call me Mr. Breneaux, pronounced brĕn-ō—also French, with the accent on the second syllable." The corners of LeGrande's lips dropped at the slight.

"Gentlemen, have a seat." Manning directed them to the couch by his desk, covered with a healthy layer of dust.

Last cleaned by slaves before the Civil War. Breneaux's cynicism segued to outright impatience when Manning circled his desk as if planning to sit down. Breneaux had been there since 6:00 a.m. All he wanted was to get the hell out.

"Del's well-liked on the Coast," Manning said, massaging his long, crooked nose. "Younger conservatives are crazy about him. Granted, they do things a little differently there. But management believes the same can work here, strengthening our ratings all along the Gulf. If Del's successful, they'll take him national—ten-to-two, right after you."

My ratings need strengthening? Breneaux felt his neck redden, his blood pressure rise. "What exactly do they do differently on the Coast?"

"We out offenders," LeGrande mumbled, too quietly to be heard.

"You what?"

"We out offenders, neighborhood by neighborhood, block by block." LeGrande shifted on the couch to face Breneaux. "What we do is—"

"I know what outing is," Breneaux said, bristling, doing nothing to conceal his disdain. He looked at Manning. "We've gone 'round and 'round on this for years."

Manning was quick to rebut. "They've shown great results from outing in the West. Huge increases in the dailies." He held up his hands in a defensive gesture. "I know . . . sex offender information's freely available. Anyone can find it, just go online. But calling them out on air captures people's attention. People won't check the Internet, but they'll listen to guys like you and Del. It's a reality-show world we live in. Welcome to reality radio."

"People want to feel safe," LeGrande added. "They want to know who's living next door. If there's a sex offender close by, they want to know. They have a right to know. We're giving them exactly what they want."

Breneaux's head was reeling. Who the hell were they to be lecturing him about conservative tastes, sex offenders, and of all things . . . ratings? If it weren't for the revenue he generated for *them*, they'd be outside on scaffolds, patching the brick. He thought to bolt, but kept his cool, assessing the situation calmly. As long as LeGrande was in the game, Breneaux would keep his eyes open and forge ahead.

He turned to Manning. "You know my position on this. It's one thing to take a conservative stance and chase the collective bogeyman all over the air. It's another to wreak havoc in the community."

"But Burn—" LeGrande caught himself. "Mr. Breneaux. Offenders wreak havoc every day. Don't you think we should stop them whenever we can?"

"Who do you think we are—the *police*? It's not our job to stop anybody from doing anything."

Breneaux saw Manning exchange a glance with LeGrande and knew immediately they'd discussed this before—sitting in this room, talking about him behind his back.

Manning leaned forward. "I know how you feel, Burn, but the decision's out of my hands. Tomorrow at ten, Del starts outing offenders."

Chapter 9

RECLAIMING THE MISSING PARTS

TEACHER of the Year, Sean thought, shaking his head. He pictured himself on a makeshift stage, shaking the hands of insincere colleagues and reaching to receive an undeserved plaque, while listening to the sound of hollow applause. *If only they knew their man-of-the-year's not only a sex offender but also a murderer.* Sean could hear Vince, laughing along.

There was no question about Sean being a good teacher, but he'd only been teaching a couple of years. Others had taught at the school for decades. It bothered him that someone truly deserving could lose on account of a schoolgirl's crush. He'd already decided to send Erickson a note, respectfully declining the prestigious award.

His students found him illuminating and engaging, judging by their attentiveness when his knowledge poured forth. In turn, their insights fortified *him*, reminding him of his past and that he had much to give. If he couldn't be a psychologist—a condition he intended to rectify—he could at least pass on to others what Vince had taught him. He entered the classroom like an athlete taking the field, leaving Erikson's threats far behind.

"The genius of Fritz Perls, father of Gestalt therapy, is evident in his theories and therapeutic approach. Perls stated that problems arise when people jettison parts of their personalities. These he called the 'missing parts'—the parts needing to be reclaimed." As Sean spoke, he scanned the room, watching Josh Braun tuck his legs under his desk, Sissy Newquest silence her phone, and Brian Bellwether remove a bowler from his head. Bellwether referred to the hat as his "bolder," a metaphor for his acting outrageous in class. Sean read in their faces the desire he had—to enjoy helping others while healing his own psychic wounds. *Good luck*, he thought, *with that healing yourself part.* They'd learn soon enough what Vince had taught him.

"What missing parts?" Aubrey Collins asked.

Sean swept his curls out of his eyes. "*Responsibility*, as opposed to blaming others. *Knowing*, versus keeping oneself in a fog. Telling the *truth*, rather than perpetuating lies. According to Perls, reclaiming the parts we've given away restores emotional health and our lives become whole. 'Gestalt' is the German word for 'whole.'"

"I once told a girlfriend I was sleeping with her roommate," Bellwether blurted to a chorus of guffaws. "After that, I went back to lies."

Sean chuckled on his way to Bellwether's desk. "Mr. Bellwether. As bold as you are, I'm surprised you didn't ask your girlfriend for permission."

"Oooos" filled the room.

Sissy Newquest raised her hand. "How do we do that—reclaim the missing parts?"

"Ahh, das ist die question," Sean said, in his best, tortured, Viennese accent. Students chuckled politely while he stroked an imaginary beard. "First vee must become avare of die parts vee've given avay."

Josh Braun spoke up. "And how do we do *that*?"

Sean smiled and dropped the accent. "Freud had patients lie on a couch, dissecting their childhoods to uncover their pasts. Perls had clients sit in a chair, retelling their dreams to illuminate the present. I'll demonstrate." He arranged two chairs, facing each other. "Can any of you recall a dream you recently had or a recurrent dream that's fresh in your mind?" James Denton, a handsome preacher's kid from Minnesota, raised a hand tentatively. "Mr. Denton. Have a seat." Denton walked to the front and sat in one chair facing the other. "Tell us your dream."

"Well, it's a little embarrassing," he began.

Sean placed a hand on Denton's shoulder and addressed the class. "When clients say they're embarrassed, tell them it's the embarrassing stuff you *specialize* in, and that it's perfectly safe for them to continue. That typically brings a smile, and they usually go on."

"I was hosting a party at my house and *you* were there," Denton continued.

"Ahhh, dreaming about the teacher," Bellwether snickered.

"We were a lot older in the dream. You were a famous psychologist, and you and I were alone in the dining room."

"Not the bedroom?" Bellwether said, with an exaggerated wink.

"I was setting the table and you were pouring champagne. Suddenly you collapsed on the floor and died. Then I woke up."

"Good, Mr. Denton. Thank you," Sean said. "Now . . . I want you to picture me as I was in your dream and imagine me sitting across from you in the chair. Talk to me in the chair, telling me the dream again, this time making sure to include every detail."

Denton stared at the chair. "You're a famous psychologist, visiting New Orleans, and you've come to my house to attend a reception. Most of the guests are sitting in the living room. You and I are in the dining room, preparing for dinner. Suddenly you collapse. Champagne spills all over the floor. I hear the sound of breaking glass."

"How are you feeling?" Sean asked. "Keep talking to the chair."

"Terrible. You're my guest. I've read all your books. And you're dying. I'm frightened. I don't know CPR. I don't know what to do. Then you die."

"Go deeper. Say how you're feeling."

"Horrible that I couldn't save you . . . that you died . . . at my house."

Sean noticed an ever-so-slight shift in Denton's expression. "Something just happened. What did you notice?"

Denton grinned. "This is *really* embarrassing."

"Talk to the chair."

"I'm sorry you died . . . But I'm glad you died at my house." Several students leaned in. "The most famous psychologist who ever lived died right in front of me on my dining room floor. That makes me a celebrity!"

Students snickered quietly.

"Close your eyes. Aside from embarrassed, how else do you feel?" Sean asked.

Eyes closed, Denton sat quietly. "Calm . . . centered . . . more honest than I usually am."

"And how does honesty feel?"

"Good. Really good." Denton opened his eyes.

"That was a nice piece of truth to reclaim. Thank you, Mr. Denton. You can take your seat." Sean scanned the room. "Anyone else?"

Sissy Newquest raised her hand and made her way to the empty chairs. "I've been having this horrible dream for over two years. I'd like to find out what it means."

"Okay," Sean said. "Relax and tell us your dream."

"I'm walking down a country road on a sunny summer day. Tall grasses form a tunnel on both sides of the road, so all I can see is the road, grass, and sky. Suddenly I hear a plane. It sounds like it's in trouble. I look up and see a jet approaching from the left, flying low overhead. Smoke and sparks are pouring out of one engine and I know it's going to crash. I think about all the people on board and feel awful because I can't do anything to save them. It disappears behind the grass on the right and explodes with a terrible boom."

"Good, Ms. Newquest. Now I'd like you to sit in the other chair and tell the dream to Sissy, as if you were the plane."

"This is going to be hard," she said.

"If it becomes too difficult, you can stop whenever you like," he assured her.

Sissy sat silently, as if gathering her thoughts. "I'm a jet and I'm in trouble. I'm scared to death I might crash. There are so many people on board, people I know I'm responsible for. I'm trying so hard to stay aloft. I'm doing everything I can to keep going."

"Say that again," Sean directed.

"I'm trying so hard to stay aloft and keep going—keep everything up in the air."

"Again," Sean said.

"I'm trying so hard . . . to keep all the balls in the air. But I can't. I'm afraid I won't be able to meet my responsibilities." Newquest began to cry. Sean approached Sissy and crouched beside her. "My Dad got a second job so I could go to school, and I'm having a hard time maintaining a C. I live in constant fear I'm going to disappoint him."

Sean handed her a tissue and talked with her quietly so no one else could hear. When he felt she was ready, he asked before the class, "What was the part you'd given away?"

Newquest took time to consider the question. "My confidence," she said, sounding resolute. She used the tissue to dab her eyes. "I know I can do it. After all, I'm a *jet!*" The class chuckled, encouragingly. "I just need to go back and change a few things."

Sissy looked at Sean. "Thank you."

Chapter 10

DEATH IN A NET

SEAN zigzagged through the parking lot toward a Pontiac Firebird, basking in the sun like a satiated lion. The 1970 was a relic by actuarial standards with removable T-tops, scoops dominating the hood, and a chrome insignia proclaiming it a Formula 400. Yet the car remained roadworthy, pinning Sean to the seat each time he climbed in and stepped on the accelerator. He appreciated its pedigree, beauty, and power, but cherished it most because it had belonged to his father.

Sean's father, John, an itinerant actor, purchased the car new, decades before, while starring in a traveling production of *Hair*. "Buying the car was a mistake," he lamented, the first time he invited Sean inside. "Never know when the show's gonna close." Then a smile crossed his face and his foot powered down. "Let's go!" he said, bolting from the curb.

Though barely able to see over the dash, Sean was thrilled as they sped through Chicago, racing beneath tracks suspended in air and zooming along a lake that looked like a sea. "Thrust" was the name bestowed on the car, presumably because of its speed and power. But Vince told Sean with a wink and a grin that his son might have had a different meaning in mind. Regardless, the name stuck. When Sean's father died, the car passed to him—not without resistance from William Hardy—and was stored by Doug's mom in a shed behind her house, where it remained until he was old enough to retrieve it.

Sean steered the car in the direction of the Marigny, the French Quarter's neighbor on the downriver side. He'd settled in that neighborhood instead of the Quarter when he found the Quarter's prices to be out of his reach. The Marigny was the "*new* French Quarter," according to realtor, Pamela Perrot—"center of the emerging music scene, with scrumptious restaurants and charming and affordable houses." "Charming and affordable," Sean soon learned, was realtor code for "badly in need of repair." He made his way along Esplanade and turned onto Frenchman, passing Café Brazil, dba, Spotted Cat, and Snug Harbor, clubs he and Laurie occasionally visited.

Laurie. Sean pictured her face as he drew closer to home, especially her smile and single pierced ear. He was eager to recount his unsavory morning and tell her, as well, about his gratifying afternoon. But he knew she was scheduled to work second shift and wouldn't leave the hospital until late that night. By then, she'd be tired and probably in a bad mood, given her recent sullenness and easy irritation. Still, he hoped, she'd be open to talk. She was his best friend and staunchest ally, bearing his troubles like he bore hers, but it hadn't seemed that way for a while. He pictured again her generous smile, unable to recall when it was last on display.

He pulled onto cracked brick that served as a drive and stared at the house they both adored. Its distinctive style—narrow but deep—was characteristic of houses in southern Louisiana. A "single shotgun," Perrot had called it, its door covered by shutters with moveable slats. Its name, she explained, drew from the fact that its rooms lay to one side of a long narrow hall, stretching all the way from the front to the back. "With a clear line of sight and no obstructions in between, you could fire a shotgun and not disturb a thing!" Perrot said gleefully, as if having done so herself.

Sean climbed the steps to the Victorian front porch and gazed contentedly at the houses all around. *"If you've taken advantage of Marci Evans . . . I'll see to it you never teach again."* Erikson's threat echoed in his ears. Sean wondered if the neighborhood, the city, and the house he owned were mere blips on a screen in a life void of permanence.

Entering, Sean heard muffled voices, a man's and a woman's from down the hall. His neck tightened. His fists clenched. Flashing on his meeting with Marci and the chancellor, he wondered what else was secretly going on. Laurie had never given him reasons to feel jealous, but her recent petulant mood and emotional unavailability had taken a toll on his sense of self-worth. He suddenly felt threatened . . . and guilty because of it.

The voices grew louder as Sean advanced. *The bedroom? She wouldn't do that to me.* Discomfort flirted with panic. He tried to reclaim the missing parts—his trust in his wife and his self-esteem— but fear intervened, blocking his aim. His legs grew heavy, his pace slowed. He recalled the boy, unable to move, terrified by the prospect of what lay ahead. Eventually the bedroom came into view. He turned. Mercifully, no one was there.

He proceeded toward the kitchen at the end of the hall. Laurie's voice was recognizable; the man's was not. He wondered for the first time if there was a chance he might lose her. *Why not?* he thought. Loss had been a constant companion. He took a last step and pivoted into the room.

Laurie and a stranger sat opposite each other, talking quietly at the kitchen table. Their serious expression was underscored by her pensive gaze downward, his body pitched forward.

Laurie spun suddenly in Sean's direction. "Honey!" She brought a hand to her chest. "You scared me."

"You're home," he said, accusatorily.

"They're doing repairs on the neonatal wing. They let us off early. This is Detective—"

"Dupree." The man rose, extending his hand. "Owen Dupree."

A detective. Relief was negated by a different kind of threat. Sean ignored the gesture and stepped behind Laurie, placing his hands on top of her shoulders. "What's this about?"

"When you moved here a year and a half ago, you registered as a sex offender, which is your obligation under Louisiana law. A little girl was raped and murdered two nights ago. When a sex crime is committed, it's my job to determine the whereabouts of sex offenders residing in Awleans Parish." He sat, pulling a notepad and pen from his pocket. "Where were you on Sunday night?"

Sean's chest wrenched. His mind raced to the time he was interrogated by police in a roundup of suspects tied to the disappearance of a girl. She was found safe and sound the following morning, camped in a "fort" she and a girlfriend crafted inside a room in the girlfriend's house. But for Sean, the psychic damage had been done.

Laurie squeezed his hand. Dupree appeared to notice.

"Here at home, preparing for class. Then I went to bed . . . with my wife."

"Sean," Laurie said softly, eyes darting nervously over her shoulder.

Sean told himself to back off and simply answer the questions. But he couldn't find a way to rise above the pain. The unexpected visit on the heels of the chancellor's threat reawakened his guilt and scraped his nerves raw.

"Your wife's version's the same as yours. She was about to tell me how you pulled offender status. All I have in the file is a ten-year-old conviction for the 'criminal sexual abuse of a minor.' You were eighteen; she was fifteen. There's also a note that your registration was extended. I'm curious what happened." Dupree waited.

Sean knew he was being tested. Certainly the detective had the answers already. Seeing Laurie lean forward as if about to talk, he jumped in. "Like I said, I was home with my wife."

Dupree returned the notepad to his pocket. "Okay, Jordan. Have it your way. I have other means of finding out. I was just trying to get a better picture. Your wife seems like a nice lady—thought maybe I could help."

"Help? I'm a registered sex offender. Why would you want to help me?"

Dupree set the pen on the table. "Jordan, I hate people who prey on kids, particularly when there's sex involved. It wouldn't displease me at all if most sex offenders were wiped from the earth. But I know we get it wrong sometimes."

"Wrong? How?"

"When the law goes fishing for sharks, it casts a wide net. Sometimes it catches a dolphin. Not supposed to. Just happens. Unfortunately after they're caught, most dolphins die in the net."

Sean removed his hands from Laurie's shoulders and took a seat facing Dupree. "What do you care as long as you catch enough sharks?"

Dupree's eyes held Sean's. "When *I* go after sharks . . . sharks are all I want."

"So what are you saying, I'm innocent?"

"No one's innocent, Mr. Jordan. It's a matter of degrees. Besides, I don't know what you did. You won't tell me."

Sean pictured himself dragging the detective into the hall, propping him up, and firing a shotgun to see if anything would be disturbed.

"Sean," Laurie repeated, her voice rising. "Detective Dupree's only trying to help."

Sean angled in her direction, spotting the lone earring. A look of surrender had settled over her face. *Where's the pirate I used to know, the one who wouldn't have hesitated to take this guy on?* He felt alone. Abandoned.

"To show you what a helpful sort of guy I am . . . Sidney Weinstat, head of registration at police headquarters, said to say 'Hi' if I saw you, and to remind you that you were required to report to him at the anniversary of your arrival in New Awlins. Apparently you're more than six months late. By statute, if you're ten days late, you're required to be fined a thousand dollars and sentenced to two years hard labor. Weinstat sends his apologies for not getting in touch with you sooner."

Sean wrinkled his brow. "Anniversary?"

"Every anniversary, Jordan. It was spelled out when Weinstat detailed your obligations. Since Weinstat hasn't gotten around to arresting you and you've continued to live in the same house, maintain the same job, and stay married to the same nice lady . . ." He glanced at Laurie with the hint of a smile. "I'm willing to prove you wrong about our unwillingness to help. I'll give you a break—this time—provided you report to Weinstat first thing in the morning." Dupree stood. He reached in his pocket, pulled out a card, and set it on the table. "My cell's on the back . . . if you change your mind. Thanks, ma'am, for your hospitality. I'll see myself out."

Sean slumped in the chair. Laurie sat and said nothing. He felt her judging him in the stillness.

"You might have been nicer," she said, breaking the silence as she headed for the sink.

"It's starting all over." He could hear the self-pity in his voice and hated himself for it.

"He was just asking where you were."

"He was asking if I killed a seven-year-old girl."

"It's his job. All you did was lie. We both lied to protect your friend."

Those were more words than Laurie had spoken to him in a week, and . . . she'd backed him when he needed it.

Still, Sean felt doom descending.

Chapter 11

THE TRUE BELIEVER

BRENEAUX listened to the familiar clip-clop of horses' hoofs, clattering atop pavers on Rue de Bienville, when the door to Arnaud's swung open behind him. He turned to see if it was the guest he was expecting and saw instead an elderly woman, negotiating the entrance with the help of a walker. Breneaux fumed. He wasn't accustomed to rubbing elbows with the riffraff, waiting for others in his party, waiting for *anything*. Typically he'd walk to the end of the hall where he'd be greeted by the staff of one of the city's best restaurants. "Good evening, Mr. Breneaux." "Good show today, Mr. Breneaux." "You're usual table, Mr. Breneaux?" Tonight, however, he'd waited in the hall as a courtesy to his guest, to be there when he arrived. But when the clock chimed seven, pretence ceased. He skirted the old woman, making his way down the hall, and impatiently summoned the maitre d'.

"It's good to see you, Mr. Breneaux. Follow me."

It was the service he expected. "Good to see you, too, Patrick. How's your family?"

"Fine, Mr. Breneaux. Thank you for asking. Table 83 in the Richelieu Room?"

"Not tonight, Patrick. Something a little quieter. Is Bacchus available?"

"Right this way." Clutching oversized menus, Patrick hastened down the hall, Breneaux following.

Breneaux took a seat at the only table in the room—an historic space behind the main dining area. Surrounding him were flickering candles and framed photos from Mardi Gras past. No sooner had he been seated when a bartender appeared, a Captain Morgan in one hand, an Altadis' Behike cigar in the other. *At least one place still practices Southern gentility.* "Thank you, Claude."

"Certainly, sir." The bartender disappeared as fast as he'd arrived.

"There'll be two of us tonight, Patrick," Breneaux told the maitre d'. If you wouldn't mind, keep your eye out for a young prick—twenty-five or so—fresh off the bus from LA. Los Angeles, that is. Not Louisiana. Thinks he's going to replace me someday."

"There's no replacing you, Mr. Breneaux. I'll keep an eye on the door. Did you tell me his name?"

"LeGrande. Something-or-other LeGrande." Breneaux slipped a hundred dollar bill in Patrick's hand.

"Thank you, Mr. Breneaux."

"My pleasure."

Breneaux had hoped to spend the evening with Charmaine—take her to dinner and let her go on about her day. But he kept replaying the line from *Godfather II*: "Keep your friends close; keep your enemies closer." By three, he'd called to extend an invitation. LeGrande accepted unhesitatingly.

Breneaux looked at his watch at ten past the hour. *Impudence! Arrogance! Rudeness!* He was certain the kid would do well in radio.

Patrick appeared in the doorway and escorted LeGrande to the table.

"Sorry I'm late," LeGrande said, removing his jacket and folding it in his lap.

An instant later, another attendant appeared. "Wouldn't you be more comfortable wearing that, sir?"

"Ah, no, I'm fine. Thanks," LeGrande said, looking up at Breneaux, who was shaking his head. LeGrande suddenly caught on. "Ah . . .

sure," he sputtered. "That would be great." He unfolded the jacket and slid it back on.

"I noticed you were a few minutes late," Breneaux said.

"I was held up by a parade and couldn't cross Canal. Why is there a parade?"

Breneaux looked at LeGrande and cocked his right brow. "In New Awlins . . . we only ask 'why' when there's *not* a parade." As an offer of peace, he tipped the Behike in LeGrande's direction. "Care for a smoke?"

"No, thanks."

"Mind if I do?" Breneaux chuckled to himself, knowing LeGrande hadn't a clue that he'd passed on Spain's finest at $500 a pop.

"No, go ahead," LeGrande said, glancing at the memorabilia adorning the walls. "Nice place. Feels like it's been here awhile."

"Nine years," Breneaux said.

"Really? I would have guessed longer than that."

"Nine years before California became a state." Breneaux took a drag, sending smoke rings sailing straight for LeGrande. "In 1990, they celebrated the building's 150th."

"What would you like, sir?" Claude asked, returning to the table.

"Club soda with a lime," LeGrande replied.

Breneaux kept his eyes on him. "Not a drinking man. Hmm. Claude, I suggest you check his ID anyway. How old do you think he is? Nineteen? Twenty? Twenty-one tops."

Claude glanced at LeGrande. "I don't know, sir. You might be right. Another for you, Mr. Breneaux?"

"In a while, Claude. Thank you."

"I'm thirty-three, *Mr.* Breneaux," LeGrande said, spinning "Mr." sarcastically.

Breneaux noted he was close, having figured him for thirty-five.

"I know you probably think I'm a punk with little experience and even less talent. But you're wrong. I dabbled in radio on and off as a kid, did a stint in the Marines—then moved to the West Coast where my numbers were strong. I can deliver an audience to sponsors—not as well as you—but well enough to make the network take notice. I don't know what the problem is here. We're on the same team. We believe the same things. We ought to be able to get along."

Breneaux positioned his rook decisively. "Tell me about the things we believe."

"Conservative causes, of course."

"There are lots of conservative causes. You make it sound like we share some *special* beliefs."

LeGrande glanced at the doorway and lowered his voice. "What we have in common is our hatred for sex offenders—teachers, custodians, doctors, priests. They live in our neighborhoods and loiter near playgrounds, laying in wait to attack kids. Hell, why am I lecturing *you*?"

Breneaux took another sip and continued to listen.

"I don't have kids, but you do. You have to be more concerned than me."

Breneaux deposited an ash on the ring of his ashtray, reflecting on his constant worries about Charmaine. Yet, of all the things he fretted about with the potential for harm, being a victim of sexual abuse never crossed his mind.

"Your career skyrocketed when you ditched gays for offenders. For me, it's the only cause I've ever known."

Claude walked to the table and placed LeGrande's drink before him. He pointed at Breneaux's glass and exited when his customer nodded.

"Let me get this straight," Breneaux said. "You believe this stuff. You actually believe it."

"Of course I do!"

Breneaux stared at his drink, at a rare loss for words, having captured the guy's queen without knowing what to do with it. He knew the arguments well; he'd employed them a thousand times. But he never lost sight of the larger truths and never wandered out of bounds. Sitting across from him was a true believer who seemed constrained by no boundaries at all.

"What?" LeGrande asked, irritated by Breneaux's silence.

"Just trying to understand where you're coming from."

"Same place as you, believe me."

"I don't think so."

Claude appeared with Breneaux's second round and a plate of fresh limes for LeGrande's club soda.

"Meaning . . ."

"I suspect we don't remotely think alike." Breneaux sent more smoke rings spiraling toward the ether. "You actually believe what comes out of your mouth. I believe ten percent of what comes out of mine. You think what you say is based in reality and that your message is actually important. I know what I say is mostly fantasy, fabricated for the purpose of entertaining my fans." Breneaux sampled his second. "And, of course, showering me with cash."

LeGrande appeared dumbstruck.

"Do you really think on weekends I pull on my waders, grab my 20-gauge, and go hunting for sex offenders? We're bound by laws, LeGrande."

"Sex offenders are bound by laws, too. Of course, thanks to the left-leaning penal codes . . ."

"Ahh . . . the left-leaning penal codes." Breneaux lowered his head.

"You say so yourself!"

Breneaux took another sip. "I find it truly amazing that you actually believe what you hear on the radio."

"So all the stuff about 'stoking the ovens,' 'burning' these guys . . ."

Breneaux studied LeGrande. "I seem to recall it didn't work all that well for the Germans. Of *course* I don't believe that crap." LeGrande appeared astonished. "Throughout human history, majorities have risen against minorities, using them as scapegoats and blaming them for their woes, creating an excuse to punish them severely. Romans fed Christians to the lions, Christians burned nonbelievers at the stake, Germans sent Jews to the ovens, and whites lynched blacks. As recently as a decade ago, straights tied gays to pickup trucks and dragged them to their deaths."

LeGrande leaned back, as if to dodge the words being hurled in his direction.

"Today, the majority *likes* black people just as the tide is turning for gays. If we attack them now like we did in the past, we'll find ourselves out, begging on the street. Those opportunities have come and gone.

"Lucky for us, there's a new minority in town. Nobody has a problem with us going after sex offenders. They *want* us to. Why?

Because America loves to hate. Look at you, LeGrande. You hate everybody, and you'll probably make a lot of money because of it. Sex offenders are our friends. If you eradicate them, we're out of business. At least for the moment, they're providing us with a great opportunity—a wave I'm planning on riding through to retirement. But it won't last forever. Someday they'll be replaced by some other hated group *du jour*."

LeGrande's black eyes sizzled. "That's bullshit. Blacks and gays don't actually *hurt* people."

"That's not what we *used* to say. Blacks were viewed as a threat to our race, mixing with whites, imperiling the purity of our bloodlines. Gays were even more dangerous, preying on little boys, and compromising the moral order by fornicating in unnatural ways." Breneaux smiled. "Those were great lines. I used them all the time. Today, nobody gives a shit what others do in their bedrooms, what holes they stick their dicks into, or what color their babies turn out to be."

"You expect me to believe that someday it'll be perfectly fine to rape little kids?" LeGrande asked incredulously.

"Of course not. But outing's not aimed at guys who rape kids, most of whom are rotting in prison. It's designed to disrupt the lives of people who have served their time and paid their dues."

"But the recidivism rates!"

"Fuck recidivism rates."

"You talk about them all the time."

"So I do. So do politicians. But the argument's bogus. I've done my homework. Sex offenders repeat their crimes *less* frequently than other criminals. We're fed sensationalized accounts in place of real statistics. If you care at all about learning the truth, you have to search things out—not listen to the radio."

"I don't believe you."

Breneaux looked up and saw the woman with the walker finally being escorted to a dining room down the hall. He felt a deep sense of shame for the better part of a nanosecond.

"You're thirty-three. Shouldn't you be checking your facts? When I lie, I at least know I'm lying."

"You sound like a bleeding-heart liberal, for God's sake."

"You won't think so the next time you tune in to my show. I'll be fire and brimstone like every other day. But never for a minute believe I haven't thought it all through."

LeGrande glared at Breneaux. "I start outing in the morning."

Breneaux gazed back. "Maybe outing's all you got."

LeGrande stood. "You're a great disappointment to me."

A smile appeared at the corner of Breneaux's lips. "You epitomize my core audience, LeGrande—true believers who never delve an inch beneath the surface." He gestured about the room at the opulent appointments and the glasses kept full by some of the city's best attendants. "It's people like you I have to thank for all this."

Breneaux overtook the trolley on St. Charles Avenue in his Rolls Royce convertible while fans stood and waved. With its charcoal exterior and red leather seats, the car was a rolling shrine, recognized by New Orleanians from the Bywater to the Garden District. He veered onto his drive at a quarter to ten, opening with a click a pair of decorative iron gates. He regarded their slow, inward roll as a grand and stately welcome, imbuing him with a sense of having arrived.

Arriving before him was Adler Huxley Hubbard, Louisiana's first steamboat manufacturer, who commissioned the mansion in 1828. Breneaux loved the house, from its two-story columns to its ornate belvedere, rising proudly above the roof like Lady Liberty's torch. After Maggie died, he considered the possibility of selling, but reconsidered at Charmaine's pleading, claiming to love it even more.

Breneaux walked in, drooping with exhaustion. The house was dark except for a spot of light, accompanying the roar of hip-hop, spilling from the second floor. Hip-hop wasn't close to his kind of music—zydeco, blues, Cajun, and jazz—but Charmaine liked it. Anything she favored, he was open to sampling. Still, he ascended the stairs like a reporter in a hurricane, bracing against the oncoming storm.

"Charmaine," he called above the din. *"Charmaine."*

The thirteen-year-old turned. "Daddy, what time is it?"

"Time to turn down the music . . ." She reached for her iPod and switched it to pause. "And give me a hug." Settling on her bed, he kissed her cheek. "Sorry I'm late. I got tied up in a dinner meeting with a new guy from work. Had to straighten him out on a few things. How'd you spend your night?"

"Getting even with Lorelei Phillips. Had to straighten her out on a few things." Breneaux smiled at the quick uptake. "She's been saying the awfulest things about me."

A warning sounded. Breneaux long feared the prospect—however slim—of Charmaine being punished for the things he said. "Like what?"

"Stuff—believe me—you wouldn't want to hear. So I decided to get even by posting a picture of Lorelei making out with her old boyfriend where I knew her new boyfriend would be sure to see it. In the caption, I wrote: 'Sometimes old is better than new.'"

"Ouch. Don't you think you might be taking things a bit far?"

"You taught me to stand up for myself and not take any shi—poop from anyone. That's all I'm doing, dishing her back a little public humiliation. It's not like saying she ought to be whipped or lynched or stoned to death."

Breneaux's ears stung. "Charity, Charmaine. Balance vengeance with a little charity."

"I get it, Daddy," she said, snuggling against him.

He loved the gesture and dreaded the day such displays of affection would slip into the past.

"Hey," Charmaine said. "There's no school Friday. Wanna go shopping?"

"What?" Breneaux's mind had drifted back to work.

"Friday. Shopping."

"Sure, baby. Come to the station at ten. I'll take you to lunch. After that, we'll shop all you want."

He kissed her goodnight and walked down the hall, thinking ahead to the following morning. He knew if LeGrande began outing offenders, charity would be the last thing on display.

LeGrande stood on the curb across from Arnaud's, the heel of his shoe pressed firmly against a lamppost. Despite the chill in the air, he was warmed by the memory of a beautiful evening—time well spent. *I've got you where I want you, old man.* He'd jumped at the chance to meet with Breneaux, agreeing the minute he got the call. It was the opportunity he'd waited for to accomplish two things: assessing Breneaux's vulnerabilities and making Breneaux believe he'd accurately assessed *his.* He'd led the man on, and Breneaux had succumbed, judging LeGrande to be ignorant rather than astute, unwieldy instead of calculated, defensive when self-assured, and committed to a cause when there was no cause at all beyond satisfying his desire for pleasure and fame. Breneaux had been right in everything he said, from minority hatred to bogus recidivism rates, but LeGrande had gained the upper hand. Henceforth, Breneaux would underestimate him greatly.

He pulled a cigar from his left breast pocket, held it under his nose, lit it, and laughed. *Who'd smoke a cheap Altadis' Behike, when he could afford a Gurkha's His Majesty's Reserve?*

Chapter 12

THE OUTING

SEAN lay in bed, staring at the ceiling, tracking cracks in the plaster from one wall to the other. He'd caught a little sleep early on, but woke with a start sometime after 3:00, one minute defending himself to the diminutive Slone Erikson, the next pitching him out of his second story window. He then scrolled to Dupree and his distrust of the man, despite the reprieve for failing to report—and on to Weinstat and his meeting at 9:00, vowing to make sure he'd arrive on time. At least it was Wednesday, Sean's morning off, his first class not starting until 1:15.

He turned toward Laurie, knowing he'd be grateful forever for her treating him like a person rather than as an adjective followed by a noun. He'd disclosed his status in the middle of their first date and was amazed when she stayed instead of bolting for the door.

"You're kidding," she said. "How does that work?"

"Not very well, actually, but I get by."

After two rounds of frozen margaritas, he shared in detail the nature of his offense and that five years remained before his status would be cleared.

"That's not fair!" she proclaimed.

"Nothing's fair," he replied. "In life, you have to fight to survive, and sometimes fighting isn't enough."

Laurie confided, months after that, it was then she decided to enter the fray. Multiplying the number of years remaining by three hundred and sixty-five, she calculated time left and began to count the days.

Their relationship flourished. For the first time since his parents died, Sean's guilt waned.

Two years later, with thirty-six months remaining, unanticipated circumstances altered the timeline. Illinois replaced three years with ten, and Sean found himself back at the beginning. Laurie retreated. Ren's birth caused her to withdraw even more. Sean remembered her asking on several occasions: "How is it possible to avoid being with children when you have children of your own living under your roof?" Psychologist or not, he didn't know what to say.

Sean studied Laurie's shoulders and the small of her back and moved in behind, settling into her warmth. He reached around, laying his hand on her breast, hoping she'd accept his gentle invitation. An instant later, she pulled away.

He shoved out of bed angrily and headed for the john. Usually he'd stop before the armoire mirror, stretching naked, Laurie sliding in behind. There, she'd wrap her arms around him and tease: "You know . . . you look even better backwards." He couldn't remember the last time she did that, any more than he could recall the last time they made love. He guessed it was about the time that Laurie stopped counting the days.

"I can't believe I forgot the anniversary," he said, concealing his anger when Laurie walked in. He wasn't prepared to deal with the problem—the one Vince said had to be addressed.

"You reported when we first moved to town, when we closed on the house, and when you started your job. Don't those count?" she asked, reaching for a brush.

"All those, and I guess anniversaries, too."

"So send him an email."

"It has to be in person, especially now that I'm out on a limb."

"It's not like you to overlook an obligation."

The uncomfortable comment caught Sean off guard. Subtle as it was, he felt the sting. He wanted to reach out and hold Laurie tight, for days if necessary until the ice melted away. But he knew if he did, she'd pull away again. "Yeah . . . well . . . lately I've had a lot on my mind."

In the silence that followed, he wondered if she'd understood.

The green and white awning of Café du Monde was visible on the sack on Sid Weinstat's desk. Sean assumed Weinstat had stopped for a snack before driving to his office at Broad and Tulane. He watched with fascination as the rotund officer, hair trailing from his ears like Spanish moss, undid the bag's folds and opened it slowly before lifting it to his nose to enjoy the smell. Like a magician, finessing a dove from a hat, he extracted two chicory café au laits and a double order of beignets in a mountain of powdered sugar. *Donuts in Chicago; beignets in New Orleans. What is it with cops, oil, sugar, and starch?*

"Here. I always buy extra," Weinstat said, handing Sean a cup of coffee and a plate full of beignets. "Never know who'll wind up eating them. That's half the fun."

Sean appreciated the coffee but had no interest in the beignets.

"So you blew the anniversary, triggawed a violation," Weinstat said, in the New Orleans dialect Sean had grown accustomed to hearing.

The words were unnerving.

"But I understand Dupree's given you a pass. Good thing. If he hadn't, things could have been worse. Eventually I would have had to have you arrested. But not today, not even if the lieutenant hadn't gotten involved. Know why? Because I'm in too good a mood. My oldest just had a baby. Here, take a look." Weinstat handed over a small framed photo coated entirely in a sticky white film. "Powdered sugar for your coffee? There's some at the bottom of the bag."

Sean glanced at the photo. "Congratulations. And no thanks." Weinstat shrugged, upending the bag, encouraging its remains into his mouth.

"Says in your file you were in therapy for five years and that most of that time you facilitated the group. What are you, a psychologist or something?"

"Something," Sean said.

Vince had taught him to be forthright at all times, stressing the importance of telling the truth. But living under the Hardys and later, registration, Sean had learned to keep his head down. No time was that more true than in the presence of police. Besides, he figured, Vince might have advised differently if he'd known there were a couple of bodies to conceal.

"What do you have, eight years to go?"

Sean was surprised Weinstat remembered. "Seven or eight."

"But your offense occurred ten years ago. I recall your registration was extended for some reason."

Sean kept quiet.

"And that you didn't want to talk about it when you first came to see me."

"I still don't."

"Your decision. Thought maybe I could help."

There was that word again. Sean scratched his head.

"Of course, I'm charged with *executing* the law. Any real changes you want to see, you have to take up with your legislators."

"My legislators?" Sean couldn't keep from laughing.

"Yeah, I know, legislators aren't about to dispute registration—point up its problems, proclaim the emperor has no clothes. Not with elections to worry about. They'd appear soft on crime. Their careers'd be over. Until the national wind blows in some other direction, I'm afraid to say, you're on your own." Finishing the last of his first round of beignets, Weinstat began eyeing Sean's.

"Here." Sean pushed them back in the officer's direction.

"You sure?"

"Yeah, I appreciate the coffee." Sean peered suspiciously at the man across the desk. "I thought sex offenders were the enemy."

"Most are. They seem nice on the surface—just like you. Then I find out what it was that they did. But I'm also concerned about the few who aren't—the dolphins who inadvertently get caught in the system. Met with one yesterday. Guy stumbles on a fight in Cabrini Park, watching an eleven-year-old beating a nine-year-old. When the older kid doesn't stop, the guy pulls him off, tells him not to do it again, and sends him on his way. Minutes later, the kid circles back, accompanied by a police officer who arrests the guy for the 'unlawful restraint of a minor.' In other words—kidnapping."

Sean shuddered.

"Guy couldn't believe it. Thought he'd fallen down the rabbit hole. Because he put a hand on an underage kid, he's prosecuted and found guilty of a sexual offense. So here I am, filling him in on his obligations under registration, when I should be pinning a medal on his chest."

One beignet remained. Sean stared at it absentmindedly, watching it disappear down Weinstat's throat.

"Most people say it's a small price to pay to keep child-raping predators off the street. Part of me agrees. Problem is, the small price society has to pay is the overwhelming price dolphins are forced to pay." He stared at Sean. "So which are you, Mr. Jordan?"

"Excuse me?"

"A child-raping predator or an unfortunate dolphin?"

The question threatened to trigger Sean's doubt. But before he could quiz himself, sliding into the abyss, four words sprang forth: "I never raped anyone."

"I figured as much. That's why I'm rambling on about this." Weinstat swatted the air. "Listen, I don't want to have to fuck with you guys any more than you want to have to fuck with me. But better me—someone who'll buy you coffee once in a while—than a guy who actually likes his job."

Sean stood. "Thanks for the coffee."

"Sure. Fill these out." Weinstat handed him paper and pen. "By now you must be an expert."

Sean headed for the door.

"Sean." Weinstat's brusque tone suddenly turned fatherly. "A word of warning. There's a new guy in town. A guy on the radio. Comes on after Breneaux. I hear he intends to out sex offenders, giving out their names and addresses on air."

"Can he do that?"

"Sure. Freedom of speech and all. It's been done in other parts of the country."

Sean felt his hands tremble. "Christ, what's next?"

"All I'm saying is, watch your back."

Sean had heard of Burn Breneaux. Everyone had. He was a conservative Republican—worshiped by some, abhorred by others. But Sean had never listened to his show. Curious, he scanned the radio, driving toward home, hoping to catch him just for a minute. He pumped up the volume when a male voice crooned, "Thanks for tuning in. We'll be back in a minute . . ." only to lower it when the voice went on, "to talk more about soufflés in our series Men Who Bake." Sean scanned further past a parade of musical genres.

"That's Mason Twain, 479 Baluster Dr.," another voice said. "Mason, welcome to New Orleans."

Sean cringed. It was a name and an address like Weinstat had warned, yet the voice was cheery, the greeting sincere. The man who was speaking sounded anything but sinister. Sean hoped there was another explanation.

"And now for number seven of today's top ten: Blake Sorensen, also new to our city. Whadaya say we make Blake feel right at home. Take him some cookies at 727 Royal, right behind the Cathedral in the heart of the French Quarter."

No reference to sex offenders. No hateful speech. No derogatory innuendo. Sean's head was spinning. If the persons named *were* sex offenders, were only new arrivals being targeted?

"At number eight, our next stop on the map: 1640 Calypso Street."

WHAT? Sean's jaw dropped. The sound of his address reverberated in his ears.

"Home to Sean Jordan. Looks like this one's in the Marigny off Frenchman. Any of you neighbors want to stop and say 'Hi'—take him a cup of sugar—let Sean know we're thinking about him?"

Sean felt a *bump!* The Pontiac lurched upward. He'd taken the curb, stopping inches before a sign. "There have to be laws!" he yelled, spitting the words. Then he flashed on his father. *Sorry about the car.*

"Number nine: Mathew Stephens. Hello, Mathew," the voice continued. "Do people call you Matt, or do they use your gay name, Math-*ew*?"

"*No!*" Sean punched off the radio, nudging Thrust back into the street. He had to tell Laurie before she heard it from others. He headed upriver in the direction of the hospital until remembering he wasn't permitted inside. Not without calling and disclosing his status—and only then in the event of a medical emergency. He spotted a Popeyes and swung into the lot, grabbed his phone, and called Laurie's cell. When the call went to voicemail, he marked the message urgent.

Waiting, he dropped into damage control. *Who else might have heard and what harm could result?* He reminded himself that he'd long been online with his picture, address, and nature of his offense. *If there was going to be fallout, it would have happened by now.* But hearing his thoughts, he wasn't convinced. Information planted in people's minds was different from that which was merely available. *What's next?* he wondered. *Having to wear a scarlet SO?*

Twenty minutes passed. Thirty. He called a second time and got the same result. He knew Laurie could be tied up with any number of things—seeing patients, doing labs, assisting in surgery, or conferring with staff. Rarely were his calls promptly returned, but Laurie always called him back. This time, he wondered if he was being ignored.

Realizing noon was rapidly approaching, Sean phoned a colleague to pin a note on his door, informing students they had scored a free hour.

Thirty more minutes passed. Sean gazed absently across the street and spotted a sign in front of a house: "Perrilliat Day Care Center." He felt like an idiot, having failed to notice. He thought about Doug, refusing to let a label supplant his freedom. But he wasn't Doug. He played by the rules. At that very moment, he was in serious violation. He started the engine, threw Thrust in gear, and headed home to await Laurie's call.

Pulling into his drive, something seemed amiss. He saw what looked like a silvery shadow in the upper-left pane of the window by the door. But on closer inspection, it wasn't a shadow, but a gaping hole surrounded by shards of cracked glass. Inside, strewn throughout the room, was a gooey concoction smelling suspiciously of egg. Indeed, a neighbor had "stopped by."

Sean peered through the window at the houses on his block, the clubs on Frenchmen, and the skyline in the distant.

"Who, God dammit?"

He knew it could be anyone.

Chapter 13

PRIVACY VERSUS PROTECTION

DUPREE empathized as he listened to Dodd, bellowing up and down the hallway. Their shared frustration was evidenced by the ache in his gut and the knot in his neck. Another day had slipped by without a break in the case.

"So, Dupree . . ." Weinstat said, sliding an afternoon coffee in the detective's direction. "Been the victim of any sexual abuse today?"

Dupree glanced at the clutter on Weinstat's desk. "No, but the day's still young." He swept a hand up and over his head, recalling the days when he'd grown his hair long. "With my good looks and this being New Awlins, at some point today it's bound to happen."

"Keep telling yourself that. From what I hear, if it weren't for the Dixie Playmates on the shit end of Iberville, you'd have long forgotten what it even looks like."

"At least I've *seen* what it looks like," Dupree fired back. He could tease Weinstat about sex all he wanted, but he was well aware that unlike himself, his good friend's marriage with still intact. Being a good husband and father was what he admired about him most.

"Sure you don't want some café au lait?"

"Please." Dupree belched discretely, ignoring the cup set before him. "I had so much before I came in, I called paramedics. Put 'em on high alert. But don't let me stop you. Have whatever you want."

Weinstat reached in his drawer and pulled out a Snickers.

Dupree winced. "Jeez, Weinstat. I feel like your enabler."

"Just a little boost to help me keep track of all our scourge-of-the-earth sex offenders," he replied, chomping down hard on caramel and nuts. "And who do I have the pleasure of keeping track of for you today?"

"No one in particular. You sure you gave me all the files? I interviewed everyone. Air-tight alibis—all except one. No one was near the waterfront when Mattie Daniels died."

He rechecked his computer. "You've got 'em all."

"Anything out of the ordinary lately with any of these guys?"

Weinstat stopped chewing to consider the question. "Nothing," he said, prying a nut from two teeth. "Of course, the guys who comply with the law and keep their registrations current are the ones least likely to re-offend. It's the others who set out to fall through the cracks and slip through our fingers that we should most be concerned with. Ever think you're after the wrong guys?"

"Trust me, Weinstat, I'm after everybody. Incidentally, where were you Monday morning around one?"

"Fucking my mistress. Now how about I *fuck you*?"

Dupree motioned toward the drawer. "Have some more candy."

Weinstat reached for the handle—then paused. "What the hell," he growled, grudgingly refraining.

"Jordan make it in?"

"Yeah, nine o'clock." Weinstat leaned forward. "Why?"

"What do you think of him?"

"How honest you want me to be?"

Dupree's interest was piqued. He waited for the payoff.

"Beats me," Weinstat said, with a grin that read "gotcha."

Dupree shook his head. "It's gotta be the sugar."

Weinstat scanned the screen. "File says he abused a fifteen-year-old. He wouldn't volunteer the rest. Maybe he's a dolphin. Maybe not. There's no evidence to suggest he's in any way dangerous. You think he's connected to the Daniels murder?"

"Don't know yet. He's got a wife and a job, but we all know how charming sociopaths can be. You know these guys better than I do. Did he get any therapy back in Chicago?"

Weinstat reached for the hard copy and handed it across the desk. "Don't you read these things?"

"I skim."

"Five years worth. Individual and group."

"Five years? I thought one or two was about max. What did he have, a crush on the therapist?"

"Doesn't say. But he does like psychology. Even practiced a bit as a kid."

"You're shittin' me."

"That's what it says."

"How does *that* work?"

"I don't know, but his shrink, Warren Andrews, let him lead the group when he was out of town. Ended up pursuing a doctorate in clinical—"

"But was dumped from the program," Dupree read from the file.

"Why are you asking about him, specifically?" Weinstat asked, leaning forward again.

Dupree cocked an eyebrow. "How honest you want me to be?"

Weinstat leaned still further.

"No particular reason." Dupree grinned. "Ha! Gotcha back."

Weinstat rolled his eyes. "I guess I deserved that."

"After meeting with him and his wife, I haven't been able to get them out of my mind."

"You said there was one offender whose alibi didn't stack up." Weinstat leaned so far forward, the desk bisected his girth into upper and lower hemispheres. "Whose?" he asked.

"His."

Dupree returned to his office and closed the door. "Dr. Warren Andrews? This is New Awlins Police Detective Owen Dupree. I'm calling to ask a few questions as part of a murder investigation of a seven-year-old girl. Do you have a couple of minutes?"

"That's about all I have," the doctor replied, clearly impatient.

Bet you'd find the time if it was your daughter who'd been killed.

"You understand HIPPA prevents me from saying much of anything."

Privacy laws! The detective grew livid. In addition to attitude, he had the Feds to contend with. He recalled how HIPPA prevented the parents, teachers, and doctors of the troubled Virginia Tech shooter from communicating with each other. If they'd been able to do so in the months leading to the massacre, thirty-three victims might have lived rich, full lives. With potentially valuable information to gain, Dupree put politics aside and checked his emotions.

"I understand," he lied. "I'm interviewing sex offenders in Awleans Parish and am interested in one in particular. Our records show he was in therapy with you for five years. His name is Sean Andrew Jordan." Dupree waited.

"I'm sorry, detective. I'm prevented from confirming or denying anyone's involvement in our program."

Dupree felt sweat beading beneath his collar. "He isn't a suspect, only a person of interest. I'm hoping to be able to rule him out. Can you tell me anything about Sean Jordan?"

"I wish I could help."

"Can you tell me if you at least know a Sean Jordan?"

"I can't."

Dupree's anger intensified. A killer remained at large, a city's safety was at risk, and some prick in Chicago was covering his ass with privacy laws.

"Listen," Andrews said, "I work with some pretty tough characters. Some of them get better over time; some don't. But I can tell you, few stay in therapy longer than a few months. Those who do, generally get something out of it. If your records show your guy was in therapy that long, I'd look instead at the guys who come once, fulfilling a judge's order, and then duck out at the first opportunity."

Dupree didn't need to be told that the murderer could be someone else. "What if a guy stayed in therapy due to a fascination with psychology—then went on to study it—but didn't get any better? Is that possible?"

Another lengthy silence. "I suppose it's . . . possible."

"And what if a guy stuck with a program—say for five years—was on his best behavior and charmed the pants off everyone, not because he was great guy but because he was a sociopath?"

"I don't see . . ."

Dupree waited for the rest of it.

"I really can't get into details. Sure, it's possible. Anything's possible."

Anything except getting this prick to talk. Dupree thought about the Jordans. Their stories lined up but their emotions didn't. She'd been conciliatory; he'd been angry. The combination didn't work. Something was off. One of them clearly was covering for the other. Dupree made a note: Ask Weinstat . . . Who continued in therapy and who dropped out? He thought it best to wait a day before calling—to give the chocolate in Weinstat's system a chance to work its way out.

"Is there something more I can help you with?" Andrews said, as if wanting the conversation to end expeditiously.

Dupree had moved on, but wanted Andrews to know he wasn't to be so easily dismissed.

"Doctor, we've just begun."

Sean sat on the floor holding a sugary sponge with slivers of glass piled beside him. He was surprised by the depth of his feelings of loneliness with Laurie and Ren about to arrive, yet they seemed an inadequate salve for his emptiness and regret. He thought about Doug and felt lonelier still, picturing him an outlaw unable to be found. He yearned for reassurance that he and Laurie would survive, but hated feeling needy even more than feeling alone. Wasn't it his job to reassure others? Find solutions to problems? Point ways to brighter futures?

He heard Laurie and Ren's laughter as they ascended the front steps. He thought their buoyancy would end when they spotted the window, but their glee continued, adding to his sense of isolation.

"Daddy!" Ren called, running across the living room. He rose from the floor with the sponge in hand.

"Sean?" Laurie said, looking around. "What *is* this?"

"We've been outed."

Ren skipped to her room at Laurie's suggestion.

"What do you mean?"

Sean dropped the sponge and pulled up two chairs, while Laurie stood staring at the freshly scrubbed couch. "Some new guy on the radio is naming sex offenders, giving out their addresses and inciting them to violence."

Laurie looked puzzled. "You showed me that information on the Internet. It's been public as long as we've been together."

"You have to search for it online. These guys throw it in people's faces. They act like it's a joke and goad people on—then hide behind the First Amendment. Weinstat warned me." Sean pointed at the window. "When I got home there was glass everywhere, mixed with sugar, flour, and eggs." *Men Who Bake* flashed through his mind. "All this time there's never been an incident. Then some new guy blows into town and suddenly we're at risk. We can't let this rest."

"But what about keeping our heads down? You've always said, 'Lay low. Wait it out.' This sounds different and it's scaring me."

"It *is* different!" Sean sprang from the chair. "Everything's changed. Don't you see? They're coming after *us*."

Sean's ringtone sounded. He reached for his phone.

"Jordan. This is Erikson. I received calls this afternoon from parents concerned about your presence on campus."

What else? Sean could feel his heart sink further.

"They told me you were named as a sex offender on the radio. I've spent the last hour defending you to the trustees, reminding them that you disclosed your status before you were hired, that there have been no incidents since you arrived, and that in fact you've been named Teacher of the Year. But they don't want to hear it. This puts me and the university in an untenable position. I have no choice but to terminate your employment. I need you to call first before coming to gather your things."

The phone went dead, sparing Sean from having to respond.

"That was Erikson," he said, hands trembling. "I'm fired." He took Laurie's hand in his, more to quell his fears than hers.

"We can't fight them," she whispered, staring at the floor.

Sean's life had been spent in the act of surrender—accepting the death of his parents and grandparents, assenting to the whims of William Hardy, and living under the rules of sex offender registration. Each eventually had come to seem normal. But there was nothing normal about the world learning of his crimes through the musings of some guy, yammering on the radio.

"Somebody has to," he replied, without a clue as to how.

Chapter 14

CONFRONTATION

SEAN stood on the sidewalk in front of WFQT radio and stared at the windows on the second and third floors. He wondered if any looked into the office of Arthur Manning, the station's general manager, he'd determined from the Internet—the person who could listen to what Sean had to say and, if he were a reasonable sort of man, do something about it.

He walked into a dimly lit, stale-smelling lobby with cracks in the ceiling and in the checkerboard tile floor. Sheets of cheap wooden paneling buckled and sagged, making it appear as if the walls were shedding their skin. On a coffee table framed by scuffed leather couches sat an ashtray overflowing with lipstick-stained butts next to manhandled magazines with pages ripped out. *Doesn't anybody tend to this place?* He tried to imagine what listeners would think if they saw the unsavory lair from which their idol's voice boomed.

He approached the receptionist, sealed behind glass, noted "Penelope" on her nameplate, and asked to see the GM. In a dazzling display of advanced multitasking, the icy young blond with tightly coifed hair adjusted her bra and dialed the phone while watching Judge Judy and reading *People* magazine.

"Mr. Manning's in a meeting," the ice queen relayed. "He said you're free to wait but it'll likely be a while."

Before Sean could ask what "a while" meant, she spun from the window, resuming her tasks.

Not only was the lobby dirty and run-down, it reeked of security from front to rear. There were shiny black fixtures concealing cameras on the walls, an airport-style metal detector forcing guests to pass beneath, and a giant steel door blocking access to the stairs, which opened at the queen's discretion with an ear-splitting *BUZZ!* Considering the incendiary nature of the station's diatribe, it clearly needed all the protection it could get.

"Burn, things like this little girl's murder prove what you've been saying all along. We've got to exterminate these guys before it's too late."

Sean looked at the speakers anchored overhead and imagined germs spewing forth, further infecting the lobby.

"And short of that?" Breneaux asked.

So that's the famous Burn Breneaux.

"I'd go for castration."

Sean felt nauseous. Different voices; message the same. He couldn't believe that day after day people actually chose to listen to such crap.

He approached the window again. "Excuse me. Do you have any idea how long the meeting will last?"

"Mr. Manning's a busy man," Penelope snapped, looking over her shoulder as Judy's verdict was about to come in. "There's no way of telling when—or even if—he'll be able to see you. He knows you're here. If you'd like to express your thoughts on the content of our programming, he'd prefer you go home and address them in an email. However, if you like, you can wait."

With few pressing engagements beyond replacing a pane of glass—a change exempt from requiring a visit to Weinstat—he thumbed through a newspaper, oblivious of its contents.

A well-groomed girl of twelve or thirteen opened the front door and marched into the lobby. She told Penelope she was there to meet her father, headed for the stairs, and was buzzed inside. Then a man walked in, roughly Sean's age, wearing a blazer and slacks above freshly polished shoes. Sean sensed something familiar about but brushed the thought aside when he watched him approach and caught a look at his face. The buzzer sounded, and he, too, was admitted.

"America is listening."

Sean considered heading home, but warned: Unless he did *something*, there might soon be no home to head to.

"Hi, Burn. I love your show," another caller began. "I wanted to let you know I'm in favor of this new outing business. When are you going to start outing on *your* show?"

"Actually, I have an outing planned for the weekend," Breneaux joked, underscored by a rim shot.

Sean looked up, spotting a delivery boy at the door, balancing flats of coffees in both hands, struggling to get in. The boy finally prevailed and angled toward the queen. When the buzzer sounded, Sean seized the opportunity. He fell in behind the boy and slid on through.

"Can I help with a couple of those?" Sean offered, as they turned and ascended the stairs.

"Sure. Thanks," the boy replied.

Sean lifted two coffees and proceeded to the second floor, stepping onto carpeting, threadbare and stained. The walls were covered with scuffed floral wallpaper beneath an acoustic-deadening ceiling, yellow from cigarettes. Dotting the yellow, to Sean's disgust, were dozens of splotches of thick black mold. He looked at the boy. "Do you happen to know which office is Art Manning's?"

"Come on. I'll take you there. It's his coffee you're holding."

They passed a conference room and two offices on the left, one occupied by a security guard, feet propped on the desk.

"America is listening," a voice boomed from above. Behind a glass wall was the source of the voice—an older man: Burn Breneaux. Sitting beside him, feet tucked under a chair, was the girl from the lobby—Breneaux's daughter, Sean presumed. He started to question whether he found her attractive. *Don't go there*, he demanded, putting an end to the thought.

The delivery boy opened the studio door, handing a coffee to Breneaux, who wore a suit and tie, and a second to a woman in bright turquoise shoes. He returned to Sean. "Follow me."

They walked into the office at the end of the hall. "Mr. Manning gets one," the boy said, motioning toward an older man, easily six-four and razor thin.

Sean handed him a cup and looked in his eyes. *What kind of a person . . .*

"And the other goes to . . ." The boy spun toward a man on a low tattered couch. *The station's equivalent of the puny chairs.* It was the man in the blue blazer Sean had seen downstairs. "I would guess . . . *you.*"

"That's fine, Teryl," Manning said, handing the boy three folded tens. "Keep the change." Sean gave the second coffee to the stranger.

"Thanks, Mr. Manning." The boy sprinted down the hall.

"Arthur Manning?" Sean looked at the manager.

Manning's smile vanished, replaced by a scowl, as if ticked that the boy's helper hadn't left with him. "Who are you?"

"My name is Sean Jordan. I'm a registered sex offender."

"Aw, Jesus."

Sean knew he couldn't blink.

"How did you get in?"

"I'm not trying to cause any trouble. I just want you to know that yesterday my name and address were given out by your station. Afterward, my house was vandalized and I lost my job. I have a wife and daughter. I'm concerned for their safety."

LeGrande stood and headed for the door. "This is between the two of you."

Manning darted in front of him, blocking his path. "Meet Del LeGrande." Manning smirked. "It's him you ought to be talking to. He's the one who outed you."

Sean turned toward LeGrande. "Why are you doing this?"

LeGrande looked at Manning. "I'm on in ten minutes. I really have to go."

Manning waved LeGrande on and turned toward Sean. "Ratings," he said. "Why does anyone do anything in the entertainment business?"

Sean's cheeks reddened.

"Did you come here thinking I'd tell you we made a mistake—that we'll never do it again? We're in business to make money, and we only make money when enough people listen to our shows that we're able to attract sponsors who want to buy airtime. Fortunately for us, there are people like you who give us things to talk about that other people want to listen to. Consequently, we have lots of sponsors. We make lots of money."

"At other people's expense."

"That's right, Mr. Jordan, at your expense. But we didn't create your misfortune. You did. Somewhere along the line you decided to invite misfortune into your life. What did you do, rape somebody? Fondle a kid? Fuck the babysitter?"

Sean felt tempted by the bait, but fury surpassed guilt. "Okay, you're right. I created my own misfortune. But that was ten years ago. I paid for my mistake. Now I have a family. We want to be left alone." Manning waved condescendingly and returned to his desk. "Obviously someone disagrees. If you paid your dues, how come you're still registered?"

The question knocked Sean off point, threatening to unleash his doubt and uncertainty. Maybe his sins *were* unforgivable, his crimes greater than what he supposed.

NO! Sean's anger clawed back. "The misfortune I suffered yesterday wasn't brought on by me. It was instigated by you and the people you work for."

Manning glanced at his call log. "Sean . . . Jordan," he read, as if committing the name to memory. "Now I'm really quite busy. I suggest you leave before I call the police." He paused . . . "Actually, security should have stopped you. I need to call them first." He reached for his phone.

"I'm leaving," Sean said. "Just know . . . people are getting hurt while you're making money."

Sean turned and headed down the hall, picturing hundred dollar bills pouring from the speakers. He noticed that the studio door was open in the hall and paused for a moment to listen and watch. Breneaux sat at the console with a headset around his neck. LeGrande stood next to him, flirting with the girl. She smiled in response, swiveling in her chair, tossing back her hair as if trying to appear older.

"Only Burn Breneaux could have produced such a ravishing young lady," LeGrande said. The girl giggled, tucking her head in her shoulder, seeming simultaneously thrilled and embarrassed.

"Christ, LeGrande!" Breneaux roared. "She's only thirteen. Pick on someone your own age."

LeGrande looked up, spotting his accuser in the hall. He turned and started toward Sean.

He's going to apologize, Sean dared to suppose.

Reaching the heavy industrial glass door, LeGrande stopped and stared, eyes filled with contempt. Without saying a word, he kicked the stop free, causing the door to swing shut with a resounding ca-chunk.

Sean lingered seconds longer, tightening his fists—then thought of the boy who used words to settle fights. *Not every situation gets fixed in a single try*, said Vince. *Some people need a little extra convincing.*

Manning would need a lot more convincing.

Sean continued down the hall, heading for the stairs, satisfied for now for having at least spoken his mind.

LeGrande sat in the studio seconds before airtime, repeating the name: *Sean Jordan.* It hadn't meant a thing when he said it the day before, but once he saw his face, he remembered from long ago.

You could complicate things if you recognized me, but chances are slim to none that you will. I remember you, Jordan. You're not that bright.

LeGrande knew every problem provided fresh opportunities. By the time his mic went live, he'd already pictured a few.

Chapter 15

THE LIE

THURSDAY *evening*, Dupree groaned, pulling out of police headquarters, heading for the French Quarter. *Four days' effort with nothing to show.* He'd started the day meeting with forensics, which had confirmed the belief that the explosion was intentional. By 9:00, the media was broadcasting the story, and by 10:00 he was again being dressed down by Dodd.

"Sweet Jesus, give me *something!*" Dodd demanded. "Mada Gras is twelve days away. People have time to make other plans."

Dodd again ignored Mattie Daniels. Dupree was livid and wanted to shove it in his face but thought: *Why? Tomorrow, he'll just do the same.* She wasn't his priority; Mardi Gras was. Dodd had to answer to the mayor like the mayor had to answer to voters, residents of a city badly in need of cash.

Despite Dodd's fits, Dupree knew he wouldn't be fired with a crisis on their hands and no one to take his place. He wished he had a substantive lead, for the city as well as the Daniels, but he didn't and likely wouldn't for a while. He knew that leads develop slowly over time. Solving the murder and bombing, like most major crimes, would take meticulous police work spanning months, if not years. That is, unless he got really, really lucky. He spun toward Dodd. "If Mada Gras's all that god damned important, I suggest you start planning next year's event."

Dupree drove downriver, headed for the Quarter, passing brothels, strip joints, and bars of dubious distinction. He parked on Iberville, half a block off Bourbon, and noted the swollen size of the crowd, the ramp-up to Mardi Gras having already begun. Adding to the size was the fact it was Thursday, New Orleanians' official start of the weekend. Unlike residents of other cities, they required an extra day to consume all the pleasures on hand. The only locals taking issue with Thursdays starting weekends were those who believed it was *always* the weekend.

Wishing to skip Bourbon, Dupree cut over to Burgundy. There was a bar he liked there. Good to locals. Good to cops. He arrived at the entrance to Shannon 'N Molly's, pushed through hanging beads, passing for a door, and settled on a stool at the head of the bar.

"Be with you in a minute, Sweetie!" Molly yelled, above clamoring patrons watching sports on TV. She moved like a cyclone from one customer to another, carrying mugs in her hands and a plastic cup in her teeth. He guessed—well, at least *hoped*—that that drink was hers. But then, with Molly, one never knew.

Dupree loved Molly dearly, and had for years, but in a different way from the way he loved Sandy. Molly was his friend; Sandy, the love of his life. But with their divorce so recent and his heart still connected, he conceded there was a chance he might feel differently someday.

Glancing down the bar, he spotted an off-duty policeman with a young brunette draped over his arm. He thought of all the cops he'd known over the years who traded families they loved for women and drugs, an occasional night out leading to days at a time. He'd often spoken up, one friend to another, pointing out the futility, encouraging different choices. But no one ever listened, no one changed course, so alluring were their rest stops along expressways to ruin. He couldn't recall one cop who, in abandoning families for flings, ever received the love, gained the satisfaction, or eliminated the pain he'd hoped for and expected.

Dupree had avoided that scene with one notable exception: Thursday nights at Shannon 'N Molly's. There he kicked off his weekends, bumped into cops, and gossiped and flirted with the barmaid in black. He never stayed late or drank too much with someone special waiting at home.

Dupree leaned back and sighed, reflecting on what he'd learned in the wake of his divorce—that all the love, kindness, and loyalty in the world couldn't satisfy a woman craving a life on her own. In an unexpected call lasting less than a minute, Sandy expressed her appreciation for all he had done while informing him she was moving on.

A brass band wailed on the street outside the bar, catching Dupree's attention, easing his disappointments. He felt a welling of gratitude and briefly closed his eyes, giving thanks for his daughter and the city he loved.

"Owen!" Molly shouted, eyes twinkling with affection. She reached across the bar, handing him a whisky over ice. "Got a new tattoo. Wanna see?"

"Sure," he replied, knowing he had little choice in the matter.

Molly rounded the bar and stood squarely before him with dozens of spectators looking on. "You're gonna want these," she said, pulling his reading glasses out of his pocket, sliding them over his ears and nose. In one grand, seamless motion, she unbuckled her pants, tugged them to her knees, unsnapped her thong, and flung it to the crowd. Patrons cheered—then fell silent, angling for the best spots from which to see. Tattooed on the area where pubic hair used to grow were four little words: "Gentlemen, start your engines!" Louder cheers rang out. Glasses rose in salute.

"There's no one else like you," Dupree officially declared, Molly wriggling her hips back into her pants.

"What are you talkin' about, Owen?" Molly replied. "The whole town's filled with people like me."

"Com'on, Moll. Not everyone does exactly what she wants—certainly not *whenever* she wants."

"This is New Awlins, Sweetie. *Most* people do. But thanks for thinkin' I'm somehow special." The cyclone grabbed Dupree and kissed him on the lips before heading behind the bar to serve a rapturous clientele. "Ready for another?" she called to Dupree.

He held up his glass. "Let me at least take a first sip of this one." Watching her work one customer after another, he imagined her serving them standard stock while pouring him brew from long hidden bottles, buried beneath the bar by Lafitte and his men.

"I don't know, Moll," he said when she returned. "Times are changing. More laws keep coming, telling us what we can and can't do."

"Nine-eleven!" Molly shouted above the din. "That's when it started, and the hurricane made it worse. A couple days after Katrina, the National Guard came in here, ordering drinks while telling me I had to clear out. Do you believe it? 'For *your* sake,' they said. *My* sake!" Dupree hung on her words. "Supplies were low, but I served every man. Then I reached under the bar for my Remington 870, aimed it at their heads, and ordered 'em to "Get the fuck out!" Never saw 'em again. Nobody tells *Molly* what to do."

Dupree laughed, thanking God for New Orleanians. Despite hurricanes, plagues, poverty, and corruption, they'd relied on their wits for three hundred years, refusing to take themselves more seriously than need be. He thanked God specifically for making one of them Molly.

Molly leaned toward him. "How's it goin', Owen? Bitch of a week, eh?" She didn't know the half of it. "Who'd wanna blow up fish?"

"I wish I knew."

Aching for a woman to open up to and confide in, Dupree longed to tell Molly everything he knew, but the details of the events were strictly confidential. On top of that, they were uncomfortably personal. He'd stood over the body of his daughter's best friend, notified her parents who crumpled in each other's arms, and immersed himself in the world of sexual predators, encountering tragedy and ugliness everywhere he turned. And, as if that weren't enough, the only lead he'd been able to develop was a man who possessed barely a record, let alone one of kidnapping, rape, or murder. His body felt raw, skin scraped to the bone.

But this is Molly, he told himself, the girl guys talked to about hopes and dreams, girlfriends and wives, failures and regrets. Dupree had leveled with her on numerous occasions. But even as her eyes glistened, pleading for facts, he couldn't bring himself to do it. Not tonight. He needed to preserve the little he knew—just this once—and use Molly's for escape.

He barely had a chance to settle into that thought when he remembered the photos from Weinstat's files. He pulled them out of his pocket and shuffled them in his hands. "Actually, I *could* use your help."

"Now *there's* a line I've never heard."

"I'm serious. You know lots of people—practically everyone in town."

"Unless they moved in yesterday." She lit a cigarette. "Wednesday's my day off."

"If I show you some pictures, could you tell me if you recognize anyone?"

"Is this for God and country, or do I get paid like a real detective?"

Dupree laughed. "Sweetheart, trust me. You want to make money? Stick with bartending." He handed her the photos and studied her reaction. She took her time, examining each.

"Hey! Can I get a drink down here?" a customer shouted.

"Not '*Can* I,'" Molly shouted back. "'*May* I!' Didn't ya momma teach ya nothin'?"

The customer stood corrected. "Okay, *may* I have a drink?"

"No, I'm *busy!*"

Molly's eyes grew large. She found a dry patch in front of Dupree and slapped a photo on top of the bar. "Him."

Dupree gulped. "Are you sure?"

"With eyes *that color*? Don't remember his name, but he was in here with a friend. Think the friend's name was Doug."

God dammit! Does every road lead to Sean Andrew Jordan? Dupree downed his drink, pushing suspicions aside. *Only means the kid hangs out in hipper places. Nothing at all to do with the murder.* He was pissed with himself for having shown Molly the pictures.

But like a moth drawn to fire, he couldn't leave it alone. "When? A while back, right?"

Molly appeared to concentrate, gazing past fresh Mardi Gras decorations further cluttering the room. "Sunday night. Around midnight. Stayed 'til after the explosion."

Dupree levitated off his stool, the alcohol in his system, evaporating in an instant.

"He seemed afraid of it . . ." She took a long drag. "Showed no interest in going to see what happened, almost as if he knew about it already. His friend seemed pissed, trying to get him to leave. And get this . . ." She grabbed an ashtray, crushing out her cigarette. "The friend said it was a '*different* explosion.' What do you think he meant by that? Oh yeah, and—"

"There's *more*?"

"Something about killing his parents."

Dupree's head snapped back, mind racing to make sense of it all. "You're sure it was Sunday?"

"Well, Monday morning if you wanna get technical about it. I took Satan to the vet just before 9:00. Your guy mentioned he had to go to work. Couldn't have gotten more than a couple hours sleep. What's this about anyway? The aquarium? The murder? I bet he killed a whole bunch of people—hacked 'em up into lots of little pieces. Better still . . . pulverized them with his X-ray eyes. Come on, Owen. What did he do?"

Dupree stared straight ahead.

"He lied."

Chapter 16

THE BRACELET

SEAN jerked awake and stared at his phone until the number on the screen registered in his brain. *Weinstat.* He wasn't sure which was worse, being awakened by a cop at seven-thirty in the morning or being in contact with him so often, he recognized his number on Caller ID. They'd spoken most recently just forty-eight hours before, at which time Sean informed him that nothing had changed. Weinstat must have heard he'd lost his job. Or maybe he couldn't sleep. Who could on a diet of sugar and caffeine?

"Weinstat," Sean said, before the officer could identify himself. "Tell me you're calling with a lead on a job."

"Wish I could help, but that's not why I phoned. I realized I overlooked a couple of things. Need to see you one more time. Can you get here by 9:00?"

"What things?" Sean demanded.

"I can't get into it over the phone. See you at 9:00."

The phone went dead. *I'm not your slave, Weinstat!*

As soon as Sean backed out of his drive, flashing lights appeared in his rear-view mirror. He steered to the curve, expecting the police car to pass. Instead, it angled to the curve and pulled up behind him. A thirty-something cop, eyes hidden behind mirrored glasses, sauntered to Sean's car and stepped to the window.

"Can I see your license?"

"What's the problem, officer?" Sean handed it over.

"You have a broken tail light. I noticed it when you pulled into the street."

Thrust! He'd make it up to his father. He moved to open his door, but the cop held it shut.

"I'd like you to remain in your car," he said in a vaguely hostile manner.

Sean glued his eyes to the side-view mirror, watching as the policeman walked away. *Not allowed to inspect my own car?* Moments later, the cop returned.

"For the equipment violation, I'm issuing a citation."

Sean turned to the officer. "The car's a classic in perfect condition. I just want to get out and take a look."

The cop glanced up and down the street, repeating harshly, "You're to remain in your car."

Sean warned himself to back off. "Sure, whatever. How about giving me a warning?"

The officer brought his nose to within millimeters of Sean's. "You want a warning? I'm happy to give you one. If I ever so much as see you *talk* to a kid, I'll shoot you on site as an act of community service. Do you understand?"

Sean froze. Reaching through the window, the cop dangled a blue ticket in front of Sean's face. Light filtered through it. Then a brighter light. Blinding. White hot. And stars.

Sean regained consciousness sometime later, blood streaming from his nose, nerves erupting in pain. He guessed he'd been in some sort of collision and hoped that no one else was hurt. He tried to open his eyes. One was glued shut, the other a mere slit. Everything appeared white like a snowstorm in Chicago, the windshield an opaque, crystal montage. Minutes passed. Throbbing set in. He felt for the wheel, fingers fumbling in air. He knew he needed to be seen by a doctor, but approval hadn't been granted to head to an ER.

Shapes and shadows began to emerge while details of what occurred remained elusive. Praying he wouldn't hit anyone on the road, he put the car in gear and tapped lightly on the accelerator. He made it to the corner—then crept another block. Block by block, he inched his way to Broad Street, managed somehow to park, and found his way inside.

"Jesus, what happened to you?" an officer asked, standing guard by an overhead metal detector.

"I have an appointment with . . ." Sean couldn't recall, names drifting in and out without landing.

"Who?"

"I think . . . Wein—" His mind went blank.

The officer handed him a round plastic container. "Put your metal objects in here—phone, coins, pens, glasses. Remove your belt and hand me your wallet."

Sean reached for the container but couldn't seem to find it. It was the last thing he remembered before everything went black.

Sean returned to the world in a series of stages, like gauze unraveling one layer at a time. Through the haze, he detected a nearby voice, a spoon being dropped, a motor turning on. He faded out—then came back . . . back to wherever back was.

"Sean . . . *Sean* . . ." a woman's voice kept repeating. The name sounded familiar, but he couldn't quite place it. One eye lifted grudgingly, permitting him to see: medical equipment lined up against a wall, a person in white with braided hair, and the shoulder of a man, standing in a hallway.

"Mr. Jordan?" the woman said, taking a different tack.

Sean recognized the name as that of his father. Were his parents there? Had they all been hurt in the same explosion?

"Mr. Jordan?"

"Yes," he was aware of responding.

"You're at University Hospital. You were out for nearly an hour. Do you remember what happened?"

"An explosion, I think," he mumbled, lips barely moving while aching in pain.

"I didn't hear about an explosion. Let's try again."

Hadn't he left the house, pulled out of the drive, and been stopped for something? "A cop hit me," he said, barely above a whisper.

"A cop hit you? I see. Must have been an awfully big cop. The doctor was here a while ago and said he expects you to heal nicely. Looks like you're quite a handsome guy under all that swelling."

He guessed she was a nurse but couldn't tell for sure. He watched her cross the room toward the man in the hall. When she disappeared, the man came in. He was wearing an overcoat, his face a blur.

"Feeling any better?" the man asked.

"Not better than yesterday."

"Do you recognize me? I'm Detective Owen Dupree. We met at your house Tuesday afternoon."

"De-tec-tive." Sean repeated, words forming slowly. "You said you wanted to help."

"Tell me about this cop."

"Did you send him to hurt me?"

"Of course not. Tell me what happened."

"Weinstat called. He said to meet him. Then a cop stopped me and gave me a ticket." Sean opened his left hand. "I had it right here."

"Is this it?" Dupree asked, handing him a blue piece of paper covered with blood. Sean stared but couldn't bring it into focus. "It's a ticket all right. Except it's blank on both sides."

Sean closed his eye. "The guy on the radio started it. Why aren't you talking to him?" Sean turned slowly in Dupree's direction. "What did Weinstat want?"

"He didn't want anything. *I* did," Dupree said. "We were waiting for you in his office when you collapsed downstairs. I had you brought here."

"What did *you* want?"

"I wanted to know why you lied to me."

Sean tried to recall their earlier conversation—then remembered. "I don't know what you're talking about."

"You told me you were with your wife Sunday night at the time Mattie Daniels was killed."

"She told you the same thing."

"I know," Dupree said. "That disappoints me as well. I don't like being lied to."

"Leave Laurie out of it!" Sean wrenched forward and grimaced in pain.

"I can do that for now *if* you tell me where you were Sunday night."

Doug's face came to mind. "You tell me."

"Okay. Try the bar at Burgundy and Conti, Shannon 'N Molly's. You arrived about midnight with someone named Doug. Stayed until the explosion."

That was that. He'd been stripped of an alibi on the night of the murder. How easy it would be to simply tell the truth, clearing his name in a matter of minutes. *One lie leads to another*, Vince always said. But Doug's freedom hung in the balance.

"I told you before, I was home with my wife. I didn't blow up your aquarium or kill any kid. Why don't you go chase real bad guys for a while, like the one who landed me here?"

"You're not a suspect, only a person of interest. Rest assured we'll identify your attacker. As regards Mattie Daniels, sooner or later I'm going to nail the bastard who killed her. The night she died, you were at Shannon 'N Molly's. I was hoping for your cooperation. Guess I'll have to find some other way to determine who you were with and what you were doing. I'm guessing your wife's covering for you. Maybe you're covering for somebody else."

Sean's head sank into the pillow. "Did you ever have a friend, Lieutenant?"

Before Dupree could answer, the nurse marched back in. "Good news, Mr. Jordan. No internal injuries, no neurological damage. Only miscellaneous contusions and abrasions. You'll be out of here this afternoon after the doctor takes a final look."

Straining to sit up, something tugged on Sean's leg. *A heart monitor? Drip?* He ripped back the sheet. Attached to his ankle was a gray plastic bracelet. "What's *that*?"

"GPS," Dupree said. "It's going to let me know where my person of interest is at all times."

"You can't do that!"

"You're a sex offender who's lied to the police. I have no choice." Sean tried to kick free. "Be careful with that. You break it, you own it. Besides, there are plenty more where that one came from."

Sean struggled like an animal caught in a trap until the pain in his head thwarted his efforts.

"Perhaps you'd be willing to comment on one other thing."

Sean stared at the ceiling, his other eye opening.

"What did your friend mean by '*another* explosion' and something about you 'killing your parents'?"

Sean turned his head and closed his eyes, shutting out Dupree and the rest of the world.

Chapter 17

SUMMER CAMP

JORDAN . . . angry and uncooperative. Guilt palpable. Dupree felt certain there was something going on. Sure, he'd have been angry, too, if a rogue cop had smashed *him* in the face. But his suspect had lied. Lying was significant in Dupree's book. He refused to believe there were little lies. Lies were always big, even false smiles. If you were a liar, you were a cheat, and if you were a cheater, you were likely a thief. So on and so forth up the criminal chain. Lying was merely the tip of the iceberg—the thing that revealed the lack of integrity that lay at the heart of everything else, up to and including murder.

"Jas. Get in here," Dupree called from his desk.

Jas raced inside, clutching a folder to his chest.

"Before you say or do anything . . ." Dupree said, scanning his eager beanpole of a partner. "Gain some weight and lose some hair."

"Yes, sir."

"You contact the leads I suggested?"

"Sure did, Lieutenant."

"So?"

Jas remained standing, crackling like a fuse. "He went skinny dipping."

"Skinny dipping," Dupree repeated.

"According to the Lee County Sheriff's Police west of Chicago where the incident took place, Jordan stated at the time of his arrest that he'd met a girl at summer camp and that the two of them had gone skinny dipping the night before she was to head back home. She was attending the camp; he was working in grounds and maintenance. He denied any malicious intent—said they'd developed a mutual crush and kissed a couple of times. He claimed that on the last night they were together, she unexpectedly took off her clothes and waded into a river. He followed. She touched his penis and he responded by embracing her. End of story, according to Jordan. No sex. Not even close."

"You don't *believe* that?"

Jas looked startled by Dupree's quick dismissal. "I don't know."

"If you were eighteen and got caught fucking a fifteen-year-old, would you admit it to authorities?"

"Probably not."

"Go on."

"When the police asked him how old she was, Jordan shrugged and said he didn't know. He hadn't asked."

Dupree threw up his hands. "Right. I'm not buyin' any of this. Skinny dipping with some random kid in the woods."

"Well, not exactly random, Lieutenant." Jas held up the file. "Her father's a big-league Chicago businessman—sports stadiums, race tracks, entertainment venues, you name it. And he's black. He apparently didn't relish the idea of his black-is-beautiful baby girl cavorting naked in the woods with some low-class white boy. Guy pulled out all the stops."

"Wouldn't you, if your underage daughter gave it up to a stranger three years her senior?"

Jas shrugged. "I don't have an underage daughter." Dupree rolled his eyes. "But the girl was never interviewed."

"No interview?" Dupree scratched his head.

"No one ever asked her to tell her side of the story."

"If there was no interview, there was no trial. Why no defense?"

"Remember the 'other explosion'?"

"Yeah."

"Turns out there *was* one—gas, seven years earlier. Leveled Jordan's house. His parents died instantly while he was delivering the morning papers. Investigators traced it to the furnace but never determined what ignited it."

"How'd you uncover *that*?"

"Internet: Jordan/explosion. Led me to the archives of his hometown paper."

Dupree did the math. "The kid would have been ten or eleven—young enough that the police might have overlooked him as a suspect. Was there any evidence he'd ever been questioned?"

"None."

"Kids that age have been known to off their parents."

Jas wrinkled his brow. "Yeah, but usually not by blowing them up."

"What happened to Jordan?"

"He went to live with an aunt and uncle, Arabeth and William Hardy—she's a decorator, he's an attorney—and his cousins, Russell and Trent, both about his age. Stayed with them 'til he landed in jail. No police record, according to . . ." Jas deciphered a note. "An Officer Sanford in Wheaton, Illinois. No indication of any kind of mischief. His cousins, on the other hand, both had records—minor stuff . . . curfew violations, underage drinking, knocking up girlfriends, that sort of thing. I called the high school and spoke with a Vice Principal Evans. Jordan graduated first in his class."

"You're kidding."

"Kid was so smart, the psychology teacher let him co-teach a course. Then I checked the loner angle. Not a chance. Good-looking kid. Girls threw themselves at him. The only kids who picked on him were his cousins—teasing, roughhousing, nothing over the top."

"You said his uncle was a lawyer? He would have been the one to provide a defense, or at least refer the case on."

"He got involved, but there's no record he did anything but enter a guilty plea."

Dupree stared at the ceiling. "You're telling me the uncle railroaded his own nephew—a kid he raised like a son."

"Some lawyer."

"Some uncle."

"I don't have all the details, but it looks like he pleaded the kid guilty in exchange for supervision," Jas said.

"And registration—ten years of it. The uncle must have known there was more to it—that Jordan had sex with the girl—maybe even raped her."

"That's still no excuse for not providing a defense."

Dupree stood and began pacing the floor. "Did he bother to inform his nephew that registration would likely ruin his life?" He looked at Jas. "Go back. What did you say about the cousins— something about knocking somebody up?"

"Three somebodies, in fact. The police were contacted on three separate occasions by parents of daughters impregnated by Trent Hardy."

"Busy kid."

"The vice principal said he thought Trent was trying to prove to the world that he wasn't gay like his brother, Russell, which was a huge embarrassment for the Christian Hardys."

"I assume all three girls were underage," Dupree said.

"Yep, but charges were never filed, or if they were, they were quickly dismissed. Guess who handled all three adoptions?"

"William Hardy."

"He's rumored to have made out like a bandit."

"So the uncle had the know-how to make his *kid's* sexual screw- ups go away. He just didn't extend the favor to his nephew. Why?"

Jas shrugged. "Beats me."

Dupree rapped his knuckles on the top of the desk. "The uncle *must* have known there was something more."

"Maybe it was jealousy. Competition. Evans made it sound as if Jordan topped his cousins on every front."

"You're suggesting? Let me guess . . . The uncle's ego soars when the kid hits a snag, finally providing evidence of the Hardys' superiority over the Jordans. Hmm. Plausible, but not likely. Have you reached Uncle William? Any of the Hardys?"

"They've moved from the area, but I have a lead on Russell."

"Good so far. What else?"

"While I had the school on the phone, I asked about our mysterious Doug."

"Speak to me."

"His name's Douglas Wile, Jordan's best friend. Evans said they were inseparable from the time Jordan's parents were killed. Wile's father died two years earlier when Douglas was nine. Afterward, he and his mom lived hand-to-mouth. The school credits her with keeping him on track. Good kid. B student. Passionate. More of a rebel than Jordan, according to Evans, who learned about Jordan's offense and kept track of both boys for a year after high school. His exact words were: 'They had each other's backs.'" Dupree stroked his chin. "To show you what kind of friend Wile was . . . When Jordan missed his first year of college because he was confined in juvenile hall, Wile sat his out, too. He put the University of Illinois on hold for a year, moved Jordan in with him and his mom, helped him get a job, and encouraged him to reapply the following year."

"Does our super-friend still live in Chicago?" Dupree asked.

"Did until a year ago. After college he got a job with a small manufacturing firm. Worked there four years—then suddenly disappeared. Told co-workers he was heading to New Awlins. He never returned."

"What about his bills?"

"Ran his credit. Up to date on everything—rent, utilities, student loans. Guess who's been writing the checks."

"Sean Jordan."

"Bingo, Lieutenant."

Dupree smiled. "Keep this up and you'll become a *real* detective someday."

Jas beamed.

"One hand washes the other. I get that. But where's Wile been that he's needed Jordan to pay his bills? Have you tracked down the mom?"

"Working on it. I haven't been able to find her."

"Keep at it and locate that prick, William Hardy."

"So what do you think?" Jas asked.

"You tell me."

Jas pursed his lips. "One thing bothers me."

"Only *one*?"

"If girls threw themselves at Jordan and he was that experienced, why would he be messing around with a fifteen-year-old and then hold the line at a little kissy face?"

"He wouldn't."

"Unless . . ."

"Unless?" Dupree echoed.

"He *wasn't* that experienced." Jas gazed upward as if trying to remember. "Evans said girls threw themselves at Jordan. He never said that Jordan took the bait. Growing up under William Hardy, Jordan might have dodged girls altogether, considering the trouble they represented. Once out from under his uncle's eye, he might have given himself permission to follow the first pretty girl he felt something for. Except he didn't know what to do. Didn't even know what to ask."

"Like her age."

Jas nodded.

Dupree's skepticism spread across his face. "He was the brightest kid in town. Went to therapy and took over the group. That takes communication skills better than mine. How could he *not* know what to say?"

"I'm just saying it's possible." Jas set the file folder on the desk and leaned against the wall. "So . . . is he a dolphin or something worse?"

"If he were a dolphin, why would he have lied? And why was he forced to register for several more years? Jordan's guilty of something. Never trust anybody who was first in his class."

"Guilty of something doesn't mean he's capable of murder."

"Neither does it mean he isn't. Every predator had to start somewhere. Answers, Jas. Bring me more *answers*. I wanna know where Wile's been for a year, and why the two of them were at Molly's the night of the murder."

"Yes, sir."

"And what Jordan did to get his years extended."

"I'm on it."

"And most of all . . . whether or not he lit the match."

"The match, Lieutenant?"

"That blew his parents to smithereens."

Chapter 18

THERE'S SOMETHING I WANT YOU TO SEE

"BE at Fiorella's in fifteen minutes. There's someone I want you to meet."

Sean recognized the phrase, the cadence, and the urgent command, ordering him to rush right over. If it wasn't "There's someone I want you to meet," it was the alternate: "There's something I want you to see." Either way, Doug's enthusiasm was infectious and compelling.

"Watch this," Doug said, the first time Sean came at his bidding. With an eleven-year-old's glee, Doug broke open a firecracker two inches long, exposing a mound of silver-grey powder. He set it on the stoop in front of his house and knelt as if officiating at some ancient celebration. When the firecracker was lit, it spun like a pinwheel, spewing colorful sparks in every direction. Sean knew from then on to trust Doug's zeal. There was a good reason to come whenever he called.

Another time, upon hearing, "There's something I want you to see," Sean rushed over to find Doug alone in his room, sprawled across his bed wearing only his briefs. "I just found out about this.

It's the coolest thing ever." Doug stripped off the rest, leaving Sean embarrassed and bewildered. His eyes drifted to Doug's penis which was half-erect and redder than the times he'd glimpsed it at the Y.

"Watch what happens when I do this." Doug grasped his penis, stroking it gently, looking at occasionally as if checking it out. His breathing deepened, his eyes glassed over, his pace quickened, his penis swelled.

Doug suddenly shuddered. A moan escaped his lips. From the tip of his penis clear fluid streamed forth in five quick bursts wetting his stomach, chin, and chest. He continued stroking, gently, lovingly, until finally his penis withered in his hand. Sean expected him to bolt upward, saying, "Wasn't I right?" or "Wasn't that great?" Instead, Doug remained still, eyes mostly closed, lips parted, breath deeply flowing.

It was Sean who spoke first, later regretting what he asked. "Can anyone do that?"

"I think so," Doug whispered.

That night in his room, Sean confirmed Doug's assessment—his discovery *was* one of the coolest things ever. From Vince, he thought he'd learned everything about sex. He couldn't imagine why he'd failed to include that.

"I can't," Sean told Doug in response to his demand. "I promised Laurie I'd take her and Ren to lunch. Then we're headed to the Ponchartrain Parade. A lot of shit's been coming down. I owe them. Can we make it tonight?"

"Not a chance. It took an act of Congress—no, *God*—to get this guy to meet us. You'll understand when you get here. Hang up and come."

"I'll try."

Sean approached Laurie with a revised itinerary: dinner after the parade, and was surprised when she agreed.

He crossed Governor Nicholls and spotted Doug, sitting at a table with a young man in a suit. Sean trusted Doug, but after the week he'd had, the sight of a well-dressed stranger filled him with suspicion.

Doug sprang from his chair, stepping out from under an umbrella. "Sean, meet Brian Monteleone." The man extended a hand. "Brian's an aide to US Senator Brandon Meyers. Brian, this is my best friend,

Sean Jordan—no relation to Michael, despite their both hailing from Chicago." Doug looked at Sean's face. "What the hell happened to you?"

"I cut myself shaving." Sean wasn't about to let on to a stranger. He shook the man's hand with little conviction.

Doug continued to stare. "What were you using, a lawnmower?"

"Something like that."

Doug leaned toward Sean and spoke in hushed tones. "Brian's here to help us." Sean fixed his eyes on Monteleone. "Like you and me, Brian's a sex offender."

Jesus. Sean drew a quick breath, aghast that Doug would out him to a stranger without his consent. Monteleone might be a pedophile who could recognize the same in him. He even looked the part, with slicked-back hair and an insinuating smile—the type Sean thought could easily seduce kids.

"Yet all three of us are innocent," Doug went on, Sean discounting the supposition. "Brian's passed the ten-year mark and no longer has to play their game. You're solidly in the middle, to which your face attests. And then there's me—a conscientious objector."

"You're serious about not registering," Sean said.

"At midnight tonight it'll be official. I'll be New Orleans's newest fugitive from the law."

Sean's thoughts raced for a way to get Doug to reconsider, but he knew him too well.

A young waitress in a catsup-stained apron, sporting multiple piercings in each of her ears, strolled to the table and asked for their orders.

"What do you recommend?" Brian asked.

"What do you like?" the waitress replied. "We're a Southern-style restaurant. Home cooking. Everything's good."

"Fried chicken," Doug said. "Cornbread. Lots of butter. A side of red beans and rice. And . . ." To the waitress's amusement, he hoisted his sleeve, revealing the parrot whose bill mouthed: "a Coke."

She had all she could do to contain herself. "'A Coke.' Did I get that right?" She was talking to the bird.

"I'll try your salmon salad," Brian said. "Do you have Perrier?" The waitress looked stumped as she headed for the kitchen.

"It's a soul-food restaurant!" Doug wailed. "Where'd you do your time—Marin County?"

"And what were you in for exactly?" Sean said, failing to conceal his disdain.

Brian glanced at Doug, as if wondering if it was safe to go on. Doug nodded. "It happened when I was seventeen. I had a crush on my lethally attractive college-bound comp teacher without realizing she had an even bigger crush on me. One day she invited me to study at her place—then asked me to stay for dinner. For dessert, she made me an offer I couldn't refuse."

Doug grinned. Sean found nothing funny about it.

"It wasn't a big deal for either of us. We knew what we wanted and went for it. I never dreamed she'd show up at school the next day and brag about it in the teachers' cafeteria. By noon, the place was swarming with police. At 1:00, I watched her being led away in handcuffs."

"You were the minor," Sean said. "How does that jive with registration?"

"When they interviewed me—the poor victim—I thought I could dispel the whole thing by telling them it was consensual, and that besides, neither of us was a virgin. What a stupid thing *that* was to say. In no time they had the names of my other partners, one of whom was sixteen, and all of a sudden, I'm a victimizer too, even though the sixteen-year-old claimed she was a willing partner as well. My teacher got three years in Angola. I got probation with registration."

"What does it feel like, coming off registration?" Doug asked.

"I wish I could say it's a whole lot better, but registration does a number on your head. You spend so many years looking over your shoulder, wondering if and when another shoe's going to drop, that feeling guilty and worried becomes part of who you are. Things get better, but deep scars remain."

Okay, so maybe he isn't a pedophile. Sean wondered if, like himself, Monteleone questioned his innocence regardless. Of the scars he referred to, likely self-doubt was one.

The waitress returned, setting their orders on the table. Doug picked up a wing. "The reason I've gathered us together today is to figure out a way to fuck the bastards, fight back, and live free. Brian here's the man who's gonna make that possible."

"How?" Sean asked.

Doug took a bite. "In OPP, I met other offenders. Real creeps. Guys who'd strangled hookers. Guys who bragged about having sex with kids. But a handful of others weren't guilty of shit. The guards called us 'Dolphins.' It means—"

"I've heard."

"In private, legislators acknowledge registration's flaws," Brian said. "But everyone's afraid to publicly renounce it, fearing for their reputations, fearing for their careers."

"What if we *are* guilty?" Sean said. "We *did* break the law."

Brian glanced at Doug and Doug turned to Sean. "You're right. Everybody's guilty. But to put our sins in a category with murder and rape suggests to me that *something* is flawed."

"Senator Meyers is sympathetic to dolphins," Brian went on. "He's retiring in three years. Re-election's not an issue. He's seen what registration's done to guys like us—guys who don't know how or lack the resources to defend themselves."

Sean looked at Brian. "Why would a retiring senator with a legacy to protect stick his neck out to defend a bunch of criminals, minor as we are?"

Doug cut in. "Who knows and who cares? Maybe he played doctor with his sister when he was five. Maybe he lost his virginity at fourteen to a seventeen-year-old on a moonlit night. Maybe he groped women on Bourbon Street, or took a leak along a highway because he couldn't hold it any longer. Maybe he did all those things and went on to live a normal, happy life, and now sees others doing the same and getting shafted for it. I don't care about his reasons. The guy wants to help, and he's the only angel we have."

"He's already met with law enforcement officials, psychologists, and community leaders, discussing alternatives to registration," Brian continued. "But mostly he wants to hear from people like us." Brian looked at Sean. "The Senator has my story and part of Doug's. Would you be willing to sit down with him and tell him yours?"

Mine? Mine's nothing like yours. I was an adult; she was fifteen. Sean read the pleading on Doug's face. The last thing he wanted was to jeopardize their friendship, but he knew if he told part of his story, he'd have a hard time containing the rest.

Brian handed Sean his card. "I'll be in Baton Rouge on Monday. Call me if you're willing and I'll set up a time for you to meet with the Senator."

The waitress returned and dropped the check on the table. Brian handed it back with a fifty dollar bill. "This one's on the federal government. We'll be in touch." Brian shook their hands and headed up Governor Nicholls.

"So what *really* happened?" Doug asked, eyeing Sean's face.

"A cop hit me." Doug stared, transfixed. "A lot's happened since Sunday. I wanted to call but there's been no time." Sean took a deep breath. "Some radio guy outed me over the air."

"Come on."

"I lost my job, the house was vandalized, and Laurie seems on the verge of taking a hike. On top of that, I'm worried about you."

"Me? Stop worrying."

"You're messing with two years hard labor."

"That's only if they catch me. I'm planning on making sure they don't. Tell you what. Come to my hideout tonight. Have a couple of beers. I'll give you a chance to work your psychology." Doug scribbled an address on a piece of paper.

"Tonight? I don't know—"

"You gotta come. There's something I want you to see."

Chapter 19

THROW ME SUMPIN, MISTA!

"DADDY! Daddy!"

Sean peered upward at an ecstatic Ren, arms held high, legs dangling over

his shoulders.

"The parade's coming!"

He turned toward Laurie and stared down the street at dozens of floats, snaking in their direction. Thousands of spectators erupted with a roar, drowning out brass bands if only for a moment. Sean stopped to think: *What other cities' parades rival these?* Rio came to mind along with New York and Chicago, boasting monstrous balloons and a river dyed green. But none was more impressive than the spectacle rolling by with men bearing torches shooting fire into the sky. So mesmerized was Sean that he forgot for a while the cop who beat him up, the pain in his face, the device around his ankle, and Laurie's reaction to it all.

He'd hoped to leave the hospital long before she got home, giving him a chance to apply a bit of makeup to soften his appearance. But when he arrived, she was already there, lying on the sofa, curled in a ball.

"Lor, what's wrong?"

Laurie sat up with a great deal of effort, seeming to require every bit of her strength. "It's never been easy." She sounded distant and scripted. "I always thought we could handle anything that came along. But these last few days . . ."

Sean took the blow, a sledge hammer to his chest. "I know lately . . ." The words lodged in his throat. "I've been caught up in myself. I haven't spent enough time thinking about how all this is affecting you." When he reached to embrace her, Laurie pulled away. Turning, she spotted his face. He expected her to recoil. Instead, she studied him calmly.

"I'm sorry all this is happening, but the 'you and me against the world' stuff isn't working anymore." She glanced down the hall. "It's no longer just the two of us."

"What does that mean for us?" he asked.

"I don't know," she answered.

The words terrified him. *Vince, help me here.*

"I pulled Ren from preschool," Laurie went on.

"What?"

"Two parents heard your name on the radio. They called Suzanne, demanding Ren be expelled. Suzanne assured me she'd stand by us regardless, but I couldn't let her do it. Her life is that school. She's too good a friend."

Sean erupted in anger. "Ren doesn't deserve this!"

"Daddy!" Ren called from her private box seat, the envy of everyone watching the parade from the ground. "Suzanne's here!"

Suzanne DeMarco, at five-foot-one, was an effervescent blond with a naughty, cherubic smile. The New Orleans' native—twice married and divorced—knew a little bit about men, a lot about children, and nearly everything there was to know about dogs. Brielle, her French Poodle, accompanied her everywhere she went—everywhere, that is, except parades. "Too hawd on the ears," she explained, with an accent like Weinstat's. "Poor Brielle . . . missin' out on all those lovely rear ends." Suzanne walked up beside them and tugged Ren's feet.

Sean remembered her calling the previous year, inviting the family to attend a Mardi Gras parade.

Parade? He thought. *Parades are for kids.*

"It's the first of the season," she chirped in his ear. "You *have* to go. *Everyone* goes. I've packed a cooler and I'm coming right over."

The moment they joined up with ten thousand others, Sean understood what Suzanne had meant.

"Daddy, *look!*"

Sean pivoted toward a float, rolling in their direction, with a ten-foot-tall chicken nesting on five-foot-long twigs. Spectators hollered, "Throw me sumpin, mista!" and the chicken complied, throwing miniature footballs and green plastic cups. Suzanne leaped in the air and snagged her first prize, smiled at the chicken, and blew him a kiss. "And this is only a warm-up parade!" she reminded everyone, standing around her. "The *big* parades are still a week away!"

Sean gazed at the men throwing beads from the floats, each masked and costumed in dazzling array. Together they formed *krewes,* or "secret societies," that produced the parades year after year. Hidden behind masks, Sean had been told, were the leaders of the community—New Orleans's elite.

"Daddy," Ren called. "Look what I caught."

"What did you catch?" Sean helped her to her feet.

"Blue ones. Like your eyes. Look!" She held up a string of cobalt-blue beads.

"What are you going to do with those pretty beads?"

"Wear them to dinner with Mom and Suzanne."

"Can I come, too?"

"Oh, Daddy. You're silly."

"Let me help you with those." Sean triple looped the strand so Ren could manage.

"Thank you, Daddy. Up!" He hoisted her back onto her perch.

The word "Daddy" resonated deeply with Sean. Whenever he heard it, he turned around, expecting to see Ren standing nearby. Occasionally it would be a different child calling, trying to capture some other parent's attention. Any child's plea touched a chord inside, whisking Sean back to the time he was free, hosting salons, gathering friends, meeting kids' needs, and handing out hugs. It reminded him, too, of his greatest disappointment—having only one child instead of three or four. *At least not now. Not under these circumstances*, he and Laurie decided long ago. It was tough enough living in constant fear that, at any time and for no discernible reason, the child he had could be taken away.

He looked at the kids along the parade route—laughing, shouting, and teeming with glee—and couldn't imagine being a threat to any of them. He'd done his best to meet his obligations, avoiding places where children would be. But despite those obligations and the risks involved, he refused to deprive Ren of the city's ultimate thrill.

Sean glanced to his right toward the next float in line and saw something unexpected: a krewe member unmasked. The man had removed it to rub his eye—just for a second, but a second was enough. Sean recognized him instantly: Burn Breneaux. Riding next to him was the girl Sean had seen, Breneaux's daughter in a golden gown. While her eyes were concealed behind a multicolored mask, there was no mistaking her dimples and upturned nose.

"Lor, look up there." Sean pointed. Laurie glanced skyward. "The guy dressed in green. See him?"

"I guess so," she said, barely paying attention.

"That's Burn Breneaux!" he shouted above the crowd. "The guy on the radio who hates sex offenders. His station's the one that outed us."

"*Sean!*" Laurie snapped, eyes darting anxiously. "Do you really have to broadcast it so everyone can hear?"

"Throw me sumpin, mista!" Ren yelled to Breneaux.

His mask reaffixed, Breneaux threw a string, sending it tumbling in Ren's direction. He continued to watch as she made the catch—then lowered his gaze, ever so slightly, as if to check out the person on whose shoulders she rode. His smile went cold. The float quickly passed.

As Breneaux disappeared, Sean pondered the moment:

Two dads. One on a curb with a noose around his neck, worried about the future, trying to survive. The other on

*a float with the noose in his hand, secure in a future that
brightens with each turn.*

"Daddy, look at these!" Ren called. He reached up again and
twirled her to the ground. "They're long. Tie 'em for me, Daddy." Sean
looped the strand just like the others. "I look like a rainbow."

"Prettiest rainbow I ever saw."

Trombones hit their peak with *South Rampart Street Parade*,
signaling that the parade was nearing its end. Sean took Ren's hand
and headed down Royal with Laurie and Suzanne close behind.

He remained deep in thought throughout most of the walk,
grappling in silence with the questions that plagued him. Would he
be able to find a job suitable enough to provide for his family? Would
any school accept Ren knowing her father was a sex offender? Would
Laurie come around before things went too far?

He thought too about the man riding on the float. Had Breneaux
recognized him and would he turn him in?

Dozens more questions demanded answers as well, none more
insistently than: What did Doug want him to see?

Chapter 20

THE OVERSIGHT

SEAN pulled up in front of the weather-beaten abode—a creepy old Victorian that seemed to growl when he approached. *What better place if you don't want to be found?* It was the second house off the corner on a dark and gloomy block lined with shot-out streetlights and wrecked, abandoned cars. Sean had steered clear of neighborhood called Tremé since warned of its danger by Pamela Perrot. "It's experiencing a renaissance, but it's going to take time. Don't go there alone and never at night." Only for Doug would he disregard the advice. He was relieved to find parking steps from the door.

Tremé was home to musicians and cooks, teachers and social workers, gangsters and crooks. It was one of the close-in parts of town where drug deals went bad and drive-by shootings took place with obscene regularity, at least according to the *Times-Picayune*. But it hadn't always been that way. Two hundred years earlier, it gave birth to a sound in a sacred place called Congo Square. There, slaves were permitted to assemble on Sundays, sharing rituals, music, food, and dance, combining rhythms from Africa, melodies from the Caribbean, and instruments from Europe in a gumbo called jazz.

Sean tugged the car's handle—then tugged it again, in order to make sure he'd locked it securely. He worried about leaving it even for an hour, knowing if it were vandalized, his father would kill him. *Then again . . .* He shrugged. *Turnabout's fair play.*

The house was as dark as the rest of the block, barely visible behind shrubs and piles of debris. Outlining the property was an old iron fence beneath years' worth of vines that had gone unattended. A decorative wooden bracket swung loosely from the peak, its nails scraping siding, emitting an endless haunting screech.

Sean found a gate to a path beside the house and navigated its length to a courtyard in the back. The backyard smelled sweetly of lush vegetation, fertile soil, and fragrant island spices—surprising for a place bereft of most simple pleasures. He hesitated. *What if the address is wrong? What if inside there's a drug deal going down?*

"Ahoy, mate!" Doug called, throwing open the door at the top of the porch. "Welcome aboard the HMS Bounty."

The tension broke, Doug's high spirits reassuring. For a second Sean thought he was back in Chicago, meeting Doug at his mother's house. He stepped inside into a dark and dreary kitchen, Doug fiddling with a bulb at the end of a frayed cord. The light sputtered—then held in a death-defying display, once again sending the Grim Reaper packing. The porcelain sink, linoleum floor, and rounded appliances echoed the 50s, the last time the house had likely been remodeled. Nothing was original except the chandelier, hanging valiantly over the kitchen table. Pointing at it, Sean asked, "Does this work?"

"Nothing works," Doug replied.

Advancing from the kitchen to the rest of the house, they passed gang signs scribbled across wallpapered walls; needles, set atop scorched marble mantles; and razor knives cast off due to broken blades. Doug led on. "I know it's a dump, but it's home." In a sitting room absent anything that could be called "furniture," they sat on a futon in the middle of the floor.

Sean looked around, taking in his surroundings. *HMS Bounty? More like a half-eaten Orca at the end of* Jaws. "Invest half a million and you might have something."

"Right . . . on top of first buying the place."

With Doug's appetite for the better things in life, seeing him on the floor filled Sean with sadness. "You realize this sucks . . . you living here."

"I can live wherever I want."

"Sure, like a Morlock in a cave, worried that everyone in daylight is carrying a badge."

"Damned if I do, damned if I don't?"

Even in the darkness, Sean sensed Doug's smirk.

"By the time Meyers and Monteleone get around to fixing this, you and I will have long been forgotten."

"So hide with me," Doug said. "There's plenty of room."

"How do I hide a four-year-old and a wife? Laurie's job is the only thing keeping us going. Why don't you register and play it straight for ten years? I'll give you the benefit of everything I've learned. We'll help each other get back on our feet. I'd even be willing to join you and your friend to see if there *is* a way to change any of this."

Doug appeared to consider—then declined. "I have to do this my way." He flexed his muscle, the parrot repeating: "My way."

A hush lingered for what seemed an eternity, Sean's thoughts drifting to his mother and father.

"I think about them too, you know," Doug said, with uncanny timing, "parents who loved you and encouraged your desires, only occasionally reeling you in. I remember everything you ever told me about them and about Vince and the way things used to be."

The words hung in the air.

"Come with me," Doug said. "There's something I want you to see." He flicked on a lighter and held it in the air, illuminating a corridor covered with dust. At the end of the corridor was a hulking room with chunks of plaster littering the floor. At one end stood an antique buffet housing several cracked plates and chipped crystal glasses. Doug knelt before it and opened a door. Removing a false panel, he reached inside, extracting a Roi-Tan cigar box with unicorns on the lid.

"What's that?" Sean asked, afraid to find out.

"An insurance policy." Doug blew dust from the top and opened the box, the flame illuminating the barrel of a gun.

"What are you doing?" Sean asked.

"Surviving. Any way I can. You keep saying you're worried about me. Maybe now you won't worry so much."

"This isn't right," Sean said, shaking his head. "You with a gun—" He suddenly remembered. "And me with—" He pulled up a pant leg, revealing the bracelet.

"*Fuck!*" Doug shoved the box back inside.

"What's wrong?"

"If they know where *you* are, they know where *I* am. Why didn't you tell me?"

"I didn't—"

"SHHH!"

A thud was heard, coming from outside. Doug dashed for the kitchen. Sean followed, heart galloping. Peeking through curtains, they saw a person by the fence. Another appeared, standing in the courtyard. A third stepped to the door and knocked with his fist.

"Don't let anyone in," Doug ordered.

There was a second knock, considerably louder. "Sean Jordan. This is Detective Dupree. I know you're inside. I want to talk to you."

Sean's thoughts raced wildly. Maybe they didn't know Doug was there, or that there even *was* a Doug. He wanted to reassure his friend—reverse his stupid blunder. But when he looked at Doug and saw the disappointment in his face, he found it unbearable.

"Give me two minutes before you answer the door," Doug said, speeding down the hall.

Sean walked to the door and listened. A louder pounding caused him to jump.

"Jordan. Open up or we're coming in."

"Okay!" Sean hollered back. He delayed a few seconds then reached for the knob. "What do you want, Dupree? I haven't done anything."

"May I come in?"

Sean was about to look over his shoulder but caught himself. "I—" His tongue faltered. "I don't see why not."

Dupree entered and looked around. "I didn't accuse you of anything. I only said I wanted to talk."

"It's Saturday night. Even sex offenders are entitled to a social life. So talk."

"Who are you with?" Dupree asked.

None of your fucking business. "Maybe I'm alone."

"Some social life." Dupree leaned on the counter and pulled out a pad. "Let's see, you had lunch at Fiorella's with a couple of people we haven't identified. From there you went home, picked up your wife and daughter, and headed uptown to the Ponchartrain Parade. There you met a Suzanne DeMarco, owner of the Little People Preschool on Olympic. Then you walked to dinner at Mona Lisa on Royal. You waited until dark to drive to this location. Why, Jordan? Why would you drive to an empty house in this neighborhood in the middle of the night?"

"It's eight-thirty!"

"I'm guessing you're here with someone. I just don't know who."

Sean's voice grew calm, non-combative. "Dupree, I let an underage girl touch me ten years ago. I've been a Boy Scout ever since. When are you going to leave me alone?"

"When you start telling me the truth. I've got a murder to solve and no better lead than a sex offender who persists in avoiding my questions. When I get some answers and if they line up, I'll be glad to leave you alone. Now who are you with?"

"Lieutenant!" a voice called from outside.

Dupree headed for the back door. Sean followed. Sprawled on brick pavers in the middle of the yard was Doug, a gun inches from his head. Holding the gun was a plainclothes officer, a badge hanging loosely at his waist.

"I found him climbing out a second-story window," Jas told Dupree.

A second officer took over for Jas. "Get up . . . slowly," he ordered. Doug stood. The officer patted him down and removed his wallet. "He's clean."

Dupree steadied the light, flickering above the sink, and motioned for Doug and Sean to sit at the table. "You live here?"

"Yeah," Doug muttered.

"Want to try that again a little louder?"

"Yes, I live here."

"Pretty anxious to get away."

"When creeps come around, you get away as fast as you can."

"What made you think we were creeps?"

"It's Tremé. We have a lot of them." Doug glared at the detective. "You think I'm gonna wait around and sort people out?"

"Your friend did," Dupree said. "How do the two of you know each other?"

Sean stared at the floor. After what he'd just done, he was keeping his mouth shut.

"From dealing drugs? Planning sex crimes? What?" Dupree continued.

"We're best friends from Chicago," Doug said softly, his voice carrying a hint of submission. Jas's eyes widened. He turned in Dupree's direction.

"So why are you here in New Awlins?"

Doug and Sean looked at each other.

"Lieutenant." The second officer entered, handing Doug's wallet to Dupree. "His name's Douglas Wile. He was arrested a year ago: public indecency. Served twelve months in OPP and was released a week ago Wednesday."

Jas slapped his forehead. Dupree shook his head.

"By the way, Lieutenant," the officer continued, "Wile hasn't registered."

Dupree began counting on his fingers.

"I already did the math. Tenth day is today. He's got three hours before he's in violation."

Dupree turned to Doug. "Well, I'd say it's your lucky day, Wile. We happened along just in time. In time to remind you to register. Might even be able to rustle up the paperwork so you can sign before the day runs out. But hey, it's up to you. If you'd rather not, we'll hang around, drink some coffee, and give you a lift downtown. What's your pleasure?"

Sean couldn't believe what he'd done to his friend. He'd spent a lifetime attempting to overcome guilt. Now *this*. He felt as if death were claiming him inside, each of his organs shutting down in succession. He tried to apologize, if only with his eyes. But when he looked at Doug, bracing for a deadly stare, Doug gazed past, as if in another world.

The second officer returned with papers and a pen. He set them in front of Doug and pointed. "Start here."

Doug picked up the pen and began to write.

Chapter 21

DETAILS

SEAN climbed a ladder at the front of the living room, pulling broken glass from its hundred-year-old frame.

"Details, Sean. Pay attention to details," he heard Vince chide (like remembering a bracelet that establishes one's whereabouts, and noticing a cough that lingered for months). *How long, Vince, did you know you were dying? Is that why you mentored me—to be a sort of legacy?*

"Psychology is the handiwork of the devil!" William Hardy railed, forbidding Sean from engaging in its practice. "For how long?" Sean asked. "Forever!" Hardy answered. Fortunately, Vince had taught Sean there *was* no forever, and that *every endeavor chooses its own time.* So Sean waited patiently, lessons on hold, expecting that someday his time would come.

Standing by helplessly while Doug signed the papers, Sean felt his time had come and gone.

He'd disappointed Doug on so many occasions, especially when bowing to Hardy's whims. "Girls chase you all around the school, and you won't even date, because of that prick, William Hardy," Doug once said, to which Sean replied: "You think he hates psychology? Guess what he thinks about *sex*. I'm not taking any chances. William Hardy knows who the sinners are."

Disappointing Doug was one thing. This was another. Forgetting the bracelet was an act of betrayal.

Sean entered Doug's number the third time in an hour, only to be greeted by voicemail again. He'd done all he could. It was time to back off. Doug knew he was trying, that he loved him and was sorry.

Breneaux settled in early, ahead of the incompetents, to catch up on news and drink his coffee in peace. He was actually fond of the technical crew—people who were hired to do *real* jobs, like pointing fingers, pushing buttons, fiddling with wires, and plugging things in. He especially liked Marilyn, who amused him each day with her quick wit, wardrobe, and generous sense of humor. It was management he loathed, Manning in particular, who had no conception of what a real job was. As for LeGrande . . . Breneaux tried to hate him but could muster only pity. *Sooner or later, the kid's gonna get creamed.*

He leaned back, closed his eyes, and pictured the guy he'd seen at the parade—the guy he'd caught a glimpse of when he came to the studio—the guy he'd not been able to put out of his mind. He had a child—a beautiful young girl—who'd ridden on his shoulders the way Charmaine once had ridden on his. When she shouted: "Throw me sumpin, mista!" he'd accommodated, tossing opalescent whites, Charmaine's favorite of all the colored beads. He recalled Charmaine, laying her beads on her bed, remembering how and from whom she caught every strand. Those were great times—the *best* of times. He thought about the guy's face, swollen from scalp to chin, bruised bright red and purple in the shape of a crab, its spiny pincers flexing when he turned his head. The wound hadn't been there a few days before. *No doubt less than great times for him.*

Then again, the guy was a registered sex offender, loitering at a parade attended by kids. Under normal circumstances, he'd have called the police. But there was something about the guy. Maybe it was his desire to protect his family. More likely it was his courage to stand up to Manning.

Protect his family. Breneaux felt sadness and a wrenching in his gut. He'd done everything he could to protect Maggie and Charmaine. But his efforts weren't enough when Maggie died from a disease he'd never heard of and couldn't pronounce. Soon after, anxiety and depression set in. He began overlooking details while worrying excessively. His only salve was his beloved Charmaine. It was she who kept him sane. It was she he worried about most.

"Mornin', boss," Marilyn said, walking from the control booth into the studio.

Breneaux looked at the clock. He was on in five, his few minutes of peace having slipped away.

He changed gears in a heartbeat, greeting the world, reminding it that Mardi Gras was a mere eight days away. Lights on the phones began blinking through the glass, informing him that the world was greeting him back.

"Mr. Breneaux," a woman began, "my daughter came home crying last night because friends posted pictures of her on the Internet."

Breneaux's eyes sparkled, the first call of the morning breaking his way. "These wouldn't be *compromising* pictures, by any chance?"

"I guess you could say that."

"Exposed shoulder and back compromising pictures, or vagina in a limousine compromising pictures?"

"More like the limousine."

"How old is your daughter?"

There was a moment's hesitation. "Twelve."

"Twelve! Who took the pictures?"

"She did."

Sexting. Better still. "Was anyone with her when she flashed away?"

"No, she would have been too embarrassed."

"Too embarrassed to be seen *taking* the pictures, but not too embarrassed to send them through space."

"She thought they'd only be seen by her boyfriend."

"Who must be about . . ."

"Fourteen."

"Huh. I was going to guess forty. What do you think she wanted to accomplish by sending naked pictures of herself to a fourteen-year-old boy?"

"I don't know," she said. "Maybe to impress him."

"You've seen the pictures. Are they impressive?"

"She's my daughter. I don't know what to do."

"Your daughter knows her way around a camera, has figured out how to impress boys, and even landed one. So what's the problem?"

"She thinks he's the one who posted them online."

"Ahh . . ."

"He's not a bad kid. He was just showing off for friends."

"Not a bad kid . . . except for plastering your daughter's vagina all over the Internet. Did he send back any pictures of himself?"

"Well . . ."

Breneaux hit the off-air switch to contain a burst of laughter. "Pretty hot, eh?"

"I can't really say."

"Sure you can. Go ahead."

"I just want to know what to do."

"You're calling a radio station to find out what to do? It's the police you should be talking to." Breneaux chuckled. "Tell them a person living in your house is producing child porn with a fourteen-year-old accomplice."

The woman began to cry. "But she's only *twelve*."

"And she's a criminal. Depending on where you live, they might go easy, but in at least fifteen states, she's committed a felony. Did you ever sit down with her, have a mother-daughter talk, tell her to keep her clothes on when cameras are in the vicinity?"

"No."

"Well then . . . By the way, when you call the police, tell them there's an adult in the house, too, checking out pictures of her daughter's fourteen-year-old boyfriend." Marilyn held up both thumbs before dutifully dropping the call. "America is listening . . ."

Breneaux finished his show and was making his escape when Manning caught him and stopped him in the hall.

"It's been nearly a week. What do you think?"

"About what?" Breneaux sneered.

Manning cocked his head in LeGrande's direction. "About *him*."

"I don't think about him at all." Breneaux dodged Manning's hand, slithering toward his shoulder.

"Got a few minutes?"

"No. What do you want?"

"I think this kid's got something: chutzpah—like yours. Lots of talent. The dailies are coming in stronger than we expected. We're anticipating, next period, that the ten-to-two ratings will blast off the chart. Know why?"

"Because the kid's got chutzpah."

"No, because the audience loves outings."

"Stop. I don't want to hear about it. We're in the entertainment business."

"My point exactly. Why not give the audience more of what it wants?"

"You know why." Breneaux did nothing to conceal his scorn. There was no getting through to the greedy bookkeeper with another dollar still to be squeezed from the air. "Entertainment ends where vigilantism begins."

"We're not rounding people up and shooting them, for Christ's sake."

"If you keep this up, it's only a matter of time. People were harassed his first day on the air—or have you forgotten the guy who was here?"

"He was a nut job."

"Didn't seem like it when I saw him with his daughter on Saturday. Apart from his face being battered and bruised, he looked like any guy enjoying a parade with his kid. Think that's justifiable in the name of ratings?"

"You make it sound like it's our fault. *He's* the sex offender."

Breneaux could feel his cheeks blazing red. He knew the plays, the dodges, and every conceivable word game. "Manning, Elvis is more likely to return to the building than you are to stop chasing a buck." He turned to leave.

"I'm not the only one getting rich off this."

The attack crossed the line. Breneaux halted but continued facing away.

"Listen, Burn, I didn't mean anything by it. Your fans love you, corporate loves you—*I* love you. It's just that we're receiving more and more e-mails asking why you're not outing as well. Corporate's hoping you'll jump on the bandwagon. This morning, I told them I'd talk to you."

"As you have," Breneaux said, continuing down the hall.

LeGrande's cell phone rang as Marilyn cut to a commercial.

"This is Danny . . . Danny Hurt," the caller announced in a cocky tone of voice.

"Officer Danny! NOPD." LeGrande had been in town less than a week when he began fielding calls from committed sympathizers, haters of sex offenders inspired by his words. The same had happened when he worked in LA, where tips from cops scored him unprecedented ratings. LeGrande heard from Hurt his first day on the air, saying he and his friends would help in any way. *Any way?* LeGrande loathed their naivety but welcomed their generosity. "What do you have for me today?"

"New registrations . . ." Hurt began.

LeGrande scribbled a list of names and addresses.

"Last one's named Wile. W-i-l-e. Got busted on Bourbon for indecent exposure."

LeGrande wrinkled his nose. "I know I'm new here, but I heard *everybody's* indecent on Bourbon Street."

"You heard right. We usually look the other way. But sometimes we make an arrest to show crowds we're payin' attention. Then we let 'em go. He must've lipped off or something to make it downtown. Spent a year in Orleans Parish Prison and was released a week ago."

LeGrande jotted Wile's address.

"Also, he didn't bother to register on his own. We think he was hiding and planning a dodge when we stumbled across him in the company of another offender. The two of them were friends in Chicago."

Chicago. Twice in one week? "What's the other guy's name?"

"Hold on a minute," Hurt said, rustling papers in the background. "Here it is. Well, what do you know . . . the first guy I told you about: Sean Andrew Jordan."

LeGrande broke into a smile. "Danny. Just curious. Why do you hate sex offenders?"

"You kiddin'? Old guys fuckin' little kids?"

LeGrande had a hunch. "*Besides* that."

Hurt lowered his voice. "I have my reasons."

"Thanks. I'll take it from there." Hurt had *personal* reasons. That made him an even greater ally.

So, Jordan . . . LeGrande leaned as far back in his chair as he could. *You again. I'm starting to enjoy this.*

Chapter 22

I LOVE YOU

SEAN woke with a start, eyes assaulted by sunlight streaming through slats in the bedroom shutters. His first thoughts were of Doug and how his calls had been ignored. Even if Doug were angry, it wasn't like him to stay away.

He turned to Laurie, sleeping beside him. "I love you," he whispered, not knowing if she heard. He wanted her to respond as she always had, first arguing that clearly, she loved him more—then pummeling him with a pillow, as if winning a pillow fight proved her claim. Regardless of who won, they'd be naked in seconds, choosing sex over assignments, classes about to begin, and patients waiting anxiously for blood to be drawn.

Sean's *I love yous* were rooted in a romanticism so deep, their expression rendered meaningless all that was superficial. He wanted stopping power when he said it—the rhino to fall in its tracks, the world to cease its rotation, his partner to reply in kind. But once Sean received extended registration, Laurie's *I love yous* were said only in response, tainted by a laugh or other affectation of lightness.

"I have to get up," she said, climbing out of bed.

"Why? It's only six."

"They called a special meeting. Then, I have to find Ren a school."

"I'll do that," Sean said. "You've got enough going on."

Laurie headed for the bathroom, leaving Sean staring in space.

It was the first time his *I love you* had elicited nothing at all.

Sean set fresh fruit and a bowl of cereal before Ren, with an apron around his waist and a paper towel draped over his arm. "Mademoiselle, would you prefer milk or cream on your Honey Nut Cheerios?"

"Sir, I really, really, really wanted blueberry pancakes." Ren played along.

"But there's a shortage of pancakes throughout the empire. Pancake seeds were planted early in spring, but the ensuing draught caused the crops to fail. In addition, South Eureka—the world's biggest source of blueberries—is still at war with Outer Veracity. Until that's resolved, it's anybody's guess when blueberries will again become available."

"Daddy, what are you talking about?" Ren said, feigning exasperation.

"*Blueberries!* he exclaimed, eyes crossing to Ren's delight. "Maybe we'll have pancakes tomorrow." Sean walked to the sink and began doing dishes. "Today, there are things we need to do."

"What kinda things?" she asked.

"A bath for starters—then finding you a new school."

"But Daddy, I like my old school."

Sean felt her disappointment. "I know, Sweetie. I like it too; and I like Suzanne. Glad she decided to join us at the parade. Wasn't that fun?" The segue worked; Ren's disappointment faded.

Sean filled the tub, checking the temperature frequently. Turning to remove Ren's clothes, he was pleasantly surprised to find she'd gone ahead and accomplished the task. "You're getting to be quite the independent girl."

"What does that mean, Daddy?" Ren asked, shoving a slew of rubber ducks into the water.

"'Independent' means taking care of yourself. That's what big girls do—big girls like you." He grasped her waist and lifted her into the tub, recalling how much less she weighed weeks before. Her rapid growth and blossoming personality presaged the future, inciting his fears: *What if someday, I'm attracted to my daughter?* He recoiled from the question, hating the circumstances that elicited it.

Ren stood and faced him with arms at her sides. "Dry me off, Daddy."

He wrapped her in a towel and hoisted her into the air. On her way down, her feet found his lap. There, she pranced on his jeans, giggling with abandon. Sean soon realized his body was responding. Worse than that, it felt good.

He removed her immediately, hiding his panic, and suggested she get dressed and watch TV.

"She was a wiggling mass of exuberance, dancing on your penis. Of course you're going to respond," Andrews assured him from Chicago. "You knew how that worked by the time you were ten. Have you forgotten everything your grandfather taught you?"

"I know, but—"

"There are no buts about it. You *love* your daughter; you don't have a 'thing' for her. I've worked with hundreds of pedophiles in my career. Trust me . . . you're not one of them. Isn't it time you stop doubting yourself?"

If only it were that easy. Sean thanked him and hung up, anxiety lingering, not only about his nature but also about Doug. *Why hasn't he called?* He knew he should back off and respect Doug's silence, but a voice kept telling him time had run out. He'd call again, he decided, when the dishes were done.

He switched on the radio next to the sink—*Static. How apropos*—and nudged the dial until a voice was heard, belonging to the guy in the blazer and slacks. Reaching to turn it off, he hesitated for a second, curious about the psychology of the person on the air.

"New outings for Monday, February sixteenth," the guy said, followed by an insertion of heralding trumpets.

Sean was disappointed but not the least bit surprised that Manning had chosen to ignore his pleas.

"Bobby Jones. Lives in Uptown off Carrolton. Write this number down. Says he spent three years in Angola . . . for fondling the babysitter *in front of her house!* Bobby. How smart was *that*? Why not a big open field? Her junior high parking lot? Somewhere—come on—where the neighbors couldn't watch. Didn't you know it was a Neighborhood Watch Community?" A rim shot sounded.

Sean felt disgust, not only for the speaker, but for the voyeuristic listeners cheering him on.

"Our second newcomer is Douglas Wile."

"Jesus, *NO!*" Sean wailed.

Ren ran into the room. "What's wrong, Daddy?"

"Nothing, honey. I have to hear this." He turned up the volume.

"Says he did a stint in OPP. For what? *Public indecency?* Seems a little stiff for flashing a homeless person in Jackson Square. Maybe that's why. Maybe he was stiff." Another rim shot was heard. "Douglas. You must have done something more creative. Give us a call and tell us what you did. Lines are open."

Sean punched off the radio, dizzy with self-loathing. He had to call and warn Doug, having fucked up far worse than he'd even imagined. He dialed the number and left a message again, this time pleading with Doug to call.

Not good enough, he thought. He had to see him.

Sean grabbed his wallet and reached for his keys before remembering how dangerous Tremé could be. Since he couldn't take Ren, he had no other choice but to call Laurie and wait for her to return. He entered her number and left a message.

"Doug?" Sean answered, when his ringtone sounded.

There was a momentary pause. "No. It's Laurie."

"Lor. Oh. Thanks for getting back to me. I've got a problem."

"What? Is Ren all right?"

He grimaced at having set her up for a scare. "She's fine. It's Doug. They outed him, too. I have to warn him. I called him again and he's still not picking up. I'm too leery of his neighborhood to take Ren along."

"Don't even *think* about taking her there!"

Sean shuddered at Laurie's aggressive response. It wasn't like her to misunderstand. "Did you hear what I said? I'm *not* taking her." His comment was followed by unnerving silence. "I can't get to Doug until you cover for me with Ren. Is there any chance you can watch her over lunch?"

More silence ensued, as if she were thinking. "I didn't know you had called. I was calling you to tell you I'm having lunch with Troy Madison. My job's in trouble."

"Shit."

"Is that shit, I hope you don't lose your job, or shit, I want to go hang out with my friend?"

Sean felt the hair on his neck stand on end. "Of course I don't want you to lose your job. It's my fault Doug's in trouble."

"I know, Sean, everything's always your fault. It's always about you." His blood ran cold. "Like the meeting this morning. I can't even go to work and be judged on my merits. Your situation overshadows everything."

"You're losing your job on account of me?"

"He didn't come out and say so, but it felt like an ultimatum—you, or the job."

"Jesus. They can't do that."

"They hate sex offenders, Madison on up. They can do whatever they want. With you out of work and me providing for Ren, I can't take any chances." Sean put up a hand like a shield against the words. "When we met, you had five years to go. Now you have eight. I can't do this anymore."

"I love you," he said. It was all he could think to say.

"I know you do, and I know you want me to tell you the same, but they'd be empty words. I can't find the feelings anymore."

Sean slumped at the table.

"You can stay in the house if you want for now. Suzanne's got room for Ren and me. We'll have to see from there."

The phone fell silent.

Emotion surged, obliterating thoughts of Doug. What remained was swirling darkness. Sean pictured Ren, her future uncertain, and settled into a sorrow that eclipsed any he'd known.

Chapter 23

RESPECT FOR THE DEAD

"SUZANNE. It's Sean. I need your help." He filled her in on Doug, and she agreed to watch Ren. "There's just one thing . . ." Vince prompting, *Learn from your mistakes.* "The police have me in an ankle bracelet. They're tracking my every move. Do you mind them knowing I stopped by your house?"

"Not at all," she laughed. "I've nothing to hide but a few grams of pot. I'd sure like to see them try to find that."

Sean and Ren were greeted by an exuberant Brielle, who lunged at Sean, dousing him with kisses. "You're definitely her favorite." Suzanne held Brielle's cheeks and looked her in the eyes. "Aren't you ashamed— throwing yourself at a man?" She set the dog down and mussed Ren's hair. "What can I get you two vagabonds to drink?"

"What's a vagadon?" Ren asked.

"That would be more than you, Sweetie," Sean replied. "Suzanne'll explain." He hugged Suzanne, Brielle jumping between them. "Thanks for everything. I have to go."

"Good luck. I'll call Laurie and let her know Ren's with me."

Sean sped to Tremé and rapped on the door. He waited and

rapped again, but no one answered. He returned to the car and waited some more until he couldn't sit a minute longer. He scribbled a terse note and shoved it under the door.

"Doug: You were outed on the radio. Call me."

Stomach growling, Sean headed down the street toward Two Sisters Restaurant a half mile away. He heard it was a favorite of city personnel—firemen, mailmen, meter maids, and cops. He sat opposite two middle-aged women wearing wide-brimmed hats trimmed with brightly colored flowers. They smiled broadly and voiced their approval when he ordered a turkey leg with gravy, grits, and greens. "That man shor knows how to eat," one said to the other. "My name's Belle." She waved from their table. "This here's Juleen."

Sean heard a marching band playing in the distance, ambling up the street in fits and starts. He asked if it was another Mardi Gras parade, spurring the women to laugh at his foolishness and naivety.

"Honey, where ya from?" Belle asked, with a critical expression.

"Chicago."

"Well, that explains it. That's no Mada Gras parade. It's a jazz funeral. Starts with a dirge to show respect for the dead—"

"Down here, we respect the dead more than the living," Juleen added.

"Then the band kicks up its heels to celebrate life," Belle went on. "Friends and bystanders fall in behin' . . . dancin' and hollerin' like there's no tomorrow. They're what we call a 'second line.' Come take a look."

Sean dropped twelve bucks and walked outside, following the women into the street. The band was playing "Just a Closer Walk with Thee," providing just enough energy to move the procession along. Behind the band was an antique hearse that was drawn by a team of sleek black horses. "Cemetery's only a block away!" Belle declared. Doug hadn't called, so Sean tagged along.

He watched as the casket was removed from the hearse, and a minister in robes read the Twenty-Third Psalm. If it weren't remarkable enough that the deceased was ninety-nine, he was eulogized by friends who'd cracked a hundred and one. His body was lowered carefully into the ground, cuing the band to blast, "When the Saints Go Marching In." Sean was amazed by the gaiety of the response, with people pouring out of houses to march along—singing, dancing, and waving white handkerchiefs, turning death and loss into celebration and triumph.

Doug has to be back.

It occurred to Sean if he'd stayed at Doug's house, he might have protected it from "well wishers"' maliciousness. He waved to the women who blew kisses in return, broke from the parade, and headed for his car.

Driving up Esplanade, a chill coursed Sean's spine. *A message from Vince?* Something felt wrong. He tried to wipe away the uncomfortable feeling, but the incessant gnawing continued to grow. Without thinking, he eased off the accelerator, hesitating like always, not wanting to know.

This is ridiculous. He resumed his speed.

He rounded the corner with increased trepidation until spotting Doug's house up the street on the right. Everything seemed normal, quiet, and calm.

Suddenly, without warning, quiet gave way.

There was a flash of white light and a deafening roar, followed by a fireball, rocketing into the sky.

"NO!" Sean screamed. *"NO!"*

Dupree put his hand on Peter Pell's shoulder in front of the chef's restaurant on rue de Dauphine. He valued their long, enduring friendship since meeting as kids, doing dishes for Pete's dad. In no time, he found himself reminiscing. "Remember the days," Peter said with a smile, "when 'blackened' referred to a steak being burnt, and a 'Creole' was a person rather than lunch?" Enjoying an encounter with the fragrance of bougainvillea, Dupree was annoyed when his radio squawked.

"Sorry, Peter. Crime's calling." Dupree crammed into his too-tight Ford, turned on his lights, and headed for Tremé.

Dispatch informed him of another explosion—residential this time, near where he'd last seen Jordan. There, he choked on smoke-filled air, watching flames shoot unmercifully through a once-grand home. He made his way around rubble and four-inch hoses to confer for a moment with the fire chief. "Any ideas?"

"Gas, no doubt. Almost always is with these old places. We'll know more when we get inside."

Dupree turned and looked across the street. Each time he entertained Jordan's innocence, his person-of-interest reappeared. Jas walked up beside him. "Lieutenant, don't you think it's a little strange—"

"Yeah. Check the place out."

Dupree turned back toward the still-blazing fire in time to witness a geyser of sparks. A dozen firefighters scrambled to make it to safety as the roof and second-floor gallery gave way.

"Lieutenant?" Jas called on the radio. "Better come over. I hear it's pretty gruesome."

Dupree clenched his teeth and turned toward the Victorian. Whatever was inside would be anything but pleasant.

"There's a body in there," a passing officer reported. Dupree hoped it wasn't Jordan. Hoped it wasn't either of them. Wished whatever had happened . . . hadn't.

The kitchen hadn't changed since Dupree was there last. The same dirty dishes lined the counter; the same stale odor soured the sink. Another officer, bounding from upstairs, nearly collided with Dupree as he entered the room.

"What do you have?" Dupree asked.

"Male Caucasian. Appears to have suffocated."

"Suffocated?"

"Upstairs. Take a look for yourself."

"ID?"

"None in the room. We're working on it." The officer exited.

Dupree climbed the stairs and headed down the hall, flashing cameras punctuating the scene. "Suffocated" could mean a lot of things—usually that a guy hung himself with a bed sheet, rope, or belt. *Jordan? Wile? Because they couldn't hack registration? Doubtful.* But if it were true, *they should've thought about that a whole lot sooner.* Dupree caught himself, embarrassed by the knee-jerk sentiment. Who knew better than him that nobody deserved to die over a moment's pleasure on Bourbon Street?

His thoughts turned to the body. Since it wouldn't have been moved pending his arrival, he braced to see it hanging off a pediment or chandelier. He turned and entered the room.

Jesus God Almighty! Dupree's legs went numb. The horrific scene before him was anything but a suicide. A naked man lay face up on the floor, spread-eagle with limbs stretched to stakes around the room. Where his penis and testicles used to be was now nothing more than a dark pool of blood, with more blood visible surrounding his mouth into which his genitals had been forcibly stuffed. His face, eyes open, angled grotesquely to one side—*no doubt to avoid seeing his executioner's work.* Glancing at the eyes, Dupree quickly turned away, wishing they could reveal the last person they saw. "Who?" he muttered.

"What's that, Lieutenant?" an officer from the lab asked.

"Find every bit of DNA—hair, bits of flesh under his fingernails, *everything.* I want to know who else was here."

"Yes, sir."

"And check his ass for semen."

"Not a problem."

Dupree landed his fist against a wall, shattering plaster into good-sized chunks. He'd seen drug deals go bad with bodies piled atop bodies; kids killed by parents—then tucked peacefully into bed; and drive-by shootings, mothers wailing for their babies, dismissed callously by reporters as "unintended victims." But he'd never seen brutality the likes of this. Already he could feel the scene seeping into his marrow, enticing him to the dark side to which cops sometimes surrendered. But Dupree understood he needed to absorb it—the big picture and the small, the personal and the impersonal, the caring as well as the not giving a rat's ass.

He wondered how one human being could do such a thing to another. He didn't want to accept that men were basically animals, hiding beneath a thin cultural veneer. But he couldn't come up with a better explanation. It would mean that the forces that held men in check, replacing chaos with order, balance, and stability could suddenly and inexplicably dissolve in a flash. He felt a loss of control, and it frightened him.

Jas walked into the room, scanned the scene, and, appearing nauseous, turned away. "We found this in the flowerbed."

Dupree lifted the bracelet out of Jas's hand. It was sheared in half and covered in mud. "Jordan doesn't want us to know where he is."

"Want him brought in?"

"No. Find him and tail him."

Another officer approached with a paper in hand. "We think we've determined who owns the building. Should be able to ID his renter."

"Don't bother," Dupree said, tossing the bracelet aside.

"His name is Doug Wile."

Chapter 24

ONLY A MATTER OF TIME

BRENEAUX stared at the microphone, reflecting on the previous day when a moronic general manager tried to tell *him* what to do. He'd lain about in the afternoon watching tapes of his games at LSU, taming his emotions with a pint of Drambuie. Afterwards, he'd recounted his numerous accomplishments, concluding his life had been a life worth living, rich in achievement and even richer in love. His beloved had borne him a beautiful daughter on whom he doted and who he adored.

Breneaux reflected fondly on his work, as well, grateful he still enjoyed it after so many years. It wasn't the message that excited him any longer, or the opportunity to flaunt his quick, sardonic wit. It wasn't even the money, knowing he'd never spend what he had. It was possessing the knowledge that he was the best, checking off the scorecard *measured* in money. He was a man getting paid for doing what he liked. *One of a very lucky few . . . compensated for breathing.*

For a whole afternoon he'd put out of his mind the new kid in town with the questionable morals, and the kid's idiot boss with no morals at all. He hoped today he'd escape unscathed.

"Good mo'nin' . . . *N'Awlins!"* his voice rang out. "Mada Gras revelers have already descended with one week to go before the big day arrives." He paused for coffee, stealing a quick sip.

"Last night on my way to a restaurant in the Marigny, I ran into a crowd at Bourbon and St. Anne—the gayest intersection in all of New Awlins. I stopped for a minute, just to watch, curious about what it was they were doing. Hundreds of men—I presume they were men—were down on their knees in the middle of the street. I thought, perhaps, they were holding a vigil, but when I took a closer look, no one was praying. So then I figured . . . down on their knees, facing each other . . . they must be proposing. I mean, what else would they be doing?" He mugged through the window. Marilyn gestured with her tongue. "When I finally got close enough to hear what they were saying, I realized they were proposing all sorts of things." The rim shot sounded.

"Marilyn's sticking her tongue out at me. Does that mean you want to kiss me, or are you trying to remind me this is a family show?"

Marilyn blew a kiss through the window.

"Gay marriage . . . Next thing you know *three* people'll want to get married—then four people and a cow. How 'bout half a dozen kids and a sex offender? America is listening."

"Mr. Breneaux, this is Justin in North Carolina. I'm part of a poly relationship."

"Oh, boy. Lemme guess: you raise parrots."

"No, poly means 'many'. I'm in a relationship with two women and one other man. We love each other and hope to get married someday."

Breneaux sighed. "Like I was saying . . ."

"Laws are changing to accommodate gays. We in the poly community hope to be next."

Breneaux shook his head. "Let me get this straight. The four of you live together."

"Right."

"And have sex together."

"Yeah."

"How does that work exactly? I mean, I know how it works. But how do you decide who sleeps with whom?"

"Most nights we alternate. My male partner's with one of our female partners while I'm with the other. The next night we switch."

"Oh, *that* sounds romantic. Let's see—is this a Monday-Wednesday-Friday week or a Tuesday-Thursday-Saturday week? I can only imagine what happens on Sundays. What about you and your male partner? Do you have sex?"

"Occasionally. Not regularly."

"Why? Don't you like it?"

"I like it a lot. He's my partner. I love him, so touching him's no problem. It's just that he and I are more attracted to women."

"Share and share alike. Like communes in the 60s. Like commun-*ism*. Listen, I was married to one woman who satisfied all my needs for forty plus years. I don't get why you need more than one partner to satisfy yours."

"Everybody has something different to offer."

"So why not marry everybody?"

"I'm not in love with everybody. I'm only in love with a few."

"And what happens when the four of you fall in love with a dozen more?"

"I guess we'll add on."

Breneaux signaled Marilyn to drop the line. "Marry everyone on your block. Simply *add on*. America is listening."

"I'm calling about my grandson who spent time in jail for touching a girl," a woman began. "He's out now, but our minister won't let him attend services or take communion. He says it's because they have youth programs on weekends and day care during the week. But that seems like an excuse. I think he hates my grandson and wants him to go away."

"And the problem with that is . . . ?"

"He's a minister. He's supposed to love everybody and bring them Jesus's forgiveness. I thought Christians were compassionate."

"He's *being* compassionate. He's showing compassion for the kids in his church by keeping your grandson away. Somebody has to protect them. Sounds to me like he's doing his job."

"I'm just afraid my grandson will lose his faith."

"If he's going around touching little kids, no doubt he already has." Breneaux cued Marilyn who cut to a commercial.

"Have you seen the *Times-Picayune*?" Marilyn asked off-air.

"Yeah," Breneaux replied. "Another explosion . . . saw it on the news."

"And the body?"

"What body?"

"Page two."

He adjusted his glasses and thumbed to the page. "Sex offender found murdered." He scanned the first paragraph and read Wile's name. *God DAMMIT!*

He flew down the hall and burst into the last office, Manning and LeGrande's eyes falling to the floor. He slapped the paper on Manning's desk, his fist landing beside it. "When were you going to tell me?"

Manning stood. "Now listen, Burn."

"You *weren't* going to tell me." Breneaux wrenched in LeGrande's direction. "A guy you outed was murdered yesterday. Don't you *care*?"

LeGrande shrugged.

Breneaux shoved a finger in LeGrande's face. "It was his fault, right, because he was a sex offender." He spun back to Manning. "I told you this was going to happen."

"Burn . . ."

Breneaux bolted for the door. "Boy Wonder's got an extra shift. I'm gone until further notice."

Chapter 25

GETTING OFF

DON'T you care?

LeGrande peered from his balcony, overlooking Jackson Square, revisiting the question that had haunted him for years. The moment Breneaux asked it, LeGrande pictured his father, hollering the question before smashing his jaw, breaking it in two places, rendering him unable to reply. He'd long since forgotten his offense at age twelve, but not the searing in his face, the bits of torn flesh, the blood streaming from his chin, and his laughing through it all. "You think it's funny?" his father, an engineer, howled. "You've embarrassed me for the last time. One way or another, you're gonna learn right from wrong." He ordered him to strip and began beating his bottom with a foot-long crucifix on a steel rod. "You just don't get it, do you?"

LeGrande *didn't* get it; that was the problem. He was being brutalized for things he couldn't comprehend and to which, as a result, he was unable to comply. He was like a child unaware of his ADHD, thinking constant fidgeting was perfectly normal; or a kid oblivious of being visually impaired, believing words on blackboards were mere meaningless scrawls; or a child unmindful of his prevailing autism, aghast that other kids actually liked to be hugged. He wondered if *all* fathers beat their kids for doing the things that were beyond their understanding. *Yes*, he decided. *Fathers are monsters*. Did he care? Not at all.

Not caring was LeGrande's defining characteristic. As far back as he could remember he *wanted* to care, meet expectations, and be like everyone else. But concepts others got, he found elusive—telling right from wrong, being a good person, controlling oneself, and doing unto others. He grasped the theory: If people do as they please, civilization will unravel and be thrown into chaos. But he couldn't *relate* to it—didn't feel it in his gut—failed to sense when trampling on a thousand social tenants, which, in their entirety, defined acceptable behavior. He'd wonder: *What puts smiling in the "plus" category and frowning in the "minus" . . . rescuing a baby bird "good" and snapping its neck "bad?"*

He recalled crying himself to sleep after setting fire to a poodle, watching a young girl wail hysterically while he felt nothing but glee. He cried, not because he cared about the dog or the girl, but because he didn't care at all and knew for some reason he should. He was vaguely aware that something was broken inside, something frightening, rendering him inadequate and incomplete. Yet hard as he tried to muster compassion, attend to others' feelings, and put himself in their place, he couldn't.

Besides . . . chaos was a lot more fun.

LeGrande's laughter grew louder, tears coursing his cheeks with each swing of the crucifix landing harder on his butt.

"Still not getting through to you?" his father bellowed. "Let's see if this does the trick." Bending the boy over, crucifix in hand, he spread his son's cheeks and inserted the Son of God. The pain was excruciating and exquisite at the same time, awakening in LeGrande worlds he'd never known. The last thing he remembered before finally passing out was the hardening of his penis and his father wailing: "You little shit!"

LeGrande's additional defining trait was his extraordinary intelligence, which he viewed as compensation for the part God left out—like a blind person endowed with superior hearing, or an idiot savant graced with astounding musicianship. As he began to indulge his soaring desires, he embraced his intellect, harnessing its strength, in an all-out attempt to learn right from wrong. He set about cataloguing the social tenants, determining how to act appropriately in order to fit in. To do so, he read everything he could find on etiquette, psychology, politics, and religion, devouring biographies of people society revered.

It was while studying psychology that he learned he was a sociopath, finding relief in knowing why he was the way he was. *I don't care because I'm not supposed to care. It's not in my nature. It's not the way I was made.* That led him to profile others of his ilk, specifically sociopathic killers: Ted Bundy, Jeffrey Dahmer, John Wayne Gacy, and Charles Ng, with the intention of determining how each had screwed up. He found that none had done his homework, cataloging the tenants and memorizing the behaviors, in order to learn right from wrong. In a hurry to satisfy their escalating desires, they accelerated their timelines with reckless abandon, tipping off the world to their deadly deeds. By contrast, LeGrande vowed to slow himself down, never stray from the catalogue, and follow a plan. When he felt like plucking the wings off butterflies, he'd do so in private, tamping down the rush of sadistic gratification. Desire itself could never set the pace. *He* needed to be the one to control the timeline.

Further . . . To avoid letting on that he didn't care, he'd project to the world that he cared a great deal, just as he had over drinks at Arnaud's.

No, he *didn't* care that a seven-year-old had been strangled and that a sex offender had been tortured, mutilated, and killed. Neither did he care that they both died at his hand.

LeGrande heard his phone and went inside.

"He destroyed police property and they said: 'Let him go'?"

"That's what I heard," Hurt said. "Word came down to leave Jordan alone."

LeGrande settled on the sofa in his brightly lit apartment, reflecting on the guy he'd met years before. *Classic brown-noser. Sucked up to the shrink. Distinguished right from wrong without giving it a thought. Something about him and a fifteen-year-old at camp. Probably fucked her. No. Not Jordan. That'd take balls.*

Jordan hadn't recognized him. But from the moment LeGrande saw *him*, he knew that to shield himself something had to be done. He'd sicced a cop on him, hoping to scare him out of town. But that hadn't worked, friend and family providing too stable a base. So he took out the friend, hoping Jordan would go nuts. Maybe kill somebody. Better still, kill himself.

But all Jordan did was smash a bracelet and run. *You're not gonna make this easy for me, are you? Have it your way.* He couldn't put it out of his mind: Sean Jordan was still in the game.

LeGrande reached forward and picked up an object, held it by a wire, and twirled it in the air. It was a sophisticated switch he'd modified for the military while assigned to demolition due to his "cool detachment." His ability to engineer solutions put him on a path to success. But the path was diverted when he once abandoned the catalogue, getting caught raping an eight-year-old on a weekend pass to Thailand. The military went easy, sparing him the brig, slapping him instead with a dishonorable discharge. They sent him packing with a one-way ticket to Chicago and the requirement of counseling for no less than a year. It was a costly lesson but an important one. Sporting long hair, torn jeans, a mustache, and a beard, he was put in a group of pedophiles headed by a doctor named Andrews. Sitting beside Andrews was his "assistant," Sean Jordan.

Pedophiles. He bristled at the thought. There was no way he was a pedophile, having tortured people of all ages with equal abandon. After two boring sessions, he dropped out of the group, shaved his face, and headed to LA.

It was a quarter past ten. LeGrande was feeling the itch. He reached for the remote and turned on the TV. An image appeared of an Asian teenage girl, walking slowly down a hotel corridor. She knocked on the door at the end of the hall and was admitted by a Caucasian in his mid to late fifties. She handed him an envelope. He opened it and read:

"My name is Nhia. The Royal Hotel owners
appreciate your business. I am their gift to you."

He escorted her into the room, shutting the door behind him.

LeGrande slid off his slacks and grasped his cock firmly. He watched the man throw the girl on the bed, tear off her clothes, and force open her legs, while the girl struggled to escape the unexpected roughness. LeGrande stroked himself faster, breath quickening. The girl remained pinned, head wrenching from side to side. LeGrande reached for his chest and played with his nipples, but instead of getting harder, his cock went soft.

"Mother FUCK—!" He paused, slamming his fist angrily against the couch. No longer could he finish with a few quick strokes and repeat the feat twice in a single day. He'd simply seen too much, done too much, raised the bar to a ridiculously high level. Torture alone was no longer enough.

He pressed another button to produce a split screen. Adjacent to the girl was a series of explosions—M-80s blowing up cats, to the obliteration of Hiroshima. LeGrande moaned, eyes darting from scene to scene in a dizzying blur of escalating violence.

He sat, basking in the combination, until the bar was scaled and resistance gave way, his body pitching forward, fluid spewing forth.

It took longer, requirements greater, but he finally got off.

It was the only way he could.

Chapter 26

A DECLARATION

SEAN was awakened by the screech of a gull. Not a lazy, fly-by, contented screech, or an excited, see-something, dive-for-it screech, but rather the frantic, tortured screech of a terrified animal pleading for its life. "Die and be done with it," Sean sneered, rubbing sand from his blood-shot eyes.

"Ha—eech!"

Sean uncoiled his stiff, aching frame and peered at the bayou through mud-splattered windows. A flock of blue herons raced between reefs, vanishing in the distance behind tall marshy grasses.

He wondered where he was and how long he'd been there, the sun having risen above the horizon. He recalled being awakened by images of Doug, lying on his deathbed, face wrenched in torment. He'd found him that way hours before, the picture forever seared into his soul.

"I'm SORRY!" he'd hollered, standing over Doug, writhing in guilt, sobbing uncontrollably. He wanted to join him on the other side where he could apologize every day for all eternity. There, he could say "sorry" to his parents as well, and to his beloved grandfather for ruining his legacy. Sean's guilt agreed: It was a good time to die. Who deserved death more than Sean Andrew Jordan? He'd thought about the gun in the dining room downstairs and the relief he'd feel turning it on himself. Then he pictured Ren. *"Look at these, Daddy!"* He couldn't let her learn he'd put a bullet through his head.

He'd jumped in the car in front of the Victorian, raced home and found that no one was there. Suzanne's house dark and quiet as well, though he thought he saw a figure, lurking in the shadows. Thrust invited a quick getaway, but Sean couldn't think of any place to go. Mind reeling, he put the car in gear and allowed it to take him wherever it liked. The car passed the airport and headed into the country on ever-diminishing roads that vanished in the bayou.

He peered through the window. *What better place to die? Here, I wouldn't bother a thing.*

"Ha—eech! Ha—eech!" The plea intensified.

"You're ten years too late. I don't save anyone anymore."

"Ha—*eech!*"

Sean opened the door and attempted to stand, but his legs buckled as the ground gave way, submerging him in mud and vile murky water. He grabbed Thrust's door and used it for support until his legs found a spot firm enough to hold him.

"Ha—eech!"

"All *right!*" He took a tentative step, then another and another, heading in the direction of the terrible sound. *What the hell am I doing?* He stared back at Thrust, covered in mud, and vowed to have it cleaned to satisfy his father.

"Ha—eech!"

A sudden, chaotic flailing of wings caused Sean to tumble into the green plankton slime. He scrambled to right himself and saw that the sound came not from a gull but a pure white crane. It stood on one leg, feathers matted, unable to break free from something unseen. Sean advanced with considerable caution, talking reassuringly to put the bird at ease.

"Ha—eech!" it answered, unfurling its wings, as if inviting Sean to come closer still.

Sean inched forward and lowered his gaze. The bird's foot was snared on a fisherman's line, tethered to the stump of an old cypress tree. "Don't worry," he said, his hand raised in peace. But when he reached for the line, the crane lunged, piercing Sean's shoulder half an inch deep.

"*Fuck!*" Sean recoiled, stumbling in retreat, thrashing to escape, beyond the bird's reach. "Okay, then *you* do it!" He inspected his shirt and the torn flesh beneath, the green soup that covered it, and the blood that spewed forth. *Animal psychologist—Ha!* "In case you've forgotten, it was you who called *me!*" He stared at the bird with steely blue eyes, considered his options, and decided to leave. "Too bad," he said, arms thrown in the air. "That's the way it is. Everybody dies."

"*Ha—eech!*" the crane wailed, lowering its head as if begging an appeal.

Sean held his stare. "One more chance."

Slowly and carefully he crouched before the crane, inspected the stump, and gathered the line. He tugged several times but the line held tight. Spotting a pair of smooth round stones, he placed one above the other with the line in between and began rubbing furiously, eyes glued to the bird.

"Here goes," he announced.

The line frayed—then *snapped.*

The crane spread its wings in a majestic stance, declaring its independence to the entire world. Sean watched him take flight and soar overhead, a last piece of line falling free from the sky.

"*Eech!*" the bird trumpeted.

"That's it? You're just gonna *leave*?" Sean waited, half-expecting the bird to return. But it kept on going, soaring away, until after a few minutes, it could no longer be seen.

Sean headed back and was startled to see Thrust's tires submerged in the mud. He circled the car in search of firm ground and spotted a patch directly to the rear. Though covered in slime, he climbed inside, started the engine, and shifted to reverse. Tires spinning, mud splattered the car like thousands of projectiles shot from guns. Still, the car didn't budge.

Come on. His heart raced. *I didn't feed and protect you all these years to watch you die and be buried in some God forsaken swamp.* He eased up on the accelerator and tried again. Once more, the wheels spun aimlessly. He applied the brakes and shifted into drive, inched forward—then switched to reverse. The car rocked, ever so slowly—then suddenly grabbed hold, lurching to higher ground. Sean felt the tension release in his neck as if he were the bird, free of what held him.

A *WHOOSH* was heard, followed by a *SHUDDER*. Sean watched in horror as the ground gave way, the Pontiac sinking, earth rising above him. *"NO!"* he screamed, fists pounding the wheel. He slammed against his door but the mud sealed it tight. He reached for the other and wailed against it, kicking and prying to no avail. He hit the switch for the electric windows. Likely shorted out by the mud and slime, the motors wouldn't engage; the windows stayed in place.

Surrender beckoned like a fast-acting drug, enticing Sean to join Doug and relinquish his burdens. He took a deep breath and closed his eyes, peace seducing him, whispering to let go. Sitting inert, his body shut down. He ceased all efforts to save his life.

Light from somewhere suddenly burst through, illuminating Sean's tomb, now bustling with activity. Vince appeared, escorting Sean into an office, passing dozens of clients waiting to be seen.

"Vince, is this heaven?" Sean asked.

"No, it's Iowa," Vince teased. "Of *course* it's heaven."

Sean wrinkled his brow. "Do people in heaven have problems, too?"

"Sure. Lots of problems. Enough to keep you and me busy forever. And get this . . . with no heaven after heaven for clients to fall back on, it's a whole lot easier to get their attention."

"Are you okay?" Sean asked.

"Never better. No disease. No early retirement. No licenses to obtain. Up here, it's strictly talent that counts. How soon can you get here? I'm a little backed up."

"Eech!"

The sound was unmistakable. Sean opened his eyes and adjusted his gaze. A sliver of light streamed through mud-splattered T-tops. Circling overhead was the pure white crane. "Go away," Sean mumbled, "I've made up my mind."

"Eech! Eech!"

"You hear me, bird? Let me die in peace." There was resignation in his voice aside growing anger.

"*Eech!*"

"*You hear me?*" he repeated, fury mounting. He realized the T-tops kept the bird from hearing. "Well, god dammit, you're *going* to hear." He lunged for the glass above his seat, using his shoulder like a battering ram, but the glass held firm. He grabbed for a screw driver under the dash and pried loose the rubber surrounding the glass. Raising his legs above his head, he kicked the glass repeatedly until the panel gave way. Another few kicks and the T-top broke loose. Sean gulped fresh air, rushing in around him, and pulled himself up onto the roof.

"*Eech!*"

"Go away!" he shouted, raising muddied fists. "Take your clean white feathers, your care-free life, your freedom to do whatever you want, and fly the fuck away!" He was looking at the bird but picturing his father. He braced to feel guilty for his anger *and* the car. Strangely, he felt no guilt at all.

You're doing well, Vince cheered. *Feel into your core. Deliver your truth.*

Sean stomped on the car in an uncontrollable rage, hastening the vehicle's final descent. "It's *your* fucking car! I'm sick of caring about *it*, and I'm sick of caring about *you!* There's nothing I can do. *I can't bring you back!*"

The crane circled again. Sean's fists punched the sky. "You left me to live with William Hardy! Do you really think that was the best you could do?" He spun on his heels and kicked the other T-top free, the car settling beneath him deeper into the slime. "Because of him, I'm an animal in a zoo with people walking by, throwing rocks at my cage!"

"*Eech!*"

Sean looked up. "And in case you haven't heard . . . my wife's about to leave and my best friend died! What the hell am I supposed to do?"

Sean stooped, hands on his knees. "I was just a boy," he said, words tearful and labored. "I know it was my fault, but I didn't mean for it to happen. I loved you and needed you." He slowly shook his head. "I *still* need you. Why did you leave me?" Tears became a torrent.

Sean cried for nearly an hour until there were no more tears to be shed. Slowly, he became aware of everything around him: the sun bearing down, the breeze lapping his face, the smell of the marsh, and the gulls circling above. His chest grew expansive, his breathing deep and still. He gathered himself slowly and dried his eyes, feeling the emptiness of the moment as well as the fullness. He looked at the roof, an inch above the water, bent down, and reached inside.

"Eech!"

The crane circled again with a downward gaze.

"Go away," Sean murmured.

Not to the bird but to everything else.

Chapter 27

THE SENATOR

SEAN stood on wet ground, reading a number off a card. "Brian Monteleone?" His phone found a signal.

"Yes."

"This is Sean Jordan. We met over lunch in the French Quarter."

"Sean. I've been waiting for your call."

The comment surprised him. "How's that?"

"I read about Doug. Terrible."

Sean pictured Doug's face. "I'm calling because . . . I need help."

"Terrible," Brian repeated hours later, escorting Sean down a hall in the Capitol Building.

"You weren't there," Sean said. "The papers didn't—couldn't describe . . ."

Brian had sent a driver with GPS after offering Sean a place to stay. When the driver arrived, Sean realized he could be tracked and hurled his phone into the marsh.

"In here," Brian said. He ushered him into an anteroom leading to the Senator's chambers.

"I killed him," Sean said, his voice barely audible.

"What?"

"I led police to his house. His address became public."

Brian eyed Sean critically. "If this isn't a good day for you, we can reschedule." He took Sean's arm. "Listen, Jordan. Senator Meyers knows how badly you've been fucked over. That's why you're here, to tell your story so we can formulate a plan. But if you're not thinking straight because you're mired in self-pity, I suggest we not waste the Senator's time."

Self-pity! Sean tasted bile rising in his gut. It was his friend who'd died, not the other guy's—the guy with a shirt, suit, and fancy job. He thought to demand an immediate apology but heard Doug whispering, *Brian's right.* "Okay," he said, grudgingly, bitterness trailing.

Brian knocked once and slipped inside, leaving Sean staring at a photo of the Senator, shaking hands with President Ronald Reagan. Glimpsing his reflection in the framed piece of glass, Sean was appalled by the condition of his hair, as well as his clothes that were covered in stew. He raised each arm and sniffed underneath. *Great way to meet a US Senator.*

"Sean Jordan! Welcome." The Senator greeted him with outstretched arms, clasping and shaking his soiled hands. He was a big man, taller than Sean by a good six inches, and muscular—certainly for a man in his seventies. His hair was as white as the crane's white feathers, his shirt, tie, and shoes crisp to perfection. "I'm Brandon Meyers. Welcome to Baton Rouge." Brian stood at the Senator's side. "I'm glad we were in town at the same time. These days, I'm almost always in Washington." The Senator motioned for Sean to sit on the couch.

"I don't want to ruin the sofa."

"Don't worry." The Senator smiled. "We have good help."

Brian and Sean sat at opposite ends.

"I'm sorry about your friend. Brian filled me in. This is what our national hysteria has led us to. I'm truly sorry."

Sean nodded.

"Brian also told me a lot about you." The Senator took a chair facing the couch. "But I'd like to hear firsthand how you've faired in the system."

Sean's head was spinning. Things were moving way too fast. One minute he was committing suicide in a swamp, the next, being interviewed by a US Senator. His thoughts were with Doug, but the conversation had fast forwarded. He wanted to run, but knew to stay, Brian's admonition holding him in place. "I'm not sure where to start."

"Take your time," the Senator said.

Summer camp seemed as good a place as any. For the better part of an hour, Sean recounted all that had happened.

The Senator, who'd taken notes throughout, moved his reading glasses to his head and looked at Sean compassionately. "You've had a tough time of it, Jordan, from the uncle who failed to defend you, to the school that blocked you from achieving your goals."

Sean had said nothing about school. "How did—"

"I had Brian do a background check. I wanted a preview before we met." The Senator opened a folder, repositioning his glasses over his eyes. "From what Brian determined, it looks like you paid for a doctorate but walked away with a master's degree."

Sean felt dismayed that strangers could know so much about him.

"The trustees of the Midwest School of Psychology had a policy in place prohibiting sex offenders from attending—in their words: 'to protect the public as well as the profession.' Just before you were to get your degree, they learned of your status and were furious for having not been informed. You countered, claiming you'd fully apprised your undergraduate school and had directed them to forward all your records to Midwest. You assumed your past had been fully disclosed. But as it turned out, *that* portion of your file had been withheld due to HIPPA. The trustees of Midwest terminated your enrollment and contacted the Board of Licensure to bar you from the exam. Without taking the test, you couldn't become a psychologist. Then they went a step further. They contacted the police, reporting the *'fraud'* you'd perpetrated on the good people of Illinois. As a result, the clock was restarted: ten years of registration from that day forward." The Senator stood and walked to the window. "Jordan, we've done you a terrible injustice."

Even though he'd lived it, Sean reeled at the recitation. Hearing it expressed succinctly rekindled his fury. At least the Senator seemed to be shouldering some of the blame.

Meyers returned to his seat and continued. "When I was ten, growing up on Staten Island, I'd hop the ferry to Manhattan with my best friend, Dave. We'd take money we earned from our newspaper routes and wander through Macy's, catch a movie in Times Square, stop for a burger, and head back home. Imagine today, allowing a ten-, twelve-, even fourteen-year-old to travel to New York unaccompanied by an adult. Yet, looking back, that early independence contributed greatly to the life I've enjoyed."

At ten, I was counseling couples on how to get along. At eleven, I was giving advice on a late-night radio show. And here I am today. So much for early independence. What's your point?

"In the late 70s and early 80s," the Senator went on, "a handful of kids were kidnapped and murder. Responding in a way it hadn't before, TV broadcast the lurid detail and discovered an audience eager for more. That led to sensationalizing story after story about kids in jeopardy—missing or abducted. Headlines read: 'Strangers stealing kids by the tens of thousands." But when the Department of Justice analyzed the claims, it found that stranger abductions were continuing to occur at the same miniscule rate as decades before. Nothing had changed except the launch of cable news and its desire to compete head-on with the networks."

The Senator shook his head. "Unfortunately, parents took the bait. They believed what they heard, and hysteria ensued. Fearing for their kids, they began curtailing their movements—riding bikes around town, walking to and from school—while demanding of legislators, protection at all cost. We, in response, similarly rushed to judgment without taking the time to check the facts. We enacted more laws on top of those on the books, which already addressed child sex, kidnapping, and murder, extending sex offenders' punishment beyond time served, whether the crime was rape . . . or skinny dipping on a warm summer night."

The Senator peered over his glasses at Sean. "You're screwed, kid, and I'm as responsible as anyone for doing the screwing."

Sean was only half listening, his thoughts fixed on Doug, his family, and the ache in his soul. Talk of innocence and guilt—dolphins and monsters—only added to the pain of not knowing which he was.

The Senator stood and circled his desk. "Here's where I'm coming from . . . I'm a conservative. Looking back, I realize I've botched a few things, like preserving kids' independence to venture out on their own. In my day, playing doctor was a way to learn about life. Today, it's a ticket to a life destroyed. Before I'm laid to rest, I'd like to right a few wrongs—restore the sanity that was jettisoned a quarter century ago."

Sean stood. "When I was a kid, I had all the independence in the world. Today, I don't have any. Because of your laws, my life is over."

The Senator peered at Sean, eyes deadly serious. "It's not over yet. I have work for you to do."

Chapter 28

CONCILIATION

"OKAY, you win." Breneaux lived to hear the words, three of the sweetest in the English language. He loved the sound they made when spoken in succession, like Spanish doubloons scooped out of old wooden chests, released in clattering showers of gold piling atop gold. He'd heard them often over the course of his career and knew he would again by the end of the day. Dressed in a jacket, trimmed in deep red velvet, he stood at the end of his palatial kitchen, holding a wine glass in one hand, his cell phone in the other. He glanced at a clock: nearly four-thirty. *Sure are taking your sweet Jesus time about it.* He had the network over a barrel, earning more than the kid ever could. He raised his glass to his custom-built Sub-Zero, designed to his taste, dispensing ice, water, and booze. "To always maintaining the upper hand."

Breneaux loved to win, whether upgrading his contract, upending a caller, or nailing management to the wall. It was all about selling and its subset, *timing*, he being the undisputed master of the game.

He recalled time spent learning "the art of the deal" after demolishing his knee at LSU. He'd been hired by the owner of a radio station in Orleans Parish, not to *fill* airtime, but to sell it. The self-impressed owner, Christian "Vern" Tetherman, was a crew-cut-shorn veteran with a passion for bowties. Breneaux couldn't remember ever seeing him without one, in addition to his ever-present seersucker suits. Taking a liking to the young football star, Tetherman gave him a chance to show what he could do, hustling *off* the field instead of on. Burn was intrigued. He was to be enrolled in a course called "The Magic of Sales," a two-week program Tetherman was particularly fond of. After that, he was expected to sell ten "spots" per week to banks, clothing stores, and other retail establishments.

"What about car dealerships?" Burn had asked.

"Not a chance!" Tetherman yowled, waving his war-ravaged hand. "The Ridley family owns every car company in town. It's Ridley or nobody."

"Nobody," Burn echoed.

"Old Man Ridley sold Packards in the '20s. Then he acquired Ford and Chevrolet. Joshua, his son, added those shit-box beetle things and is now talking about selling a car from Japan. *Japan!* I fought those sons-a-bitches at Guadalcanal! Don't even think about car dealerships. For years I pushed the old man to advertise with us. Not a chance. It's useless."

"Useless," Burn repeated, fully inspired.

He paid close attention throughout the class, his future in focus, dollar signs in his eyes. He'd thought about becoming a radio personality, but couldn't figure out how personalities made any money. Selling, on the other hand, was straightforward and simple. Somebody said yes and the other guy got paid.

The assertive aspect of selling appealed to him most. "Not *aggressive*," his teacher, Dr. Hemmingworth, maintained. "Forget all that hard-sell, beat-'em-bloody nonsense, sticking your nose in customers' faces, pushing, pushing, pushing. Instead, simply state your case and ask for the sale. Asking is assertive," he emphasized, "pushing is aggressive."

"But what if they say no?" Burn asked.

"Then you assess *why* they said no, restate your case in a way that handles their objection, and once again, ask for the sale. They're called 'trial closes.' Keep repeating the cycle until all objections are resolved. Once you've satisfied them all, they *can't* say no."

"Isn't that aggressive?" Burn asked.

"*Pushing* is aggressive! Who said anything about *pushing*? We're talking about a pleasant conversation, handling objections, asking for business."

I can do this, Burn thought. *I've always done this.* The formula seemed so remarkable in its unremarkability. He wondered why the name of the course was "The Magic of Sales." Asserting himself, he asked.

"You want a little magic?" Hemmingworth smiled at the group. "Here's the best I've got. It's the first rule of sales. And yet only the best salespeople stick with it." Burn picked up a pen. "After you state your case and ask for the business . . ." He paused until the last student stopped writing. "You *shut up*. The first person who talks . . . loses."

Burn didn't get it. Judging by others' expressions around the room, neither did anyone else.

"Here's an example," the doctor continued. "Burn here tells his prospect that if he advertises with his station, he'll increase his sales revenues by fifteen percent. He shows him various charts that support his claim. Then he asks, 'Would you be willing to commit to four sixty-second commercials?' The prospect falls silent to consider the question. The silence lengthens. Burn, who doesn't *like* silence, is troubled by it. He begins to rock back and forth in his chair. He has difficulty breathing. His palms start to sweat. His knees rattle and shake. Unable to stand it a second longer, he jumps in and says something fool-ass crazy like, 'I know you've advertised on the radio before,' to which his prospect responds, 'Not now; try me next year.' Burn goes home empty-handed, pissed with himself for his lack of grit. If, on the other hand, he'd continued to remain silent, filling the time by repeating to himself: 'I love silence. Silence is my friend. I'm winning. He's going to say 'yes' . . . his *prospect* would have finally broken the silence, most likely uttering a simple: 'Okay.'"

Burn got it . . . down to his marrow. Being assertive and waiting for the *loser* to talk first was going to make him a winner, time and time again.

A week later, Burn sat in Joshua Ridley's dining room, eating barbecued chicken and sipping champagne. He hadn't bothered to tell Tetherman he knew the Ridleys well, having dated their daughter and been entertained in their home. He and Maggie Ridley met at LSU.

"Care for some more chicken?" Joshua asked, passing the platter in Burn's direction.

Burn appreciated Ridley's lavish generosity—cook-outs on the bayou, boat rides on the lake, wadded bills pressed into his hand when he and Maggie went on dates—as well as his gregariousness. The forty-five-year-old head of the Ridley Automotive Empire was a storyteller *par excellence* who loved a good audience. The only thing he enjoyed more was being entertained by others who could tell stories as well. He later confided being impressed with Maggie's beau for brightening conversations and telling stories of his own. Burn usually matched Ridley story for story, but tonight would be different, the first rule of selling reverberating in his head.

"Thank you. I've had my fill," Burn said, handing the platter to Mrs. Ridley. "But there *is* something I'd like to talk to you about."

"Shoot, Breneaux."

"Advertising."

"What about it?"

Burn told Ridley he understood the logic of advertising on larger stations with their bigger audiences and broader demographics. But in addition, he pointed out, "I think you'd do well to saturate high school sports. With the lower advertising cost of a smaller station, you could *own* Friday and Saturday nights. Eventually, every high schooler in New Awlins would be a customer of yours."

"What are you suggesting?" Ridley asked.

"That you commit to a hundred spots a week spread across sports throughout the year. Would you be willing to give that a try?"

There. He'd done it—made his case and asked for the business. *One thousand one, one thousand two, one thousand three . . .*

"Did I ever tell you about the time I nearly lost the boat down in Barateria?" Ridley said.

Burn waited patiently, listened to the story, and refrained from responding with a story of his own.

"Which reminds me of the time . . ."

Again Burn waited, body still as death, eyes toward the floor.

"You don't seem to have much to say tonight," Ridley finally noted.

Burn refused to respond or even look up. *Two thousand one, two thousand two . . .*

"About that proposal of yours . . ."

Burn held his breath for what felt like eternity.

"Let's do it!"

They shook hands, Burn bursting inside.

"Is there anything *else* I can do for you tonight?" Ridley asked, sarcastically.

"As a matter of fact, there is," Burn said. "I'd like permission to marry your daughter."

Maggie and her mother shrieked.

Burn fell silent.

Breneaux leaned against the island in the center of his kitchen, dismayed by the fact that the gift of the moment—his chance at putting Manning, LeGrande, and the network in their place—resulted because a person had died. At least *he'd* spoken up, stood by his values, refused to screw people for a few bucks more. LeGrande, on the other hand, had struck a deal with the devil. Breneaux knew it was too much to expect that his head would roll, but muzzling him would be its own sweet victory.

The phone rang. Breneaux noted the time at five minutes to five.

"No more outing," Manning declared, sounding upbeat, cheery, and resolute, as if he were the one who came up with the idea. Breneaux pictured him hog-tied, limbs bound behind his back, face forced downward into the dirt. "You were right. We never should have gone there. Maybe it works in California. People listen, laugh, consider it entertainment. Here—I guess they take things more seriously. The network agrees. We're cooling it for now, returning to conservative rhetoric without making it personal. We need you back. *I* need you back."

Four more words Breneaux loved to hear. He took a long sip of wine, emptied the glass, and drank the last inch straight from the bottle. "What about the kid?"

"I handled it. I sat him down and spelled out the rules going forward. He wasn't happy, but he knows the word came from on high. It's out of my hands and his."

Breneaux ate it up. "How unhappy was he? Big scene?"

"I'm not gonna hand you a play-by-play. He was unhappy."

The star's heart grew lighter.

"Can I count on seeing you in the morning?" Manning asked.

Breneaux took pleasure in the trial close, the same as when his contract came up for renewal. "That depends," he said.

"On what?"

He knew Manning expected to hear money, cars, and vacations— anything but LeGrande's head on a platter. "An apology," Breneaux said. "A public apology to the people of New Awlins."

"He won't do that!" Manning blared.

"Then . . ." Breneaux waited, the first rule of selling doing a tango in his brain.

"I'll figure it out."

"When you do, call me." Breneaux segued to the second rule of selling: *When you have them by the balls, hang up.*

A moment later, the phone rang again.

"Okay. You win."

Chapter 29

A SEXUAL SORT OF THING

FOR the first time after a staffing since the aquarium took its bow, Dodd hadn't stormed out in a fit of anger. He'd actually been upbeat, and Dupree knew why. By late Tuesday, Dodd had ascertained— from airlines, Amtrak, hotels, and restaurants—that despite constant coverage of the murders and explosions, cancellations were few. There'd even been talk, given all the attention, that some were coming specifically to see a luxurious cruise ship, listing to one side, and a hundred-foot crater that used to house fish. Thousands were anticipated to arrive today, followed by tens of thousands on Thursday and a couple hundred thousand on Friday, primed to enjoy the Mardi Gras bash.

After the meeting, Dodd hurried by, telling Dupree simply, "I'm counting on you." Protecting tourists was never the goal. The real priority was making sure they showed up.

The Duprees had shown up the year before to celebrate Mardi Gras with the Daniels family. On a second-floor balcony they rented on Dumaine, they barbecued ribs, drank margaritas, and threw beads to clamoring revelers below. Dupree thought about all that had changed in an instant, recalling his visit to Hal and Lynette. "Find him for us!" Hal pleaded, clenching his teeth. "Find the guy who killed our Mattie."

Dupree entered Weinstat's office without bothering to knock.

"You again?" Weinstat reached forward, offering pralines.

Dupree lifted his shirt, exposing his chest. "See this?"

Weinstat adjusted his glasses. "What?"

Dupree pointed. "Scar."

"Yeah, I see it—from the bullet you took that time in Mid-City."

"Exactly. Lemme tell you, it's a bitch to remove lead."

"So?"

Dupree pointed at the praline in Weinstat's hand. "Pure lead, as soon as you swallow."

"Fuck you, Dupree. It's the Wednesday before Mada Gras. I've got work to do. Is there some way I can help?"

"Thought I'd give you an update on Jordan."

Weinstat perked up. "I guess that *is* my work. Go on."

"We followed him to Baton Rouge. Ended up at the capitol."

Weinstat's coffee went down the wrong pipe. "The capitol?" he croaked. "What the hell would he be doing—"

"I was hoping *you'd* know."

"Haven't a clue." Weinstat frowned. "Wait a minute. You followed him? We got him in a bracelet."

"Not anymore. He smashed it outside Wile's house. I decided to let it go—"

"Without my permission?"

"I'm here asking for it."

"You got it. Go on."

"I wanted to see where he'd go if he thought we weren't watching."

"The capitol . . ." Weinstat stared at the ceiling. "Haven't a clue."

"You're no help."

"I'm just a clerk. You're the detective."

"How about this?" Dupree's voice turned serious. "There were two explosions. Two homicides. Both sex crimes. Each explosion happened within spitting distance of each murder—both, it turns out, at nearly the same time."

"Too big a coincidence," Weinstat said. "The murderer and the bomber have to be the same guy."

"That's what I've been thinking." Dupree leaned back.

"The bombs were intended to draw attention from the murders."

"Or maybe, draw attention *to* them."

"Why would anyone want to call attention to his own crimes?" Weinstat asked.

"That's the $64,000 question."

"God, are you *that old*?"

Dupree ignored him. "I'm waiting on DNA."

A pretty police officer, Darla Grey—young and black with a take-no-prisoners attitude—appeared in the doorway. "Lieutenant? Here are the lab results you requested."

Dupree and Weinstat burst out laughing.

"What did I say?" she asked.

Her flustered look caused them to laugh again. "It isn't what you said, Officer Grey," Weinstat said, "it's your timing. The lieutenant here leads a charmed life."

Dupree shrugged. "Ask and ye shall receive." Rolling her eyes, she dropped the folder and left. Dupree opened it and read.

"Well?" Weinstat said.

"Same guy, both homicides. Same semen. Same DNA."

"Still doesn't prove the murderer's the bomber."

"I'd stake my life on it."

"As opposed to something of value?" Weinstat huffed. "Has to make your life easier knowing there aren't *two* crazies out there you need to be concerned about."

"Trust me, Weinstat. There are *dozens* of crazies I need to be concerned about."

Weinstat tapped his pencil repeatedly on his desk. "I can't figure why a murderer would do it."

"Do what?"

"Blow things up." Weinstat leaned back, fingers interlaced behind his head. "Maybe he just likes explosions."

Dupree perked up. "What do you mean?"

"You know—like firebugs—guys who get off on setting fires."

"Get off . . . Like a sexual sort of thing?"

"I suppose," Weinstat said. "Hell, I don't know. That's out of my—"

"The guy gets off on explosions. He gets off on murder. What if he literally gets off . . . at the same time the explosions occur?"

Weinstat nodded. "The same time he kills."

"Explosions—up close and personal—ones he can feel, see, hear. *Weinstat!*"

Weinstat jumped. "*What?*"

"You oughta rethink that clerk thing." Dupree's fingers detected a second report tucked behind the first. "And what do we have here?" He scanned the page. "I had Jordan's DNA sampled in the hospital."

"And . . . ?"

He handed the report to Weinstat. "We need to be looking for somebody else."

Dupree hadn't been gone ten minutes when the phone rang in Weinstat's office. "Sure, I'll hold. For Senator *who*? Senator *Meyers?*" He sat up straight.

"Is this Sidney Weinstat?" the Senator asked.

"Yes, *sir.*"

"I think you have a registrant in the Parish named Jordan."

"That's right."

"I'd like you to do me a favor and forget about him for a while—keep this between you and me. I know he's required to check in when he moves, but I need him. We're working on something together."

"You and Sean Jordan?"

"Right. He'll be working with me and residing with my assistant. Are we in agreement?"

"It's an unusual request."

"*Unique*, Weinstat."

"It's a unique request. Yes, sir. They pay me to be a stickler on details, but under the circumstances . . ."

"That's great. I truly appreciate it. Keep up the good work in New Awlins." The Senator hung up.

Forget about Sean Jordan? He'd just agreed to do the antithesis of his job. Weinstat's eyes sprang open. *Shit!* He wanted to inform Dupree but didn't know if he was allowed. In the excitement of the moment, he hadn't thought to ask.

Chapter 30

THE REVERSAL

BRENEAUX hurried to the studio under pink and gray skies, dodging 5:00 a.m. raindrops threatening his Bally Canisio shoes. He was met along the way by gutter punks and drunks, begging dollars from bystanders to fund final drinks. "Get a job!" he'd bark, any other day. But today, still high off yesterday's win, he greeted the lot with hundred dollar bills, relishing their surprise each time he let go. Otherwise, North Peters was quiet and calm, the new day's celebration yet to begin.

He'd checked on Charmaine before leaving for work and found her asleep, curled in a ball, sheets in disarray, light blasting from her laptop. Creeping into her room to lower the screen, he flashed on calls from the previous day. *Sexting. No way. Not Charmaine.* Yet he braced as he approached, hoping what he'd see was PG. He tapped the mouse and her picture appeared, surrounded by clothed friends with glistening smiles. His guilt was eclipsed by a sense of relief. He wished he hadn't doubted even for a minute.

"America is listening."

"Good morning," a male caller said, opening the show.

"Yes, it is. It's a very good morning."

"I heard you say the other day it's time to stoke the fires to burn all the sex offenders."

Ouch. The expression sounded uglier when someone else said it. "Go on."

"They used to say that about Jews. You could get away with it in Nazi Germany because Jews were the hated minority."

It was the same argument he'd made with LeGrande. Perhaps the public was wising up. Maybe the tide was turning sooner than he hoped. Or maybe the caller was a Massachusetts professor.

"There was a time in this country when you could lynch blacks—"

"Stop!" Breneaux said. "Try comparing apples to apples. A Jew is a person of a particular heritage. A black is a person of a particular race. A queer—excuse me, *gay*—is a person who's confused about his sexuality. They're not everybody's cup of tea, but they don't go around raping and murdering little kids. Sex offenders aren't apples, they're kumquats—it's a whole different category—the convicted felons' category—the dangerous convicted felons' category. Next time you decide to employ an analogy, try using a coherent one." Breneaux waved his hand. Marilyn dropped the call. "America is listening."

"Mr. Breneaux?"

"That would be my father. He was here a minute ago. Let me see if I can find him." Breneaux leaned from the mic—*"Dad?"*—then came back. "I guess he left. Anything I can do?"

"That last call—I wish you'd let him make his point."

Breneaux guessed the man to be in his thirties. "But his point was *pointless.* Sex offenders aren't Jews." He smiled at Marilyn. "Well, maybe some of them are." Marilyn shook her head. "Let me ask this. Do you have kids?"

"A daughter, six."

"Okay, so think ahead ten years. She's asked out on a date by a Jew. What are you going to say?"

"How would I know he was Jewish?"

"Because his name's Silverstein. He has kinky hair and a big nose and says his father's a lawyer in the entertainment business." Breneaux paused; the caller said nothing. "So what would you say? Would you let her go out with him?"

"Sure, if he seemed like a nice guy."

"Now a black shows up. Surprise! What are you going to say when you meet him at the door?"

"'Come on in. She'll be down in a minute.' If we can put our country in the hands of an African American, I suppose my daughter can date one."

"Maybe *you* put our country in the hands of an African American. We'll save that for another show.

"Now a gay comes to the door. Yeah, right. Skip. A twenty-something man walks up the steps with flowers in hand and asks if your daughter's ready to go out. You recognize him from your search of neighborhood sex offenders. What are you going to say . . . 'Come on in. She'll be down in a minute. You're really gonna like her because she's only sixteen'?"

"I'd invite him in, tell him I saw his picture, and ask what he did to receive sex-offender status."

"Oh, for God's sake!" Breneaux started laughing. "You're a social worker. Tell me you're a social worker. Or worse—a *psychologist.*"

"I'm not a social worker. I'm a supervisor in the steel industry."

"A steel-industry social worker. I'll bet your job is to help people solve problems."

"Well . . ."

"Right every time. So he's not a violent sex offender. He's merely standard issue. You're saying you'd still let him take her out."

"If what he did is a thing of the past, probably . . . especially if he didn't deserve the label to begin with."

"Je—*sus!* He goes all the way through the criminal justice system, a verdict's handed down, and you think that somehow you know better. We'll be right back." Marilyn cut away.

Manning walked past and flashed two thumbs up. *He'd better like the show. I'm fucking on fire.*

LeGrande sauntered down the hall looking harried and worn. Breneaux gauged his expression and knew he'd soon have his apology.

Following LeGrande toward Manning's office was a stocky man carrying a wooden briefcase. *I know that guy.* Breneaux tried to place him and finally recalled: *Elliot Broom, attorney for the network. Now what?*

Commercials rounded out the hour at three minutes 'til ten. LeGrande entered the studio. "How are you?" Breneaux asked.

"I'm all right."

Breneaux waited for a "How are *you?*"

"Manning wants to see you," he said, pulling headphones over his ears.

Manning stood, unfolding his gangling body when Breneaux entered the room. "Burn, you remember Elliot Broom."

"Right. It's been a while." Breneaux and Broom shook hands and turned to sit on the couch. "What's this about?"

"As we discussed yesterday, there will be no more outings. Corporate agrees with you. In this market today, it's simply too dangerous. But as far as a public apology is concerned, there isn't going to be one."

Breneaux felt the slap, yet remained calm.

"Corporate can't allow it," Manning went on. "It'd be construed as an admission of guilt—that we were responsible for Doug Wile's death."

"It'd be corporate suicide," Broom asserted.

Despite his feelings, Breneaux understood, knowing if he were in their shoes, he'd make the same call.

The door opened and LeGrande walked in. "I've got five minutes."

"Del, sit down," Manning said.

Breneaux had no idea what was going on.

LeGrande angled in Breneaux's direction, glancing up from the floor only for a second. "I'm sorry."

They're making him apologize to ME?

LeGrande stumbled for words. "For . . . not heeding your

warning. I didn't appreciate the difference in markets." He glanced at Manning—then at Breneaux. "You were right. I was wrong."

Breneaux sensed LeGrande's seething under the surface, being forced like a child to apologize for his sins. Apologizing was obviously a whole-new experience, akin to passing a kidney stone or eating a roach. Breneaux knew LeGrande's words didn't mean a thing. Still, the performance filled him with glee.

"Is that it?" LeGrande asked Manning and Broom.

"Thank you, Del," Manning replied. "Knock 'em dead out there."

LeGrande left the room and headed down the hall.

"That's the best we can do," Manning said.

Breneaux shrugged, unable to contain his laughter. "Everybody wins a little; everybody loses a little. That's how the game's played. Right, boys? Just remember, you owe me."

"Thanks for understanding." Manning sounded relieved.

"No more outings," Broom reconfirmed. "Just stay on message."

Breneaux pivoted toward him. "And what message it that?"

Manning and Broom looked at each other as if unsure how to answer.

"Conservatism!" they replied in a simultaneous burst.

"Hatred," Breneaux corrected. "Conservatism doesn't sell."

LeGrande settled in his chair and stared at the mic, congratulating himself on his loser performance. Convincing them his ego had taken a hit moved him one step closer to overtaking the king. Breneaux alone had moved up the timetable. *Go ahead, old man. Make it personal. I was prepared to be patient, but you changed my mind.*

He pictured various ways to dispose of Breneaux, but knew the man couldn't simply go missing. *If he did, the cops would turn to me. No one else has as much to gain.*

Sean Jordan again popped into his mind. *I wonder . . .* He pictured Jordan and Breneaux side by side, bit his tongue, and began to laugh.

I'll deal with them both in a single play.

Chapter 31

. . . AND MANY MORE

"HAPPY Birthday," Laurie said in a cool, distant voice, glaring at Sean at the foot of the bed. Ren entered the room, oblivious of her father, and hopped into bed with her mother and a stranger. Doug then appeared and tossed Sean a gift the size of a cigar box wrapped in shiny gold foil.

Sean bolted upright, drenched in sweat. Not even sleep could provide a safe haven.

"Hey, you bum." Brian pummeled Sean with a towel. "What are you doing, lying in bed?"

"I was having a bad dream."

"*That's* no excuse . . . Look at me—jacket and tie. Look at you—Fruit-of-the-Loom."

"They're Calvin Klein."

"Whatever! You can't dress that way. You're on the payroll of the United States government." Brian grinned and departed.

Pain and emptiness unabated, Sean wanted badly to go back to sleep. But he owed his hosts an honest day's work in exchange for food, clothing, and shelter—not to mention, keeping the cops away.

The Senator's questions, far-reaching and thorough, were a search for skeletons other than camp. A surprise indiscretion, rising from Sean's past, could render the truth moot and scuttle the hearings. Sean answered each question fully and honestly and even confessed that he might be a pedophile. The Senator replied he wasn't surprised that Sean didn't know if he was or he wasn't. "How could you possibly *not* doubt your innocence when everything around you points to your guilt?"

"You don't understand," Sean fired back. "I really *was* attracted to the girl at camp."

"So what?" the exasperated Senator said. "What could be more normal—a boy and a girl? You've been so thoroughly jerked around, you don't even know what normal is." The Senator vociferously exhaled his frustration. "However, you need to find out fast. Ambiguity like that could cost us your testimony."

The day was alternately a striptease and a catharsis, but in the end Vince was right: It felt good to come clean. Sean took a chance, confiding everything he could remember—all except killing the parents he loved.

Sean called to Brian on the capitol steps: "What time are we meeting the Senator today?"

"We're not. He left for DC last night. Next couple of weeks we're on our own."

"Doing what?"

"He wants a written record of the story you told, making sure to include every detail. Then he'd like the same for Doug. I have a few recollections. You have far more."

Doug. The morning's nightmare replayed in Sean's mind, down to the cigar box disguised as a gift. Suddenly he remembered: It *was* his birthday—his golden 29th on February 29th. The leap-year date had provided the Hardys an excuse to ignore all his birthdays but two, the highlight of those being angel food cake, topped with sickly colored frosting and cardboard-tasting stars. While birthdays had lost their appeal for a time, this one felt special in a strange sort of way. He wanted people to know and to share the day. But the few people who knew didn't know how to reach him, while those who could find him remained unaware. *Doug would have moved mountains to be here if he could*—just as Sean had joined him the previous year, celebrating his birthday behind prison walls. *God, I miss you. Isn't there* something *in heaven you want me to see?*

"Leap year birthdays are the best of all," his father said over cake the day he turned five. "An extra day's needed, every four years, in order for the calendar to align with the stars. If it weren't for you and your extraordinary birthday, the seasons would inch forward year after year 'til we'd barbecue in January and build snowmen in July." Sean made a note. "It's you who keeps the planet on schedule."

Me, Sean thought, *and a girl named Tyne.*

He'd known a few others with leap-year birthdays, but the only one who mattered was the girl from camp. While they'd sat on a hill overlooking the river, she mentioned her birthday and its special date. *"Really? You too?"* It dawned on him that it was August 29th, the half-year anniversary of their special date. Later that night, he snuck into the kitchen, decorated two cupcakes, and handed one to Tyne. The party lasted a mere handful of minutes, but he remembered thinking it was the best he ever had.

Sean spent the day detailing his life, focusing especially on the times he died—on Jennings Street, standing amidst mounds of rubble; in jail, awaiting his uncle's wrath; in the Marigny, watching his marriage derail; in Tremé, kneeling over the body of his friend. He tried to picture the good times, but horrors kept intruding.

Sean thought to invite Brian to join him for dinner until he realized he'd be paying with Brian's cash. Instead, alone, he ducked into a dive and sat in a booth, facing a wall. He stared straight ahead, lost in thought, when Tyne slid in on the other side.

Vince, I'm losing it, here.

Talk to her, Vince advised.

There was an otherworldly quality about her, luminescent in black and white. "You look nice," Sean said, "exactly as I remember." He felt strangely at peace, appreciative of her company. "It's our birthday . . . and here you are." As hard as he tried not to stare, his eyes kept returning, tracking hers slavishly. "I wanted to tell you . . . what happened after camp . . . it was my fault, not yours. Your father had every right to be angry." Tyne acknowledged with a nod, black eyes radiant. "I'm starting to know how fathers feel, being married now with a daughter of my own."

A thousand what-ifs crossed Sean's mind. What if his parents, instead of dying, had been there to meet Tyne's and appeal for understanding? What if her parents had gotten to know him, judging him to be a worthy friend? What if he and Tyne had met years later?

But that would negate Ren, Vince whispered in Sean's ear. *Most things in life happen just as they're supposed to.*

Sean couldn't take his eyes off Tyne's girlish smile. Pedophile or not, he felt alive in her presence, his heart connected irrevocably to hers. He was about to lift his glass in honor of their birthdays when a waitress walked up and reached across the bench. In one, quick gesture, she removed the extra setting, leaving only Sean's, lying before him. "What can I getcha?" she asked.

Sean stared ahead. "A fresh start on the last ten years."

"Sweetie, wouldn't we *all* like that!"

Sean looked up at the middle-aged woman, her harsh life apparent in dark sunken eyes. Despite her difficulties, he sensed her kind, gentle spirit. "It's my birthday," he said, sounding like a child. "I guess . . . I just wanted someone to know."

"I'm glad you told me. I'll be right back." She returned moments later carrying a cupcake and candle.

Sean swept his curls out of his eyes. "A real birthday," he said. He took her hand. "Stay a minute. Celebrate."

"Why not?" she said, sitting where Tyne had been. "It's a quiet night."

Studying her face through different eyes, he was aware this time of the beauty he'd missed.

Just like you used to teach, Vince noted. *Open your heart to those who show up.*

"Make a wish," she prompted, lighting the candle.

Sean blew out the flame and broke the cupcake in two. "Here."

She took the first bite, a tear falling from one eye. "I almost didn't come to work today."

Sean cupped her hands in his.

"Who woulda figured . . .?" she said, laughing and crying. "A washed up old broad, invited to a party by a handsome young man. You made my day." She squeezed his hands back and rose to leave.

"Can I give you a hug?" Sean asked.

"I sure could use one."

Sean gathered her frame in his outstretched arms and brushed her cheek with his soft, warm lips. "Thanks for making this one of my best birthdays ever." She walked away, dabbing an eye with her sleeve.

Make a wish.

Because of the years he missed in between, Sean felt he deserved several instead of just one. He decided to make two and keep the others in reserve.

He wished for the waitress happiness and serenity and wished for himself knowing Ren was okay.

Chapter 32

FRAGMENTS OF A PLAN

LEGRANDE left the studios under a sunny afternoon sky with fragments of a plan swirling in his head. *Jordan* and *Breneaux*. He liked the sound of it, as well as the symmetry. He'd heard Jordan was hiding in Baton Rouge and had even spent time with a US senator. No matter. *I'll manage.* LeGrande always did. If he could double his listener base in a few short weeks while rivaling Katrina in wreaking havoc on the city, he could certainly handle Sean Andrew Jordan.

"How long were ya on the list?" a voice boomed behind at the entrance to his apartment.

LeGrande spun around toward a plump older woman in a red velvet hat with a white flowered band. "Excuse me?"

"Just wonderin' how long ya'ad to wait. Takes fifteen years to get a place in the Pontalbas. *Twenty*, sometimes."

LeGrande shrugged. "I didn't wait at all."

The woman staggered backward, her hand on her heart.

He rushed to catch her arm to keep her from falling. "Are you all right?" he asked, feigning concern. "The apartment's leased to people I work for. I needed a place and they gave me the keys."

"Oh, for goodness sake," she said. "That makes all the difference."

For a plan to come together, LeGrande knew he had to learn everything he could about the city's peculiarities. He already knew he lived in the oldest apartment building in America, across from its twin on Jackson Square. Now, in addition, he'd come to find out: To live there, regular folk had to wait in line.

"Ya probably noticed the Ps," the woman said.

"The what?"

"The *Ps!* all along the balconies. The Baroness Pontalba, in 1840—"

That much knowledge he didn't need. LeGrande ducked inside, made his way upstairs, and unlocked the French doors that led to his balcony. From there he looked down on the afternoon crowd with strains of "Struttin' With Some Barbecue" filling his ears. *Gimme sumpin, New Awlins. Sumpin I can work with.*

Grabbing sunglasses and a cap, he went back to the street, pausing by the cathedral to watch the activity. Beneath its colorful slate roof and towering steeples, a brass band roared, entertaining thousands nearby, including fortune tellers and voodoo queens, portrait artists and pie ladies, and hordes of shirtless boys, tap dancing for tips. Tourists swarmed the band like honeybees on magnolia blossoms while locals walked by, dodging the circus all around.

People carried alcohol up and down the streets, and even more surprisingly, from one bar to another. *You can't do* that *in LA.* Spotting a pair of little girls at a makeshift stand, LeGrande figured they were selling pink lemonade. But when he got closer and saw beans, standing in the cups, he took time to read the sign: "Bloody Marys . . . 5 bucks!"

Dogs suddenly appeared, costumed in a parade, marching behind a banner reading: "Krewe of Barkus." *Isn't that Bacchus?* LeGrande shrugged. Seconds later, the pun settled in. In addition to dogs, there were *people* in collars, leashed to dominatrixes sporting handcuffs and whips. He'd been told during Mardi Gras, people do crazy things. But it was five days away. *How much crazier can it get?*

"Hey!" a man called, wearing a ten gallon hat, passing Rouses Grocery at Royal and St. Peter. He used one hand to hoist a thirty-two-once beer and the other to steady a stumbling brunette. "Can you tell me where a guy can get tater tots with cheese?"

LeGrande logged *tater tots* into his head. "Head to Boise—then turn right toward Wisconsin."

He heard a roar and headed in its direction, winding up on Bourbon among a sea of revelers. Girls on balconies were screaming for beads, flashing their breasts, and dropping their pants. Guys were flashing too, up and down the street, exchanging glances of their flesh for anything they could score. A blond overhead, wearing a red sequin top, hollered at a guy standing next to LeGrande: "Show me some dick!" When he complied, she refused to throw beads. Instead, she demanded: "Now make it hard!"

Tough bitch, LeGrande thought. He kept on walking.

Heading up Bourbon, he caught the eye of a girl, meandering alone in the opposite direction. He pegged her immediately at twelve or thirteen—likely a runaway, definitely a prostitute. He could tell from her shorts—micro cut to her crotch—and by the see-through fabric tied loosely about her top. As soon as they passed, curiosity made him halt. He turned and had his suspicion confirmed; she'd stopped too and was staring at *him*. She walked back and asked, "Wanna go someplace?" *Of course. Who wouldn't?* he thought, heart rate quickening. But he'd never take such a ridiculous chance with her pimp likely watching from a doorway nearby and police cameras scanning every inch of the street. *Doesn't she know she ought to be more careful? After all, a girl could get killed.* Amused by the irony, he continued on his way.

"Harper," he whispered, the name escaping his lips.

The prostitute's age, build, and stringy blond hair reminded him of a girl he'd known long before—the only one for whom he'd ever felt affection. He was fifteen; she was twelve. He supposed he had a crush on her but never knew for sure, crushes failing to be addressed in the catalogue of social tenants. It wasn't that he cared for her; he didn't care at all. But from their first encounter in City Park, he felt an affinity and a tug that were more than just sexual. She seemed his soul mate, if there were such things—someone who understood him when no one else did—someone who liked him exactly as he was. He couldn't explain their connection at first. Then a curious tingling at the base of his spine informed him that she, too, lacked the capacity to care. He'd never encountered such a person before. In Harper, he found a friend to share the darkness.

By the time they met, she'd already progressed from shoving kids down stairs to cutting herself for fun. She reveled in showing him all her fresh wounds, especially the ones from which blood still ran, bragging how each surpassed the last. For months they got together as often as they could to conjure violent scenarios, dare each other to carry them out, and fuck.

LeGrande enjoyed Harper immensely, but the thought of *liking* her was a festering problem. Liking conveyed expectations, and he wasn't to be counted on by anyone. Furthermore, while she no doubt liked him, she didn't care about him. That meant she could turn on him at any time—rat him out—tell the world she knew somebody who . . .

He couldn't let that happen.

The next time they met, he said he had no other choice. She could pick the method, but he was going to kill her. Harper giggled in response and set about helping him plan.

Using a red felt marker, she drew a circle around her neck and made ten small Xs where his fingers were to go. Meticulously and dispassionately, she positioned his hands, cupping them around her neck, fingers tight against her throat. "You're afraid," she told him, slapping him hard across the face. "Do it. It's only scary once. Next time it'll be easier. Think of all the fun you'll have." With his hands poised, she thanked him for killing her, demanding he have sex with her after she died.

He strangled and revived her quite a few times, adding to her suffering just like they'd planned. It wasn't until her body fell limp, face turning gray from newborn pink, that he knew for certain he'd completed the act.

He stared at his hands, teeming with power, and howled like a banshee: "I FINALLY FUCKING DID IT!" Adrenaline streamed through his brain; blood surged to his cock. It would be his last time with Harper—his first with a corpse. He ripped off her clothes in a ravenous attack, like a starving animal set upon meat. He shrieked and thrashed and plunged and roared, until finally he finished, his promise kept.

Like always, he thought to fill her in on the details—what he'd felt, how hard he'd come—until he realized his soul mate was no longer there. All that remained was a crumpled shell.

From that day forward, he was haunted by the memory—not of her death, but of her far greater courage. Unlike Harper, he was afraid to die. Each time he'd backed down when they pledged to kill themselves together, unable to imagine himself not in the world, even a world in which he didn't fit. Before Harper died, he apologized for his cowardliness. She clucked like a chicken and laughed in response.

Turning onto Canal Street, LeGrande encountered a parade. "Another parade?" he called to a bystander.

"Every day between now and Fat Tuesday."

A float passed by, towering overhead, replaced by others in an endless chain. "Who makes the floats?" LeGrande asked the bystander.

"Guy named Morel. Vincent Morel. His studios are upriver off Tchoupitoulas."

LeGrande sensed a plan drawing near.

A sudden burst of sunlight caught his eye, reflected off a window across Canal. The window was on the second floor of a grand old building, one of the remaining jewels in the historic downtown. Intrigued, LeGrande attempted to cross the street, but was directed by a policeman to head downriver past the point where the parade disembarked. He reached the building, an unoccupied shell, with a sign on the door reading: "No trespassing by order of New Orleans." He fixed his gaze on the second story windows and felt the last piece of his plan fall into place.

"Floats," he whispered. "Lots of floats."

LeGrande studied the scene for nearly two hours, staking out the building and scrutinizing the parade. When the sun finally set behind balconied buildings, it gave rise to a shivery, wintery chill. The last float rolled by, jettisoning a flurry of beads, with a couple of strands landing at LeGrande's feet. *What the hell.* He draped them lazily over his head and shoulders and headed down Royal on his way to the Marigny.

The house was dark when LeGrande climbed the steps and stared through the window on Jordan's back porch. Wrapping his hand with his sleeve, he punched the glass once, breaking it to let himself in. He made his way from one room to another, memorizing the layout, noting photos on the walls. *Who'd they use for a decorator, Mother Theresa?* Opening the medicine cabinet, he spotted a comb—better still, one with hairs in the teeth. He sealed it in plastic he'd brought from home, slid it in his pocket, and stepped outside.

"Happy Mardi Gras," a couple hollered, laughing as they walked.

"Happy Mardi Gras," LeGrande echoed, tossing them his beads as if he'd lived there forever.

Chapter 33

MARDI GRAS WEEKEND

"GOOD mo'nin' . . . *N'Awlins!* This is Burn Breneaux, coming to you from the Crescent City, where we're celebrating the start of Mada Gras—the *greatest free show on earth!* He hit a button, sounding a cheering crowd. It's Friday, which means half a million of you freaks'll be arriving today." He inhaled loudly, parodying Arlo Guthrie from Woodstock. "The freeway's closed, man. Can you dig it? Four hundred thousand people, man. Can you dig it?" He resumed his own voice. "Hey Arlo, I'll see your four hundred thousand and raise you a quarter million. Come one, come all—eat, drink, and be merry." Breneaux looked through the glass. "Marilyn, what do you think merry's a euphemism for? With a name like Mary-Lynn, you've got to be merry."

Marilyn's voice came over the air. "No. I have kids."

Breneaux laughed. "Marilyn!"

"In Metairie, we celebrate a kinder, gentler sort of Mada Gras. Lots of food, music, and good clean fun. What about you? How merry do you get in the Garden District?"

"I'm *always* merry; I'm just a merry sort of guy. Of course, living with a teenage daughter, I have to set a good example." Breneaux spotted LeGrande, walking by the window. He noted his crisp gait and the start of a smile, in sharp contrast from the day before. "Now there goes a truly merry person. Ladies and gentlemen, Mr. Del LeGrande." LeGrande did a one-eighty and opened the door. Breneaux hit the button and the crowd cheered again.

"I thought I heard my name," LeGrande said, leaning into a mic.

Breneaux raised his hands. "Not in vain. I wasn't using it in vain. In fact, I was commenting on your exceptional mood. Does it have anything to do with the start of Mada Gras?"

"Oh, yeah." LeGrande's eyes glistened. "I've got plans."

"Being single, I'll bet you do. That's right, girls, here sits one of New Awlins's most eligible bachelors. I'm sure you'll enjoy yourself whatever you do."

"Thanks, Burn. Same to you."

As LeGrande exited, Breneaux felt uneasy, LeGrande's forced smile making his blood run cold. "America is listening."

"Good morning, Burn," a man began. "I've never been to Mardi Gras. We came close this year to packing up the kids, but with the aquarium and the murder, my wife was too scared. What are the police saying?"

"I don't know. They're not in the habit of filling me in. However, if I were in charge, I'd investigate Democrats opposed to animal rights. Who else'd target a whole bunch of fish?" Breneaux scanned page one of the *Times-Picayune*. "Hmm. Seems I was wrong. According to today's paper, the person who killed Mattie Daniels likes to blow things up. A murderer *and* a bomber. Looks like we've uncovered a whole new species. America is listening."

"Am I on the air?" a woman asked.

"Only when you speak."

"I was thinking . . ."

"Marilyn. Are we still giving out points for thinking? I thought I saw a box of thinking points in the storeroom a couple of weeks ago."

The woman laughed. "Wouldn't a guy who likes to murder kids and blows things up be easy to find? I mean . . . they keep profiles, don't they, on people who commit unusual crimes?"

"Listen up, Police Chief Dodd. We have a listener calling with a really good idea. What you need to do is profile the guy." Breneaux addressed the woman. "Maybe you ought to call the chief directly. I'll put you on hold so we can give you his number. And don't forget, when our producer comes on the line, be sure to tell her where to mail those points."

Breneaux checked the time and released a long sigh. The Mardi Gras luncheon of the Krewe of Rex was scheduled to begin in a couple of hours. Held annually at Antoine's since before he was born, Breneaux greeted the event with giddy enthusiasm. At least he had, every year until now. He pictured the Krewe, circling like sharks, hungry for details not publically known. Being a member of the press and having nothing to feed them, he imagined the sharks eating him instead. The Lord of Talk kept conversations flowing. But on this particular subject, he was all talked out.

"So, Burn, any fresh leads on the murders?"

Breneaux hadn't been in Antoine's one full minute before Henri Renalde took the first bite. Henri, a descendent of the cotton Renaldes, was well into his sixties, old-moneyed and conservative, typical of members of the Krewe of Rex. He was the kind of man who never told a joke but could be counted on to laugh when someone else did.

Breneaux's family fortune was built on banking, dating to his great-great-great-grandfather's earliest endeavor, the founding of a bank in 1809. Breneaux's choice of radio over the business of banking was an affront to his family and a scandal throughout town. Even into the twenty-first century, the city's elite frowned on native sons, pursuing anything that was viewed as breaking with tradition. If boys stayed within ranks, they could be drunkards or rogues, but if they stepped outside, they were kept outside. Breneaux's rise as a celebrity helped his cause, but his family never stopped feeling a twinge of disgrace.

"Renalde, if I knew anything, I'd tell you." Breneaux took a seat at a table for four, one of twelve such tables in a room designed for six. Entering behind him was his friend, Tom August, captain of the lead float in the Rex parade—the float on which Breneaux rode as well. With his salt-and-pepper beard, bushy white sideburns, white linen suit, and white leather shoes, he seemed more the captain of a paddlewheel steamship than he did the captain of a Mardi Gras float. When he walked into a room, mischief hung in the air.

"Burn!" Tom called, making his way to the table. "Wait 'til ya see what we planned this year." With a bugle fanfare and roll of the drums, twenty bandsmen in uniforms burst through the door, unaware they'd been hired to march into a closet. The Krewe laughed heartily when the band stumbled in, bumping into each other and everything else in sight.

"Nice job," Breneaux yelled, over "Mercy, Mercy, Mercy." The musicians concluded with an ear-shattering blast before fighting their way out of the ridiculously tight space.

"And they're known for precision maneuvering!" Tom exclaimed, to the riotous applause of everyone nearby.

"So, Burn, what are you hearing on the murders?" Tom asked.

"Jesus, you guys, this is supposed to be a celebration!" Breneaux grumbled, slumping in his seat. Spotting a man he'd hoped to see, he perked back up and waved him to their table. "Owen. Over here." Dupree got up, crossed the room, and stood, hovering above the others. "Pull up a chair. Relax awhile. Tom and Henri are asking for updates on the murders. They're questioning me and I don't know a thing."

"I thought you were an expert on everything," Dupree said, taking a swipe at Breneaux.

"Boys!" Henri cut in. "We're here to have fun."

"I don't think I've seen you since last year's parade," Breneaux rejoined, with a swipe of his own.

Despite his family's fortune and status throughout the South, Dupree shunned privilege, remaining an outcast among the elite. Only once each year did he enter their world, to ride in Rex, an unquestioned right. For a few hours annually, he was one of them—then, and when any of them got into trouble, looking down their noses giving way to respect. When requests for help were reasonable and legal, he'd suck up his pride and do what he could. But when pleas were trivial, excessive, or illegal, his refusals of aid were swift and harsh.

"Too busy fighting crime," he said, brushing the comment aside.

"Especially this week. Right, Owen?" Tom said, raising his glass for the first toast of the afternoon. "Here's to solving crime, once and for all."

"Crime's part of what we love about this city," Henri weighed in. "I'm not sure we want it to all go away."

"I wouldn't worry about that," Dupree said. "Between what happens on the street and how it gets stoked by the media . . ." He looked straight at Breneaux.

"Are you referring to me?"

"Boys, boys . . . It's Mada Gras." Tom reminded them again. "Be calm. Take a breath. Have a drink. Have five drinks."

"I'm referring to that boy of yours. What's his name? The one who's been causing all the trouble," Dupree said.

"Yeah, yeah . . . He's not my boy. The network brought him here. I'm the one who muzzled him. Badmouthing sex offenders is one thing. Outing's another."

"What if a guy's labeled a sex offender but doesn't deserve it?" Dupree said.

"Oh, here we go. On Mardi Gras day, when people hold up banners reading: 'Give 'Em Hell!' *I'll* throw beads. When they flash signs reading: 'Go Bleeding Hearts!' *you* throw beads."

Henri, already a bit tipsy, pointed in Breneaux's direction. "If you ask me, I'd say Burn Breneaux's the best thing that ever happened to this town. No, make that the whole damn country. Too much spending. Too much crime. Look who we've got in Washington. Look who's living in the White House. The whole country's gone socialist! Keep givin' 'em hell, Burn."

"Excuse me." Dupree rose and moved to another table.

Breneaux tried to find his watch under the sleeve of his jacket, but the cuff was too tight and it wouldn't give way. "Shit," he said. "I can't find my watch. What time is it?" He stood and wobbled on liquidy legs, returning to the chair to avoid tumbling on the floor.

"You all right?" Tom asked. "You gotta be sober by Tuesday to help me with my float."

"*Your* float?"

"Okay, *our* float. Have another drink."

Breneaux tried to focus. "Where are we?"

"Oooo, maybe you've had enough. We're in Hotel Monteleone, remember? The Carousel Bar? The one that goes round and round?"

Breneaux didn't need to be reminded of anything that went round and round. "How'd we get here? Weren't we at Antoine's?"

"That was four stops ago. Remember dinner at Arnaud's?"

"Yeah," Breneaux said. "Couldn't tell you what I had, though. Did I like it?"

"Arnaud's? Did you like it? You asked for rack of lamb and they said it's no longer on the menu, but for *you* . . ."

Breneaux again wrestled with his sleeve. "What time is it?"

Tom removed a gold watch from his vest. "It's quarter to nine. Why?"

"I promised Charmaine I'd call after school. I broke my promise." Breneaux rose again, this time slowly, steadying himself on the back of his chair.

"I'm sure she'll forgive you. Stay for one more. Then I'll call a cab."

Breneaux's head was swimming. "I think I better call now."

A United Cab driver drove through the gates, pulling up to Breneaux's front door. "Can you make it from here, Mr. Breneaux?" he asked.

"*Can I make it into my own goddamn house?*" Breneaux reconsidered. "I'm not sure."

The driver guided him onto the stoop. Breneaux gave him a twenty and walked inside.

"Charmaine?" Breneaux warned himself to lower his voice before realizing it was merely a whispery whine. "I'm sorry, Charmaine." Slowly and with great effort, he started up the stairs. Charmaine's door stood open, light streaming from her room.

Char-*ma-ine*?" He took a step forward and slid on the floor, slamming his nose against a closet door. *"Fuck!"* Finally, he reached Charmaine's room.

The mess before him was incomprehensible. He tried to make sense of it, but sense was elusive. *Is Katrina back? Where's Charmaine?* "Charmaine," he repeated. He heard nothing but silence. A computer was tipped upside down with books, blankets, and pillows strewn about the floor. A reddish-brown streak was visible on a sheet, on top of which lay a clump of hair. Next to the hair was a small black comb, the kind that cost a quarter and only boys used.

Breneaux clung to the banister on his way down the stairs, fog lifting a degree at a time, enough to let the terror sink in.

God, help me. He rifled through papers in his kitchen drawer. *I gotta find the number of that prick, Dupree.*

Chapter 34

THE PERFECT SUSPECT

DUPREE was awakened by the blare of his phone, piercing the groggy, semi-consciousness that held him in its spell. Middle-of-the-night calls were an occupational hazard, but he'd come to welcome them lately, hoping for a break. "Yeah," he muttered, expecting Jas's voice or Dodd's. Instead, he heard nothing at all.

"Hello!" he barked, noting it was 2:13.

"Du . . . pree?" the caller droned, drunk as a worm in mescal. "This is Breneaux."

Dupree rolled his eyes, waiting for the rest.

"There's been a . . . break-in."

So what? Call the police. Again, Dupree was conveniently one of them. He was in no mood to sit and suffer a drunk and was about to say so when he heard Breneaux wail . . . *"Charmaine's missing!"*

Dupree ceased to breath. "What do you mean missing?"

"Someone messed up her room and now I can't find her."

"Don't touch a thing. I'm coming right over." Dupree hoped in Breneaux's compromised condition that he'd simply overlooked her and would find her soon. At the same time, he told himself: *They always come in threes.*

The instant he pulled into the drive, he knew in his bones something was wrong. The house felt forlorn, doors secretive and sad, shutters framing windows, vacant and drawn. He couldn't explain why, but the week before, the Daniels's house imparted the same dreadful feeling.

When Dupree entered the foyer, Breneaux lay on the floor. "Where's Charmaine's room?" Breneaux pointed upstairs. Dupree dashed to the landing and down the hall. He returned minutes later, squatting beside Breneaux. "Burn, I know how hard this is. Do you have any idea where she might be?" He waited. "Who could have done this?" Breneaux shook his head. "Was Charmaine dating anyone?" Silence continued. "Did she have any enemies?"

Breneaux looked up, cheeks puffy and streaked. "People hate *me*. Everybody loves Charmaine. Find her for me, Dupree," he sobbed. "God dammit! Find her for me."

Sean tossed and turned at a quarter past five, plagued by nerves and unending conversations. With listlessness, hopelessness, thoughts of suicide, and no sleep, his diagnosis was simple: anxiety *and* depression. *So, what are you going to do?* He thought to reclaim the missing parts. But lying awake, pondering which they were, he realized *all* the parts of his life had gone missing.

"*Depression equals inactivity,*" Vince had said. "*Get out of bed. Get active. Get busy doing something.*" He pulled himself up and rubbed his eyes. *Okay, you're right. That's good for depression. But while I handle that, what do I do about my fears?*

"Anxiety is the gap between the present and the future," Perls told clients in a film Sean once saw. "We fill the future with catastrophic expectations. The present, by contrast, is safe and calm. To return to the present, take a moment and breathe." Sean closed his eyes and took a deep breath. The present, however, remained out of reach. His head was stuck in the not-too-distant future, certain that authorities were closing in.

He climbed out of bed, his mind on Ren, wanting more than anything for a chance to reassure her. Yet he knew if he returned, he was certain to get caught. He had hoped to see Brian the night before to pour out his soul and ask for advice. Instead he found a note on the kitchen table saying Brian had been called to Washington as well. Brian's hasty exit smelled like a setup, giving credence to Sean's fear that the police were on their way.

There was a *THUMP* at the door.

Heart pounding, Sean crept to a window and peeked out, expecting to see officers crouching with guns. Instead, lying on the porch was the morning newspaper, rolled and held together with a rubber band.

Sean pulled it inside and tossed it on a chair. But when he did, the rubber band broke. The paper unraveled; the headline caught his eye:

"Murders linked to bombings!"

Then they can't *suspect me! I'm a sex offender, not a bom—*

He began to tremble, Dupree's words rushing back: "What did your friend mean by '*another* explosion' and something about you 'killing your parents'?"

He was caught in the crosshairs of intersecting trajectories with a history of explosions as well as sex. Sean knew he was, in fact, the perfect suspect.

Dupree poured bourbon into a paper cup and leaned all the way back in his living room chair. He'd left his team, tagging evidence at Breneaux's, Jas assuring him he'd have answers by dawn. Though exhausted from weeks of sleepless nights, he thought it pointless to go to bed. Mattie's murder was bad enough. Now he had a kidnapping on his hands. Mattie could wait. The only thing that mattered was finding Charmaine.

He sipped his drink and stared at the phone, waiting impatiently for the lab to call. He had the murderer's DNA, which meant he had the bomber's. What he didn't have was a national data bank match.

Dupree woke with a start when the phone finally rang. Despite his intentions, he'd fallen asleep.

"Dupree? It's Dodd."

"What time is it?"

"Quarter to six. I want to give you a heads up. Vincennes called in the Feds. I argued against it, but we had no other choice. Breneaux's involved. The whole country's watching."

"Yeah, whatever," Dupree managed.

"You're still heading our case, but the FBI's involved as well. You sound tired."

Tired! Dupree hung up. He looked around for the paper cup, finding its contents spilled on the floor. The last time he felt as miserable as this was when his wife said she was leaving for a twenty-one-year-old named Miguel.

The phone rang again. "*Now* what?" Dupree snarled.

"Lieutenant? Spencer at the lab."

"Sorry. Thought you were . . . never mind."

"Got a print off the comb. Hair was still wrapped around it. Should have DNA soon."

"And . . ." Dupree waited for a name.

"Your boy, Sean Jordan."

Dupree hung up, feeling like a fool. Maybe it was good they'd brought in the Feds. He'd botched the case from the very beginning. *Sean Jordan, convicted sex offender. Lied about his whereabouts the night Daniels was killed. Covered for a friend who later wound up dead. Destroyed government property before skipping town. Left his fingerprints in the room of the daughter of the man whose station outed him over the air. And I let him go . . . for no other reason than to see what he'd do.*

Dupree got up and stretched his legs, rotating his shoulders, shaking the sleepiness out of his head. *On the other hand . . . DNA rules him out of the murders. When he runs, it's into the arms of a Senator! Now, a fingerprint? What the hell's going on?* He clenched his forehead, deepening lines on his brow. *How many prints?* He redialed Spencer.

"One, Lieutenant. No others of his were found anywhere in the house."

"Thanks."

"Hope your APB pays off."

"What APB?"

"For Jordan. I just heard it. I figured you called it."

"You tell anybody else about the comb?"

"No, Lieutenant. My lips to your ears. Nobody else."

"Let me know about the DNA." Dupree ended the call and entered Jas's number. "Still dickin' around with your evidence bags? Take a break. Meet me in half an hour."

"Half an hour, Lieutenant?" Jas sighed with fatigue.

"Ah, poor baby. Make that fifteen minutes!"

Dupree strained to remember if he let something slip, mentioning Jordan to someone in the same breath with Breneaux. He hadn't.

Well, someone *did.* Someone *authorized the APB. It couldn't have been the Feds. Where would they have gotten the information?*

No, he decided. It was somebody else.

Chapter 35

NORMALCY AMIDST CHAOS

COFFEE. Espresso. Anything with caffeine. I'd trade my kingdom for a single cup. Sean reached in his pocket and counted the change, concluding a cup was about all his kingdom was worth. He took a quick look in Brian's cabinets, searching for instant if nothing else. Finding none, he remembered a place—CC's Coffee House close to the Capital. Minutes later, he was standing in line.

"Charmaine Breneaux, the thirteen-year-old daughter of national conservative radio talk show personality, Burn Breneaux . . ." Sean's eyes wrenched up toward an overhead TV. "Was forcefully abducted from her home last night in New Orleans' famed Garden District."

Sean *knew* the girl—had seen her twice—lovely, with pretty eyes and a radiant smile. Probably had the personality to go along. *Please don't let anything happen to her.* He shuddered, seeing her picture, plastered across the screen.

"New Orleans Police have yet to say whether this constitutes a new development in their recent spate of homicides and bombings. In the meantime, they've issued an all points bulletin for a person of interest, a registered sex offender, Sean Andrew Jordan, thought to be living in Baton Rouge."

Sean blanched at his name and couldn't breathe.

"May I take your order?" the barista asked. Before Sean could answer, *his* picture appeared. *Forget the coffee*, Vince commanded. *Turn slowly. Get out.*

Sean ran to Brian's, lungs gulping air. He had to find a way out of Baton Rouge. He reached for his wallet and counted the bills, barely enough for a one-way trip. *To where?* He grabbed his toothbrush and headed for the door, stopping at a table piled high with beads. On top of the pile was a green leather mask. He donned the mask and slung beads over his head, glad he at least had a rudimentary disguise. He recalled the bus station he'd seen in town and took off running in that direction.

Sean entered the building, lined with old wooden benches, relieved to find he was nearly alone. Two buses were scheduled in a couple of hours, one to Galveston, the other to New Orleans. His gut voted for Texas, but he had to see Ren.

"Happy Mada Gras!" a voice called from across the room. It was a girl's voice crackling with enthusiastic good cheer. Sean turned and saw a young girl wave, her pigtails framing a mask of gold. Next to her sat a good-looking woman, likely her mother, Sean supposed. "We're goin' to New Awlins," the girl announced.

Sean appreciated her exuberance, reminiscent of Ren's, and the fact that she, too, was wearing a mask. Still, he tensed at her sudden, gleeful greeting, knowing he was forbidden to engage with kids.

"Where are *you* going?" the girl asked.

The mom smiled repentantly in Sean's direction, as if apologizing for invading his space. He thought to steer clear and maintain his silence but figured: *What's a little conversation compared with murder?* "That's where I'm going, too," he said, sliding in beside them. "I have a daughter named Ren. She's four."

"I'm Daisy. I'm six."

"Daisy. What a nice name. I bet your mom gave you that name."

"Actually, her father came up with it," the mother said. "I was hoping for *Lorraine*, same as my mother. We compromised with Daisy Lorraine."

"Daisy Lorraine," Sean repeated. "You're lucky to have two such pretty names."

"Are you going on the bus?" Daisy asked.

"I am. I promised Ren I'd take her to the Rex Parade." Sean was moved by the rare moment of normalcy, talking to a child not his own.

"I saw a parade once. The floats were gitanic!"

"Gi-*tan*-ic. That's a good word. I'll have to remember it."

A police officer entered. Sean looked away, normalcy hijacked instantly by terror. He felt for his mask, praying it would protect him. Footsteps drew closer. Panic surged. Sean's sense was to bolt. Then it occurred: *I won't seem a killer if we continue to talk.*

"How big is gitanic?" he asked, dizzy with dread.

Daisy's arms stretched wide. "*This* big."

"That's really big. And how tall?" He glanced at his legs, shaking involuntarily.

The officer walked up and stopped.

Daisy reached upward as high as she could. "*This* much."

"Wow, that's a lot."

The cop stared at Sean with eyes like augers. "What's your name?" he demanded.

"Richard Muller," Sean said, pulling a name from the air.

"Let's see some ID."

Sean reached—then feigned remembering . . . "Sorry. I forgot. I left New Orleans without my wallet. I remembered it last night when I stayed with a friend. I'm heading home to get it now."

"Muller," the officer repeated, never breaking his stare.

"He's going to the Rex Parade!" Daisy related. "His daughter's name is Ren."

Shit! How could I be so stupid?

"That's Mr. Muller's business, darlin'," her mother said. "Come sit on my lap."

Sean held his breath, awaiting the verdict. The cop dropped his gaze and looked at the mom. "Ma'am," he said, tipping his hat.

"Happy Mada Gras," she replied, nodding back.

The cop turned and headed for the door.

Sean exhaled like a burst balloon.

"A couple days in New Awlins should do us both good. I'm Darlene," the mother said, oblivious of what happened. "We were in Baton Rouge for a—" She lowered her voice. "Custody hearing."

"Sorry," Sean said.

"Didn't go too well. I didn't think he should have unsupervised visitation. The judge disagreed."

From the age of ten, Sean made it his mission to be available to anyone with things to sort out. He could tell that the woman wanted to talk—people always did once they sensed he was a listener. But he wasn't sure he could as he continued to shake, overwhelmed by the things *he* needed to sort out.

You have a gift, Vince said. *You can't deny it because of problems of your own. Just like the waitress, the mom showed up. Open your heart and you'll feel good about you.*

Sean knew with certainty that Vince was right. He hadn't a clue what awaited him back home. The bus ride might well be his final free hour. Why spend the time, cowering in fear, when he could serve else someone who needed a hug?

Chapter 36

THE HANGING JUDGE

"JAS!" Dupree yelled, storming toward his office. "Did you know an APB was issued for Jordan?"

"Well . . . *yeah*."

"Who the fuck authorized it?"

"I thought *you* did."

"And why would you think that?"

"Because you're in charge."

Dupree wheeled toward Jas, faces inches apart. "It's an illusion, kid. Nobody's in charge." He opened the door and moved toward the desk. "Find out who issued it and leaked his name to the press. But before you do, get Brandon Meyers on the phone."

"Yes, sir."

Minutes later, Dupree's phone buzzed. "Senator Meyers. This is Detective Lieutenant Owen Dupree, NOPD. Thanks for taking my call. I understand you have a relationship with Sean Jordan."

"Yes, Lieutenant. We heard about Breneaux's daughter and guessed you might be calling. You and the city certainly have your hands full.

I'm planning to convene a Senate subcommittee and hope Jordan will testify. I've spent time with him. Frankly, I think he's okay."

"Do you know where he is?"

"Haven't any idea. I saw him last on Wednesday before heading to DC. He's been staying in the home of my assistant, Brian Monteleone. When Brian had an associate check on him this morning, he'd left. Still, I can't see him being involved in any of this. His life hasn't been easy. He's bitter. But who wouldn't be? Kidnapping? Murder? Let me put it this way, I'd trust Sean Jordan with my kids and my grandkids."

Dupree thanked him for his time.

Jas rounded the corner, eyes dragging on the floor.

"Where's the Eagle Scout who was in here ten minute ago? You look terrible."

Jas kicked the filing cabinet with a sudden violent burst. "I should've figured. *Dammit!* I wasn't prepared."

"Prepared for what?"

"Constance Wile. Douglas's mom. I've been tracking her all week and finally got through."

"And . . . ?"

"She starts telling me about Jordan, what a great guy he is, how hard it was for him after his parents died to adjust to the 'crazy Hardys'—her words. Said she never heard a soul suggest Jordan was in any way responsible. Then . . ." Jas pivoted and kicked the cabinet again.

"*What?*"

"She asked how Doug was doing."

"Christ."

"First thing I did when she came on the phone was express my condolences. I guess she thought I was referring to jail." He shook his head. "I should have made sure."

"This isn't the first time the duty's fallen on you."

"But I've always been prepared. I assumed after a week, she'd already heard. I just stood there, stammering into the phone. I can imagine how hard it must have been for you to tell the Daniels."

"Welcome to the grownup world, Trevor."

The phone rang. "Lieutenant, is Jas in your office?" an officer asked.

Dupree hit *speaker*.

"He has a call on two from a Russell Hardy in San Francisco."

Dupree and Jas looked at each other. Jas took a seat. "Put it through . . . Hello, Russell?"

"This is Russell."

"Good morning. I'm Detective Lieutenant Owen Dupree. I'm sitting with Officer Trevor Jas. You're on speaker."

"Good morning. I got your calls earlier this week and . . . well . . . I've kinda been blowing you off. But when I saw Sean's picture on television this morning, I figured it was important."

"You grew up with Sean Jordan. Is that right?" Jas asked.

"From the time we were eleven."

Dupree leaned toward the phone. "Do you know he's a suspect in a pair of murders, a couple of bombings, and a kidnapping?"

"That's what they said on the news, but it's bullshit. Sean Jordan was the only sane person in our household. Does his being a suspect have anything to do with that sex offender business?"

Dupree glanced at Jas. "I suppose it does."

"You know my father screwed him."

Jas flashed two thumbs up. "How so?" Dupree said.

"My father's a religious nut case. He thinks he's the only righteous person on the planet. When he thought his clients were guilty, he did everything he could to sabotage them, all the while pretending to represent and protect them. Forget due process. Throughout his career, he fashioned himself counsel, judge, and jury. He'd have welcomed being the executioner, as well, if someone had handed him the switch."

"Did he do the same to Jordan?" Dupree asked.

"For years he tolerated him 'cause Sean always behaved to his standards. But the moment Sean ran into trouble, my father pounced. He let him sit in jail for three days and nights before finally meeting to discuss his case. He *wanted* him to suffer to atone for his sins."

"Why didn't Sean seek other counsel?" Jas asked.

"He didn't have the resources. He wouldn't have known where to turn. On some level, I suppose, he trusted my father—figured he'd step in if he ever really needed help. What he failed to fully appreciate was that William Hardy would rather hang sinners than defend them, especially sinners who lived under his roof."

"So he handed him a stack of papers and said, 'Sign here,'" Dupree said.

"That's exactly what he did. My father bragged about it afterward, like sticking it to his nephew was some great achievement. When Sean asked what signing meant, my father told him it was a gift—that he'd called in a lot of favors to secure probation over prison—but that there was nothing he could do about the initial sentence of ninety days. What Sean never knew was . . . it was my father who arranged for him to be held those ninety days. It was his idea. He pulled in favors, all right—not to help him, but to crush him. Those ninety days cost Sean his first year of college."

Dupree sighed. "You're not too fond of your father."

"It gets worse. The real poison was registration. Sean never should have gotten it. The prosecuting attorney thought the same, and registration was taken off the table. But my father never informed Sean. Instead, he handed him the original set of documents. Signing was the biggest mistake he ever made."

"Where's your father now?" Jas asked.

"Naples, Florida. He moved after my mom left him three years ago. He's facing charges of professional misconduct in Florida and Illinois. He thought he could get away with fucking people forever."

Dupree and Jas again exchanged glances. "Thanks for getting back to us," Jas said.

"One more question," Dupree interjected. "Did Sean have anything to do with the explosion that killed his parents?"

Russell laughed. "Are you kidding? The day they died was the worst day of his life."

"You've been most helpful, Russell," Dupree said. "If we need anything further, we'll be in touch." Another call rang through. He pressed the flashing button.

"This is Spencer. The hair on the comb's a match for Jordan."

226 |

Dupree hung up and stared at the floor. "Dodd and the Mayor ought to be worried. Whoever's trying to frame Jordan has a lot of information and a shitload of capability. I'm guessing his next target's already been chosen." He stood and thrust a finger at Jas. "Find out who leaked Jordan's name, and who authorized the APB."

Jas got up and stopped by the door. "I guess that settles it in terms of Jordan killing his parents."

"I still think he did. The guy's guilty of *something.*"

"Wile would have been able to tell us. Unless Jordan's willing to talk, the mystery dies with him."

"Forget Wile and Jordan," Dupree said. "There's one other person who knows all about it."

Chapter 37

CLOSING IN

SEAN peered from the bus on its approach to the Convention Center, half expecting SWAT to parachute from the sky. After all, it was the bus from Baton Rouge, where the infamous Sean Jordan had been hiding out with a Senator. Surely they'd have sent *someone* to greet it.

Apparently not.

Sean and Darlene hugged as they disembarked, her thanking him for his counsel as well as his caring. She'd acknowledged her concern wasn't triggered by abuse, rather by the parade of girlfriends her ex brought home. "I don't want Daisy exposed to people I don't know."

"Darlene," Sean said. "None of us can control our ex's choices, especially when it comes to choosing their friends. But you can invite Daisy to come to you, to share concerns safely, where they'll be met with love." He held Darlene's hand and looked in her eyes. "No one can replace you as Daisy's mom. You're the only mom Daisy will ever have."

Darlene took Daisy's hand in hers. Turning to leave, she called over her shoulder, "Ever consider a career in counseling?"

Sean smiled, noting the suggestion.

He crossed into the Quarter and headed down Charters, picturing Ren at home, cameras trained on the house. He thought about necessities, namely food and shelter, with few dollars in his wallet and no place to stay. At least he'd enjoyed a couple nights' reprieve, complements of Brian and Senator Meyers. He guessed, with his status as a "wanted man," there was little further help even they could provide. Weinstat had helped too, treating him squarely, offering to share and warning him of trouble. Dupree was the one person Sean couldn't trust after syncing him to GPS while he floated in the ether.

Spotting WFQT on trucks parked next to a building, Sean realized he was standing in front of the station. He thought about Manning, who valued money over life, and pictured Breneaux—not there, but at home—waiting by the phone for word of Charmaine. Sean couldn't imagine a more horrible fate.

Then there was that other guy: Del LeGrande. *What an asshole.* It was his actions that led to Sean losing his job, Ren losing her school, and Doug being killed. A half-empty Coke can beckoned from the street. Sean grabbed it and hurled it against the side of the building. *Not smart for a guy needing to remain inconspicuous.* But it felt good— really good.

Winding his way toward Bourbon Street, Sean encountered revelers numbering in the thousands, beads about their necks, drinks in hand. Among them were police, both state and local. Dozens were visible, parading in uniform. Others, he imagined, were hidden in plain clothes. He thought he caught a glimpse of the FBI—guys in black suits and dark skinny ties. But a closer check showed they were people in costumes that looked like Will Smith and Tommy Lee Jones. Turning onto Bourbon, he headed down the street past hot dog stands, reeking of onions; seedy-looking bars, promoting "Big Ass Beers!"; strip club barkers shouting, "Check out the girls!"; and an evangelical, rebuking the crowd, screaming, "Reservations in hell are now being taken!"

The street was awash in music of all kinds, from Dixieland to techno, zydeco to jazz. Dancing to the pulse were girls overhead, any of whom could have been the one who lured Doug.

Sean heard a *CRACK*, followed by a *WHIZZ,* and ducked at once into a crouching position.

Screams rang out, thousands scattering amidst gunfire. Sean assumed gangbangers had invaded the Quarter until two men in black appeared, charging in his direction. He spun to the right and dove into the crowd, clawing his way toward the middle of the street.

Sean peered around heads, spotting a club he'd been in, with a patio in the rear and a balcony upstairs. He dashed inside, house music blaring, sharpshooters visible, heading his way.

He considered the patio, but it felt too confined. Instead, he fled to the second floor. There, music poured from dozens of speakers above hundreds of partiers shoehorned into the room. A young, bare-breasted girl approached, holding a tray full of shots and a fistful of cash. "Two bucks a pop," she barked at the crowd, "or five if you care to lick it off my tits!" Eyes darting back to the top of the stairs, Sean looked in horror as a marksman reached the landing.

He fought through the crowd, making his way onto the balcony, where a fire escape connected the second and third floors. Going up seemed his only chance. But the ladder was blocked by a throng of onlookers, cheering two naked girls avidly making out. He broke through the crowd and swung in behind, grabbed hold of the ladder, and began his ascent. Hearing the crowd roar, he looked down and saw they'd turned from the girls and were now cheering *him.*

He reached the third-floor, gasping for air, and was met by fresh revelers greeting his arrival.

Now what?

He looked around in every direction, options dwindling, time running out. He could enter the building and head down the stairs, hoping the Feds had lost his trail. He could climb the fire escape onto the roof and search for a way down on the other side. Or . . . *Are you kidding?* He could leap from his balcony to the one next door, trusting he'd land without breaking his neck. The gap was at most three to four feet, but at thirty feet up, it felt like a mile.

Suddenly the crowd streamed back into the building. There could be only one reason: they'd been ordered inside. Sean climbed on the railing to a few stragglers' gasps, steadied himself, leaned forward, and jumped.

He landed with a roll and sprawled on the floor, catching his breath while checking for broken bones. From behind iron balusters, he watched agents next door peer at the balcony above and the street below. Where the agents weren't looking, just as he'd hoped, was at the balconies on the buildings on either side. Sean crawled through a window and scrambled down the stairs, disappearing once more into the crowd-packed street.

"There he is!" a man shouted, pointing a finger at Sean, while an agent ran toward him, pointing a gun. "He's wearing a green mask!"

Sean spotted an opening in the middle of the pack, plunged through the hole, and flew down the block. He stopped at the entrance to a gay bar on the corner, reputedly one of the best in town.

"Ten bucks to get in," a man barked at the door, muscles exposed in a shirt with no sleeves.

Sean pulled out two fives, the last cash he had, handed them over, and sped inside. He spotted at once naked men on the bar, dancing with towels held loosely about their waists. Every few seconds they let the towels fall, enticing patrons to pet genitals with five dollar bills. Behind the dancers were large-screen TVs, blasting videos of Madonna in a never-ending stream. Sean reached the stairs at the back of the room and turned to see the agent charge through the door.

Sean took the stairs and rushed into the room, expecting hundreds of dancers to be crammed onto the floor. Instead, occupying the better part of the space, stood an enormous plastic tank, teeming with wet, naked men. Bubbles rained down from dispensers above while the men climbed a slide to plunge into the foam. Movement inside viewed through thick, foggy panels evoked images of a squid waving tentacles of flesh.

"I take it you've never tried it," a voice called from behind.

Sean spun toward a young man in black leather shorts. "I don't even know what it is."

"It's a *foam party*. Check it out."

Sean preferred not to die at the bottom of some tank, but with few other options . . . "What do I have to do?"

"Take off your clothes and leave them with me."

"What? *Here?*"

"Sure! You can leave your underwear on if you want. Some do and some don't."

"Thanks . . . I think." Sean stripped to his Calvins with an eye on the door. "You're sure they'll still be here when I get out?"

"Don't worry about a thing. I'm Justin. Look for me when you're done."

"What do I do now?"

"Climb aboard!"

Sean started up the steps with one eye across the room. Ahead of him was a patron, sitting on top of the slide. Sean waited anxiously, expecting him to let go, but instead he just waved and called to his friends. "Listen, would you mind sliding down?" Sean pleaded.

"What's your rush? Lemme guess. You're a bottom in heat, and your top's waiting below."

"Something like that." Sean hadn't a clue what he was talking about.

"Well, why didn't you say so?"

Sean glanced again and saw the agent by the door. "Please!"

The guy turned around. "I love when men beg." He released his grip and slid legs first, disappearing into the frothy foam below.

Sean jumped to the top and held his breath, hesitating for a second before letting go.

The music's pounding beat was instantly replaced by the underwater drone of water-filled ears. Inches in front of him, splashing in the goo, were dozens of legs, some hairy, some smooth; decorative underwear, the likes of which he'd never seen; penises and asses pressed firmly together, and . . . He looked again. A *vagina?*

A hand reached down, pulling Sean to his feet. "Were you planning on staying there the rest of the day?" the girl asked, flanked by a pair of male companions.

"I was considering it," Sean said. He looked across at the Plexiglas panels, realizing it was as hard to see out as to see in. Yet despite the plastic, fog, and foam, he knew at any moment the tank could be drained, its inhabitants ordered out and lined against a wall.

"It's our first foam party," the girl said. "Isn't it fun?"

The next cloud of foam, wafting from the ceiling, settled over the tank, concealing them entirely. When the bubbles finally settled, the three of them were gone, replaced by others, laughing and squirming, rubbing bodies against bodies in slick liquid Joy.

Sean made his way to the side of the tank, wiping a spot clean on the foggy plastic panel. He peeked through the hole—then immediately recoiled. Talking to Justin—studying him intently—was the agent, standing right next to the glass! When the agent turned, diverting his eyes, Justin kicked Sean's mask under the slide. He tapped the agent's shoulder and pointed toward the stairs. The agent grabbed his radio and headed outside.

Sean felt a splash, announcing another partier's arrival. He turned to see Justin, standing in the slime.

"Don't worry," Justin said. "I sent him to the river. I told him the guy in the green mask ran in, asked for directions, and ran back out." Justin shrugged. "He must have believed me."

"How did you know I was in trouble?"

"The way you kept looking over at the stairs, you were either anticipating a spurned lover's arrival, or . . ."

"But that was the FBI. Why didn't you rat me out?"

"I don't much like cops. Want another reason?"

"Sure."

Justin reached forward and tousled Sean's hair. "You're fucking adorable."

Sean laughed. "I owe you."

Justin beamed. "Any chance of collecting now?"

"Ah . . . listen . . . I . . ."

Justin held up a hand. "No problem. I understand. But I want you to know . . . tonight in bed, I plan on loving you in absentia."

"Knock yourself out," Sean said, returning Justin's smile.

They climbed out of the tank, dried, and dressed. *If anyone deserves a hug* . . . Sean hugged Justin warmly at the foot of the tank.

"No more green," Justin said, handing Sean a black mask. "Green undermines your cobalt blues."

Sean exited the building and fled into the crowd.

Nothing seemed real, Sean thought as he hid—not the terror of being shot at by the FBI, the panic of flying through air without a net, or the horror of being wanted in a child's abduction.

Inches away, two men stood kissing. Sean thought about Laurie and then about Tyne and finally about the best friend he no longer had.

A notion occurred. *Why not?*

LeGrande stared through a window overlooking Canal, pleased with the vantage he'd carved for himself, inches above the top of the floats. He'd accessed the building through a window in the rear and unlocked the loading dock door from inside. In the largest of several rooms upstairs, he found a mannequin in one corner by a box labeled "shirts," beside a bulletin board filled with thirty-year-old ads. This had been The Clinton, according to the ads, "offering woman's apparel since 1917." What remained of the building was a cavernous brick shell, with cracked plaster ceilings and walls bleeding dust.

LeGrande approached a girl, handcuffed naked to the wall, and dangled a piece of chicken in front of her nose. "If you promise to be good, you can have a little dinner." He unlocked an iron cuff and handed her a wing. She threw it in his face, pieces cart wheeling across the floor. "Nice. I *like* that. Come Mardi Gras, the two of us are gonna have a really good time." He reattached the cuff, stuffing a second wing in her mouth. "Better eat and stay strong, with three days to go. I won't be back again until sometime tomorrow."

She spit out the chicken, aiming it at him. "My father has friends! You'll be sorry you did this."

LeGrande dabbed a spot of grease that landed on his shirt. "Warning duly noted."

"I know what you did. You're the one who killed that girl."

LeGrande nodded. "You're pretty smart for thirteen."

She tugged with her wrists, struggling to break free.

There was a faint sound of scratching behind LeGrande's back. He turned and saw roaches, dashing for the meat. "At least someone appreciates the gifts I provide. Hope you enjoy the rest of your evening."

Chapter 38

THE REUNION

SEAN woke abruptly to the sound of gunshots, unaware of where he was. His mind returned to the pure white crane, picturing its feathers covered in blood, its lifeless body a trophy on display—not on hunters' walls, but on the FBI's. He caught his breath and looked around. He'd returned to Tremé and slept in the Victorian. His head was dizzy, his stomach sick. The smell of chlorine permeated the house, struggling to mask the stench of death. He hadn't gone upstairs and never would. Not again, under any circumstance.

He stumbled into the bathroom and looked in the mirror—shirt stained, eyes swollen, hair tangled above a two-day-old beard. *Beards.* Sean hated beards. It was the guys in therapy with mustaches and beards who hid behind hair and one excuse after another. He opened the medicine cabinet and reached for Doug's razor, wondering why and for whom he was making the effort.

Looking in the mirror, an apparition appeared—Doug's face hovering next to his, as if his friend were by his side. He glanced at the face, feeling guilty and ashamed, and thought to turn away, but Doug's image held his gaze. He searched Doug's eyes, expecting anger and blame, but was surprised to find love and understanding instead. Then his parents appeared, their faces beside Doug's, followed by his grandparents and relatives he barely recalled. Others showed up, too—students and friends, and still more whose names he'd long forgotten. Like Doug's, their faces were filled with affection, lifting Sean's spirits, lightening his load.

He closed his eyes and breathed into his core his ancestors and allies, friends new and old—all who had come to assemble before him. He lingered for a time in the comfort of their presence, breathing easily, finding peace. Exhaling, he let go from the depths of his being, imbued with fresh hope, feeling not so alone.

When he opened his eyes, the faces were gone, all but his own, lustrous and determined.

Find Ren. Reassure Laurie. Help Charmaine.

Sean found a shirt lying in the parlor, pulled it over his head, and headed down the hall. He knelt in the dining room, hesitating for a moment, staring at the cigar box, knowing what was inside. Resolute, he tipped open the lid, reached for the gun, and inserted the clip. He raised and lowered the weapon on the way to the back door, trying to get used to its weight and feel.

"Relax," he said to the kitchen sink. "I'm not gonna kill ya. I'm only gonna wash my hands." He seized a windbreaker that hung from a hook, put it on, and slid the gun into the pocket.

The Sunday before Mardi Gras began quietly enough with business as usual at police headquarters on Broad. Officers sipped coffee as they walked through the corridors, processing Saturday night's brawlers, pickpockets, and pimps. But business as usual wasn't to last. A few hours later, chaos ensued.

The media got hold of a clip of the Mayor talking to a clerk beneath a camera outside his office, commenting that another explosion was sure to occur. "Bigger than the aquarium," he seemed to boast. "Tell you what I think," he told the young woman. "Burn Breneaux can kiss his kid goodbye."

The clip went viral in less than an hour, with the mayor's folly blasted all over the world. No one could fathom how the mayor of a major city could be so callous toward its own national star. Despite his concern for Charmaine and New Orleans, Dupree struggled to keep his amusement in check.

Furious hotel managers and restaurateurs descended on City Hall to no avail, fuming over locked doors and useless phone messages: "Please call back during regular business hours." Republicans flooded talk shows seeking revenge, claiming Charmaine's disappearance was a plot to silence conservatives, while Democrats concurred that indeed there was a plot, but that it was staged by Republicans as a way to discredit *them*. The president phoned the governor and conferred with the FBI, requesting hour-by-hour updates, offering whatever assistance he could. Everyone waited anxiously with the same questions in mind: Who was behind it, and what was going to blow up next?

Following his chewing out by an embarrassed and angry governor, Vincennes was publically contrite but privately enraged. He demanded from Dodd the name of the bomber as if expecting it to be lying on top of Dodd's desk. He demanded to know, too, the details of the next explosion—the one he alone had publically predicted. Apparently clairvoyance went only so far. Finally, he ordered the chief of police to find the person behind the leak. The chief, in succession, hammered Dupree.

"The mayor's a madman," Dupree said to Dodd. "He brings in the Feds, who open fire on Bourbon Street!"

"Jordan's a wanted man."

"He's a *person of interest!* Since when do we give shoot-to-kill orders for *them*? If you ordered that, you're no better than Vincennes. Dupree spun and headed for the stairs.

"I didn't hear that," a fuming Dodd called.

"Jas!" Dupree roared, not knowing he was standing beside him.

"About the APB, Lieutenant. The chief ordered it."

"What? Nobody knew about the comb except Spencer and me."

"Correct. The chief found out about the comb *after* issuing the APB. Said it proved him right."

"He acted before he had the evidence."

"He said he had to do something—that the heat was on from above and below. Jordan was all he had."

"What do you mean 'below'?"

"He said the guys were talking about it in the locker room—that they couldn't understand why he wasn't leaning on Jordan."

Dupree shook his head slowly. "The girl had barely been taken from her house before Jordan's name was plastered on the news. I want to know about 'the heat below'—who has the chief's ear, who's running the show. Now!"

Sean followed the fence to Suzanne's back porch, keeping an eye out for movement of any kind. He hoped she was home but worried about her disposition, fearing the news might have turned her against him. He walked to the door and peeked through the glass, detecting light and motion at the end of the hall. Heart racing, he knocked.

"Who is it?" Suzanne called, above Brielle's boisterous greeting.

"Suzanne, it's Sean."

"Sean!" She sailed through the door, arms spread wide. "Is that you behind that good-looking mask?"

With a surge of relief, he lifted a corner, glancing over his shoulder at the neighbors' backyards. "Can we go inside?"

"Of course. Sit down. Let me get you some tea." She reached for a cup, pulling tea from the cupboard. "You must know by now you're a wanted man." Brielle barked, seeming to second the fact. "I've never entertained a wanted man before . . . well . . . except for Cleve, my dearly departed husband. Turns out he was wanted by every woman in town." She handed him a cup of chicory tea and took a seat at the table. "It's really good to see you. Laurie's been worried. Ren asks about you all the time."

"Are they here?" he inquired, removing his mask, craning his neck toward the front of the house."

"No, they're out."

"All that stuff on the news . . . I didn't have anything to do with it."

"That's what Laurie keeps saying."

"I have to let them know I'm all right. Where are they?"

Suzanne shook her head. "I don't know, Sean."

"You don't know?"

"I don't know if Laurie would want me to tell." Suzanne lowered her eyes as if gathering her thoughts. "She's angry . . . and scared. She's constantly worried that the police are going to arrest her in order to get you to turn yourself in. She asked me this morning if I'd take care of Ren . . . you know . . . if anything happens."

"Jesus." Sean leaned in, eyes pleading. "I need to see them just for a minute. Then I'll leave. I won't cause any problems."

Suzanne sighed, squeezing Sean's hand. "They went to the Crescent City Parade Museum to see the floats being readied for Tuesday."

Sean recalled Ren asking to go the year before. He'd turned her down because children would be present.

"Thanks, Suzanne." Sean readjusted his mask and rose to leave. Suzanne pressed a few bills into his hand. "I can't—"

"Nonsense," she said. "You look like you haven't eaten in weeks."

Sean bent down and kissed her on the cheek. "Suzanne, you're the kindest person I know."

"Well, aren't you the dear. Happy Mada Gras, Sean."

"Happy Mardi Gras."

Sean headed upriver along Decatur, avoiding Bourbon and a repeat of yesterday. He paused in front of the French Market Restaurant, where a short, skinny black man in a Tabasco-stained apron scooped bowls of jambalaya out of a huge steel pot. Famished, Sean told him to "make it a double," handing him a wrinkled ten dollar bill.

He ate and walked until he reached the museum, a towering structure upriver from Canal. He was ushered inside by a man wearing a tie in Mardi Gras colors: purple, green, and gold.

The staging area seemed to go on forever, with dragons and jesters looming overhead. Beneath were the floats, nearly two stories high, filling the rest of the cavernous space. Hundreds of tourists milled about while fabricators applied last-minute touches.

Sean scanned the room for mothers with kids. Several moms pushed strollers; others held kids' hands. In the distance, stood a woman and a girl, the girl straining to touch the nose of a clown. Though they were facing away, their movements seemed familiar. Sean continued to watch and slowly approached.

"Laurie," Sean said in a calm, quiet voice.

"*Sean?*" Laurie responded. Her eyes darted about as if scouting for danger. "What are you doing here? Everyone's looking for you."

Her anxious reaction, while reasonable and measured, bore none of the relief he'd hoped to find.

"Is that Daddy, Mommy?"

"Shhhh," Laurie whispered. "Yes, it's Daddy."

Sean scooped up Ren and placed her on his shoulders. "I want you to know . . . I had nothing to do with any of it."

Laurie looked in his eyes. "I never thought you did."

"Are you and Ren okay?"

"Daddy," Ren hollered. "Bounce up and down!"

A uniformed cop started in their direction. Sean felt for his mask to make sure it was secure—then realized he alone was wearing one. His knees began to shake like they had in the station. The cop drew nearer, placing a hand on his gun.

"Happy Mardi Gras," Sean said, shaking getting worse.

The cop glanced repeatedly between Laurie and Sean.

God, please.

He finally reached up and gave Ren a high five. "Happy Mada Gras," he said, and continued on his way.

"We're fine, Sean, but you have to go," Laurie urged.

"Bounce higher, Daddy. *Higher.*"

Sean's thoughts were reeling. *Death by a thousand cuts.*

Taking a moment to gather himself, he spotted a man in a costume beard, rolling from under a gilded float, lying on his back on a mechanic's dolly. Sean might not have noticed if the beard's string hadn't snapped, exposing the man from WFQT. Sean hadn't recognized him with a clean-shaven face, but seeing him in a beard, he instantly remembered: He'd worn one in therapy ten years before.

"LeGrande." The name escaped Sean's lips. He lifted Ren from his shoulders and stood her gently on the floor. "Daddy'll be back soon." He kissed her, squeezed Laurie's hand, and followed LeGrande out of the building.

What's he doing, the fucking prick? A radio personality under a float? A guy who loves attention, hiding behind a beard? He followed LeGrande to a parade, rolling down Canal Street, and assumed he'd cross, heading into the Quarter. Instead LeGrande stopped *before* the parade, and headed up Canal. One block. Two. Three. Four.

What am I doing? Sean suddenly thought. Finding his family had been his focus for days. Once he did, he left them behind, pursuing a near stranger without purpose or provocation. What did he hope to gain?

A bit of satisfaction. The chance to fuck with a sex offender who goes around attacking other offenders. LeGrande's hypocrisy was utterly appalling. *No, that's not all.* Sean didn't want to just fuck with the guy. For what he did to Doug . . . Sean felt the urge to kill him.

LeGrande turned at a corner away from Canal—then pivoted again into an alley. Maintaining some distance, Sean traced his steps, reached the alley, and found it deserted. Two doors down was a big empty building, its loading dock door left ajar. He surmised LeGrande had gone inside.

At the end of the alley, people continued to pass by, drinking while drunk, finding humor where there was none.

"Happy Mardi Gras!" students cheered, wearing TKE-emblazoned sweats.

"Happy Mardi Gras," Sean murmured, minimizing his voice.

Struggling to stay vertical, they lined up their beers, unzipped their pants, and peed by a dumpster. "Hope you don't mind," one turned and said, as if apologizing for pissing on Sean's private lane.

Half a dozen more dolphins the moment they're caught.

Sean heard the screech of an old rusty door. He made sure not to turn and remained deathly still. Seconds later, LeGrande hurried by, clipping Sean on the edge of his shoulder. "Sorry," he muttered without looking back, sounding as if he couldn't care less.

"No problem," Sean said, adrenaline surging. He watched LeGrande turn, heading back toward Canal. This time he felt no compulsion to follow, his attention drawn to the building instead. He squeezed through the door into a large empty room, dusty and dirty, but ordinary enough. No one had done business there for quite some time.

He climbed up the stairs and encountered a smell, pungent and stale like the frat boys' piss. Stepping into the space straight ahead, he was blinded by light, streaming through the windows. Muffled shrieks emanated from across the room like a desperate animal caught in a trap. He proceeded cautiously in the direction of the sound, blinking repeatedly to restore his sight.

Beneath the windows in a pool of urine sat Charmaine Breneaux, naked and terrified.

LeGrande! Son of a bitch! His urge to kill doubled as he loosened Charmaine's gag.

"I wanna go home!" she cried, eyes filled with tears.

"I'm gonna do all I can to make that happen." Sean inspected her wrists. The iron cuffs that bound them pinned her to the wall. "This takes a skeleton key. Does he keep it with him?"

"No," she sobbed. "It's hanging over there. He told me he wanted me to be able to see it."

Sean dashed for the key.

"Hurry, *please.*"

The key caught and turned. The cuff fell away. He unlocked the second and lifted her gently, carrying her to a table above a box marked "shirts." He ripped it open and handed her one.

Sean's emotions soared with a sense of triumph, reminiscent of moments from a life long gone. He did what he'd intended with Ren, Laurie, and Charmaine. The only thing left was to return her to safety. "Let's get out of here."

A noise behind them was followed by a scream. Charmaine's contorted face was the last thing he saw before he felt something heavy land against his skull.

Chapter 39

LUNDI GRAS

BURN Breneaux lay on his back, eyes shut, mumbling to greet another day. *Was it a dream?* Voices in the hallway negated the possibility.

A nurse stepped inside. "How are we feeling today, Mr. Breneaux?"

"What day is it?" he asked, through a sedated haze.

"Monday morning," she answered, far too cheerfully.

Lundi Gras. Charmaine's been gone three days. He felt a howling, rising in his gut. He rolled on his side away from the nurse. *"Charmaine!"* he wailed. *"I love you. I'm sorry."* He thrashed, shrieked, and sobbed until exhaustion descended.

"Would you like another shot, Mr. Breneaux?" Without waiting for his answer, she lifted the sheet and sent him soaring to a galaxy light years away.

"Del. When you have a minute . . ." Manning stood glumly at the studio door.

LeGrande feigned concern. "Now's a good time." He followed his boss to the end of the hall. "How's Burn?"

"How would *you* be?"

Whoops. Perhaps not concerned enough. "I can't imagine," LeGrande said, lowering his head.

"He's fucked up. At least for the time being. I just got off with Corporate. Breneaux's their man, but in light of all this, no one knows when or if he'll return." Manning stared across the desk, his expression a mixture of pride and reservation. "Beginning Wednesday, after the holiday, they want you in his slot until further notice."

Two weeks and two days. Could anyone have done better? LeGrande pictured Caligula upon Tiberius's death, rising from a minnow to a veritable god.

"It's your national shot. No long-term promises. Just a chance to look good. Think you can deliver?"

He flashed a look of grief and sorrow—pages seven and eight in the catalogue of social tenants. "Not as well as Burn Breneaux. Not ever. But I'll do my best."

Dupree pulled from his drawer a picture of Molly, studied it for a moment and set it on his desk. Her hat and feather were cocked to one side, her lips moist, prepped for a kiss. He wanted to call her—hear her tell him not to worry, and to remind him of the fact that he was a good cop. But he didn't have time, and neither did she. Not this time of year. Not during Mardi Gras. He imagined her scrambling from one customer to another, while yelling at couples to stop fucking in the john. *"I don't do that when I come over to your house!"*

If Shannon 'N Molly's was a padded cell, police headquarters was a full-blown asylum. Calls for the mayor's impeachment escalated throughout the day, while police clashed with Feds over every aspect of the case. Reporters begged scraps to inflate into scoops as negotiators stood by, awaiting calls that never came. Hollywood writers were brought into town to scheme like madmen to generate leads. But each time one hit on a brilliant idea, he squirreled it away for his own future script. Psychics arrived on the scene, as well, requesting bits of Charmaine's clothes or locks of her hair. With those, they argued, they could pinpoint where she was more accurately than they could, reading cards, charts, or palms. A voodoo queen from Rampart Street also marched in, cloaked entirely in feathers atop dirty bare feet. "I'm Ruby St. John," she proudly proclaimed, flashing a wide, toothless grin while adjusting her tall beehive wig. "Fo'*get* the reward! *I'll* tell ya where she's at. Only cost ya a mere *twenty-five dollars!* Just gotta make sure I get paid in advance."

That was yesterday's cast of characters. Dupree could only imagine who he'd encounter today. While he stood at a urinal on the second floor, Jas stepped beside him. "And . . .?"

"The officers who were circling, gnawing on the chief, were Peter Boutreau, Tom Harrigan, and Danny Hurt."

"Hurt." Dupree zipped his pants and washed his hands. "I know that prick. On the force about ten years. Suspended twice for beating up gays. Bring him to me."

"I checked. It's his day off. But I have something else: Mrs. Jordan's calendar and phonebook. Called every entry trying to find her."

"Skip the smug look. And . . ."

"Remember Suzanne DeMarco? The Little People Preschool on Olympic. Jordan's kid went there 'til a week ago when her mom pulled her out. DeMarco said she didn't know where they were hiding. I asked what made her think they were hiding. The phone went silent. I pushed harder. She admitted the wife and kid were staying with her while Mrs. Jordan sorts out her marital difficulties. She was adamant that she hadn't seen *Mr.* Jordan."

"Had you asked if she had?"

"Not once."

"Uh *huh.*" Dupree made a note. "Where's the wife?"

"Children's Hospital. DeMarco said she's a nurse. I'm about to head over."

"You'd be wasting your time. Mondays, she works second shift."

"How do you know *that*?"

"She told me, first time we met. Think you're the only one who knows stuff?"

Jas pulled up in front of a pink Creole cottage. "I'll handle this," Dupree said. "You find Hurt. Piss on his day off. I don't care if he's on a plane to the Bahamas."

He walked up the steps and knocked on the door. "Police Lieutenant Dupree," he called inside. "I'm looking for a Ms. Suzanne DeMarco."

Laurie, dressed in a nightgown and robe, opened the door and invited Dupree in. "I'm not surprised you found me, Lieutenant, with everyone in the city, searching for Sean." She sounded calm, voice free of antagonism. "You seem like a good detective."

The compliment felt natural, neither calculated nor forced, impressing him like she had the first time they met. "I'm sorry about the toll this trouble's taken on your marriage, but I have to ask a few questions."

"I understand. Would you like to sit down?"

The two sat opposite each other, a coffee table in between. "Do you know where he is?"

Laurie shook her head. "No."

"When was the last time you heard from him?"

She hesitated. "Yesterday."

"Where was he calling from?"

"He didn't call. I was with him."

You were what? Dupree concealed his surprise. "Where was that?"

"Inside the Crescent City Parade Museum. He found out I was there and wanted to see me."

"What did he say?"

"That he was okay. That he loved me. That he didn't have anything to do with the stuff on the news."

"Did you believe him?" Dupree asked.

"Of course," Laurie said. "Sean never lies."

"Ahhh . . ."

"Just that once to protect his friend. He spent all year beating himself up for the trouble Doug got into. Now . . . he'll never forgive himself."

Dupree pulled a pad and pen from his pocket and settled his glasses on the end of his nose. "What else happened at the museum?"

"Nothing. We were together only a minute. He was staring at something. Then he left."

"Any idea what he was staring at?"

"Not really. It was like he was distracted."

"Can you recall anything that might have distracted him?"

Laurie thought. "He was staring in the direction of the floats." Dupree waited for more. "That's all, Lieutenant. He was staring at the floats."

"What was he wearing?"

"I didn't pay much attention. Jeans. A jacket, I think. I was mostly aware of his mask."

"Mask?"

"Black. Not very fancy. That's all."

Black mask, Dupree noted. Searching for a needle in a thousand bales of hay was better than searching for one in a million. "Did you make arrangements to meet again?" Laurie shook her head. "Give you a phone number? Anything?"

"Nothing, Lieutenant . . . except . . ." Dupree waited. "When he was distracted, he said something."

"What was that?"

"'A grand' . . . I think."

"A thousand dollars?"

Laurie shrugged. "I don't know. I might have gotten it wrong."

Dupree stood. "Thank you, Mrs. Jordan." He turned—then spun back. "It's only my opinion, but I think you still love him."

Laurie looked away as if to conceal tears. "Sure. Maybe. I don't know. I just know I can't live like this any longer."

Dupree placed his card in the palm of her hand. "Keep this . . . in case something else comes to mind."

Jas turned the key and pulled away from the curb. "How'd it go, Lieutenant?"

"Fine. What do you have?"

"Hurt's expected at a barbecue at his in-laws' in Gretna. He's not answering his cell. They'll have him call as soon as he arrives."

"If he hasn't called in an hour, call back. Call every ten minutes 'til you reach him."

"Yes, Lieutenant. What'd you find out?"

"Sean Jordan likes floats."

Chapter 40

RAISING THE STAKES

"I'M sympathetic to your plight, ma'am," LeGrande told the caller, "but if your son wanted to avoid jail, he should have kept his pants zipped 'til his girlfriend turned eighteen." He felt a vibration in his pocket and checked caller ID. "Do you have other kids?"

"A daughter, fourteen."

"Better send her to a school that teaches abstinence only." He cut to a commercial and returned the call. "Hurt. What do you have?"

"Jordan's still on the loose, but the department's located his wife. She's holed up with a friend. Want the address?"

"Sure." LeGrande took down the number. "Anything else?"

"No, man, but listen, somethin's comin' down. My in-laws took a call from headquarters. Somebody's tryin' to find me. If it turns out to be trouble, I might need your help."

LeGrande bit down hard. "My help?"

"Well, after all, I've helped you since you first came to town. Gave you some pretty choice stuff."

"That's funny," LeGrande snarled. "I thought I was helping *you*. I could swear you said you wanted me to nail these guys—set 'em up for you and your buddies—that we're fighting for the same cause."

"I'm just sayin'. . . I don't know why headquarters is callin'."

"It'll be nothing," LeGrande decreed, putting a period at the end of the conversation. "For the cause. Right, Hurt?"

"For the cause."

LeGrande hung up. *What do the authorities have on Hurt, and what if they press him into a god damned confession?* Seconds later, he'd figured a cover. *Hey, I only pick up the phone. Say "hello." Never solicit a thing. Never pay anybody a nickel. The caller gave me a tip, trying to be helpful. If the police can't muzzle their own, that's their problem, not mine.*

Still, it bothered him.

Sean's eyes fluttered open. He heard himself groan. He'd been on a distant planet but had no idea for how long. It was daylight. Something smelled. The space around him was cavernous and dusty— the air, moldy and damp. He had no memory of having been there before. "Where am I?" he mumbled, thinking he was alone.

"Somewhere downtown," a woman's voice answered. "Are you all right?"

Sean turned too fast, igniting a firestorm in his head. "*Fuck!* What happened?"

"You don't remember?"

He turned again, slowly this time, exercising his eyes to bring the woman into focus. As the haziness lessened, he realized at once: It wasn't a woman but a child! Her face was captivating, her body nude. She looked familiar, but no name came to mind. Their hips were touching, sitting side by side, legs stretching outward into the room. Inspecting further, he realized he was naked, too.

He tried to sit up but met resistance, his wrist stuck, tied, or pinned to something behind him.

"This time," she said, "he chained us *both* to the wall."

Yanking his arm, he felt a tearing where iron encircled his wrist. The girl's right hand and his left were cuffed to the wall. Their "free" hands were tied together with plastic restraints.

"He only has two handcuffs . . . So we get to share."

"Who?" Sean asked.

"Del LeGrande, the *murderer*. I guess I'm next."

Sean looked at her, surprised by her spunk. "Not if I can help it." Clouds cleared. "You're Charmaine Breneaux."

"Yep, and you're Sean Jordan. Del said you're a sex offender. Everyone in New Awlins thinks it was you who took me."

"Del?" Sean looked at her quizzically. "You called him Del, like he's your friend."

"What else am I gonna call him? After what *he's* done, I don't think he deserves to be called 'Mr. LeGrande.' Should I call you, 'Mr. Jordan'?"

Sean looked down at his hairy legs, shriveled penis, and half-exposed testicles cramped between his legs. "Under the circumstances, Sean'll do fine." He turned too quickly again, reigniting the pain. *"Ow!"*

"My daddy says we're supposed to learn from our mistakes. Are you gonna keep doing that?"

"No. That time I got it." He looked at her skeptically, as if she were forty masquerading as a kid. "Listen, LeGrande says lots of things. I wouldn't pay any attention."

He began to size up their situation. The bank of windows behind them was high off the floor—too high for anyone to hear if they hollered. LeGrande must have come to the same conclusion, chaining and stripping them while dispensing with gags. Sean's clothes were visible but just out of reach; Charmaine's, by contrast, were nowhere to be seen. He looked for something sharp, bits of broken glass—anything he could use to cut their restraints.

"Well, I was there. You didn't kidnap me. *He* did."

"Bet you change your story when we get to court."

"Ha-ha. Are you really a sex offender?" she asked, coiling matted hair. "You haven't tried to touch me or anything."

Sean didn't know what to say. Few people had ever been so blunt. He wished there was a way he could tell her the truth without admitting there was a chance he might find her attractive.

"Yeah, I am . . . But don't worry, my offending days are over."

"I wasn't worried," she said, "even though my daddy says: 'Once a sex offender, always a sex offender.'"

Jesus! Even here I'm confronted with Burn Breneaux. "Well, your daddy's never met me. If he ever does, he'll have to reconcile his beliefs with me, the exception to the rule."

"What does 'reconcile' mean?"

"Shhh!"

Footsteps were heard emanating from the stairs.

Sean's fright was rivaled by his rapidly mounting fury as he was about to come face to face with the man behind it all. He welcomed the encounter as much as he feared it.

LeGrande appeared and surveyed the scene, crouching before them, holding a brown paper sack. He seemed to revel in his superior position, grinning broadly like a Cheshire cat. "I see you're back with us. How's your head?"

Sean stared back. "You're gonna blow up the parade."

"Brilliant!" LeGrande laughed, staring up at the windows. "When the first float makes it to right about . . . here . . ." He cocked his finger as if pulling a trigger. "Kablooey."

"You killed my best friend, you fucking prick!"

"Yeah, and I gotta admit I enjoyed every minute of it. *Many* minutes in fact. He didn't die easily."

Sean spit at LeGrande, his spit falling short.

"Nice. Keep it coming. I *want* you to fight."

LeGrande's delight sent chills up Sean's spine. He was a textbook sociopath who killed strictly for fun—his missing part, a conscience, that could never be reclaimed. So fascinating was the disorder, Sean had longed to see it firsthand. However, being chained to a wall with the sociopath holding the key wasn't exactly the circumstance he'd had in mind. He glanced at Charmaine, determined to let nothing harm her.

"It's a great plan," LeGrande said, talking to himself. "Drive my competitor crazy by stealing his daughter, while tying her disappearance to the other thorn in my side." He angled toward Sean, setting the sack on the floor. "What I hadn't counted on was you stumbling in here. Yet, what could be better? When they find pieces of your body embedded in hers, the police will have their man and the case will be closed."

"What about your need to abuse kids, LeGrande? They'll catch you eventually; it's just a matter of time." The words felt true, psychology the only weapon Sean had on hand.

"*You're* the pedophile, Jordan, not me. I enjoy having sex with people of all ages. Think of me as an equal opportunity destroyer. You, on the other hand . . . How old was she? Thirteen? Fourteen? It's been so long, I can't remember. I can imagine what she looked like, though—perfect skin, tiny nipples, gently protruding belly, lovely little ass—just like Charmaine here. You loved it, Jordan. *You're* the one who has to have it."

"If that's so, why do I never go after it?"

"Like you said, it's just a matter of time. You know, I'm surprised all this talk isn't getting you excited. Here, let me help." LeGrande scooted forward and reached between Sean's legs.

Sean leaned sideways, defending himself with his knee. He attempted to break loose, but the restraints held tight. He spit again, striking his target. He expected retribution, but LeGrande laughed instead.

"I get it. You'd rather have Charmaine."

The thought sickened Sean. Pedophile or not, he'd never do a thing to harm this or any child, just as he wouldn't torture LeGrande like LeGrande tortured Doug, even if somehow their situations were reversed. What he *would* do, if he were able, was put a bullet through his head.

LeGrande grabbed for Sean's penis a second time.

Sean drew his leg back and kicked with all his might, landing his foot squarely at the base of LeGrande's balls.

LeGrande recoiled, writhing in pain—then struggled to his feet, dissolving in laughter. *"Now that's fun. That's what I mean. What else you got? Kick me again!"*

Sean was staring at a wild animal, its excitement fueled strictly by violence. He *wanted* to feel pain. He wanted to feel *anything*. A thought came to mind. Sean saw a way to play him.

"You liked that, LeGrande—the pain, the rush. I think maybe, finally, I'm starting to understand."

"You'll never understand me, Jordan. You have too feeble a mind."

"There's nothing at your core except pain, LeGrande. Above that, you're numb. To feel anything, you have to produce ever-increasing highs, requiring levels of violence even you can't achieve. The path's unsustainable. You're an addict, LeGrande. Finding satisfaction will soon be impossible."

LeGrande's face hardened.

"What happened? Did your parents beat you? Did you lose the girl you loved?"

"I don't need any of your psychological bullshit!"

"That's it, isn't it? Was she pretty? Did you love her? Was she your first?" Another thought came to mind. "Did you kill her, too?"

"SHUT UP! JUST FUCKING SHUT UP!"

"You killed her, LeGrande, the girl you loved. What was that like? Do you think about her and miss her and wish she were here?"

His exterior penetrated, pain oozed from inside. He began to hyperventilate in the middle of the room.

"You're a walking dead man, LeGrande," Sean pushed on. "A vacant shell. Since your life's almost over, why not finish the job today? Kill yourself and terminate the emptiness. Do it right here. Treat us to the pleasure of which you're so fond. *Now, LeGrande, while the two of us watch.*"

LeGrande paced like a tiger preparing to pounce.

"End your pain now. You deserve to be free."

"Deserve?" LeGrande shouted. "No one deserves anything. Shit happens!" His face broke into another inappropriate grin. "But then good things happen, too . . . like being bound to a naked thirteen-year-old nearly sitting in your lap. What did you do to deserve that? *Nothing.*"

Sean wasn't taking the bait. He felt the vulnerability of his opponent's psyche. "Lots of random things happen. What I'm talking about is intentional—taking your life to end your pain. You're afraid. Is that it? Might cause you an instant's suffering? You prolong the agony when you take your victims' lives, but you're afraid to take your own with no pain at all. Have you always been a coward, LeGrande?"

LeGrande picked up the sack and threw its contents on the floor: two wrapped sandwiches and a small bottle of water. Without saying a word, he headed for the stairs.

"LeGrande!" Sean called. LeGrande paused. "Maybe I am a pedophile and maybe you're not, but I like myself. You loathe yourself and are scared to do anything about it."

LeGrande pivoted, eyes narrowed to sinister slits. "We'll see who's scared. Wait 'til you see what I've planned just for you.

Chapter 41

ROOTING A MOLE

A grand, Dupree repeated, the word circling in his head. *What could he have seen that cost a thousand dollars? A giant jester's head? A mountain of beads? What use would he have for either of those? Maybe he saw something he thought was grand. A float? Hell, all floats are grand. A grand day? Grand to be with his family? Grand to be alive? God dammit.* Something *had to be grand*.

Hurt strolled into Dupree's office at a quarter past three, eyes stern, arms crossed, as if warning Dupree that his time better not be wasted. His hair was military-short, his complexion cratered. A tattoo of a cross graced his exposed right arm. A fake diamond earring pierced a swollen left ear. Either would have earned demerits on company time, but he was on his own. "You wanted to see me?"

Attitude, as expected. Dupree hated pricks like him—entitlement cops—guys who believed the world owed *them*. Taking him down was an easy task—getting the answers he needed, much tougher. With nothing to grasp but shadows and ghosts, Dupree hadn't a clue where to begin. Regardless, after years of trial and error, he trusted his instincts and went to work. "Sorry to call on your day off, but my back's against the wall."

"I know," Hurt said. "Sean Jordan."

First thing out of his mouth. Dupree had the right man. "Thought maybe you could help."

"Whatever you need."

"Sit down." Dupree took a seat on the edge of his desk, one foot dangling, the other on the floor. He leaned toward Hurt, who slouched in his chair. "First of all, I have to make sure."

"Sure of what?"

"This is a special assignment, Hurt . . . covert . . . sensitive. It'll take an exceptional cop to handle it. You know what I'm saying?"

"Not really."

"Lemme put it to you this way . . . You do hate sex offenders, don't you?"

Hurt sat taller. "Hell, yes. Ask anybody in the department."

Dupree noted the enthusiasm, as if his prey were applying for a job. "Is that so?"

"Yeah, everybody knows."

"So, I can count on that."

"There's no one who hates sex offenders more than I do."

"No one?" Dupree asked.

"No one I know."

Dupree breathed deeply, his expression hardening to steel. "Do you hate them enough to kill one or two?"

Hurt's head jerked back. "I don't know what you're talkin' about. You don't think *I* had anything to do with this?"

"With what, Hurt?" Dupree studied his movements—fingers fidgeting, legs pulsing like pistons.

"Nothing."

"I think you're up to your eyeballs in it. I'm just not sure how."

Hurt forced a laugh. "I can't believe this. My day off—fucking *Lunda* Gras—and I'm bein' accused of *murder.*"

"I got a stiff in the morgue who used to be an offender."

"Not my problem."

"You said you hate offenders and that everybody knows it."

"The guys know how I feel."

"Do they know you hate gays and blacks as well?" Dupree dropped a folder in Hurt's lap. "I also read you beat up a cop—a *female* cop. Was there any particular reason or does everyone know you hate women, too?"

Hurt squirmed. "That was a long time ago. The charges were dropped."

"'A long time ago,' meaning you've changed? That you morphed somehow into a regular sort of guy? Or that you moved from blacks, gays, and women to concentrate on sex offenders?"

"I don't know why we're sittin' here." Hurt's voice grew louder. "You hate offenders as much as *I* do. I heard the Daniels were your friends."

It was a sucker punch Dupree hadn't seen coming. He wanted to lean forward and throttle the prick, but checked his anger and settled down. "I know why *I* don't like sex offenders. But what about you?" The question felt solid. Pay dirt potential.

"I don't like people doin' stuff to little kids."

"No one likes shit coming down on kids. Let's get personal here, Hurt. Why do *you* hate sex offenders?"

"Like I said—"

"Not good enough."

"Fuck you."

"That's right, Hurt. Show that temper."

"I hate 'em for the same reasons everybody else does."

"Not everybody, Hurt. We're talking about you. Why do *you* hate sex offenders?"

The cop stared at the floor. "I have my reasons."

"I'm sure you do. No doubt good ones." Dupree felt the opening. "Look at me!" he yelled. *"Why do you hate sex offenders?"*

"Fuck you!"

"Look at me!"

"I'm not goin' there."

Dupree felt the moment's potential. He knew, now, there was a "there" to go to. He returned to his chair and sat quietly.

"I didn't kill Wile," Hurt said, voice resolute. "But if Sean Jordan walked in here right now, I'd consider it my duty to drive a dagger through his heart."

Dupree wondered: *Is there something about Jordan that elicits such hatred, or is he merely a symbol and easy prey?* He continued without responding. "When Charmaine Breneaux turned up missing, who told you to finger Jordan?"

"I don't know what you're talkin' about."

"The chief issued an APB for Jordan after a hundred guys told him Jordan was involved. We tracked the source of the talk to three: Harrigan, Boutreau, and you."

"Yeah, that's right," Hurt said, "I heard it from Boutreau."

"No, you didn't. Both have been in here already," Dupree lied. "Each fingered *you*. They said *you* were the one who insisted it was Jordan. Why was it important they spread the word?"

Hurt's fidgeting increased. "Everyone knew he'd lied to you—that he'd been near the aquarium and was connected to Wile. The guy was connected to everything. So we assumed—"

"Not we—*you*—perched at the top of the pyramid. Why?"

"*You* knew he did it. You were the one who ordered the bracelet. You knew he was guilty. *Everybody* knew."

"But it started with you. You told everyone it was Jordan."

"It wasn't me. I want to talk to my attorney."

"There's no time for that. A girl's life's at stake. I want the truth, Hurt. Why did you finger Jordan?"

Hurt flew out of his chair. "Because he's guilty of it all!"

Dupree remained seated, let it breathe. He was getting closer but wasn't close enough. Dead ends loomed—then he remembered . . . "Not the first two."

Hurt calmed. "What are you talkin' about?"

"You seem to know everything that goes on around here. How'd you overlook that the semen taken from Daniels and Wile was DNA-negative for Jordan?"

"I—"

"Kind of an important one to miss, don't you think?"

"The comb. They found his DNA on the comb."

262 |

"It was a plant, bright guy. Not one additional scrap of evidence linked to Jordan was found in the house. Somebody planted the comb—somebody who hates sex offenders, somebody who wants us to think Jordan did it, somebody who wants Jordan out of the way. Somebody, I think, who's covering for himself. When we figure out who *that* somebody is, we'll find Charmaine Breneaux." The color drained from Hurt's face.

"Sit down," Dupree demanded. Hurt obeyed. "I'm only going to ask one more time. *Why do you hate sex offenders?*"

Hurt hung his head, his voice barely audible. "My stepfather raped me when I was five."

The words hung in the air, Hurt's motivation clear. "Did you plant the comb?"

"No," Hurt whispered, face toward the floor, "but I might know who did." Dupree's eyes were like lasers. "The guy at the radio station. The guy after Breneaux."

Sure, blame a radio personality. What better way to deflect attention than to name a celebrity who rants against offenders? Dupree knew Breneaux's rants were staged for entertainment. The same had to be true for the other guy. Then again, it was he who named Jordan the day outing began. "What's his name?"

"LeGrande."

Dupree's eyes sprang wide. His head shot back. *Not a...grand. Le... Grande! Did Jordan see him at the museum? And if he had, how would he have known him?* Dupree returned to Hurt, placing the thread on hold. "Let me guess. New guy comes to town who hates sex offenders. He needs an insider. You have a reputation among the force. You find each other and get married. You think he's come to lead the charge, rooting out people you and your buddies despise, when in fact he's using you to advance his career and, at the same time, cover his tracks. Close?"

"Something like that."

"Who smashed Jordan in the face—you, Harrigan, or Boutreau?"

"Give me a fuckin' break. I gave you LeGrande. I'm not rattin' out a fellow officer."

"He's no longer a fellow officer. Put your shield and gun on the desk. You're finished."

"I'm takin' this to arbitration!"

"Be my guest." Hurt placed the items on top of the desk. Dupree locked them in his drawer. "Where does LeGrande live?"

"I don't know," he said, all fight gone. "He's off for the holiday, back on Wednesday."

"Wanna make book on that?" Hurt rose to leave. "Sit down."

Dupree summoned Jas and filled him in, telling him to track down the station's manager and find out where LeGrande lived. He then called Dodd and brought him up to date, recommending he contact the press, with Jordan no longer a person of interest. He also pushed delaying an APB for LeGrande, hoping to catch him at home unaware. He phoned Weinstat to ask for background on LeGrande—in particular, were there sex crimes, lurking in his past. Finally, he asked an officer to phone Tom August, letting Tom know Dupree would miss the parade. "Now you can stand," he said to the rogue cop. They stood and headed for the door.

Dupree's phone rang. "Hold on," he told Hurt.

"Lieutenant, there's a woman on the line," his secretary said. "She sounds hysterical. Insists on talking to you."

"Put her through."

"Lieutenant, this is Laurie Jordan." Her voice was reed thin, high pitched, terrified.

Dupree froze. "Yes, Laurie."

"I stopped at home. Suzanne's dead!"

"Dead? What happened?"

"I found her upstairs—" she said, gasping for air.

"Are you all right?"

"No!" she shrieked. "Ren's missing!"

Every hammer in Dupree's brain pounded in succession. *God DAMMIT!* "I'll be right there."

He looked at Hurt, standing by the door. "Your hero's struck again. You're under arrest."

Chapter 42

A WORLD OF THEIR OWN

CHARMAINE lifted their hands and grabbed for a sandwich, devouring it in a series of ravenous attacks. It felt queer for Sean's hand to move on its own, queerer still to be feeding a thirteen-year-old. He grasped the other sandwich as soon as she was done, unwrapped it with his teeth, and guided it to her mouth. She attacked it, too, and chased it down with water, offering Sean the few drops that were left.

At least we're pulling in the same direction. Feeding Ren as a toddler had been more like a contest, both holding her spoon but with different agendas. Yet, it was in the give and take of those mealtime ballets that they learned to sense each other's rhythms, accommodate each other's temperaments, and appreciate each other's desires while deepening their bond. Here he was, learning another child's rhythms, tethered to her wrist, handcuffed to a wall. Sean couldn't imagine a stranger scenario. *Weinstat would have a field day.*

"Sorry you had to see that," he said.

"Believe me, I've seen worse."

"Really? Where?"

"On the Internet!"

Sean rolled his eyes.

"Was it yucky when he was grabbing at your . . . you know . . . like that?"

"Everything about that man's yucky. That's why I need to stop him."

"Good luck."

Good luck is right. Sean sat, reviewing their situation, guessing there was little chance LeGrande had accepted his challenge. *Bound to a naked thirteen-year-old nearly sitting in your lap.* The words echoed in his head. When he and Charmaine talked, the thought never entered his mind. But in moments of stillness, they crept back in, resuming his questioning, reigniting his doubt. Sure, he was attracted to her. Who wouldn't be, with her sparkling eyes, dimpled cheeks, and budding body hinting that womanhood was near? *It's perfectly natural for people to feel that way,* Vince had professed, seconded by Andrews. But why did other men remain disinterested, at least until girls turned eighteen?

Voices urged him to imagine having sex with Charmaine. He knew if he did and *wasn't* aroused, he'd dismiss the results with a new set of excuses: *disgusting surroundings, lives on the line . . .* If, on the other hand, he did and he *was* . . . He couldn't go there, the thought too frightening.

It has *to be more than a natural attraction.*

Sean arched his head and closed his eyes.

He wondered if, under Vince's wing, he'd grown up too soon, forgoing his childhood, seeking to relive it by befriending kids. Or if in the act of killing his parents, he'd been frozen in time, stuck at eleven, forever preferring friends that age. But each time he paused to consider the possibilities, he realized his friends were all his age or older.

Theories, Vince said. *Intriguing, but wrong.*

Sean glanced at Charmaine. Maybe sex wasn't why he found her attractive. Maybe it was her mix of innocence and grit. She seemed a young lady who could take care of herself even under the most arduous conditions. In addition to her spirit, he appreciated most, her openness toward him despite knowing his status.

Charmaine moved closer, pressing her hip against Sean's. He began to squirm, warmth permeating his body. He felt a rippling in his penis, its hardening horrifying. *She'll see. She'll know! There's no way to cover up!* Vince's words returned: *Penises rise and fall on their own, only sometimes signaling sexual desire.* There was no way he wanted sex with Charmaine, any more than he did with Ren. Still . . .

He told himself he wasn't excited—that he wasn't enjoying the sensuousness of the moment. But as hard as he tried to deny his feelings, Vince kept intervening: *Embrace the truth.*

Embrace the truth? My God. I CAN'T!

Why not? Vince said.

She'll know who I am!

So?

SO?

Despite your old wounds and inconvenient erections, if you live in truth, you'll find you're not a bad guy.

Sean closed his eyes and attempted the impossible: surrendering fully to his deepest truths. He opened slowly to the warmth of Charmaine, tentatively allowing his feelings to emerge. He expected to be aroused but instead felt enlivened by her youthful energy and radiant vitality. *Breathe them into your soul*, Vince whispered. *Allow her spirit to nurture yours.*

Charmaine moved closer. Panic returned. But this time, rather than push fear away, he let it in, too, and gave it free rein.

Something shifted. His heart rate slowed. Worries remained, but they didn't control. Taking her in, he was imbued with a glow centered not in his genitals but deep in his heart. He lingered in the moment, breathing in and out, feeling her essence, nurturing him within. With one long, final exhalation, he let Charmaine go, knowing he neither needed nor wanted anything more.

Sean opened his eyes and laughed.

"What?" Charmaine asked.

"Your toes. The smiley faces."

"Oh, yeah. Cool, huh?"

"Way cool."

Still think you might be attracted to young girls? Vince asked. For the first time in years, the question seemed absurd. Sean loved the girl sitting at his side, fully and unconditionally, and would do anything to protect her. He was attracted to her in the way he'd been to friends in fifth grade—excited by their spirits, sparked by their potentials. Attraction was part of what made him a good psychologist, but attraction was neither the point nor the goal. His purpose was to nurture, mentor, and guide—to father any child needing support.

Sean was amazed and heartened by the insight and wondered why he hadn't seen it years before. Then he realized: Sex offender registration had made all his attractions suspect. He exhaled again, feeling calm and serene, a decade's worth of questioning having come to an end. At long last, knowing had overcome doubt.

"We have to get out of here," he said.

"Right, but how?"

Sean held up their hands and studied her wrist. It was wafer thin, but the cuff was secure. "If only we had something to slice through the ties."

"There's nothing. We've already looked."

Beside a few mannequins, the table in the corner, and the old box of T-shirts tucked underneath, Sean's clothes were the only objects in the room. Closest to them was the nylon jacket.

The jacket. The GUN! The blow to his head must have caused him to forget. "I have to reach that," he said, motioning.

"What can you do with a jacket?"

"You'll see. We have to work together." He lay on the floor, his left leg stretching as far as it could reach.

"What should *I* do?" she asked.

"Tell me how far away I am. I can't see from this angle."

"You mean math?"

Sean rolled his eyes. "Yeah, we're working on *measurement.*" Spreading her thumb and index finger, she held them up so he could see. "Looks like about two inches. What do you think?"

Charmaine shrugged. "Two, I guess."

He stretched again, iron tearing his wrist. She shoved forward, too. *Inch, inch and a half . . .* He kept pushing, stretching, fighting for every sixteenth. He felt the veins in his neck pulsate, the muscles in his leg contract. *"Dammit!"* he said. He lay back, drained.

"Maybe if you try harder," she said.

"Harder?" He laughed. "It's no use."

"What are we gonna do?"

There's got to be a way to move it. He sat up and stared, studying the jacket. "See how the collar's standing on end, tipping in our direction rather than facing away?"

"Yeah. So?"

"The collar's width has to be at least two inches, right?"

"Maybe."

"If I could get it to fall toward us, it might give us the length we need."

"But *how?*"

"The jacket's lightweight. It wouldn't take much." Charmaine began to whistle. "Well, more than just whistling."

"Whistling's how I think. You oughta try."

Sean settled against the wall and attempted to whistle, a rite of passage he never quite mastered. His partner flashed several disapproving glances until he finally sounded a reedy toot. The first was followed by two or three more. "You might be on to something," he said, staring into space.

"Told you. Come up with anything yet?"

"I'm thinking," he said, and whistled again. Suddenly, he bolted forward.

"What?"

"No. No. I *couldn't.*"

"What?"

"I can't."

"Can't *what?*"

He threw his head back, laughing. "But I *have* to."

"Have to *what?*"

"PEE! I've been holding it forever."

"I held it forever once. I think it was in third grade."

"Listen, Charmaine, I know it's gross, but it's the only thing I have to work with."

"*Pee?*"

"We're short of the jacket by an inch and a half. The collar's standing, bending in our direction. See the pucker in the middle? That's the lowest point. If I aim just right and hit the indentation, I have a chance to bring it down, closing the gap."

"Yeah!" Her face lit with excitement.

"Sorry about this. Just close your eyes."

"Are you kidding? There's no way I'm gonna miss *this!*"

He shook his head, disbelieving. "Suit yourself." He studied the situation. "I'll have to get on my knees." He tucked one leg beneath him, shifted his weight onto it, and pulled in the other. "Another thing . . ." he sighed, tugging their mono-arm in his direction. "I need this hand to direct it."

"Not a problem."

The daughter of Burn Breneaux is helping me piss and it's not a problem.

He stared. Concentrated. Waited. But as badly as he had to go, he couldn't.

"What are you waiting for?" she said. "Do it!"

"I'm *trying!* Would you please close your eyes—for *my sake?*"

"Oh, all right."

He concentrated again, picturing himself wading in cool water. His urine began to rise.

"*Wait!*" she shouted.

Agony. "*What?*"

"I was at this pissing contest once. Boys in the neighborhood were showing the girls how far they could pee. The boy who won started real high and came down slowly, like this." She moved her head in an arc. "Thought you'd wanna know."

"Thanks. Anyone get arrested?"

"Heck, no. This is New Awlins!"

Sean concentrated some more. Finally, a few drops trickled forth, followed by a torrent.

"You hit it!" Charmaine exclaimed.

He ignored her and focused, driving the stream forward to the edge of the jacket. Still, the collar remained erect. He feared he'd hit it in front by mistake, forcing it to fall in the wrong direction. He concentrated on the spot in the center and aimed. There was a ripple and a splatter and finally collapse. When the center of the collar plummeted, he aimed side to side, pinning the rest, fast to the floor.

"Quick," he said. They lay on their backs, stretched, and strained. He could feel the wetness under his heel. "Not enough," he said. "Stretch some more." He felt something different, wrinkly and cold. He attempted to tug but his foot slipped free. He stretched one more time, coming down harder, securing the jacket under the heel of his foot. Another tug. The jacket gave way.

"It moved!" Charmaine yelled.

He pulled with his leg, drawing it toward them, bringing it to rest within their reach. *What if LeGrande found the gun?* He guided their hands into the pocket.

"Eww," she said, scrunching her nose.

"Trust me," he said, reaching deeper. Seconds later, he eased out the gun.

Charmaine's eyes widened. *"Cool!"*

"It *would* be if only I knew how to use it."

"What are you gonna do?"

"I haven't thought that far ahead."

"Why don't we shoot out the windows? Then we can scream and somebody might hear."

"I suppose we could try." Sean gripped the gun solidly and raised it in the air. He pointed. Squeezed. Nothing.

"They work better when you release the safety," Charmaine advised. "See the little slider alongside the grip?"

"Let me guess. You and your friends were at a shooting contest once . . ."

"No. My daddy taught me."

Sean again raised the gun, steadied it, and fired, the explosion shattering the silence of the room. But despite the wall being mostly glass, he missed and hit brick, leaving a trail of red dust pouring from the hole.

"You *don't* know how to shoot, do you? She snickered, gleefully. "It's *my* turn!"

"*Your* turn?"

"Yeah. I can at least hit windows."

Sean set the gun down so Charmaine could retrieve it. Without hesitation, she pointed, aimed, and fired. The bullet pierced the glass, but failed to shatter it, creating nothing more than a very small hole. The two of them laughed, and laughter felt good. "Let's think of something else," he said. "I'd hate for someone to get hit by a stray. Also, we need to stop wasting bullets."

Charmaine laid the gun down, Sean shielding it under his leg. He offered a few ideas and she added her own. They talked, planned, and rehearsed for hours. By the time the sun set, Sean felt ready.

Together they listened to a Dixieland band as gaslight flickered on their prison walls. There was a party going on one story below, attended by thousands unaware.

"Sean . . . Jordan," Charmaine said, moonlight streaming through dusty windows.

"Present."

"You don't have to answer this, but . . ."

Sean smiled. "It's not like we've been keeping a whole lot of secrets."

"How did you get to be a sex offender anyway? I mean, like, what did you do?"

Sean closed his eyes, bringing Tyne into focus. "I had a crush on a girl at summer camp. I was eighteen. She was fifteen."

He told her what they did and what she'd meant to him . . . and how a moment of discovery had changed his life. He told her about the Firebird and how he'd stomped it into the ooze; about Laurie and Ren, fearing he might lose them; about Doug and Vince and how he planned to become a psychologist; and about the unhinged Hardys and killing the parents he loved. He told her everything and he cried.

Charmaine sat silent, taking it all in. He expected her to say, "That's not fair. You're *not* a sex offender. You didn't mean to kill your parents." But she refrained, her silence providing far greater support.

Sean's heaving chest yielded to slow, deep breaths as he felt his nakedness, solely on the inside. It was a good feeling . . . the feeling of being known.

Charmaine drew closer and laid her head on his shoulder. "Thank you for not staring."

"Staring?"

"At my body. Every time you look at me, you always look in my eyes."

He watched her fingers on their mutually bound hand inch to the side and interlace his—the same thing Ren did every night before bed.

She squeezed gently.

He did the same.

Chapter 43

CONFIRMATION

RETURNING to the cottage he'd stopped at hours before, Dupree noted the change in the poodle's disposition. The dog had last greeted him with barks and kisses. This time she shook with her tail between her legs, whining pitifully before settling into silence. He bent and stroked her but couldn't bring her peace.

He'd expected to find Laurie flailing with emotion, but by the time he arrived, she'd slipped into shock. "Do you have any idea who might have done this?" he asked. She stared past him, gaze vacuous. "Does the name Del LeGrande mean anything at all?" She barely moved her head. "Have there been any calls—demands for money, threatening messages warning not to call the police?" She continued to stare, presence unavailable. He guessed she hadn't a clue about what was at play. Even if she had, he wasn't going to find out. He offered encouragement, telling her he had leads, but even as he did, her eyes grew more distant.

He descended the front steps, passing members of his team. "The victim's upstairs. The mom's just inside." He approached the ambulance driver angled in the parkway. "The woman needs a doctor. Check her for shock."

Streetlights declared there was no time to waste, Lundi Gras day having turned into night. But a moment of waste was what Dupree's soul craved. Pausing a second as a brass band blared, he spotted a man, paunchy and old, dressed in nothing more than a shiny gold thong, his butt cheeks jiggling in a full-on display. "Toto, we're not in Kansas anymore," Dupree whispered, grateful for a laugh and a moment squandered.

He drove around the Quarter, avoiding ankle-deep trash, and pulled in front of headquarters, greeting Weinstat at the curb. Weinstat struggled to squeeze into the car—then yanked on the belt to buckle himself in. When the belt wouldn't stretch, he threw it aside. "*Hell* with it!" he barked. "Be careful how you drive."

"Happy Lundi Gras to you, too," Dupree said, slamming hard on the pedal, causing a visor full of beads to fall in Weinstat's lap. "Those are for you. Please don't do anything to earn them."

Weinstat winced, sweeping the pile to the floor. "It *was* a happy Lundi Gras 'til I heard from you. Something about duty and friendship. Which is this?"

"It certainly ain't friendship."

They were seated moments later at Dooky Chase, ordering fried chicken, cornbread, and tall lemonades. "What do you have?" Dupree asked.

"Del LeGrande. Sex offender all right. Registered in Chicago a decade ago—then went AWOL. Hasn't surfaced 'til now."

"Not his real name, I'd bet."

"You'd bet right. Try Eric Sax. Dad was an engineer; mom stayed home. He joined the Marines at nineteen after killing his father with his fists."

"Really."

"An argument escalated and the old man lost. The kid claimed self-defense. Had the scars to prove his father nearly killed *him*."

"The sins of the father . . . ?"

"Maybe," Weinstat said, adding extra sugar to his lemonade. "But don't forget, some monsters are made; others are born. If you're dealing with a bad seed, it wouldn't matter if the Cleavers were his parents."

Dupree nodded. "Anything else?"

"I'm just warming up. In the military, he was assigned to explosives. Learned his trade well. Even received a few commendations. Would've continued to prosper if he hadn't gotten caught raping an eight-year-old while on leave in Thailand."

"Girl or boy?"

"At eight, there's no difference."

The waitress arrived with two platters of chicken. Dupree listened and ate; Weinstat talked with his mouth full.

"After the military kicked him out, he returned to Chicago, entered sex offender therapy, and immediately dropped out."

"Jordan."

"Exactly."

"But there's no way to prove the connection."

"You're gonna kiss me for this. I already have."

"How?"

"I called your friend, Andrews, the shrink in Chicago, and explained the situation—two girls kidnapped, another one murdered, and the likelihood of another bomb going off in New Awlins."

"That's all it took? Reasoning?"

"That, and I told him I was married to the daughter of Chicago mob boss, Anthony DeCiloni, and that I'd stop at nothing to find out if Jordan and LeGrande had been in therapy together. They had. After that, the doctor spilled everything. I couldn't get him to shut up."

"Your cheek, your ass . . . What do you want me to kiss first?"

"Save it for when we can be alone. About the other thing. You were right. Andrews was the one other person who knew about Jordan killing his parents."

"And?"

"The night before they died, there'd been a storm. The electricity went out. Scared, Jordan lit a candle and made his way to his parents' room where he heard noises."

"What kind of noises?"

"Fucking noises—moans, shrieks, sighs . . . the kind *you* used to make. His father must have seen the light in the hallway. He told him to wait while they covered up—then invited him in. The three of them sat, listening to the storm, with the candle cradled in Jordan's lap.

"The following morning, the furnace blew. Jordan couldn't remember if he'd blown out the candle. He assumed he hadn't—that a spark had escaped and he was responsible.

"Except for Wile, and much later Andrews, he never whispered a word of it to anyone, especially William Hardy. But because of his uncle's fire-and-brimstone speeches, vilifying among others Jordan's free-spirited parents, Jordan came to believe that somewhere along the line, he and his parents had done something wrong. The explosion was not only proof of their sins, but also the punishment for it. According to Andrews, years of therapy failed to convince him otherwise."

Dupree sighed. "Ninety days in juvie must have seemed a mild sentence for a minor crime, if Jordan actually believed he'd killed his parents."

Jas entered the restaurant and walked to their booth.

Weinstat stood to leave. "I'm catching a cab. Gotta get back to the family." He looked at Dupree. "And since you currently have no family—just a job at several pay grades above mine—you need to get to work. Don't bother to get up."

"*Hey!*" Dupree barked before Weinstat reached the door. "Is there a Chicago mob boss, Anthony DeCiloni?"

"Sure hope not, with me droppin' his name all over town."

Dupree turned to Jas. "Tell me something I don't already know."

"Station's general manager's a guy named Manning. I left messages the past couple of hours—finally caught him a few minutes ago. Defensive as hell. But I got him to give me LeGrande's address and cell number. He's subletting in the Pontalbas. St. Anne and Chartres, second floor."

"You didn't call the number, did you?"

"And tip him off? No way, Lieutenant."

"Good." Dupree phoned Dodd to report LeGrande's location.

Dupree fought through traffic to get to Jackson Square, finding tactical police already in position. In camouflage fatigues, helmets, goggles, and boots, they looked like everyone else battling zombies around town. Dupree gave the command. The police broke through the door. Del LeGrande was nowhere to be found.

The apartment was clean with nothing out of place, its modern motif contrasting with the building's grace and age. Dupree opened the refrigerator and peeked inside, half expecting to see skulls, dissolving in acid. But everything seemed fine. Anyone might have lived there. Anyone, that is, with lots and lots of money.

Checking under the bed, he found stacked magazines, the first featuring a woman, hanging by her wrists, the second showing a man, killing animals with an axe. *Jesus! He has to be our guy.* In the living room, he found a cabinet with DVDs. None had labels. All looked homemade. He pressed "open" on the player and found one loaded inside.

An unimaginable picture sprang onto the screen: a woman being raped beside a man being beheaded. Dupree grabbed the remote, desperate to turn it off, fingers hammering all but the right buttons. He threw it on the floor and stared at his hands, as if checking to make sure they hadn't become infected. Feeling his stomach convulse, he rushed to the john. *Charmaine. Ren.* He knew what could happen.

"Can I do anything for you, Lieutenant?" Jas asked, holding evidence in latex-wrapped hands.

"I'm fine," Dupree answered, struggling to stand. He headed for the balcony in need of fresh air. Sprawled beneath him was the world's greatest party, yet when he looked out, all he felt was afraid.

"Miguel?" Dupree kept his lips close to his phone, speaking loudly enough to be heard above the crowd.

"Señor Owen?"

Dupree could barely hear. "How are you? Are you all right?"

"I'm fine, señor."

"Is Sandy there?"

"No, she went to a party."

"Then where's Jenna?" He'd called to *calm* his nerves, not magnify them.

"Say again, *por favor.*"

"*Jenna!* Where's *Jenna?*"

"She's right here, next to me, asleep on the couch." Dupree's shoulders slumped. "Do you want me to wake her?"

"No, let her sleep, but do me a favor. Keep a close eye on her, and . . ." He pictured himself wrapping his arms around the girl. "Kiss her on the forehead for me."

Jas stepped onto the balcony and reached out his hand. In his palm was a green and brown object, screws protruding from one end, wires from the other. "What do you make of this, Lieutenant?"

Without his glasses, it looked like a toy. But when Dupree put them on . . . *Fuck!* He recognized it immediately from seminars he'd attended, staffed by ex-military working for Homeland Security. It was a sophisticated fuse, part of a remote detonating device. Its purpose: to wreak havoc from a distance without dirtying one's hands.

Dupree ordered the officers to stand guard at the building and took off once more into the cool night air.

Chapter 44

NOTHING TO LOSE

LEGRANDE entered Ren's room with a sedated girl in his arms and laid her gently across the bed. *Asleep in her own room—the one place no one would look.* He felt madly euphoric, trippy, and vengeful. *"Walking dead man." "Empty shell." Jordan, who do you think you are? You're the one facing extinction, while I've got it all.* All except Harper and her stringy blond hair.

Harper. He pictured her face and felt a longing. *How did Jordan know? Is he really that smart, or does psychology imbue him with special powers? And if* he *knows, how soon before* others *know? Maybe it's true. Maybe I am an addict, the bar to satisfaction rising precipitously. I can't come without violence. When that no longer works, what next?*

LeGrande cautioned himself to stay the course, remain disciplined, and work his plan. He reviewed what remained to be done in the morning, as well as what he'd done that afternoon. He'd spent hours at the museum with unrestricted access after flashing his press pass at an unsuspecting guard. There, he located the floats for Rex, planting explosives under each of the axels. Finally, he found the perfect place to hide a four-year-old on route to her final destination.

Straightening Ren on top of the bed, he tucked a sheet under her chin. "Sleep tight," he said. "Tonight we're going to a *museum*."

LeGrande heard a roar emanating from Bourbon Street, enticing him to join the raucous celebration. *Not tonight, boys. I've got more exciting things to do.* He crossed Decatur at Cafe du Monde and saw what looked like armed guards by the Pontalbas. Scanning the block, he spotted three more. A bloated police presence was expected under the circumstances, but this was different. Something was wrong. Drawing closer, he saw another—this one kneeling below his balcony. His eyes ascended to the second floor. The doors to his apartment were standing wide open!

What the FUCK!

He lowered his head and kept on walking. *It can't be. How could anyone have found out?* He felt dizzy and disoriented. Everything was a blur. He dashed into a souvenir shop, donned a mask and wig—then shoved his way back into the middle of the throng.

"What are you doin'?" someone yelled, pushing back.

LeGrande stumbled to the ground, taking a young couple with him. After struggling to stand, he turned and bolted, running headlong into a horse ridden by a cop.

"*Hey!*" the policeman hollered, flashing a threatening glare, yanking on the reigns to keep the horse from stampeding. The horse turned and reared, taking the cop with him, providing LeGrande an opening to disappear. He turned down Conti, fought his way up the street, spotted a bar, and ducked inside.

"What can I getcha, good lookin'?" Molly yelled, over the heads of dozens of clamoring customers.

LeGrande wanted only a place to rest, but was directed to the sign: "One drink minimum." "*Coke,*" he shouted, over the drunken roar.

A TV screen hanging beneath photos of the Saints went blank to the disappointment of the spirited crowd, resuming seconds later with a "Special Bulletin."

"*Quiet!*" Molly demanded.

A picture of Jordan appeared above the scroll: "No longer a person of interest in the abduction of Charmaine Breneaux."

LeGrande's mind raced, scrambling for a clue, trying to make sense of what might have happened.

The scroll continued . . . "Popular radio talk-show personality . . ." Then *LeGrande's* face appeared.

"FUCK ME!" he screamed, attracting no more than a few sideways glances. In an instant, he'd lost it all—a spectacular career and the freedom to do as he pleased. He'd played it smart, respected the tenants, acted cautiously, and taken his time. Yet none of it mattered. Jordan was right. There was no time remaining. His life was done.

He ducked into the bathroom and pictured his father. *"It's your fault, you bastard. You never understood."*

He felt a strange feeling—a tingling of emotion. Maybe it was what people felt just before they cried. He'd spilled tears when his father brutalized him as a kid, but he beat them back, vowing retribution. After that, he never cried again, not even when he realized Harper was gone. He shook off the feeling and returned to the bar.

All that was left was his final play—one last thrill before the itch went away. He reached for his cell and dialed the police. "This is Del LeGrande, the guy you're looking for. Give me someone important." Seconds later, Dupree was on the line. "I don't know how you did it . . . I'm sure you think you won, but don't forget . . . I've got the girls. This Mardi Gras's the one *everyone*'ll remember."

LeGrande threw his phone into the trash and headed for the Marigny to pick up Ren.

Dupree called Jas. "Still have LeGrande's number?" Jas rattled it off. "Same one I've got. He just called. Find out from where."

Lundi Gras was nearly over. LeGrande would strike tomorrow. A terrifying image entered Dupree's mind: Charmaine screaming for help, her arm straining to reach him—then a buzzer going off with a game show host blathering, "Oh, too bad. Better luck next time." It felt to Dupree as if his luck had run out.

The phone rang. "You won't believe this," Jas said, sounding out of breath. "The call originated from Shannon 'N Molly's."

Dupree leaped in his car without saying a word and sped toward the bar, red lights blazing. *"Get out of the way!"* he yelled, waving revelers aside as the car took the curb, bumping up onto the sidewalk. He felt for his gun but kept it in its holster, approached the front door, and stepped inside. His eyes swept the bar. The crowd seemed engaged, enjoying the festivities. If the killer was there, his presence was undetected.

"Molly!" Dupree shouted.

"Hi, Owen. Be with you in a minute."

He raced to where she was standing. "This can't wait. We tracked a guy to a phone call placed here. Anything unusual happen in the last half hour? Anyone you don't recognize?"

"Owen, it's Lundi Gras. Half I recognize; the rest are from Pluto." Molly's face suddenly lit. "There was a guy a while ago. Ordered a Coke. Stood talking to himself—then disappeared into the bathroom. When he came out he looked wasted."

Dupree glanced around. *"Everyone* looks wasted."

"No. Different from alcohol. *Upset* wasted. Last time I saw him, he was standing over there."

Dupree dashed to where Molly was pointing. Nothing seemed out of the ordinary. No one looked suspicious. Next to him was a trashcan, teeming with bottles, with cigarette butts floating in liquid remains, and . . . He looked closer. Wedged between a Dixie Blackened Voodoo and an empty bottle of Jack was a shiny new cell phone similar to his own. Dupree pulled it out and waved it over his head. Molly smiled. Jas met him at the door.

"No LeGrande. Just his phone." Dupree slapped it in Jas's hand. "What was he doing at the museum, where's he holding the girls, and what's he planning to blow up next? Hopefully that'll give you some answers. You said the station manager was 'defensive as hell.' Why?"

Jas shrugged.

"I'm gonna find out."

Dupree rolled into Manning's drive minutes past 11:00. He was greeted at the door by an aging Southern belle. The woman in a green robe and gold-trimmed slippers glared, grumbling about the late-night intrusion, particularly the lights left flashing on his car, providing grist for neighborhood gossip. She informed him that her husband had gone to bed, having lost both his breadwinners in a span of three days.

Dupree didn't care. "We all have our problems, ma'am. Kids' lives are at stake." She hesitated seconds longer—then let him in, escorting him not to a bedroom, but to an office down the hall. The station manager lay sprawled across his desk, a tumbler of whisky clutched in one hand.

"I hope you can help him," she said with despair, leaving the opulent room through ten-foot-tall doors.

Helping Manning was the last thing on his mind. "Wake up," he yelled, wrenching the glass from his hand. "I'm Detective Lieutenant Owen Dupree. I need answers and you're going to give them to me." Manning moaned, raising his head off the desk. "What brought LeGrande to New Awlins?"

"*I* did," he roared, hands flapping in air. "He was hot in LA, but the network wanted him here—to groom him for the day . . ." Manning slumped and whispered, "LeGrande sped up the timetable."

"What do you mean?"

"He took Burn's kid to cripple him."

"Why?"

"To *take over*. I knew he was ambitious, but—"

"When he was outing people on the radio, did you know he'd been convicted of raping a child?"

"*Fuck you*," Manning replied.

"I'll take that as a no."

"Radio was dying. iTunes killed music. The Internet threatened news. That left talk. We tried liberal, but everybody kept agreeing—it was *kumbaya* every day of the week. Who wants to listen to a goddamn love fest? So we went conservative, rode the anger of the Bush years, pumped up the volume with Obama, and made lots of money. Hate sells. Who would have thought?" Dupree looked around at the mahogany French doors, Venetian candelabras, and gold chandeliers, picturing them paid for in human suffering. Manning's head started to roll. "I just never expected . . ." The rest was unintelligible.

"How does Sean Jordan fit?"

Manning steadied himself. "I don't know," he said, speech halting and sing-song. "He came to the office."

Dupree's ears perked. "Why?"

"To complain."

"About what?"

"Us outing him."

"What happened?"

"I gave him the facts of life and threw him out."

"Who else was there?"

Manning stared into space. Finally he remembered. "Burn . . . Del . . . Marilyn . . ."

"Back up. LeGrande was there?"

"Yeah, why?"

"Did he and Jordan see each other?"

"Of course. I introduced them."

Dupree hid his surprise. "So they got a good look at each other."

"Yeah, so what?"

"Did they recognize each other?"

Manning looked perplexed. "Why would they? They just met."

Dupree paced the room. *If Jordan had recognized LeGrande, LeGrande might have killed him to prevent him from talking. But if Jordan hadn't recognized him, LeGrande might have murdered Wile to scare Jordan out of town before the connection could be made. But Jordan didn't cave. He smashed the bracelet as an act of defiance. LeGrande must have known. But how?* Dupree slapped his forehead. *Hurt.*

Manning lay with his head on the desk. Dupree took him by the shoulders. "Wake up, old man. How do you know LeGrande took Burn's kid?"

Manning shrugged. "I saw it on television."

Jesus. Dupree scuttled a laugh.

LeGrande was smart, planting Jordan's comb in the girl's bedroom and Jordan's name in Hurt's warped mind. Just not smart enough to sustain a career full of potential.

"We searched the Pontalbas. He wasn't there. Where else might he be?"

"Who the fuck knows? I never want to see the prick again. Now . . ." Manning mumbled, bloodshot eyes glazed. "Do you have what you need?"

"I'll have what I need when every kid in this city is tucked in bed safe at home." Dupree headed for the door. "You might want to rethink that format of yours. Hate's gonna cost you more than your love fest ever did."

Dupree sat on the drive feeling his body shut down. He knew he needed to somehow keep going, but couldn't focus a minute longer, gallons of caffeine having lost their effect. *Two hours rest. Then I'll be good*. He pulled into the street and headed for home.

His clock read: 12:00.

"Happy Mada Gras," he whispered, to no one but himself.

Chapter 45

MARDI GRAS MAMBO

FLOATS. What's Jordan's fascination with floats? Dupree lingered in the shower an extra five minutes, watching yesterday's filth drain to some other part of town. He'd awakened to Charmaine Neville's *Mardi Gras Mambo*, blaring from his radio at a quarter past six. He'd scrambled out of bed and checked for calls, hoping in vain that LeGrande had been found. Then he dashed for the shower. Now he didn't want to leave.

Jordan was looking at floats when he spotted LeGrande. Sure, floats are fascinating. But what was it about them that caught his attention? Maybe he was surprised to see them built on wagons, instead of on cars like in high school parades. Maybe it was more about their massive size—large enough to accommodate a krewe, equipment, and supplies. Maybe he was drawn to one of the giant heads, filled with cups, beads, and Spanish doubloons.

No. Dupree flung back the curtain and grabbed for a towel. *Jordan's leaving had nothing to do with floats. He didn't say, "Floats." He said, "LeGrande." But how had he recognized him if he hadn't at the studio? More importantly, what was LeGrande doing hanging around the museum?*

Museum. The guy's got a thing for museums. He's already blown up one. Dupree wondered why he hadn't thought of it before. The parade museum, filled with tourists and floats, was one of Mardi Gras' leading epicenters. Everything originated there. LeGrande and the girls could be lying in wait at any of a thousand locations close by.

Dupree called Dodd and spelled out his suspicions.

"Are you sure?"

"No, I'm not sure, but it's the best I've got. The pieces fit."

"I'll take it from here. How soon can you get there?"

"Twenty minutes . . . unless I get hung up by a parade."

Dupree arrived with planes flying overhead, news trucks racing into position, and police keeping onlookers at bay. Cameramen scrambled for superior vantage points while bomb-sniffing dogs strained to be released. SWAT appeared, armed and ready, and wasted no time surrounded the building.

Dupree spotted Dodd and sprinted in his direction. "What's going on in there?"

"Wished to hell I knew. I've been calling the museum for the past half hour. All I get's a recorded message." Dodd wiped sweat from the back of his neck. "Keep your eyes open. It's showtime, folks." He reached for a megaphone and raised it to his lips.

"This is New Awlins Chief of Police, Clarence Dodd. The museum is under police protection. We want everyone inside to line up single file and quickly and calmly exit the building." Everyone waited— SWAT, police, reporters, and bystanders—expecting to see hundreds, filing out of the building. Nothing happened as two minutes passed.

"This is Chief of Police Dodd. Everyone inside, line up in single file . . ." No one responded. "What is this?" he said to Dupree.

A shadow appeared in the window by the entrance. Seconds later, the door creaked open. A lone man in uniform stepped outside, hands behind his head in a show of surrender. A police officer charged in the man's direction, handcuffed his wrists, and delivered him to Dodd.

"Who are you?" Dodd demanded.

"Richard Speers, security for the museum."

"What the hell's goin' on in there?"

The guard shook his head. "Nothin'. There's nobody inside."

Dupree couldn't believe it.

"Where are all the goddamn floats?" Dodd bellowed.

"They left hours ago," the guard said. "By now, they gotta be all over the city."

Dodd threw down the megaphone and pivoted toward Dupree. "Any more bright ideas? I'm as good as canned."

Dupree reached in his jacket and handed over his shield. "Here, give him mine while you're at it. On second thought . . ." He yanked it back. "I'll deliver it myself so I can shove it up his ass."

Dodd kicked the ground. "God *dammit!*"

"We took our best shot. We know LeGrande was at the museum. Why . . . if he didn't intend to blow the place up?"

"Who knows?" Dodd huffed. "Maybe he likes floats."

"Or maybe . . ." Dupree tightened his fists. "He likes *groups* of floats. He could do a lot more damage and create a lot more terror, blowing up a parade flanked by thousands of spectators."

Dodd thrust a finger in Dupree's face. "If you think I'm gonna disrupt every parade in town, scaring half a million people because you have another idea . . ." They looked up in unison as a helicopter roared by. "You're *nuts.*" He turned and stormed off.

Dupree thought about the girls. There was no other option. If he had to, he'd search every float himself.

Chapter 46

PARTNERS

THROUGHOUT the night, Sean had reassured Charmaine, who'd awakened frequently to the sound of her crying. "I'm afraid," she'd whimpered, to which he'd replied, "There's nothing to be afraid of," desperate to make it so.

Sean didn't want to die. Realizing so was a revelation. He'd courted death repeatedly since the day Doug was killed. Now he wanted to live . . . to experience life without asking the questions, free of the doubt that accompanied the asking. He wanted to walk from his prison walls, knowing he was good man despite others' opinions. He wanted to wrap his arms around Ren, kiss her on the cheek, and be the father he wished to be. He wanted to deliver Charmaine to safety, thanking her for being the gift that she was, especially for enlightening him to the truth of his nature. He wanted to fly like the pure white crane, appreciating life like he had as a kid.

Once Charmaine settled in a restful sleep, Sean grew drowsy and nodded off as well. His dreams were filled with frustration and longing. Then his parents appeared, comforting him by their presence. They were sitting on their bed, propped against the headboard, faces aglow from the flame of a candle. The candle was nestled between Sean's legs atop a small China plate with a butterfly border.

Without any warning, the room fell dark.

"I'm afraid!" Charmaine called out in the dream—her voice recognizable, her presence unseen. She climbed into bed, hands searching in the darkness, finally squeezing between Sean and his mom.

Talk to her, Sean, Vince said in the dream.

"My parents are here. They'll keep us safe."

"No!" she cried, "I can't see a thing. Everything's black. I must have gone blind."

"You haven't gone blind. It's dark for me, too."

"But why is it dark? Something *terrible's* happened."

I'm lost here, Vince. What should I say?

You're not lost at all. You're inches away. Simply tell her the truth.

What truth? Sean asked, still sound asleep.

Charmaine's not asking, "Why is it dark?" You are. Replay the dream. Remember what happened.

"Trust me, Charmaine. Everything's fine."

He pictured himself entering the room, holding the candle, and climbing into bed. He looked at his parents, covered by a sheet, and noticed the warmth in both their expressions. He gazed at the candle cradled in his lap, took a deep breath, and—

"If everything's fine," she cried, *"why is it dark?"*

"Because I . . . I . . . blew out the candle."

Sean woke with a shock, eyes flaring wide. He'd looked through a portal and recalled it all—extinguishing the flame, smelling the sulfur, positioning the candle securely on the nightstand.

It wasn't a dream.

Memories poured forth, flooding his senses, confirming the truth he'd buried for years.

"I didn't kill my parents."

"Of course not," Charmaine said, still half asleep. "Nobody kills their parents, even when they want to. Happy Mada Gras."

"Maybe the best ever," Sean replied.

"Best *ever?*" Charmaine stretched as well as she could.

"Yeah . . . well . . . *maybe*." His voice was upbeat. "We've got a lot going for us, don't you think? Like a gun. And a *plan*."

"What time is it?"

"Close to noon, I imagine."

"I'm scared," she said, leaning her head on his chest.

"Me, too, a little. But you know what? When this is over, you'll have amazing stories to tell your friends."

"Like being protected by a sex offender."

"See," he said. "They'll think that's way cool."

"Martina will."

"Who's Martina?"

"A friend . . . some of the time. She's kinda the school slut."

"Really," Sean said. "What makes her a slut?"

"For one thing, she never stops talking about boys. And at least once a week, she colors her toenails."

"You're a great kid, Charmaine." She burrowed her head in the crook of his arm, heartbeat palpable through the tips of her fingers.

"What are you gonna tell *your* friends when you get back?" she asked.

"I don't have as many as I used to—mostly Laurie and Ren. I'm gonna tell them I love them and hug them every day for a week."

"Why not a month?"

"Yeah—a *month*. That's a great idea."

"If you want, I'll be your friend," she said. "That way, you'll at least have three."

Sean squeezed her hand. "Done deal."

A *CREAK* sounded at the top of the stairs. LeGrande had chosen to live another day. They glanced at each other—then across the room, Sean telling himself he had to remain calm despite knowing how easily things could go wrong. Together they needed to work their plan. He squeezed her hand. She squeezed back.

"*Good mo'nin' . . . N'Awlins!*" LeGrande called out, mimicking Breneaux as he bounded into the room. He studied his captives, leering at their nakedness. "If you aren't the coziest peas ever to share the same pod."

Sean felt like meat, being inspected by a butcher. Charmaine inched away, affording access to the gun.

"So, Dr. Freud, how was Charmaine?"

"Knock it off, LeGrande."

"The pedophile didn't take a *turn?*"

"I know who I am." The words felt right. It was a new feeling— rock solid and true.

"Whatever you say. Half an hour from now, Rex'll lumber down Canal. That leaves enough time for me to deliver on my promises."

"How are you going to do it?" Sean asked. *Keep him talking. Buy some time.*

"Do what?"

"Blow up the parade. Is it set to a timer?"

"EEEEE!" LeGrande squawked, imitating a buzzer. "Wrong." He pulled the detonator out of his pocket and dangled it inches in front of Sean's face. "There's no way to know exactly when the floats'll pass by. With a detonator, I'm in control. Learned that in the Marines. See this cover?" Sean cocked his head to look. Before he could answer, LeGrande flew into a rage. *"I asked you a question!"* He drew back his leg and kicked Sean in the gut.

Choking with pain, Sean pictured the gun. He wanted to grab it, but wisely refrained.

"Let's try that again. See this cover?"

"Yes," Sean managed, gasping for air.

LeGrande flipped it open, turning the device on its side. "See the little red button?"

"Yes."

"Press Mr. Red . . ." LeGrande shrugged. "No more parade." He played catch with the mechanism, tossing it like a toy. "So what are we waiting for? Let the games begin!"

LeGrande moved cautiously, retrieving the key, removing his shirt, unbuckling his belt. Then, without warning, he lunged for Charmaine.

Sean tapped her finger and felt her tap back. LeGrande grabbed her legs.

"*NO!*" she wailed.

Sean glided their mono-hand inches to the left, felt the steel of the gun, and wrapped his fingers around it. Together, they raised it to within an inch of LeGrande's face.

"Don't move," Sean ordered.

"What are you doing?"

"Considering whether to blow your head off."

"You wouldn't."

"I would. I'm highly motivated," he said, voice steady.

LeGrande's eyes darted about the room.

"If you're thinking about running, think about this. While you were blowing stuff up for the Marines, I was training sharpshooters— the elite of the Infantry. I can hit a quarter at a hundred yards. Here's what you're going to do. Keep your eyes fixed on Charmaine's." LeGrande glanced to one side. "*ARE YOU LISTENING?*" LeGrande's eyes returned. "Better. Now. Very slowly, unlock Charmaine's cuff. One slip, the gun goes off."

LeGrande tried to slide the key into the mechanism, frustration mounting as he struggled to find the hole. "*Fuck this.*"

"Patience, LeGrande. The parade isn't due for fifteen more minutes. Uh, uh . . . eyes on Charmaine." LeGrande looked at the girl—then at the gun.

"How do you expect me to unlock it if I can't look at it?"

"Find a way." The key slid in place. The cuff sprung open. Charmaine's arm fell flaccidly to the floor. "Now, on hands and knees, back up ten feet." LeGrande complied. Suddenly he leapt and bolted for the stairs.

Sean pulled the trigger. The gun fired with a roar. LeGrande stood frozen in the middle of the room.

"That was a warning," Sean improvised. "Next time I'll put a bullet through your head. Back on your knees. Slide the key to Charmaine." LeGrande crouched and glided it in her direction.

"I can't pick it up," she cried, fingers failed to work.

"You're doing fine." Sean kept his eyes on LeGrande. "Shake your hand a few times. The blood'll return."

Within seconds, she was able to grasp the key and use it as a wedge to pry loose the tie. Slipping her hand free, she inserted the key, unlocking Sean's cuff with one quick turn.

The whoosh of freedom was electric. "Now, slowly take the detonator out of your pocket, set it on the floor, and crawl back six feet. If you lift the cover, I'll shoot you between the eyes."

Suddenly, excruciating pain erupted. After days of disuse, Sean's arm begged surrender, the weight of the gun becoming unbearable. His face contorted. His grip went limp. The gun fell from his hand, crashing to the floor. LeGrande seized the opportunity and dashed for the stairs.

Sean reached with both hands and grasped the gun, firing as LeGrande reached the stairs.

A wail rang out. Tumbling was heard.

Charmaine turned to Sean. "I thought you couldn't shoot."

"I can't. I wasn't aiming at anything at all."

Muscles numb, they struggled to stand, leaning on each other to keep from toppling. Sean grabbed a shirt from inside the box and tossed it to Charmaine along with his briefs—then threw on a tee and tugged on his jeans. They staggered toward the stairs the best they could, appearing like partners in a two-legged race. Reaching the landing, they carefully climbed down, following blood into the alley.

Sean opened the door and gulped fresh air. None had ever tasted so sweet. They rounded the corner, heading for Canal, and spotted a young officer with a serious expression. "This is Charmaine Breneaux," Sean said to B. Shipley, according to the nameplate fastened to his shirt. Shipley turned away without saying a word, failing to hear in the din of celebration. "Charmaine Breneaux! The girl who was kidnapped."

Shipley caught on and stared in amazement. "Breneaux?"

"Yes, and you found her." Sean imagined the citation the officer would receive. "Please take her home."

"Of course. Right away."

Sean turned to Charmaine and ran a finger down her cheek, sealing her in his memory, bidding a silent goodbye. She threw her arms around him and held on tight, tears flowing freely down to her chin. "I'm really glad you didn't kill your parents."

"Me too," Sean said, feeling his own tears stir. "Thanks to you, I don't need these anymore." He retrieved from his pocket the keys to the car and laid them gently in the palm of her hand. An instant later, he disappeared into the crowd.

Sean reached for his wallet, praying Dupree's card was still there. He found it tucked behind a picture of Ren, and turned toward two guys standing feet away, their hats turned sideways, their pants half-way down. "Listen, can I use your phone? I gotta call the police."

The pair flashed back incredulous expressions. "You're ax'n us for a phone to call da po-*lice*?" said the one whose pants rose a little higher.

"Somebody's gonna blow up the Rex Parade."

"Rex? Shit. We're goin' to *Zulu!*"

"Really!" Sean said. "I have to use your phone. One minute is all I'm asking."

The other, with the more exposed rear end, took out a phone and slapped it in Sean's hand. "One minute."

"Dupree. It's Sean Jordan."

"Who? I can't hear a thing."

"Sean Jordan!"

There was a moment of silence on the other end of the phone. "Are you fuckin' with me?"

"I'm calling the number you gave me. I didn't have anything to do with it. The guy you want is Del LeGrande. Charmaine's safe. I handed her over to an Officer Shipley. LeGrande's got a detonator. He's gonna blow up the parade."

"Which parade?"

"The *Rex* Parade." Sean heard a roar rise in the background. He looked up Canal at the lead cops on horseback, signaling that the parade was rounding the corner. "The detonator's remote controlled. You have to disperse the crowd—get everyone off the floats."

"Where are you?"

"Canal Street. Ground zero."

"Sean."

"Yeah?"

"You need to know this."

"Know what?"

The words stuck in Dupree's throat. "LeGrande's got Ren."

Chapter 47

DESPERATION

ONE girl was safe; another was in jeopardy. So were thousands more, with the parade inching toward the river. Dupree knew he had to stop it, even if it meant lying in the tractor's path. But could he do it in time? *The girl*, he kept thinking. *The girl* . . . Sprinting toward Canal, he reached for his phone: "It's the Rex Parade!" he told Dodd. "We gotta get everyone off!" There was no answer. He looked at the phone in time to see one bar disappear, replaced with "no signal." Seconds later, two bars returned. He entered a different number and quickly pressed *call*.

"*Tom. It's Owen,*" he hollered over the crowd.

"Hey, Owen. Happy Mada Gras! Where *are* you? It ain't the same without you and Breneaux."

Dupree bent at the waist, gasping for air, his voice a mixture of croaks, pants, and whispers. "Tom. Listen to me. You gotta get off that float. The floats are rigged with explosives."

"What's that, Owen? It's real hard to hear."

Dupree held up the phone and shook it in anger. "*Explosives!*" he shouted. "*Get off the float!*"

"Okay," Tom said.

Dupree felt a massive wave of relief.

"See ya 'round four. And don't forget the barbecue sauce."

Jesus have mercy! Dupree raced to Canal Street, air searing his lungs. He heard cheers ring out and watched spectators lunge forward as the lead float approached with Tom at its helm. Dupree ran toward him, waving his arms—then realized *everyone* was waving their arms.

He tried Dodd again but his screen fell dark. In the turmoil he'd forgotten to charge his phone. *What else can go wrong?* Without his phone, he was on his own.

The lead tractor was key. If he could signal the driver and get him to stop, everything behind would be forced to halt. He finally stood opposite the front of the float, but remained separated by a six-foot-deep crowd. He dove in, shoving desperately, clawing at revelers to break through to the street. "What the hell are you doing?" one shouted. "We've stood here for hours!"

A cop working the crowd grabbed Dupree by the sleeve. "No, you don't. You're coming with me."

Dupree scrambled for his badge and reached to present it. Just as he did, he took an elbow to the ribs, knocking the shield from his hand to the street. Bending to retrieve it, he looked down in horror as someone kicked it sideways onto the grate of a sewer. It lay, inches away, balanced precariously on narrow slats. He broke free and lunged, but was snagged again by the cop. *"I'm NOPD!"* Dupree shouted. *"A detective!"*

"Show me your badge," the cop snapped back.

Dupree looked down. The shield was gone. There was no time for proof or disbelieving cops. He broke free again and fought through the crowd, making his way to the front of the tractor. He called to the driver, but the driver swerved, seemingly in an attempt to shake the intruder. Dupree grabbed hold and mounted the step, prompting the driver to land a carefully aimed blow that sent Dupree reeling to the street once more. With three cops approaching, reaching for their guns, Dupree scrambled to his feet and grabbed onto the float.

"Owen, what are you doing?" Tom shouted.

"The float's a rolling bomb!"

"*What?*"

"Get everyone off!"

The cops climbed aboard, guns aimed at Dupree. "You're under arrest. Turn around. Spread 'em."

Dupree knew if he did, they'd all die in seconds.

LeGrande's got Ren. Dread turned to terror. Sean stood, frozen, knives plunging into his heart. *Not this. Please. Anything but this.* A torrent of memories flashed through his mind—Ren placed in his arms as soon as she was born, eyes eagerly greeting their first rays of light . . . It was heartbreaking enough losing his wife. Losing Ren . . . he'd never survive.

He felt wild, psychotic, out of control. *"WHERE IS SHE?"* he hollered at the top of his lungs.

A young girl walked by, accompanied by an adult. In the crazed, warped reality of Sean's altered mind, he was convinced it was Ren being whisked away. He lunged at the man, holding her hand, grabbed his shirt, and wrestled him to the ground.

"What the fuck!" the man shouted.

"Daddy!" the girl hollered.

The sound of her voice, much deeper than Ren's, wrenched Sean back from the depths of delusion. "I'm sorry," he said, hurrying from the scene.

Despite Vince's comments about handling problems of his own, he knew if he didn't handle this one, no one else would. Sean did his best to pull himself together, craziness doing nothing but impeding his intent.

The last he saw of LeGrande was his blood outside the building. He ran to the ally and picked up the trail. Quizzically, it led back to Canal. *If you're going to blow up the parade, why run toward it? Do you have another building with Ren chained to a wall?* LeGrande's words came back: *"Wait 'til you see what I've planned just for you."*

Sean passed a discount electronics store, his attention drawn to a bank of TVs. On each TV was the face of LeGrande, along with the words: "One child still missing."

Everyone knows.

Sean's eyes glazed as he instantly understood. *LeGrande's a condemned man. A* desperate *man. He's gonna blow himself up and take Ren with him.*

"Officer, I know this man," Tom said. "He's a member of our krewe. He belongs on this float."

"He says he's a cop."

"A *top* cop in fact. Meet Detective Lieutenant Owen Dupree."

"Lieutenant?"

"Check under the float." Dupree commanded.

All three cops made their way down the ladder, followed closely by Tom and Dupree. The lead cop knelt. His face paled. "Holy *fuck!*"

"You three stop the tractor. Tom, clear the float." Cops broke rank, running to Dupree. "Disperse the crowd," he commanded. "Evacuate these buildings."

Revelers didn't need to be told to disperse. Seeing krewe members leap from both sides of the floats, they fled on their own, flooding streets off Canal like water surging at the height of a hurricane.

Watching them flee, Dupree roared with jubilation over the thousands of lives that had likely been saved. A second later, he remembered . . . *Ren.*

Chapter 48

THE OFFER

THOUSANDS of people sped past Sean toward neighboring streets, promising safe passage. In their wake, a ghost town remained, knee-high litter substituting for tumbleweed. A lone, disheveled figure stood in the distance. Sean recognized him immediately: *Owen Dupree.*

They ran to each other and grasped hands soundly, nerves frayed, eyes cluttered with tears. There were dozens of things Sean wanted to say, but not now. Maybe never.

"I shot LeGrande and tracked his blood to the parade."

Dupree gazed up Canal. "We gotta search the floats. I'll go to the back. You start here."

"She's *my* kid, Lieutenant. *I'll* check the floats."

"All *those?*" Dupree pointed at dozens, trailing into the distance. "Like I said, I'll go to the back. Still have the gun? Next time, shoot to kill."

Sean climbed on the first, beads strewn about. He listened intently, but there was no movement or sound. He peered at the jester head's mocking grin before proceeding up one aisle and down the other.

Nothing. Sean's heart sank. Despair threatened to set in.

There were too many floats and not enough time. *And what if she's not on any of them?* Starting down the stairs, he glanced at a step and noticed a small, red, glistening spot—then a second, then a third. *Blood.* He turned and followed it to the jester's head.

"Ren?"

"Daddy!" Her voice rang out.

Sean eased the gun out of his pocket. "I'm here, sweetheart," he said, tone measured and calm. "I'm coming." He spotted a hinge at the rear of the head, lifted a latch, and stepped inside.

"Sean, come in. What a wonderful surprise." LeGrande sounded like a host at a cocktail party.

Sean's chest seized at the sight of Ren, sitting in LeGrande's lap, playing nonchalantly.

Ren stood and stepped forward, legs streaked with blood. Sean gasped before realizing she'd been sitting in LeGrande's blood. LeGrande reached out and quickly retrieved her.

"Daddy!" Ren cried, straining with outstretched arms.

Sean suffered the blow. "It's okay, Sweetie. I'm right here. Stay there and show me all of your beads."

Ren lifted a strand. "Blue ones. Look at these." Her eyes appeared heavy, enthusiasm dimmed.

Sean raised the gun, sighting it between LeGrande's eyes. LeGrande raised his arm, revealing the detonator.

"It appears we have a standoff," LeGrande said calmly. "Well, not exactly. I have the advantage."

"How's that?" he asked, knowing only too well.

"Turns out you were right. My life *is* over. That puts me in a very powerful position. You, on the other hand, would like life to go on. Shoot me and your kid dies. Slide the gun over and she lives."

Ren was unharmed, sitting inches in front of him. Sean reveled in the miracle, tarnished as it was. He drank in her innocence and zest for life, pressing them into his marrow to be stored for all time. He wanted to grab her and never let go, but a madman with a detonator prevented that from happening. Holding a gun in the face of explosives was like waving two pairs at an opponent's full house.

Still, he held something. Discarding what he had seemed out of the question. He thought to fire—then remembered his aim.

"First let her go. *Then* I'll give you the gun."

"Maybe," LeGrande offered, "but not with it pointed at my head."

Slowly, Sean lowered his arm to his side.

"That's good. Now slide it over."

"You said you'd let her go."

"I said *maybe*."

Shit. What am I thinking? Trust LeGrande? He'd angled a concession, weakening Sean's hand. There was no way he could raise his arm, site, and fire quicker than LeGrande could push a button. The gun was history; he'd relinquished that chance. He didn't dare give up anything else.

Watching Ren, struggling to break free, Sean felt desperate to hold her in his arms. Taking a chance, he slid the gun forward. LeGrande picked it up and set it by his side.

"Have a seat. Join us. We've been enjoying each other's company."

Sean bit down hard. Ren reached for him again. This time, surprisingly, LeGrande let go.

Ren dashed for his arms. Sean held on tight, knowing the opportunity might never return.

"I was planning to go out with one last thrill. You know . . . her and me. But then *you* showed up. Hmm . . ." LeGrande held his chin between his finger and thumb, feigning contemplation, smirking all the while. "Two is never as much fun as three. Don't you agree?"

Sean saw red. "More of your bullshit, LeGrande?"

"Please. Watch what you say. Children are listening. We're a couple of bright guys. Given the opportunity your presence provides, we ought to be able to come up with *something*."

Sean knew he was being played, LeGrande getting off on each move in the game. The talk alone was likely turning him on. *Let him ramble. See what he's after. As long as he talks, Ren stays alive.*

"Oooo, here's an idea."

Sean's head rolled. "Jesus, LeGrande. Don't you ever quit?"

"Not when faced with such wonderful possibilities. Grant me one last wish. Then, I promise, I'll let you both go."

"What wish?"

"To *share!* I've never seen a father and daughter before."

Sean's gut bled acid, anger rampaging. He drew back his fist, aiming for LeGrande. "*YOU—*"

LeGrande uncapped the detonator, party host vanishing. In the blink of an eye, a monster emerged. "*COME ON! I'M READY! WANNA PLAY? LET'S GO! FORCE ME TO KILL YOUR KID! WANT THAT ON YOUR CONSCIENCE? COME ON! LET'S DO IT! I'M READY! LET'S GO!*"

The craziness of the man sliced through Sean's rage, soaking him in sweat, chilling him to the bone. *Don't be suckered. Play it out.* He loosened his fist, lowering his arm to his side, anything to avoid provoking the animal any further.

"That's better," LeGrande said, congenial host returning.

A temporary truce settled over the proceedings.

Sean needed another way into LeGrande's head, calling him out on his cowardliness no longer an option. But *what* other way? Nothing Vince taught him prepared him for this.

What does LeGrande want? That seemed clear. *He wants to have fun, which means taking us with him. What do I want? I want Ren safe and sound.* That appeared unlikely with LeGrande wielding the power. *Power.* Sean looked at Ren. *What's the source of LeGrande's power?* The answer arose swiftly: *His power's based on my fear.* LeGrande's threat to harm Ren controlled the entire situation. *If I stop fearing, LeGrande's power stops.* Sean needed to let him know they were prepared to die.

"Think about it, Sean. Twenty years from now, she'll never remember."

"If you're waiting for an answer, I can give it to you now." Sean's eyes were like daggers. "*I'd* remember." LeGrande looked crestfallen. "Do you actually think I'd harm the child I love for no other reason than to provide pleasure for a sadist?" He circled his arms tightly around Ren. "Go ahead. Kill us. We're not afraid to die. Do it, LeGrande. *Now!*"

LeGrande transformed instantly into a cyclone of fury, wincing in pain as he struggled to his feet. "If nothing else, you're going to *watch!* But first . . ." He raised the gun. "I owe you."

LeGrande fired once, blowing a hole through Sean's arm.

"DADDY!" Ren screamed, face wrenched in terror.

LeGrande flung the gun to the rear of the float, dropping the detonator into his pocket. With an arm like a piston, he snatched Ren back, tearing at her clothes, howling like a beast.

"NO!" Sean bellowed, blood bathing his arm.

"I'm gonna do this, and you're gonna watch! Watch me, Sean. You're gonna love it!"

Sean lunged.

A shot rang out.

Chapter 49

SEE YOU IN HELL

DIZZY from worry and loss of blood, Sean struggled to make sense of what had just happened. He knew for sure that a gun had gone off. Had Ren been shot? Had he, again? Who fired the weapon and would he fire once more? As soon as the chaos began to subside, he remembered seeing Ren, sliding to the ground, LeGrande spinning twice before crashing to the floor.

Sean scooped Ren in his one good arm and began planting kisses all over her face.

"Are you all right?" a familiar voice asked.

Sean turned and saw Dupree, standing in the doorway, a still-smoking gun clutched in his hand.

"I heard the shot. Got here as fast as I could."

Sean said nothing, words inadequate.

"Here, lemme help." Dupree fashioned a tourniquet out of his belt and extended his arm to help Sean down the steps.

With Dupree bracing his side and Ren clinging to his leg, Sean figured they looked like a strange new life form, descending a spaceship from another planet.

Jas appeared, heading their way.

Dupree looked up without letting go. "Body's in the jester's head. Detonator's in his pocket. Ease it out gently and bring it to me. *Carefully!*"

"Daddy has an owie," Ren told Dupree, pointing at his arm dangling loose at his side.

"I see that, sweetie. Your daddy'll be fine."

"Fine" didn't begin to express the way Sean felt. Despite the searing in his shoulder and nausea in his gut, he knew the girls were safe and the police knew the score. What more could he ask?

Laurie.

He hoped there was a chance.

"Look, Daddy."

They turned to see Jas, standing on the float, arms raised at his sides, expression perplexed. "There's no one here, Lieutenant."

Sean squeezed Ren tight.

"No!" Dupree shouted. *"Get off the float!"*

Dupree and his charges trudged toward the corner, Sean grimacing in pain with each new step. "Take Ren. I'll be fine." he said.

"No chance," Dupree countered.

"Lieutenant!" Jas yelled, pointing back at the float.

Sean and Dupree turned and looked over their shoulders. On the tallest point of the jester's hat, LeGrande sat perched, arms raised high, detonator in his hands, laughing like a loon.

Quickening their advance and rounding the corner, Dupree wedged the others between a dumpster and himself, shielding them with his frame the best he could. Despite the blare from a helicopter's rotor, they heard LeGrande holler loud and clear . . .

"I'm coming, Harper. SEE YOU IN HELL!"

A moment of stillness was followed by havoc as the lead float exploded, piercing the sky. Light was accompanied by a deafening roar, a concussion not heard since the Civil War. One after another, the floats blew sky high, block after block, up and down Canal Street. Day turned to night as the heavens ruptured, raining debris like in a tickertape parade.

Mere minutes went by but the time seemed like hours, huddled together, waiting for the calm. When the conflagration subsided, they extricated themselves, unwinding their bodies, itemizing their wounds.

Dupree was hammered hardest, sparing the others, glass slicing his arms, wood battering his skull. Sean fared much better but still took his share, hovering over Ren with her head tucked beneath.

"How bad is it?" Sean asked Dupree.

"I've been better," he moaned, wobbling on wounded knees.

Ren tugged Sean's leg. "Let's go see!"

Hobbling to the corner, they beheld an otherworldly sight: a proud and stately boulevard transformed to Armageddon. The remains of floats burned blocks on end amidst electrified wires, dancing magically on their own. Tipped over trolley cars lay on their sides, tracks twisted grotesquely, reaching for the sky. Across from the trolleys were mountains of debris where buildings had stood minutes before.

"Lookit, Daddy." Ren pointed at a statue listing in the street. It was that of a saxophone player leaning against a lamp, its head replaced by a rooster's, blown in from some float.

"Kinda looks like the mayor," a voice called from behind.

The three turned and grinned at a smudge-faced Jas, feathers protruding from both sides of his mouth.

The air was still, the street eerily quiet. All that could be heard were sirens in the distance . . . another parade on its way to Canal Street.

Chapter 50

A DIFFERENT WAY TO SERVE

HOW odd, Sean thought. *Attending a barbeque in the backyard of a cop.* Then . . . lots of odd things had happened in the course of six months.

He and Ren were the first to arrive with a boisterous Brielle, dodging their feet, her psychic wounds healing on a par with Sean's arm. While Ren played with Jenna and Brielle barked at both, Sean exchanged jibes with Owen Dupree.

"With that arm in a sling, think can you still light a grill?"

"It was you who said you wanted to help *me*. I never said anything about wanting to help you."

Dupree grinned, turned, and walked away, heading inside to fix Sean a drink.

Odd, indeed.

Sean gazed at bougainvillea, flowering around the yard, and tried to make sense of all that had happened. He recalled the day Breneaux returned to work, the press likening the event to the second coming of Christ. Sean had expected to *not* tune in but finally caved at Weinstat's insistence. Breneaux publically thanked him for rescuing Charmaine, and for—as the *Times-Picayune* subsequently quoted—"wrenching me out of a black-and-white world where surfaces go unscratched, nuance is deemed dangerous, and reason is rarely, if ever, employed."

He remembered, too, the Senate hearing, mics shoved in his face, cameras blazing. Ren sat by his side, coloring throughout, while Charmaine and her father smiled from the gallery. He was anxious at first, but quickly relaxed as he read the statement he was asked to prepare:

> "There are monsters in our midst—*real* monsters, who do monstrous things. But when we let ourselves to be seduced by the hysteria that surrounds us, we add ourselves to their ranks and hasten our own demise."

Hypocritical reporters who'd anointed him a freak changed their minds overnight, proclaiming him a celebrity. Asked how it felt to suddenly be a hero, he answered, "I'm no more a hero than I was a child molester. None of this would have happened if the system hadn't failed."

He recalled, as well, his day in court to have his status as a sex offender purged from the records. "Piece o' cake," Weinstat assured him, "considering the circumstances." Sean, however, disagreed. *If ten years can become twenty, twenty can become life. Registration is designed so that no one gets out.* Testifying in court were Breneaux and Dupree, with emails forwarded by Andrews and Meyers.

Sean recalled clearly his supporters' shock when the judge handed down his official ruling: "Sex offender registration grows more draconian each year with ever-increasing laws eroding judges' discretion. No longer can we overturn the status of an offender, even when the facts make it clear that we should. I'm sorry to say, other than presidential pardons, legal remedies for offenders no longer exist."

"But he did nothing to deserve it," Dupree said, sitting up front.

"Doesn't being a hero count?" Breneaux yelled from the rear.

The judge reaffirmed: "There's nothing I'd like better than to expunge this man's file. But based on the law, it's out of my hands."

"What about a governor's pardon?" Breneaux demanded.

The judge shook his head. "He'd still have to comply in every other state."

Half the spectators lashed out. The others sat, dumbfounded. *"Then,"* Breneaux shouted, *"we'll* get *him a presidential pardon!"*

"No," Sean said, to supporters in the hall. "I won't seek a pardon. It wouldn't be fair." He'd known since fifth grade that, in order to help friends, he had to make available a path they could follow. To gain a reversal based strictly on fame would provide no such path, leaving dolphins stranded. By remaining a dolphin, on the other hand, Sean thought perhaps he could help others survive—maybe even get ahead—in a hostile world. Thoughts coalescing, he pictured Vince, approving his decision and cheering him on.

He remembered, too, Weinstat calling soon after, encouraging him to testify at William Hardy's trial. Sean saw no reason to reopen old wounds, figuring karma would strike before a jury ever would. William died in his sleep a few days later. Sean pictured him scurrying all around hell, checking his list against the sinners he'd meet.

Sean's thoughts eventually turned to home, Laurie's exit a blend of resolve and best wishes. She said in the end she needed to be free of the scourge that had tarnished their love irrevocably.

Free. Sean breathed in the word along with its promise. Unlike the crane, he remained tied to a rock, but he remembered Vince saying: *Everyone has something to overcome.* It occurred to Sean: *Perhaps it's in the act of transcending limitations that we fully come alive and truly feel free.*

"Don't burn yourself on that," Breneaux said, walking toward the grill, the intensity of his smile matching his bright, Hawaiian shirt.

"Hi, Sean!" Charmaine called, waving from inside the screened in porch.

"How about: 'Hi, *Mr. Jordan*'?" Breneaux instructed with a growl. "Kids!"

"How's she doing?" Sean asked.

"So well it scares me. If it weren't for her exuberance when she tells friends about her 'adventure,' I'd seriously consider taking her to a shrink. Of course, being with you *was* being with a shrink."

Sean smiled. "I'm glad you're back on the air."

"Really? I wouldn't have guessed you to be a conservative."

"Well . . ."

"After I said nice things about you, I got deluged with calls, cajoling me, pleading with me, *threatening* me not to go soft. Believe me, I haven't. The only thing I changed was dropping the hate. If it's hate people want, there are other stations to choose from." Breneaux looked at Sean. "Thank you for that."

Dupree returned with Sean's drink in one hand, andouille sausage in the other.

Breneaux noted immediately the absence of sauce. "Where's the sauce, Owen? Gotta have your sauce."

"Barbecue sauce! Is that all I'm good for?"

"*Yes*, Daddy," Jenna shouted from the porch.

Breneaux eyed his host. "You know, Dupree, Mada Gras's only six months away. What do you have in store for us *next* year?"

"*Ha!* Boys, you're on your own." He pulled a travel brochure out of his pocket. "I don't know about you, but my butt's gonna be here." He pointed at a palm tree on a beach in Tahiti.

Charmaine, delighting in her big-sister role, marched into the yard, Ren and Jenna in tow. Around her neck hung two small keys, suspended at the end of a long silver chain.

Sean smiled. "Happy birthday, Charmaine."

"Thanks . . . *Mr. Jordan*," she droned, stabbing her father with barbeque tongs. "Daddy, after we finish with the cake, is it okay if I show Jenna and Ren how to shoot a gun?"

"*Charmaine!*" Breneaux roared.

Sean concealed a laugh.

"Sorry I couldn't get here any sooner," Molly's voice rang out. She burst into the yard with a birthday cake in hand. In place of her black dress and long green feather, she wore a brightly colored sundress and a broad straw hat. Sean failed to recognize her for a couple of seconds, until she hollered to the crowd, "How's everyone fixed for drinks?" Molly kissed Dupree, hugged Breneaux, and messed Sean's hair, sighing "Gorgeous" again.

Following the feast, Molly continued: "Girls and boys, it's time to light the candles!" Striking a long match, she lit the first of fourteen.

Charmaine ran to Sean and whispered in his ear, "My job's to blow. Yours is to see I get them all." Sean captured her wink and answered with a smile.

In time, the candles were lit, "Happy Birthday" was sung, wishes were made, and the flames were blown out. Sean checked to make sure.

There wasn't any doubt.

ACKNOWLEDGEMENTS

IT'S easy to recognize the fact that making a movie is a collaborative effort. It's harder to see that writing a book requires much of the same. Sure, a writer spends months alone, creating a story that's never been told. But then rewrites begin, requiring the involvement of neighbors, cleaning ladies, and people from New York. Countless individuals investing time and talent provided brilliant assistance and ruthless insight—you know who you are!—even occasionally picking up lunch. To each of you I give my heartfelt thanks. Those who contributed most seriously to the book were my editors in New York, Richard Marek and Michael Denneny; publicist, Michele Karlsberg; IT advisor, Robert McAllister; additional editors, readers, and friends, Gary DeVar, Rebecca Pastor, Carol Fetzner, Judy Kentor Schmauss, Dale Aviza, Margaret Knox, Kim Bookless, and Kathryn Hallenstein; and partner, Debbie Dietrich, who loved every word from the first draft to the last, keeping me afloat with abundant false courage.

ABOUT THE AUTHOR

CRAIG Bennett Hallenstein is a psychologist, writer, and father of five, whose blog, *Let's Talk Sex*, is a guide to conscious living and sustainable relationships. *The Dolphin* is his first work of fiction.

Hallenstein was born in Chicago into a family of journalists—his father an editor for the *Chicago Tribune*, his mother the editor of a suburban weekly. "She wanted me to follow in their footsteps; he wanted me to follow my muse," Hallenstein says. "Psychology won out, but writing waited patiently."

Hallenstein attended Beloit College and the California School of Professional Psychology, earning a PhD in clinical psychology and prompting a study of contemporary sexuality. Writing classes followed at the University of Iowa, Chicago Dramatists, and Musical Theater Building Chicago. His writing first appeared in *The Journal of Professional Psychology*. "But it wasn't until *The National Enquirer* came calling," he says with a smile, "that I knew as a writer I'd finally arrived."

Among his writing credits is a *People Finders* cover story that was optioned by Dick Clark Productions for a made-for-TV movie. His earlier blog, *Sex-Positive Parenting*, provided guidelines and tips for fostering sexual health in children.

When not writing, Hallenstein manages a successful career as a business broker and restores old houses in Chicago and New Orleans. His favorite holiday is Mardi Gras. The Academy Awards claims a close second.

CPSIA information can be obtained at www.ICGtesting.com
Printed in the USA
LVOW11s2214280316

481158LV00001B/78/P

9 780692 578834